Keeping Mum

Keeping Mum

Emma Hannigan

HACHETTE
BOOKS
IRELAND

First published in 2012 by Hachette Books Ireland
Copyright © 2012 Emma Hannigan

1

The right of Emma Hannigan to be identified as the Author of the
Work has been asserted by her in accordance with the Copyright,
Designs and Patents Act 1988.

A CIP catalogue record for this title is available from the British Library.

ISBN 978 1 444 72617 6

Typeset in Sabon MT and Aire Roman Std
by Bookends Publishing Services

Printed and bound in Great Britain by Clays Ltd, St Ives plc.

Hachette Books Ireland policy is to use papers that are natural,
renewable and recyclable products and made from wood grown
in sustainable forests. The logging and manufacturing processes
are expected to conform to the environmental regulations
of the country of origin.

Hachette Books Ireland
8 Castlecourt Centre
Castleknock
Dublin 15, Ireland
A division of Hachette UK Ltd
338 Euston Road
London NW1 3BH

www.hachette.ie

For my husband Cian and our children Sacha and Kim,
and for Denise and Philip, aka Mum and Dad,
thank you for all your love and unbending support

Acknowledgements

As always, this book wouldn't exist without my behind-the-scenes support team. Massive kudos and respect to my amazing editor Ciara Doorley at Hachette Books Ireland. This story has transformed and grown along with the characters. I couldn't have made this happen without Ciara's unwavering belief in me. Thank you. Thanks also to the rest of the gang at Hachette Books Ireland – namely Breda, Jim, Joanna, Ruth and Margaret. You're brilliant and I love working with you!

Love and thanks to my fabulous agent Sheila Crowley of Curtis Brown UK.

Huge appreciation to the dedicated people in the book trade for the fantastic support you've given me since the day my first novel graced your shelves.

Thanks to my husband Cian for all the years of love, loyalty, support and understanding, especially on the days when I've been sick, tired and about as attractive as a dose of leprosy.

Our son Sacha and daughter Kim let us know each and every day how blessed we are to have them. They also teach us patience and resilience as we've learned to continue with day-to-day life to the background tones of the electric guitar, keyboard, PlayStation, iPod docking station at full volume along with the usual 'heated discussions' they are both so good at. Most of all they've taught us the true meaning of unconditional love and all the precious privileges it brings with it. I love you both with every fibre of my being and cannot imagine life without you.

I've said it before and I'll say it again – I have the best parents in the world! Not a day goes by that they don't say or do something to enhance my life. My love, thanks and appreciation knows no bounds.

Thanks to my extended family for all the continued support. Cathy Kelly is part of my family as far as I'm concerned. Thank you for being there always.

As life goes on, my friendships have evolved and deepened. The longer I spend on this earth, the more I cherish the people who share their hopes, dreams and love with me. I don't take any of you for granted. Thank you.

My team of angels in Blackrock Clinic in Dublin should all be sainted. Dr David Fennelly and all the team in the Oncology Day Unit – Sinead, Caroline, Aoibheann, Riza, Liz and all the staff not only make my life worth living – you literally keep me alive! Words are hardly enough, but thank you all.

Since I began writing, I've been in receipt of letters, emails, Facebook messages and tweets from a vast array of readers. When you all share snippets and often large parts of your lives with me, I feel more humbled and grateful than you will ever know. Thank you all sincerely for buying my books, saying lovely things about them and reaching out to me over and over again. It blows me away and lets me know how lucky I am to have you all as my cheerleaders.

I really hope you all enjoy *Keeping Mum* and please stay in touch via Facebook (Author Emma Hannigan) twitter @msemmahannigan or my website (www.emmahannigan.com).

Wishing you all health and happiness whereever you might be!

Love
Emma

Mothers ...

1.

Ava's Story

When I think back to before I became a mother, I wonder what the hell I did with all my time. In my defence, I worked as an airhostess for a large airline so I was kept out of trouble. But I don't think I had ever experienced the true meaning of the word 'tired' until I had a child. But then, nor had I ever known that a love so pure could exist. I can still recall Justin and I staring at our firstborn, Jake, for hours on end, enraptured.

Most relationships come with baggage of some sort. We take on another person's life experience and whatever background story has shaped them. That type of love – although it's wonderful – has conditions attached. We decide to stay together. We choose one another. It's all done in good faith and we enter into relationships hoping they'll work out. But there is no guarantee. With a baby, though, there are no precursors. There is no logbook. Just a tiny infant – a clean and pure little soul with so much love to give.

I had a totally different personality before I had kids. I worked relentlessly, never wanting to take a break. I wanted to take on all the long-haul flights and was ambitious and hungry for success. I left school at seventeen and was accepted as a crewmember at Air Éire several weeks later. I loved my job and gave it my all.

I met Justin at a house party in the early eighties. I'd just returned from Boston and was feeling quite disorientated. Sue, one of the girls I worked with, was heading to a party quite near my parents' house in south Dublin and asked me to go along.

'You're hardly going to sleep at this stage, Ava. What harm will it do to come and have a couple of drinks and unwind? You might as well,' she cajoled.

So off I went, like Airhostess Barbie, still dressed in my green and blue uniform, caked in make-up with my hair wound up in a chignon.

Justin approached me almost as soon as I entered the room and smiled. 'What time's the next flight? If I assume crash position and panic a lot, will you give me mouth to mouth?'

He was eleven years older than me, and most definitely not the type of guy I would normally go for. He was smaller than me height-wise and although he had the kindest eyes and most naturally gorgeous way about him, if I'm totally honest, I wasn't instantly attracted to him.

I know I might sound like a cow, but I only stayed chatting to him for as long as I did because he made me laugh. Besides, I didn't know anyone else in the room, except for Sue. She was doing the rounds, chatting to relatives and friends. Rather than sit awkwardly by myself wishing I'd gone straight home, I stayed with Justin.

He was so clever and witty that by the end of the night, I found myself willingly giving him my phone number.

After that, he went to huge efforts to meet up with me. He was working predominantly in the UK at the time, and I was wherever work took me. All my previous relationships had brought a certain amount of uncertainty because of my frequent travelling. My sporadic time schedule annoyed most men, and it quickly became apparent that my nomadic lifestyle didn't suit. If I wasn't available every single weekend, most guys lost interest.

I didn't realise how much I'd fallen for Justin until he took me by surprise and proposed only six months after we'd met. I instantly knew the answer should be yes.

We had a small wedding less than a year later, with only thirty guests. My sister Lorraine was my bridesmaid. Mummy and Daddy were elderly when we married and were of the opinion that a woman was the responsibility of her husband once vows had been exchanged. Luckily for all involved, Justin agreed with my parents and was very old-fashioned in his ways. Maybe a bit too old-fashioned because once we were husband and wife, it became clear that he wasn't entirely happy with my demanding career.

'But what do you want me to do? Sit around painting my nails and climbing the walls, going slowly insane? It's the eighties, Justin, not the fifties. I love my work and I'm good at it,' I explained. 'Why would you want me to stop? Besides if you want me to be happy, you'll support me in my life choice.'

Put to him in that manner, Justin had known that forcing me to quit work would have made him look like an old fuddy-duddy. His mother had stayed at home, while his father had been the breadwinner. He'd just assumed his own married life would be the same, but I soon persuaded him otherwise.

When we were first married, Justin worked between Dublin and London, which was an easy commute. His aptitude for financial dealing, along with his talent in all things to do with stocks and bonds, meant he was climbing the corporate ladder rapidly. It became obvious that soon all his work would be UK-based, so Justin asked me to consider relocating to London.

As it happened, I discovered I was pregnant with Jake a few months after the wedding. Nothing in the world could have prepared me for how ill I turned out to be.

'I'm almost allergic to pregnancy,' I whispered after another violent vomiting session. I was so ill, I was hospitalised. As I lay back against the pillows in the maternity unit, one of the midwives mopped my brow.

'Just because you were a high flyer before doesn't mean those hormones are going to comply and allow you to continue. It's not the safest thing to do, jetting across the world in your state.' The nurse on duty sighed. 'You're not going to be able to work during this pregnancy unless you can hold down some food and water, my girl. This could be God's way of telling you that you need to concentrate on carrying and delivering your child.'

I was furious. How dare she tell me that my career was over just because I was having a baby! After all, I was a woman of the world with a flourishing career and could wear bigger shoulder pads than Krystle Carrington and make it look stylish.

'Who are you to tell me whether or not I'm in a position to work?' I seethed. God, when I think back now, I'm ashamed at how arrogant and ignorant I was.

'I'm not the one telling you what to do here, lovie,' the nurse responded tetchily. 'Your baby and your body will do that. Just try not to be too disappointed, that's all. Sometimes nature is our ruler.'

Things had indeed gone from bad to worse. I ended up in hospital for over a month suffering from dehydration and a nasty affliction exclusive to pregnancy known as hyperemesis gravidarum. Bed rest was prescribed, and there was nothing I could do about it. By the time Jake was born, any energy I might have had left was rapidly sapped by motherhood.

We moved to London so Justin could put in long hours in the City and still feel somewhat part of a family. I was in a daze, just trying to get through the fog of new motherhood. The day Ana joined our household was the first day that fog cleared – not only could I see rainbows again, I could see the pot of gold at the end of it. A young woman from the Philippines, Ana was like a little fairy in stature, with long shiny straight black hair and pretty, doll-like features. Looks could be deceiving, however. Ana was, and still is, like a tiny bolt of lightning. She zooms around the house, leaving everything spotless in her wake. Together, we put the house in order and worked out a system that enabled me to be a mother and get some time to myself as well.

In 1982, following another harrowing pregnancy and emergency caesarean section birth, Luke joined our family. Justin's long absences from the house because of his work meant the continuity of care rested with me, not to mention being the presence at the school plays, parent-teacher meetings and school gates. While we always tried to make sure we weren't apart for prolonged periods, circumstances often meant that I didn't see Justin for up to four weeks at a time.

On the flip side, we were fortunate to enjoy a very comfortable lifestyle and when he was home, Justin was the perfect husband and father. I had a good routine going by the time Luke was born and he slipped right into it. I also had loyal and supportive friends in London by then and my boys were my life. Nonetheless there was a dull ache niggling at the back of my mind.

I wanted a daughter.

I longed to buy little pink clothes. I imagined scenarios in my head where Justin would proudly cradle our daughter and whisper that she was his princess. I adored my sons and not a day went by that I didn't thank God for their existence, but once I admitted to myself that I was harbouring this undeniable desire for a girl, I found it impossible to put it to one side.

I had given up my career for my boys, and I knew I was in a privileged position, having the funds to do so. I had loved my job and wouldn't have guessed in a million years that I'd have ended up as a stay-at-home mum. We had a stunning home in the quiet and affluent area of Chelsea, but I still felt a sense of … incompleteness. I thought that once I had a daughter, I would never shed another tear. I used to lie awake at night and wonder what our daughter would look like. I wanted a girl so badly, it became like a dark cloud that shadowed my entire life. I knew I was being terrible and that this ache inside was something I could never share with anyone else. I feared that other mothers and even my closest friends would judge me harshly if I dared to insinuate that I wasn't content with my lot. Don't think I didn't cherish and adore my boys, because I did. But I wanted it all.

In 1985 Justin was racing up the ladder of success. Jake was all geared up for starting 'big school' in September and Luke was three and we'd accepted a place for him in the nearby Montessori. June of that year was the first time I heard the word 'PGD', and I came across it quite by mistake.

A close friend, Helena, who had one child, a boy as it happened, confided in me over a coffee one morning. She was also Irish and we'd gravitated towards one another since the first day we'd met at Jake's Montessori school. We had one of those wonderful friendships with no pressure. If we couldn't meet for days or even weeks on the trot, neither of us minded. When we did get together, we enjoyed our easy chats and felt comfortable being honest with one another. That particular day, we were discussing our children.

'I'm not sure if you were aware, but we conceived Tristan as a result of a grand total of five rounds of IVF,' Helena said as she sipped her latte.

'Wow, I never knew you had to try five times, Helena. That must have been so difficult. I had always stupidly assumed you'd gone once and hey presto, he appeared nine months later,' I admitted.

'God, if only it had been that easy, but the end result was obviously well worth it. But listen, what I'm about to tell you is to go no further okay?' Helena leaned forward.

'Go on,' I whispered.

'Have you heard of PGD?' she asked, whispering so no one at the other tables could hear her.

'No, what is it?' I asked, wondering if it was an illegal drug or something.

'It's a specialised type of IVF. It's only been developed a while and it's only available in the States for now. It's more accurate than standard IVF so with luck, it might give us a better chance of success first time. The other wonderful thing is that it enables screening against defects, as well as allowing the patient to choose the sex of the baby they have implanted, should they wish,' she finished.

I will never forget the feeling that came over me at that moment. It was as if the roof of the building had opened up and the gods were smiling down on me as the angels chorused the 'Hallelujah'!

I actually began to reel on the inside as Helena filled me in on this concept. PGD stood for pre-implantation genetic diagnosis. The two doctors who developed it had managed to successfully sex rabbit blastocysts and determine whether there were any defects present, as well as the sex of the offspring.

'It's now reached a stage where they can apply it to humans. Potential parents go to a fertility clinic in New York and undergo the usual steps for IVF,' Helen continued, 'but the difference is that the embryo is brought on until it reaches the eight-cell stage. Only then, one cell is removed for testing. They can determine whether or not there are any potential problems, and they can also tell the sex of the child. So we're going to try for a girl,' Helena finished with a guilty smile. 'We feel we're going down the IVF route as it is and this will be our last child, and we'd love a little girl to make our family complete. One of each would be such a dream, wouldn't it?'

I hugged her and told her I thought it was a fantastic idea and wished her well.

'Before I go, could I get the details of the clinic from you? Please don't ever say it to anyone, but I would give my right arm to have a daughter myself, and this could be the answer to my prayers,' I admitted. Biting my lip, I felt a rush of guilt and relief in equal measure.

I knew I had to be very careful admitting such a thing to a woman who had just told me the struggle she'd had to conceive a baby full stop, and here was I being nit-picky and saying I wanted a girl when I had two healthy, naturally-conceived children at home.

'Of course,' said Helena rooting in her handbag. 'Here's the card. I'm so glad you don't think I'm a demon for trying to plan the sex of our baby. It's so lovely to meet someone who understands what I'm doing.'

'Helena, nobody has the right to tell you that you're wrong in this case. You need IVF anyway, otherwise you can't have a baby, so why not use the technology available to you?'

'Thanks, Ava! You're a breath of fresh air,' she said, smiling.

I literally ran from the coffee shop and around the corner. I stood with my back against the street wall, gulping in air. Oh, my God, this was how I was going to get my daughter! This was the answer that I'd been searching for. I *had* to convince Justin to go along with it. I would beg him to pay the fees and come with me to the clinic in New York.

As is often the case, once a topic or subject becomes personal, it's like it crawls out of the woodwork everywhere you go. I began to notice snippets of information cropping up in the media. PGD appeared to be winking at me from all sides. 'Are you looking to create a "designer baby"?' one of the newspaper headlines demanded.

I waited for Justin to return home before I broached the subject with him. It wasn't a matter I felt could be discussed over a long-distance phone call. I'm a firm believer in fate and things happening for a reason. Justin came home a week later with news.

'Ava, I've been offered a serious promotion,' he said as he sat opposite me, nervously rubbing his hands together.

'Why are you looking so glum about it, then? That's great news, isn't it?' I felt nervous for a second.

'Yes, but … it's in America – full time. New York, to be exact.' He paused and looked at me.

'What are you asking me, Justin?' I said quietly.

'Would you consider moving with the boys to New York?'

There was a brief silence as I tried to take his request on board. 'But couldn't we stay in London and you could commute? Tons of our friends do it and it seems to work,' I floundered. I'd never harboured any desire to live far away from my roots. I know I'd flown for years and dipped in and out of many countries and cultures, but I was never one for backpacking for months on end or doing a year in Australia. I loved to *see* things and then return home.

The move to London had been a big enough step for me. But at least the culture and people were comparable to home. Besides, where we lived in Chelsea some of my neighbours were Irish, so it was like a home away from home.

'The boys are about to start school and Montessori. We've paid the fees, everything is organised. I'm not sure how I'd cope with moving them now. I wouldn't know a soul there … oh, God, Justin, I don't know,' I admitted.

Then a thought struck me. If I were in New York, I'd have access to the American medical system. That could be my way of having PGD done. It would be more of a reasonable suggestion if we were there. I know it sounds like I was being really sneaky, but I cannot express how strong my desire was for a daughter.

'Let me think about it for a few days, can you, darling?' I begged.

'That's just the issue. I need to accept or decline and I only have a week to make up my mind.'

'What do you want to do?' I asked.

Justin sighed deeply. 'I want us to be happy and I want us to have the best life we possibly can. This is a massive opportunity. If I take this job, it indicates a pretty sound future for us. I know there are no certainties in life, but it's a wonderful offer, Ava.'

My head was mush. I loved London at that time. Friends like Helena were closer to me than my own family. I had always hoped in my heart that we would return to Ireland one day, but at that exact moment in time, London was very much my home.

In order to be kept in the running for this opportunity, Justin had to make a three-day trip to New York to meet with the American bosses.

'Why don't you come with me?' he suggested. 'See the place, and that might help you with your decision.'

Ana, my trusty nanny, housekeeper and right arm agreed to mind the boys and I packed my bag for New York.

Justin and I landed in a hot and sticky New York three days later, filled with trepidation and expectation. I met with the American team. As I'd been to the city many times before during my air-stewarding days, I excused myself from their company after a lengthy lunch and ambled happily around the streets of Manhattan. I found myself in FAO Schwarz and bought Disney stuff for the boys that I knew nobody at home would have.

An invisible force pulled me towards the girls' section. As I was alone and no one knew me, I could stroke the pretty pink things and relish in the femininity of it all. The playhouses were like stepping back to Victorian times. The doll section was so vast and beautifully set out that I had to use all my resolve not to buy things. Like an addict gorging on forbidden substances, I took in every inch of the area.

Over an hour later, I meandered out of the store feeling cold and empty inside despite the muggy heat. Just across the road in Central Park, I sat and tried to imagine how it might be to live in this bustling city. Once the tears started, I couldn't stop them. I sat and sobbed for what felt like an age. The loneliness and fear I felt was all encompassing. I knew I wasn't cut out to be a NYC gal.

Justin met me back at the hotel that evening. His eyes were dancing with enthusiasm and he was more alive than I'd ever seen him.

'This company is dynamic, Ava. I would love this job. Can we at least try and live here? Even for a few years?'

I've never felt like such a cow, but those tears I thought I'd cried dry that afternoon returned.

'Justin, I can't cope with the thought of moving us all lock, stock and barrel to New York. Why don't you take this job and we'll work around it?' I suggested.

'But how can I when you're already in such a distressed state? The job and the money would both be fantastic, but not if the price I have to pay is walking away from my family,' he said. 'No. I'll turn them down. You and the children come first. I'm only doing this for all of you. What's the point in that if we're not together?'

I could see that he meant every word. I knew he would walk away from the deal of a lifetime for us, but I couldn't allow him to do that. Setting aside the financial gains, this was what he'd worked his entire life to achieve. As a man and a person in his own right, he was entitled to grasp the opportunity.

'I want you to go, darling,' I insisted. 'We'll work it out. You start the job and I'll come over with the boys for all the holidays and long weekends. We'll reassess the situation in a couple of months. Please, follow your dream. The rest will just have to fall into place.'

As it turned out, Justin needed to come to the London office once a month for five days as part of the new job.

'If I have that five days each month, I can fit in another long weekend every month, even if it's at my own expense,' Justin decided.

'And if we know we're headed for a long spell, say over two weeks, I'll come with the boys for a couple of days,' I vowed.

Thankfully, in practice, the arrangement worked for us.

On one of my trips to New York, in August of 1985, barely two months after Justin had started the job, I joined him to attend an important corporate black-tie event. On the day of the function, I found myself with time to spare. I was sitting in Justin's neat apartment, wondering what to do with myself, when I spotted a phone book. I grabbed it and looked up fertility clinics.

On autopilot, I phoned and made a few enquiries. I was astonished to discover that it seemed to be easier than I thought to get PGD assistance. Once I explained our circumstances and my desire for a girl, they seemed to think this was quite an acceptable reason.

'Can you come this afternoon by any chance, Ma'am?' the receptionist asked.

'Yes, as a matter of fact I can. I'm only a couple of blocks away,' I answered. My voice was rising an octave with every word.

I took directions and agreed to be at a three o'clock consultation.

At 2.50pm, I approached the doors of the building. My heart was pounding in my chest and my mouth was dry. I pushed open the heavy glass doors and stepped inside.

The place was more like a plush modern hotel than a hospital or clinic. An impressive fountain gurgled in the foyer and the carpets were inch-thick beneath my feet. Tentatively I approached the large reception desk, which housed several impeccably dressed ladies.

'Good afternoon, how may I help you?'

'My name is Ava Moyes,' I managed. I did attempt to whisper, but the lack of soft surfaces and vast expanses of marble made my voice carry.

'Yes, Mrs Moyes, we're expecting you. Welcome and follow me.'

Feeling sick with nerves, I found myself in a less imposing consultation suite.

'Dr Macintosh will be with you shortly. Please have a seat, can I bring you a cold drink?'

'Yes, just water please,' I rasped.

A tall dark-skinned man with a flawless complexion and deep-brown eyes entered the room. Dressed in a dark grey suit, the air of confident authority along with his unbuttoned white coat left me in no doubt he was a consultant.

'Mrs Moyes, delighted to meet you.' His voice and smile both projected a sense of confident professionalism.

I had a totally surreal moment as we shook hands. This was the person who could potentially fix it for me to have a daughter. He arranged himself in the vast leather chair opposite me and immediately cut to the chase.

'So, how can we help you to have the pregnancy you want?'

'Well, I'm … I'm here because, I … Oh, this sounds rather strange, I'm sure. Let me begin by saying that I love my children very much.' I tumbled over my words, sounding like a nervous teenager.

'I've no doubt you do, Ma'am,' he said with a very wide smile.

'I have two boys. Two beautiful, cherished and wonderful boys,' I said, wishing I could stop going on like this.

'And you would like a daughter?' he finished. The smile still hadn't faltered. There was no coldness or judgement in his voice.

'Yes,' I whispered, beyond relieved that he'd said the words for me.

'Well, that's part of what we do here at the clinic, Mrs Moyes. You are not alone in wanting to select the sex of your baby. So please rest assured that this is no courtroom. I am neither judge nor jury. But I am a fertility expert and I will gladly help, should you fit with all the necessary medical and financial requirements.'

It was like I'd been pumped with adrenalin. I joined in with the wide-mouthed smiling and felt my shoulders begin to drop from my ears.

Two hours later, following a myriad of questions, blood tests and other minor on-the-spot checks, I was given an appointment to return with Justin.

'At your next consultation, we will run through the procedure in further detail. From what you've told us today, you are the optimum age, at thirty-one, for this type of assisted fertility. The fact that your husband is forty-two won't affect the outcome, unless he happens to have a very low sperm count. But judging by the success you have had conceiving naturally, all indications would suggest a lack of problem in that area.'

I took all the leaflets and information, omitting to inform the doctor that my husband was across the city and blissfully unaware that I was sitting discussing his sperm count, or indeed my own fertility, with a consultant. How he would respond when I told him all this, I just didn't know.

When Justin returned that evening, we barely had time to greet one another before we were collected by the chauffeur and taken to the event. The ball was like nothing I'd ever experienced before. The vast space and throngs of people were a far cry from the two hundred-strong dances we'd attended in the past. The colour scheme was black and gold, which the event organisers had taken all the way through to the food. The gala ballroom was adorned with huge golden globes and shimmering black ribbons, which cascaded down the backs of each chair. Roses had been dyed black and dipped in gold glitter to create a tiny arrangement at each individual place setting. The main course was pasta made with squid ink with a sauce topped in gold leaf. The dessert was a mousse made from darkest cocoa with tiny edible golden balls surrounding it.

The other wives, along with Justin's colleagues, were courteous and friendly, but the evening was still a bit of a trial. I love meeting people and I've no problem with approaching strangers, but that evening all I wanted was to sit in a quiet room and talk to Justin about PGD.

It was after two in the morning by the time we returned to the apartment, so I knew it was the wrong moment to start any chats, especially the one I had in mind. Justin fell into a peaceful sleep and I lay next to him, fearful and excited by turns.

The next morning, as Justin emerged from the shower and padded into the living room, I was waiting for him with butterflies in my stomach.

'Can you work with me and hear me out for a few minutes? What I'm about to say to you might shock you and I desperately need for you to try and keep an open mind,' I began.

'Okaaay. Ava, you're making me nervous, what on earth are you about to say?' Justin sat, or perched to be exact, on the sofa beside me and stared at me. Lord only knows what he thought I was going to tell him, but the relief that flooded his face when I revealed my wishes was wonderful.

I was pleasantly surprised by how well he took it all. He didn't make me feel like a monster for voicing the fact that I longed for a daughter.

'Jeez, Ava, I didn't know what was coming there,' he admitted.

'I was considering using that old gay joke, you know the one where a young man tells his parents he only has a month to live? While they're sobbing uncontrollably, he yells that he's only kidding, he's just gay.'

'Sick!' Justin laughed as he fixed the towel he'd wrapped himself in after his shower.

'Do you feel the same way?' I finally asked.

'What, relieved you're not dying or gay?' he joked.

'No, silly, do you have any thoughts on fathering a little girl?'

'I've thought about it, I'd be lying if I said I hadn't. But I don't harbour the same burning desire you seem to,' Justin said honestly. 'That's not to say that I won't go along with what you'd like. If you think these people are legitimate and safe, then my answer is that I will attend an appointment. I'm not making any commitment until I see this clinic and speak with the doctors. If there is any danger to you or indeed any possible child—'

I didn't let him finish; 'There isn't, they're amazing people, Justin. Wait until you see the set-up they have.'

He held up his hand to silence me gently.

'I'll go along and we'll take it from there. That's all I can promise for now.'

'You're unbelievably calm about this, darling. Have you heard of it all before or something?' I asked, suddenly curious about his demeanour.

'I've obviously heard of IVF and I've heard a work colleague speaking about this PGD thing too, but you seem to be forgetting that we're married. I know you better than you think, Ava. Don't believe for a second that I've been oblivious to your longing for a girl.'

'Why have you never said anything then?' I looked at him incredulously.

'Because, in a way, I felt it was my fault,' he answered, his darling face filled with emotion.

'Whaat? Why?'

'Well because it's a fact that the male sperm determines the sex of the baby. Sure the egg and the womb and the actual pregnancy bit is all left up to you girls, but the determination of the sex is down to the man.'

'But it's not as if you can hold your underpants aloft and tell your willy to only produce girl babies tonight,' I giggled without thinking.

'Don't you think I know that, but at the same time, I guess I've never wanted to discuss it too deeply because I was always afraid it might open a wound that we wouldn't be able to fix.'

His honesty and understanding that first time we talked about PGD will stay with me forever.

Two days later, he accompanied me to the clinic. He was just as impressed by the professionalism of the entire service as I had been. He warmed to Dr Macintosh and I just knew that he was going to agree to the procedure.

While there was a strict format to the whole thing, it was also a lot simpler than I'd ever imagined. Due to the fact that we were not a couple in need of IVF for conception purposes, all that was required of me was to have my eggs retrieved at the optimum time. Justin was to provide a sperm sample, and they would do the rest.

That may sound awfully straightforward, but there was a bit of medical intervention involved. I had to inject myself with hormones to optimise my egg production, just the same as any other IVF patient. But the good news was that my regular cycle meant that we could begin almost right away.

I returned home and began the treatment. Only a few short weeks later, I left the boys in London in Ana's capable care and returned to New York. The only person who knew what I was doing apart from Justin was Helena. She was so supportive and excited for me. It was wonderful to have someone who understood exactly what I was going through. Happily, Helena had completed her own cycle of PGD and was pregnant with a little girl. We were like kindred spirits, sharing in this wonderful life-creating project together.

'I pray it all works for you too. Good luck and call me any time,' Helena said as she hugged me goodbye.

Timing was everything. As the process was fairly new to the mass market, once we had the money to pay, it all happened swiftly. The clinic harvested twelve eggs on that visit. All twelve eggs were inseminated in the laboratory. For several days the hands of the clock seemed to remain static. I felt like I'd walked a thousand miles – in fact I probably had. Central Park became my stomping ground. I could probably still tell you how many trees surround certain benches. I recognised most of the horse-and-carriage drivers at the main gates within days.

I couldn't bear the frantic noise and bright lighting of the massive stores. There was nothing on the shelves that I desired. I wanted the biggest prize of all – a daughter.

After eight days of cultivation in the incubator, our embryos were gently biopsied. The doctors obtained a single cell that could be used to determine the gender of each embryo. Literally twenty-four hours after the embryos were tested, I got a call.

'Mrs Moyes, we have managed to create one embryo that is female. All the rest were male. As we explained, we usually prefer to have more than one embryo to implant, but this time we don't have that option. Would you and your husband like to go ahead and have the implantation done?' Dr Macintosh's smooth voice asked over the line.

'Yes, please.' I could barely get the words out. I was mildly disappointed that there weren't more embryos available, but I had a good feeling about this. It had all slotted into place. Since that moment Helena had shared her knowledge with me, it had been plain sailing.

With a heart of hope and feeling more excited and terrified than I'd ever imagined possible, I attended the clinic along with Justin. It was eight o'clock in the evening on Wednesday, 2 October 1985. As many couples filed into fancy restaurants to share a meal together, Justin and I completed our implantation process. It was quick and without much fanfare.

'All that remains now is for you to conduct a pregnancy test in ten days' time. We wish you all the luck in the world,' Dr Macintosh said. 'I know this is not an easy thing to hear, but should your embryo implantation not prove a success, don't hesitate to contact us again.'

That was the only time that I saw a different side to the clinic. Up until that point, I had firmly believed that although we were paying royally for the service, Dr Macintosh was doing the PGD procedure because he dearly wanted to give us a daughter. During that flashing moment, clarity crashed through to my senses. This was a business. For better or worse, we had just completed our transaction with Dr Macintosh. I returned to London and to my boys. Justin remained in New York. He wasn't due to fly home for a further two weeks.

'Call me if anything unusual happens, won't you?' he said kissing me goodbye at the airport. We stood silently embracing for the longest time before I boarded the flight. That quiet hug we shared brought home to me how lucky Justin and I were in our marriage. No words were needed. The embrace we shared said it all. I knew he was rooting for me. We both longed for the same thing and even though we were going to be thousands of miles apart, our hearts were in the same zone.

Sometimes miracles do occur. I know because that's what happened to me. The PGD worked like a dream and I ended up in our en-suite bathroom at home with tears of joy streaming down my face and a positive pregnancy test in my hand.

My hands were shaking as I dialled Justin's number in New York, desperate to share the news with him.

'Justin! We did it,' I fairly shouted down the phone.

'Oh, darling, I'm so delighted,' he croaked. 'This is certainly worth being woken in the middle of the night for,' he teased gently.

'I'm sorry, darling, I just couldn't wait until lunchtime for dawn to break in New York!'

'Don't be silly. I'm thrilled you woke me.'

The next nine months were blissful in one way and pure torture in another – wonderful because I knew that every inch my waist expanded meant our daughter was thriving, and awful because I could barely contain my excitement at the thought of holding our little girl in my arms. If you can imagine placing a divinely wrapped parcel in front of a small child and telling her not to open it for nine months – that was me.

But as day follows night, nature took its course and at long last Daisy graced us with her presence. I don't remember the pain of that labour. In fact, as the contractions grew stronger my exhilaration grew. The first time I saw her little face will remain with me until I breathe my last puff of air.

All the effort had been worthwhile. I'd do it again ten times over in a heartbeat. Becoming the mother of a daughter seemed so right. I knew I was finally complete. Justin was like the cat that got the cream. He crooned at his baby girl and kissed her button nose, telling her she was his little princess. I knew from that day forward that I would willingly devote my life to making my little girl happy.

2.

Greta's Story

The tight feeling I carried in my chest a lot of the time was beginning to ease. The only way I could shake it was by exercising. Running is the best – especially outdoors. The pounding noise of my feet on the ground is like a therapeutic hammer for my mind. Each step is a step further from returning to that ugly, useless body I was once trapped inside. There is absolutely no way in hell I'm going back there.

From day one, I was the chubby one. My parents hadn't the time or energy to worry about the fact that I was putting on extra pounds – that just didn't count back then. There were six of us at home and I was the eldest. Mammy was always cooking, cleaning and trying to keep up with the mounds of washing. All the same, my first and strongest memory of her was her pretty smile. She was the most beautiful woman I've ever laid eyes on. She had sallow skin and the most gorgeous dark, wavy hair that I would have killed for. It was thick and glossy and no matter what she did with it, from piling it into a bun or letting it fall loose down her back, it looked like it had been styled by an expert. She had one of those faces that an artist would want to draw: high cheekbones and full pouting lips. She rarely had the time, or money for that matter, for make-up, but even the tiniest amount would light up her pale blue eyes. To me, she was more gorgeous than any movie star.

Daddy worked all the time as a truck driver. When he was home he was too exhausted to spend much time with us rowdy lot.

Don't ask my why, but food was always on my mind as a child. I ate all the meals I was given and everything else I could get my hands on.

'Where's that sliced pan I left there earlier?' Mammy asked one afternoon.

'I didn't mean to eat it all, Mammy,' I answered, feeling ashamed of myself. 'That jam you made was so gorgeous, I couldn't stop.'

'Ah, sure, you could be doing worse, love. Run around to the corner shop and get me another, will you?' Mammy said handing me the correct change.

I used to find ways of getting sweets, too. I'd collect up all the glass bottles I'd see lying around and bring them back to the local shop in exchange for jellies and chocolate bars. Mammy always had to buy my clothes in bigger sizes – when I was eight, I was in ten-year-old stuff. She never made a fuss of it, though. It was just the way it was.

I spent a long time telling Mammy that all the words on the blackboard were just a fuzz. Eventually, when I was ten, I got glasses. In the seventies, there was no such place as Specsavers and it wasn't considered sophisticated to wear glasses. Girl power hadn't hit the world so women weren't considered sexy and intelligent if they wore glasses. All I saw when I looked in the mirror was a flabby speccy-four-eyes. I didn't want to leave my bed, let alone the house.

I got through school by acting tough. Anyone who actually called me speccy-four-eyes to my face got a Chinese burn for their troubles. I developed a thick skin and a quick tongue, lashing out at anyone who made me feel unsure of myself. I couched it all in laughter, of course, but what I said always stung. I knew most of the girls were terrified of me as well as disliking me, but what did I care?

Martin is my Auntie Marie's son. Marie wasn't really my blood relation, she was Mammy's closest friend and the nearest thing we ever had to an extended family. Martin was just six months older than me, so we were always together when our mothers were chatting in the kitchen. Mammy and Auntie Marie used to turn up the radio and dance. I can still hear their giggles, I tell you. They were a bit touched back then.

'What are you doing?' I remember asking as Mammy and Marie did the actions to 'The Birdie Song'.

'It's called being silly, and unlike most things in life, it's free of charge!' Mammy had said, roaring laughing.

Martin had two younger siblings and we had grunting conversations about how annoying little kids were.

'I wish I was an only child,' I used to mutter, as I shoved my glasses back up my nose with my middle finger.

'Yeah. That'd be deadly. No hanger-oners. A bedroom to yourself.'

It was great with Martin because I forgot about my fat body and my bloody glasses. I could just sit with him and be myself. We'd known each other so long, all that other stuff didn't matter. I was just Greta and he was just Martin. The rest didn't feature.

When I left school, I'd no intention of going to my graduation ball. If I never saw the pack of bitches from my class again, it'd be too soon. But Martin was sent to have a word with me. Mammy was next door, having a cuppa with Auntie Marie. I was sitting at the kitchen table flicking through a newspaper, bored and feeling pretty low. I remember that day as if it were yesterday. Martin let himself in our back door and stood looking all awkward and weird.

'I'm after getting tickets to my Debs ball. Are you coming?' He didn't look me in the eye. 'You can tell me to shag off if you don't want to. I won't mind. I'll get you flowers and chocolates and all, and I won't try to shift you, I promise,' he assured me.

'Why not? Am I too fat for you?' I answered nastily.

'No, not at all, Greta. You're lovely-looking. Even if you are a bit, eh, fat.'

'That's very insulting. I'm proud of my curves. That's what people call it now – curves. Fat went out with the Rubix cube. Move with the times, Martin.'

'So will you and your curves come with me then?'

Both of us cracked up laughing.

'Ah, go on then. Sure, we'll get pissed and have a laugh. If it's really terrible, we can always leave,' I said.

'Yeah, I'll bring you for a kebab instead and you can ensure your curves don't feel neglected,' Martin chuckled.

Mammy was surprisingly excited about the whole thing. She got material and made me a dress and Auntie Marie sewed sequins on it.

'Black is a great colour for hiding the bulges and the bit of strategically placed glitter takes the eye away from the parts that mightn't be your best features,' said Auntie Marie. I was never into glitter and trimmings, but if it made Mammy and Auntie Marie happy that was fine by me.

True to his word, Martin turned up bearing gifts. God bless him, he was dressed in a cheap, hired, nylon tuxedo suit and looked like he'd a carrot up his arse, he was so uncomfortable.

'I feel like a spanner, Greta. You look smashing though. Here's your chocolates. Oh, and this is a corset. You're meant to put it on your dress. Mammy told me to get someone else to do it or else I'll mark the dress and muck it up.'

'It's a *corsage*, you twat. A corset is bleeding underwear to hold in your wobbly bits!' I said, roaring with laughter.

'Ah, sorry. I've never heard of either of them, to be honest. I wasn't slagging you. Honest.' Martin pulled at the collar of his shirt. 'I feel like I've a *cobra* around my throat.'

'You look like James Bond, Martin. Seriously, you're not as ugly as usual,' I said, taking the gifts.

'Feck off,' he said, grinning.

Mammy and Auntie Marie stood at the gate and waved to us as we left the house a while later.

'You look stunning, love,' Mammy whispered to me as I hugged her goodbye. My heart soared with pride. Even if I did look like a piglet in a satin sack, I was thrilled that Mammy thought I was lovely.

We walked to the hotel around the corner – there was not a sniff of a Hummer or a limo in those days. Martin marched straight up to the bar and bought us a pint each.

'Ah, Martin, that tastes like it came from a colostomy bag. Get them to put some lime in it, will you? A good slosh of it now. I can't get pissed on that.'

'Do you want something else, Greta? I'll drink that for you if you like?'

He looked so willing to please me and genuinely would've bought me a bucket of brandy if I asked for it. A switch flicked in my mind. Martin really cared about me.

'Can I have a bottle of Ritz instead?' I asked in a softer tone.

'Of course you can.' He returned with the drink and a box of Marlboro cigarettes. 'Want one?'

'I've never really smoked,' I said, eyeing them up. Looking around, I noticed all the skinny bitches in the room were engulfed in a personal cloud of smoke.

'Go on then, I'll try one.'

At first I felt like I was going to choke. I coughed and my eyes watered so much I had to stub it out and go to the toilets and fix my new blue eyeliner.

I noticed something though. The cigarettes immediately made me feel less hungry. I decided two things that night. One, I was going to learn how to smoke and do it more often. Two, I liked Martin. Not like, like – but *like, liked* him.

We'd a mad night together. Martin paid for every one of the fifteen bottles of Ritz I drank. Not to mention the B52s and shots of peach schnapps. I got really into the smoking thing and by the end of the night, he'd taught me how to inhale properly. I was better at it the more pissed I got, and I even had a go at blowing smoke rings. All in all, the night was massive in every way.

The following day Mammy and Auntie Marie were in the kitchen looking for all the gossip about the night, when Martin called in.

'All right?' he asked nodding at me.

'Yeah, feeling a bit rough, but it was a deadly night. Thanks for looking after me. Did you enjoy it?' I asked.

'Ah yeah. Deadly.'

'Yeah, deadly,' I affirmed.

Mammy and Auntie Marie were looking for details. Who wore what and who looked like a hooker and who was puking, fighting or snogging – all the usual.

'Fag?' Martin asked, lighting up.

'I think I will, thanks,' I said.

'Since when do you smoke?' Mammy asked.

'Martin taught me last night,' I answered proudly.

'That's just bloody brilliant, that is. Oh, so healthy and you working in a gym,' Auntie Marie tutted sarcastically.

I took the cigarette anyway and decided I liked my new habit. Once I realised that smoking also made me crap like an elephant, I was even more enthusiastic. The more I smoked, the less I felt I needed to eat, and the quicker I dropped anything I did eat. My weight took a nosedive and I decided to go to one of the step aerobics classes at the gym. I didn't have to pay on account of my being staff, so it was worth a try.

All the other women in the class were wearing bright lycra gear, with legs like pipe cleaners and washboard stomachs. For the first half an hour I hated it and was vowing to myself never to repeat the experience. But then I started to get into it, sort of lost myself in the music, and before I knew it the class was over and I wanted another go. I was hooked.

I knew the mixture of exercise and smoking was a bit of a contradiction, but the results spoke volumes. Within eight months I was a fraction of my former size. I've often thought of giving up the smoking over the years, but it's like an old pal. My little crutch, if you like. It also represents the time that I evolved from being a person I hated on the outside to the person I always wished to look like on the outside.

Martin and I had started dating properly by then. We'd even done the wild thing and hadn't felt all funny with each other afterwards. When he proposed six months later, I accepted immediately. Mammy and Auntie Marie were beside themselves and insisted they would make my dress. That was fine by me – less to pay for the whole shindig.

The wedding was a quiet enough affair. We decided to have it at home to save on expense. We pinned up the Christmas lights around the sitting-cum-dining room and everyone crammed in. By the time both our families had been invited, along with the neighbours, we'd enough to be going on with. I invited a couple of the girls from school, but only to show them I wasn't a lard-ass any more. I got contact lenses and I knew I looked transformed.

One of them, Janet something, said exactly what I was hoping to hear. 'I can't believe how skinny you are!' she screeched at me. 'Your dress is actually quite nice too.'

She'd brought a boyfriend who looked like a gangster, with a thin moustache, a pale grey shiny suit and a mouth like a sewer.

'Here, Janet, your fella sounds like he has Tourette's. Can you tell him to quit with the cursing? Martin's mother is scarlet in the corner. She's never heard such language,' I said as innocently as I could manage. In reality, Auntie Marie would make a parrot blush, her language was so colourful when she'd a couple of beers on board. But Janet was on a need-to-know basis.

My happiness that day was complete when snotty Janet had to leave suddenly because yer man she brought was so drunk. She had to prop him up and steer him outside, and he made an utter eejit of himself by vomiting in the petunias outside Mammy's back door.

They never got to taste the chicken à la king and rice Mammy had cooked.

Vinnie from around the corner was doing a nixer as a DJ and he came round with flashing lights and two record decks. We danced to 'The Birdie Song' well into the wee hours and everyone on our road agreed it was the best wedding they'd been to in years.

I told Martin from the beginning that I'd no interest in having kids. I'd grown up with siblings coming out my ears and I didn't want more little ones hanging off me. He looked taken aback, but fair play to him he just nodded and said whatever I wanted was fine by him. That was Martin for you.

Technology was advancing at a rate of knots. Martin got a job in a big warehouse-style place that was going to sell nothing but computers. I laugh now to think that I considered it a fly-by-night operation.

'Do you think it'll work out?' I'd asked him, worried off my head. 'I can't say I get this idea that everyone on the planet will have those yokes in their houses in years to come.'

Luckily, I was totally wrong on that one. The other thing I misjudged was my timing with the pill. We weren't even married a year when I got knocked up.

'I'm not giving up smoking, and I'm certainly not getting fat,' I warned Martin.

'Right, love,' he'd answered calmly.

True to my word, I kept the weight off me. I only gained a stone in all over the nine months. The pregnancy was a nightmare all the same. I used to see other women patting their swollen bellies and looking at their bumps all dewy-eyed. All I could see was fat. I hated the lack of control I had over my body. I tried not eating, but inevitably the baby would squirm along with the grumbling of my empty tummy and I'd have to have something.

I'd obviously assumed I was having a boy. Well, my sister-in-law had just given birth to her Laurence, so I think I'd just decided it would suit us all if our sons could pal around together. I'd be able to connect with a boy, too. He could play soccer and ride on his bike beside me while I was running.

When the birth was over I knew I'd never, ever go through that ordeal again.

'If you have to have your bits chopped off, so be it, Martin. Nothing about that was natural,' I said bathed in sweat, shivering like crazy and feeling as if I'd never be right again in my downstairs department. 'And we've had a girl! What am I meant to do with a daughter?'

'You'll be like two peas in a pod,' Martin said as he cuddled her. 'I can just see the two of you off shopping and gossiping in no time.'

'Eh, I've had a baby not a lobotomy, love,' I said. 'When have you ever known me to want to waste a day trotting around shops?'

The week after I'd had Tallulah, I left the maternity hospital vowing to shed the fourteen pounds I'd gained as quickly as possible.

I named her Tallulah so she'd grow up skinny and pretty. The way I saw it was this: who's ever heard of a girl called Tallulah and thought 'fat ugly cow'? The two just couldn't go together.

Martin was a brilliant dad from the second his daughter was born. He did all the bottles and night feeds. He changed the most stomach-churning nappies and never flinched. He never got tired of playing silly peekaboo games and he never seemed bored by the mind-numbingly repetitive life she gave us.

Mammy loved babies, so she happily took Tallulah during the day while I went back to work at the gym. Our two-bed house was modest, but it still wasn't free of charge. I had to bring in some money. And as Mammy said, she'd been minding babies for so long, she'd be bored if she didn't have one on her hip.

She doted on Tallulah and spent more time and energy on her than she did on me or my brothers and sister. She was always cooking and baking with her, and that was probably why Tallulah ended up looking like a baby seal by the time she started school.

I'd no interest in food at all, so Martin tended to eat at work and bring home a few chips or a kebab for himself and Tallulah to have for tea. It became their thing, and I suppose I just let them at it.

When Tallulah was five, Mammy passed away suddenly. The void she left in her wake was gut-wrenching. Of course she was my mother and I'd adored her, but the worst part was the impact it had on Tallulah. For weeks on end, she cried herself to sleep. She'd call out in the night for Nana to come back. I went through a stage where that awful feeling I'd had in school crept back, the dreadful sensation where I knew I wasn't good enough. I'd try and comfort Tallulah, but all she wanted was her nana.

It was a blessed relief when Tallulah started school. I knew she was being looked after and she was distracted most of the time. She stopped crying for her nana and latched on to Martin instead.

The older she got, the bigger she got. I tried to tell her to stop eating so much. If I told her once, I told her a thousand times – nobody likes a fat girl. But did it have any effect? No. Every time I looked at the kid, she was pushing something sweet and fattening into her pudgy little face. I'm sure she thought I was angry with her about it, but the truth was it made me feel sad and afraid, if I'm being honest. It was like looking at a slow-motion video of myself at the same age. I know I should've tried harder to put a stop to the continuous weight gain, but the whole thing scared me witless. When I looked at her, I saw what I could so easily be if I lost my hold on the reins. So I grabbed them tighter and tighter – it was the only way to protect myself.

Martin didn't seem to notice how big she was getting and would bring her treats home. The two of them would sit and watch the kids from *Fame* and munch through bags of crisps and packets of biscuits.

'You're Daddy's little princess,' Martin would tell her as they shared the sofa. They never got tired of watching their musical videos. If she wasn't being Annie, Martin had the child believing she was Mary Poppins. He'd pretend to be Dick Van Dyke and they'd prance around like two Goons.

Their relationship was so strong and they seemed so at home together, I guess I just took a step back. I retreated to a place I could control in my own mind. My weight became my main focus in life.

A new line of products came on board in the gym. They were milkshakes that were an entire meal. I thought they were the most ingenious thing on the planet. Instead of eating rabbit food or just not eating at all, I could have one of them and I was full. They had all the nutrients I needed to have the energy to keep up with my workout regime. I usually found the days I didn't eat much a strain – I'd get head spins and feel like I was going to pass out. I worried I was doing myself damage, too, so the milkshakes were the answer to all my prayers.

Martin and Tallulah wouldn't even try them. So I left them to their pies and happy-clappy movies. I figured I was being like Mammy and taking a live and let live approach. If I left Tallulah to make her own decisions, eventually she'd come to her senses, or so I hoped. But every now and again, I'd freak out and wouldn't be able to hold my tongue.

'Martin, that pie in a tin could be made from deep fried rat, for all you know. Would the two of you not try a shake?' I asked one time.

'Until I end up in an old folks' home with no teeth, I'll stick to my grub,' Martin said. 'You love them shakes and that's fine by me, pet. But it wouldn't be good for a man or a growing child to live on them.'

The odd time people would make snide comments to me about Tallulah's weight. I always ended up feeling like they were attacking me more than her. 'I lead by example,' I'd tell them, in no uncertain terms. 'She knows that she needs to drink her shakes and run. But will she listen? No.'

Tallulah's eighteen now. I can't really believe all that time has passed. We get on fine most of the time, but we're still like chalk and cheese. She's a daddy's girl and that's the way it is.

When the gym was sold and my hours were cut, the new owners banned staff from attending the classes for free. I bought a load of exercise videos instead. But what I found I really loved was running. I got more and more into it. I found the freedom of pounding the pavements gave me a new lease of life. Every run I take, I feel like I'm running another bit away from the old me. I know I haven't been fat for decades now, but I can't let go of the feeling that it could pounce on me again if I take my eye off the ball for a second. I have to maintain this level of exercise, keep drinking the shakes, keep smoking the fags. I have to be *this* Greta, otherwise I'll be destroyed.

I burned all the photos from my childhood. When Mammy died, I did a swoop of the old photo albums and took all the ones of me and burned them in the back yard while Martin was at work. I never need to be reminded of how repulsive I was. Those images are burned into the back of my mind.

The best thing about the way I am now is the sense of control. I can decide exactly what goes into my body. I can look the way I want. When I was a fat slob, I never felt good. I always felt like I needed to apologise for myself. Now that I'm thin and fit, I feel like I can take on the world. For me, being slim means I look like someone who takes pride in herself. I feel I can hold my head up and feel proud of me. It isn't easy to look like this, but I've done it.

There's only one fly in the ointment in all this. For years I thought I had it all worked out: once I was skinny, I would automatically be happy. The two things were completely interconnected as far as I was concerned. I've always believed that once my body was a well-oiled machine and my cheekbones were prominent and I had no bits that wobbled, I would be content and at ease with myself. Happy.

It's been an awful punch in the well-toned six-pack to realise that I was wrong.

3.

Mia's Story

It's odd, as a midwife I deal with babies all the time and it usually doesn't phase me at all. But every now and again I see a baby who reminds me of Amy. Sometimes it's a baby's silky dark hair, or maybe the shape of her little head, whatever triggers it, suddenly I'm back in March 1984. Over the years I've learned to live with my grief, but whenever I dare to think I have it all sorted in my head, I'm overwhelmed by the memories once again.

I'd been in labour for sixteen hours when my first child, Amy, finally made her way into the world. She was born in Galway General Hospital. Jim was at work and we'd decided that he wouldn't be there for the birth. He wouldn't have been the type to cope with it. I know from experience men fall into two categories – fainters and fog-horns. The fog-horns yell more than the woman in labour and generally upset and distract everyone. Jim would've been the other kind, the turn-green-and-pass-out type, so we thought it best he stay away from the whole birthing experience. Sure, I was so looking forward to meeting my little one, I wasn't a bit afraid, so it didn't matter either way.

Amy was a textbook baby. She slept when she was supposed to, took her feeds on time and rarely cried. I was in seventh heaven and loved dressing her in little pink outfits with tiny matching hats. Jim had painted her nursery a pale shade of candyfloss pink, the same colour as the quilt I had sewn for her during the nine months of waiting. No baby was every so cosseted as she was. We both adored her.

The morning of 4 July 1984 – at 11.36 to be precise – was the worst moment of my entire life. Amy was exactly four months old to the day. As usual, she went for a midmorning nap. She took a few moments to settle and I left her bedroom door ajar, so I would know that she'd nodded off. I knew not to leave her to sleep too long, or else she'd be out of kilter with her feeds and afternoon nap.

Looking at my watch a while later, I decided I'd go in and wake her gently. I crept into the nursery and saw her lying there, with her little arms stretched out above her head. She was face down. At that time, the general medical opinion was that babies should sleep on their tummies. All that has changed since, of course.

I opened the curtains and made my way over to the cot, ready to stroke her or tickle her little hand to wake her up. As I looked down at her, before I even put a hand to her, I knew she was dead.

At first, I was afraid to touch her. I hesitated, telling myself over and over again that she was just asleep. I think I'd convinced myself that if I didn't have full and total confirmation that she was gone, there was still hope. But I'd seen stillborn babies during the course of my work, so I knew full well what I was gazing at. I forced my hand to reach forward and I touched her skin. That was the moment I knew for sure. In a blind panic, I scooped her body out of the cot and held her tightly to my chest. A deep, hollow sound poured out of me, for all the world like the cows in labour down on the farm. I couldn't believe that noise had come out of me. As I looked helplessly at her tiny rosebud mouth and long sweeping eyelashes, knowing those eyes would never open again, I began to shake all over. That image of Amy – frozen in time, with all colour drained from her skin, leaving her with that unmistakable greyish-white pallor – will remain with me till the day the good Lord takes me to my rest. I can never, ever escape from it.

I ran to the kitchen, still clutching her body, and laid her gently in the pram. I dialled 999 with shaking fingers and managed to tell the woman at the other end that I needed an ambulance.

'My baby isn't breathing.'

I repeated the sentence over and over. The lady on the phone kept asking for my address. I kept answering with the same mantra.

'My baby isn't breathing.'

I must have given her my details before I dialled Jim's number because a squad car and an ambulance arrived in what felt like moments. Jim followed close behind. His car screeched to a halt and he flung himself out of it and up the path to our front door.

The police were very kind. There were three officers and one was a woman. She stroked my hand as Jim wrapped me in his arms and sobbed loudly. I'd never seen or heard my husband cry before. I think his open distress added to my own trauma. The entire scene was like something from a sick horror movie. Jim was a big hulk of a man physically, but he was steady in personality, never loud or booming, more of a gentle giant. He had an easy smile and was tolerant to a point of astonishment in my mind. He rarely raised his voice in all the years we shared together. So to hear such thunderous bawling from my darling man was a torture all its own.

The ambulance people explained that her tiny body needed to be taken to the hospital for a postmortem. Jim held me back as they lifted her body from her pram for the last time, and took her out of our home, away from me.

We were brought to the hospital in the police car. The only sound during that journey came from the radio. A man was hosting a chat show. They were discussing the plight of the red squirrel in Irish woodlands. I can still remember the dialogue. Neither myself nor Jim cried, nor did we utter a syllable to one another. It was as if we were frozen in time, too, along with Amy.

The ambulance drove ahead of us in silence. I remember wanting it to blare its siren, but of course there was no need. There was no hurry. The emergency had happened. The worst-case scenario had already been realised.

Perhaps it was because I was a midwife at the hospital or maybe it was the luck of the draw, but the coroner was on site when we arrived.

'I'll conduct the postmortem now,' he assured us.

We were shown to the family room, where I had brought grieving family members on more than one occasion. Any time I had retreated from that room, I had sent up a silent prayer for the destroyed family I'd just left behind me. But nothing could have prepared me for how it felt to be the ones who remained in the room while the medics departed to do their work – in this case, to carry out the postmortem on our baby's lifeless little body.

By my own request, I have never been in that room since.

Jim and I clung to one another like koalas, and very little time seemed to pass before the coroner returned to talk to us.

'The official report will take time, Mr and Mrs Byrne. As you know yourself, the paperwork must be done and you'll receive my written report. But I wanted you to know, off the record, that I have filled in "no known cause of death was found",' he said gently. 'This was a case of cot death.'

'But something must have caused it?' I sobbed. 'You can't just say there's no medical reason why Amy is dead! Please, you must be missing something. Did she have a heart defect? Was there any sign of a brain haemorrhage? Please, I need to know!' I suddenly felt panicked. I didn't want the coroner to leave the room. I needed to know what had gone wrong, to give it a reassuring medical name and know it was inevitable.

The coroner looked down at his notes and took a deep breath. Then he looked me directly in the eyes. 'There is rarely any medical explanation for this, as you must be aware Nurse Byrne.'

'But I did what I was supposed to,' I cried out, feeling a sort of rage rising up in me. 'I'm a midwife, for God's sake, my baby shouldn't have died.' My hands shook, then the rest of my body joined in. My teeth chattered and I felt Jim's large frame enveloping me once more.

'I couldn't find any distress to the vital organs,' the coroner said gently. 'There was no bleeding in the brain. I'm so sorry.' He hesitated. 'I know it would be easier for you if there was a definite explanation and I wish to God I could provide it, but I've checked carefully and nothing has shown up.'

I collapsed against Jim's chest and was lost under a heaving sea of grief. That's the only way I can describe it. It was like when I was little and went out of my depth in Galway Bay and the sense of helplessness and resignation that floated over me as I watched my family get farther away on the shore. That feeling that you're just too small to fight, let alone win. I was too small to do anything at all that day, so I just sank to the bottom and let those waves crash over me. It was useless to try to be brave or show a stiff upper lip, any of that guff. This was a grief so real, it seemed to make the world disappear from around me. There was only me and that raw, painful emotion and, somewhere on the periphery, Jim, trying to reach me and failing.

Three days later, as we went through the motions of the funeral, I was still locked inside myself, so bitterly hurt and ashamed that there was no reason for this. To this day I often have flashing images of the tiny white coffin, the hoards of well-wishers, the flurry of letters and mass cards that were sent from far and wide telling us that Amy was in many kind hearts and prayers. Those good intentions were probably what kept me from shrivelling into a ball and expiring.

For a long time, I blamed myself. I agonised over the events leading up to that moment. I turned each second over and over in my mind. But in the end I had to come to the conclusion that no amount of self-loathing was going to bring Amy back to us. That was the awful truth of the matter.

'How are you going to tend to new mammies and little babies in your grief?' Jim had asked me, worried.

'I'm not sure,' I'd answered honestly. 'But it's all I ever wanted to do and it's all I know. I'll give it a go, and if it's too painful, we'll have to reassess things,' I said, hugging him.

Amazing as it may sound, other people's babies helped to heal my battered soul. Enough, at least, so I could shunt myself from one end of the day to the next. Having daily contact with babies, instead of having the milky scent and tiny features erased from my life entirely, seemed to get me through.

A year later I fell pregnant for the second time and our family and friends rejoiced for us. Although each and every person was quick to point out that Amy could never be replaced, we all felt this new baby would give Jim and I renewed faith in the world.

When Terry arrived nine months later, I was relieved he was a boy. Even though it was almost two years since Amy's death by the time he was born, I still didn't feel ready for another girl at that time.

Terry looked totally different from Amy. Although he shared his sister's sallow complexion and shock of dark hair, he was rounder and more robust. His features were broad, like his daddy's. His fists were square as opposed to Amy's slender petite hands. His temperament was feisty and demanding to match. He fed constantly and much as I tried, I couldn't get him to stick to any kind of sleeping routine. As I think back to those early days of Terry's life, I think that was God's way of reassuring me, hour by hour, that he was still alive. I never moaned about the lack of sleep with Terry. I spent the first few weeks with one eye open. His Moses basket was right beside my head in our bedroom. I barely allowed myself any kind of decent sleep.

By the time Terry was past the six-week stage, I was so destroyed by lack of sleep, I think I would've passed out in a bath of iced water. So between the two of us, Terry and I learned to conk out on a chair, sofa, bus or park bench for any passing snatch of sleep that was available. It was like he understood that I needed it to be this way. He was a great little thing, God bless him.

Johnnie graced us with his presence in 1987, a year after Terry. Two babies under the age of two meant I had very little time for deep thinking. The sharp pain of Amy's loss eased slightly. The nightmares didn't terrify me quite as often and, over time, it was only about once a month that I'd jolt awake in the dead hours of the night, crying and weeping for a baby who wasn't there.

As the years flew by and Mark came along in 1989, followed by Bob in 1991, a major step had to be taken. The size of our family meant Amy's bedroom had to be repainted and given over to baby Bob. With a heavy heart, Jim painted over the candyfloss pink, which had faded so much by that stage it was closer to white. Her bedroom may have changed, but photos of baby Amy were on the mantelpiece, in the hallway and on our bedside tables. The boys all knew they had an 'angel sister' who was looking down on them from heaven. Jim and I would talk about Amy regularly in everyday conversation and each and every Sunday we brought the boys to lay flowers on her grave.

For the most part, I learned to live with the grief of losing my little girl, but some days, out of the blue, I'd experience a dreadful stab of deep hurt. In that moment I'd feel so overwhelmed by emptiness and sadness, I'd feel as if I couldn't go on. But then one of my beautiful boys would instinctively hug me or ask a childish question, like, 'Mama, why don't slugs have eyebrows?', and I would realise that I still had so much to live for. I learned to be grateful for what I had.

Family life kept us busy for the next few years and Jim and I came to rely on each other completely. I felt so lucky to have a husband who met me halfway on everything and treated our family as a wonderful blessing. I'd see other women's husbands at the pub for hours of an evening or off playing golf or whatever, and my heart would break for them. I couldn't have done it all if I hadn't had Jim at my side, through thick and thin, as completely devoted to our little family as I was. We were happy.

But after a while I began to long for another child. I know it might make me sound as if I wasn't content with my lot, but I just couldn't get it out of my head that there was another little one out there for us.

'Mia, don't you think you've done your bit for the population of the planet at this point?' Jim teased.

'I know most women would think that, but I still feel as if I have room in my heart for one more,' I said sheepishly.

Of course I knew, without saying it out loud, that the real reason I felt as if my life wasn't complete was down to losing Amy. I often wondered whether I'd have still felt the void as strongly had I given birth to another daughter. My lads were my world, but I still yearned for a little girl to cradle in my arms once more.

We decided to let nature take its course and leave it in the lap of the gods.

'We'll play Russian roulette and see what happens,' Jim said.

'Is that what they're calling it nowadays?' I teased him.

While I hoped and prayed to be blessed with another baby, I had no idea that my world was about to be shattered beyond recognition.

It was December 1993. I was putting up Christmas decorations and trying to find a set of tree lights that actually worked when there was a ring on the doorbell.

'It looks as if his heart gave way, Mia. I'm so terribly sorry.'

One of the uniformed officers stroked my arm as he fought to maintain control of his own emotions.

I went into a misty place in my own head that nobody could touch. An awful, dark place that I'd gladly left locked away forever several years previously. That hideous feeling of overwhelming grief I'd been lost to after Amy had left us engulfed me once again.

The men led me to the kitchen, muttering kind words in an attempt to ease my shock. As I fell onto the kitchen chair, the faces of my young sons greeted me.

'Mama? Why are you crying? What's going on? Why are the men here?' Terry asked.

'Your daddy's gone to heaven,' I heard my own voice answering, sounding like it was a million miles away.

'But why?' Terry burst out crying. He was my eldest and I ached for him, knowing a huge part of his childhood innocence had just been ripped away.

Wiping my eyes with my sleeve, I took a huge gulp of air and gathered my four boys into my embrace. I pulled baby Bob onto my lap and huddled them all as closely as I could. Rocking them gently, I'd crooned into their hair. 'Daddy had to go and mind Amy, lads. She needed her daddy, too. We had him for a good while and now he has to go her,' I explained.

'Didn't he like it here with us? Wasn't he happy?' Johnnie stuttered through his tears.

'Of course he did, darling. He loved us more than anything else in the world, but God decided He needed him to go and be an angel in heaven with Amy,' I said gently, choking back my own tears.

'But *we* need him. Who's going to bring me fishing?' Johnnie cried. I prayed silently that God would give me the strength to raise these children on my own. I hoped I would have the ability to protect and love them and turn them into caring men, just as Jim would've wanted.

As they'd done nine years earlier, the kind people of Carryway rallied around us. The neighbours sent trays of lasagne and pots of stew. They offered school lifts and practical help with ironing and cleaning. Yet again, I was blown away by the empathy and human kindness bestowed upon me at that dreadful time.

The postmortem showed that Jim had suffered a massive heart attack. At least this time, I had a sound and logical reason as to why another person I loved the very bones of had been taken away from me so suddenly. Unlike Amy's unexplained death, Jim's was easier to grieve.

The evening of his month's mind mass, I was standing in the courtyard outside the local church when the trees began to spin. All the sounds of people talking and my boys' chattering voices dulled.

Echoes filled my head. I knew before I hit the hard ground that I was collapsing, but I couldn't stop it. In slow motion, I tried to grab the handles of Bob's buggy for support, but it seemed to slip from my grasp. I wasn't able to steady myself.

As I came around, I was advised to sit with my head bent towards my knees. Most of the shocked onlookers understandably assumed I had passed out from sheer grief and exhaustion. A house call from the local doctor later that evening confirmed otherwise – I was pregnant with Jim's 'Russian roulette' child.

The doctor smiled kindly at me, obviously thinking this was a little blessing, a little gift from my dead husband that would help me through. Inside, I silently cursed Jim. I felt anger like I'd never known possible. There I was, a widow with four young children, and now I was expected to bear another child – alone.

That night, as I knelt at the side of our redundant marital bed and clasped my hands in front of my face, I dissolved into hysterical and exhausted tears. I was emotionally and physically wrung out. I felt like I couldn't take a single moment more of the black and cold existence that had become my lonely life since Jim had gone.

'How could you do this to me, Jim? I can't cope as it is,' I hissed through gritted teeth into the darkness. 'Why did you have to leave me with this mess?'

I know that might sound very stupid of me, but God help me, I honestly thought there was some sort of ration of sadness and pain that each person was allotted in life. I had convinced myself after Amy's death that her passing was the entire dose of badness that I was going to be dealt in life. As I ached for my dead daughter, I think I got myself through by deciding that I had now filled my quota of grief. I had walked through the valley of death and come out the other side, and I wouldn't be asked to make that journey again. With Jim's death, I realised that there was no such line in the sand. There was no limit to the amount of dreadfulness that a single person could be asked to bear in one lifetime.

As I knelt there on the hard bedroom floor, trying to pray, the sound of Bob crying made me rise and move with robotic movements to his bedroom. As I cuddled Bob and stroked his flaming little cheek,

I felt immeasurably sorry for the infant. He would never remember his father and now he was going to be forced to grow up and be a big brother to this new child.

'God, if you're listening, I don't understand You. Why have You done this to me?' I said aloud to the ceiling.

I won't say it was a voice in my head or anything so dramatic, but in that moment I was suddenly possessed of the idea that the tiny seed growing in my womb was a girl. It was like a tiny flicker of hope that sparked deep in the recesses of my frozen heart. Somehow, I just knew this was Jim's parting gift to me.

I loved and adored my boys. If anyone ever tried to hurt so much as a hair on one of their heads, I'd have murdered them with my bare hands. But I often feared that once they were older, I would have less in common with them. They would hopefully enjoy sports and find good partners, but it was unlikely that any of them would want to go up to Galway city with me to look at the new fashions. But a girl – a girl would be a different thing altogether. I felt that a girl would stay with me and comfort me until I left to be with Jim.

Rita, my older sister, had appeared for Jim's funeral. She'd flown in from England where she'd lived for donkey's years. After my dramatic collapsing incident in the churchyard, she felt she owed it to me to stay a while and help. Well, there was always a first time for showing concern. We'd never been close. She was nothing like me, either to look at or speak to. She lived alone in a well-to-do area of London and was 'a professional'. I always felt she looked down her nose at me for being a mother. The fact that I was a midwife seemed to please her even less. She hadn't a maternal bone in her body and when I think of her now, Lord rest her, I actually feel sorry for her.

She was the most unlikely saviour, then, to come to my aid, but that's what she did.

'I think you should come to London and stay with me until that child is born,' Rita stated bluntly at my kitchen table a few days after the funeral.

My immediate reaction was to tell her to sod off, that I'd rather stick pins in my own eyes than drag my boys to London and endure her wrath for the next few months. But the shock of Jim dying and the difficulty in balancing the household and four small boys all alone made me change my mind.

I also knew I was in severe danger of heading down a dark road of despair, where I would drown in my own grief. I figured that if nothing else, London might offer a change of scenery and, more to the point, a place where the ghosts of my baby and husband didn't reside. The space on Jim's side of the bed was so vast, the silence was so loud, I just had to get away for a while.

We packed up the car and took the boat to England. The theory was that Rita would give me some time to myself and that I'd be more relaxed and less aggrieved by the time the baby was born. In reality, I was probably more stressed than I'd ever been in my life as the children fell into instant hate with their auntie.

In order to get a bit of head-space, rather than any real need to attend, I joined the local prenatal class. I figured it would afford me the chance to meet some other mothers and maybe a few people with children the boys' ages. Because it was a 'medically associated' session, Rita agreed to mind the boys while I went. It didn't seem to occur to her that I might know much or all of the information the class was supposed to teach.

I met some lovely women, who welcomed me warmly and of course we shared the sense of sisterhood that pregnancy brings. That was also where I met a friend who helped me to clamber back out of the dark hole that had become my life.

Aoife was Irish, too, and as she was enduring a God-awful pregnancy, we became united in pain. As a midwife, I was able to advise her and help her with the physical stuff. In return she offered me a listening ear and a shoulder to cry on. Our relationship was intense and healing. We could've introduced our children and done the whole playdate thing, but both of us enjoyed the fact that we had a one-to-one relationship, which gave us much needed refuge. It was almost like we were having an affair! When the classes finished, we had the opportunity to join prenatal yoga each Monday.

Rita managed her job by taking Monday as her day off. She was never going to win an award for her natural maternal tendencies – Mary Poppins she certainly was not. She rarely smiled at me, or at the children for that matter. Fun in her presence was out the window and she barked instead of speaking, but, in fairness to her, she rearranged her life to help me out when I desperately needed it.

I decided that when the baby was born, we'd return to Ireland fairly quickly. I was anxious to be back home before the start of the new school year in September.

The day I went into labour, every emotion known to woman must've rushed through me. I longed to have Jim beside me. Even though I'd given birth five times before and had vast midwifery experience, I'd never felt more alone, or more terrified.

The nurses were fantastic, though, and rejoiced in such a heartfelt way when my baby slid into the world.

'You have a daughter! Well done, Mum.'

As my little girl was handed to me, swaddled tightly in a hospital blanket, some of the broken jigsaw pieces of my life clicked back into place. She wasn't at all like Amy in appearance, yet she had the dainty little hands and rosebud lips that none of the boys possessed.

'Have you thought of a name?' the midwife asked gently.

'I'm going to call her Felicity,' I said firmly. 'It means happiness. She's only here five minutes and she's already done more for me than I'd ever have thought possible.'

'Ah, isn't that lovely?' the midwife answered, smiling at the two of us.

As I gazed down, Felicity opened her eyes and stared right back. Most books will tell you that newborns don't focus on much for the first couple of days, but I will never forget the feelings I had when Felicity's eyes met mine at that moment. It was so bittersweet. Here in my arms was most certainly what I needed to fill the void I'd spoken to Jim about. I was just gutted that he wasn't there to share it with me.

'Watch over and protect our precious daughter, Jim,' I whispered as I kissed Felicity's downy head. 'Please stay by my side and guide me through the journey I'm about to take.'

We came home in mid-August. I had a tearful farewell with Aoife, who would be the thing I'd miss most about England. She had shown me the kind of love and understanding that only comes along rarely, and I owed her so much for that. But it was time for me to take my family home.

Almost the first thing I did when we got back was to visit the grave. I brought Felicity with me in her pram and introduced her to her father and sister. The tears coursed down my cheeks as I looked at the headstone.

Here lies Baby Amy Byrne
Died 4 July 1984, Age 4 months
A baby angel who will never be forgotten
Sleep in peace, baby girl

And also
James Byrne
Died 22 December 1993
Loving father, husband and friend
Sadly missed and always in the hearts of those who loved him
May he rest in peace

Time has been a healer in many ways. I've come to terms with my lot in life. I've made my peace with God. But I still think of Jim and Amy each and every day. I often look at girls around Amy's age and wonder where she'd be if she were alive today. I try to picture her in my mind's eye as a grown-up. Herself and Felicity were so unalike to look at as babies, that I don't gaze at Felicity and feel Amy is still here. The loss of Amy hits me at times like a physical blow, making me gasp and long for her.

I've never met another man. Odd as it might sound, I don't know if I actually want to.

Of course, everything is set to change again now. That's life, isn't it? With time, everything is different. Felicity, my baby, is now eighteen years old and she's getting ready to strike out on her own. Of course I've heard of empty nest syndrome, but you don't understand it until it's your turn and you feel what it means. What I hadn't expected was how frightened I'd feel. I'm going to have to crawl out from behind the screen that motherhood has afforded me. Raising five children has been my ticket to a strange sort of independence. It'd be rare for anyone to invite a woman and five children over for Christmas dinner. Equally, I could easily avoid any evening invitations that didn't tickle my fancy, using the lack of a babysitter as an excuse. Plus the fact that I've always worked had served as a further buffer against concerned suggestions from well-meaning people. The fact is, nobody sees me as a loner. I'm always inundated with young people. My kitchen has provided enough hot dinners to open a small restaurant. My clothesline is never bare. I am very rarely alone. But now Felicity is going to move on, just like her brothers have. It hurts like hell, but I know she's not mine to keep. She's not a possession.

Now, I am starkly aware that the time has come to dust myself off and make some kind of life just for me. I'll have to fill in the gaps for myself as they begin to form. I haven't been just Mia for such a long time. I was Jim's wife, then the brave widow raising a brood on her own. If I'm not going to be Felicity's primary carer any longer, that means I need to reinvent myself. I'm not sure I know how to go it alone. The thought of being just Mia makes me feel more afraid than I could describe to anyone. I'm not sure I even know who she is any longer.

Daughters ...

4.

Felicity

Felicity and her best friend, Aly, burst into Mia's kitchen, laughing and talking at the tops of their voices.

'Woo hoo, Mum, we're finished!' The two girls were hyper, unable to sit still. They flung their schoolbags into the corner. 'And do you know how we're going to celebrate?' Felicity asked, with devilment in her eyes.

Mia looked at them warily, wondering what hare-brained plan they'd devised this time.

'We're going to burn this damn uniform!' Aly screeched.

'What?' Mia gasped. 'Are you two mental?'

'No, Mum, just happy, happy, *happy*,' Felicity shouted, spinning Aly around.

Mia shook her head – when they were like this, she knew there was no talking to them.

It was June and the girls had just finished their last school exam. The state exams were a rite of passage, marking the end of school and the beginning of their future.

They ran giggling up to Felicity's room, flung off their uniforms and yanked on whatever was closest to hand. They rushed past Mia and out the back door, running up the field behind the house until they reached a safe spot.

Felicity grinned at Aly. 'Right, bonfire time!'

They stuffed hay into their school blouses and set them alight. Once it got going, they added their hated gabardines, jumpers and ties, lastly flinging their shoes on the flames for good measure. They created a bonfire that would've made Guy Fawkes proud. 'High five,' Aly shouted, and Felicity reached up and slapped her hand. 'What an amazing feeling,' Aly sighed, hugging her friend.

'I just hope to God I get enough points to get into college,'

Felicity said as she poked the smoldering mess that used to be her gabardine.

'You've always been a brainbox, Flick, you'll fly it. I'm the one who should be worried and I'm not!' Aly retorted. 'I'll go wherever they'll have me. I just want to have fun, if I'm totally honest.'

Felicity and Aly had applied to the same universities, hoping they'd end up at least in the same place, if not on the same course. But they both knew there was a likelihood of separation. As Aly had pointed out, Felicity had always been more studious. Aly was a good-time girl and her attitude to most things was 'feck it, we won't worry about that too much'.

Felicity wished she shared her best friend's point of view, but she did admit to worrying about things a little more. She wanted to make something of herself. Perhaps it was down to the fact that she'd grown up without a father, but her mother had instilled, by example, how important it was to be independent as a modern woman.

'You should never have to rely on any man,' Mia had said a million times. 'Your father, God rest him, would have worked his fingers to the bone for us all, but he wasn't given the chance. If I hadn't had my nursing to fall back on, I don't know how we would've survived.'

Felicity and Aly had been working Saturday jobs during the school year in Carryway, their local town – Felicity at the delicatessen and Aly at a boutique – so they'd confirmed their summer jobs well in advance. The way they had it figured, if they stayed put at home – Felicity with her mam and brothers, Aly with her parents – they'd have enough savings to enjoy university to the full.

'I'm burrowing away as many clothes as I can, too, I'll let you know when the autumn/winter samples come in. I'm sure my boss will let us have first pick, like last year,' Aly said as she crouched down to make sure her school jumper was well and truly barbecued. 'Come on, I'm starving – and I think the uniforms are cooked,' Aly said with a grin. They grabbed each other and raced back down the field.

Felicity and Aly bundled back into the kitchen. The excitement that oozed from them made Mia feel eighteen years old again.

'I don't know why you had to burn your shoes,' she said disapprovingly to them. 'There was nothing wrong with them. They were just black slip-ons, you could have worn them again.' She looked at her daughter and her friend, their eyes shining, and tried to hide a smile. 'But far be it from me to tell you two what to do.'

'Mam, we're heading into town for the end of exams disco tonight. Aly is going to stay here afterwards so we'll stagger home ourselves, cool?' Felicity asked.

'Okay, love, that's grand once I know the two of you are together. So, have you decided on the outfits for tonight yet?' Mia asked as she pulled a chocolate cake out of the oven.

'Oh, my God, Mia, that smells like heaven. Will you make the fudge frosting or are you putting chocolate rum cream on it?' Aly asked as she hugged Mia.

'Well, considering it's your special day, I'd better do fudge frosting!' Mia said smiling.

'Thanks!' Aly clapped and grabbed Felicity by the arm. 'Let's go try on stuff and figure out who's wearing what. I want to see that pink tartan mini-skirt on you, I think it might suit you better.'

'I could wear it with my knee-high socks, do a Britney kind of look on it,' Felicity said. 'You okay, Mam, or do you need a hand with anything before we go and start getting ready?' Felicity asked kindly.

'No, pet, you two go on ahead. I'll call you for a bit of food in a while,' Mia answered. She smiled to herself. They weren't going out for another four hours at least, but the preening process would take a long time.

Within minutes, Bruno Mars was booming from the iPod deck in Felicity's bedroom.

The two girls spread all the new season gear out on Felicity's bed. She'd slept in the same white painted iron bed since she was a toddler. Her room had once been more old-fashioned, with flowery wallpaper and matching curtains and bedspread, but a few years ago Mia had let the two girls redecorate. With the help of Terry, Felicity's oldest brother, the girls had covered the more traditional wall covering with a plain, dull silver paper. They'd proceeded to cover the carpet and all the furniture with sheets before adding splashes of colour – literally. Using small pots of bright, clashing paints, they had dipped their brushes in and flicked paint randomly at the walls. To Mia, it looked like tinfoil after a particularly violent paintball fight, but the girls had professed it 'so cool'.

'That lace dress is gorgeous, Aly. Can I try it on with the little white denim jacket I got a few weeks ago?' Felicity asked. The pale pink mini-dress would be stunning with her sallow complexion and dark hair.

'Yeah, go for it. I'd look like a corpse in that,' Aly muttered as she rooted around the room for the jacket Felicity had in mind. With milky white skin and red hair, Aly knew she had to be careful about wearing too many neutral shades.

'Look under the bed, I wore it with that maxi dress. I can see the top of it just there, look!' Felicity pointed. Sure enough, the white jacket was stuffed under the bed, a perfect spot for a pale-coloured item.

Aly shook it out in an attempt to remove some of the creases, then handed it to Felicity.

'If it works, I'll iron it,' Felicity said, standing on her tippy toes to give an impression of high heels. 'What do you reckon? Yea or nae?'

'I really like it, but you need to show me what shoes you're thinking of. The bare feet look isn't grabbing me.'

After more flinging and grunting as she rooted in the wardrobe, Felicity found a pink platform sandal.

'I'll get the other one in a sec, nice?'

'Yeah, love it. You need the other shoe though. I've a funny feeling it's in my house. I think I saw it last week. My mum had a meltdown and I had to do a clean up and I'm almost certain I have it,' Aly said apologetically.

'Damn, it's half-past five now. By the time we troop to your house and back, eat and do hair and make-up, it'll be too much hassle.'

'Sorry, Flick,' Aly said.

'Ah no worries, what about silver instead? I've definitely got two of those here!' Felicity tottered to the mirror in shoes so high they looked like they needed to be accompanied by scaffolding to hold her upright.

'They're deadly. Will you be able to walk in them?' Aly asked.

'Ah yeah, I'll be grand after a couple of drinks. I can kick them off if I have to and we'll get a taxi home. I'll ask Mam to drop us down to the pub. We'll go to the bar below the disco and that way we only have to toddle up the stairs. I'll be grand,' she repeated.

With Felicity's outfit sorted, they moved on to Aly. She wasn't quite as quick in her selection.

'This is manky on me. I look deformed in everything tonight. Maybe I'll just go out in a black sack,' she said feeling deflated. When she was made up and had her long hair curled with the hair tongs, Aly knew she'd look fine, but she'd never have Felicity's dark skin and elfin sparkle.

'You look like Cheryl Cole, and I look like a complete minger,' Aly moaned.

'Shut up, would you? You'll be the one with boys hanging off you like bees to a honeycomb. Don't you go all poor mouthing on me!' Felicity wagged her finger with her hand on her hip.

'Okay, help me then! I give up! I can't create any "look" today. I think my brain is fried after all the exams,' Aly admitted.

'Oh, holy shit! Can you believe we've finished school?' Felicity suddenly screamed. 'We're free! We are now officially school-leavers!'

'We can sit and have conversations over a glass of wine mentioning the time when we were in school!'

Mia giggled as she heard the thumping around and squealing from above her head. The girls were going to be whipped into a total frenzy by the time they got to the bar later on. Mia called them down for a bowl of pasta and a slice of her melt-in-the-mouth chocolate cake.

Felicity was in a tracksuit and Aly wore a dressing gown.

'What are you both wearing later?' Mia sat and joined the girls for dinner. Bob was the only boy left living at home and there was no sign of him.

'Where's Bobbert?' Felicity asked, using her pet name for him.

'I'm not sure, he might have gone to the pub after work.' Mia wasn't too worried. She knew her youngest son would turn up at some stage.

'I'm sorted with this evening's clobber, but Aly's having a bit of a trial, aren't you Alz?' Felicity said popping a fork full of pasta into her mouth. 'Gorgeous sauce, Mam, by the way.'

'Thanks, that's one of Nigella's new recipes,' Mia said, smiling.

'Yeah, I feel like a freak, Mia,' Aly lamented, rolling her eyes. 'Everything looks kind of yuck and I'm almost at the stage where I'm going out in Felicity's duvet cover.'

'Tragic, but I'm sure you'll eventually find something suitable in that bomb site,' Mia said, smiling at Aly.

'I'll have you know, I can find anything you ask me for in my room. It's just, how shall I put it, laid out differently to the way you might like,' Felicity giggled to her mother.

'No comment,' Mia said, holding up her hands. 'So, any nice fellas on the horizon?'

'No – as in none that we know about yet,' Felicity answered.

'What about that guy Logan? He has it bad for your daughter,' Aly said laughing.

'Ugh! He doesn't. He just wants a girlfriend of some sort. It could be me, you, one of the Addams Family or a blow-up doll. He's so vile, I couldn't bear to go on a date with him,' Felicity shuddered.

'I think she likes him, don't you?' Mia teased.

'Yeah, what's that phrase about protesting too much?' Aly winked.

'"The lady doth protest too much, methinks",' Mia supplied.

'Oh, yuck, you two. And now if I say anything in my own defence, you'll think I *do* fancy him.'

They moved on to who would be there and what the other girls might be wearing.

'Well, Kate and Susan were in the shop last Saturday and they both bought maxi dresses. Annie will be wearing a stripper style outfit, as usual,' Aly said raising an eyebrow.

'She's not that bad, is she?' Mia looked shocked.

'Mam, last time we went to the disco, just before Christmas, she was wearing a strip of tinsel and very little else.'

'And without wanting to sound like a total bitch, she needs a hell of lot more decorating that that. Those thighs weren't designed to be on show,' Aly said cringing. 'I'm not even half her size and I wouldn't go out in the state of undress that one seems to deem decent.'

'Well, isn't it just so handy that you two are perfect?' Mia said dryly.

When the girls were fed and the kitchen cleared, Mia went through the list of people she needed to call on. She knew there were at least two new babies requiring the heel prick test over the next three days.

As the thundering of heels came down the stairs, Mia braced herself. She loved seeing the girls all dolled up, faces filled with anticipation.

'Well, give me a twirl. Oh, wow, you both look stunning!' Mia gasped. They did, too. The delicate pink, lace, baby doll dress made her daughter look divine. Aly was svelte and gorgeous in cream skinny jeans with a silver bandeau-style top and stilt-high glittery shoes. Both girls were so different looking – Aly was a pale-skinned, red-headed Irish beauty, while Felicity looked like she could've been plucked from Spanish shores with her dark eyes, hair and skin.

Perhaps because they were so radically different, they never fell out over clothing or boys. They made a great little team, though Mia knew the clock was ticking as far as the girls were concerned. She had this last summer to immerse herself in their wonderful young world and then they'd be spreading their wings and leaving her behind. If Mia was honest, her heart hoped that Felicity wouldn't get her first-choice university as it was 130 miles away in Dublin. But her head wanted her daughter to fulfil her highest ambition.

They all climbed into the car, and Mia smiled as she listened to the excited banter and tried not to sneeze and splutter.

'Jeepers, girls, how much perfume and hairspray have you put on?'

'My hair won't stay in the GHD curls without a ton of lacquer,' Aly said, poking her head between the two front seats to look in Mia's rear-view mirror.

'Sit back, you minx, if I brake suddenly, you'll fly through the windscreen,' Mia scolded.

'I just need to make sure I don't have fuzzy hair at the front,' Aly said sitting back reluctantly and clicking her belt in place.

'You're stunning, Aly, and don't even *think* about poking your hair. I've spent ages on those curls,' Felicity warned, leaning behind from the front seat.

When they reached the bar, the two girls kissed and hugged Mia, then slammed out of the car and linked arms, facing into their first night as post-school adults. Mia envied them, if she was totally honest. They had their whole lives ahead of them. The best was only beginning. They had finished the pressurised and nerve-wracking state final exams and university lay ahead, all going well.

Mia also felt immense pride swelling in her chest. She had raised Felicity and the boys alone, and as she inhaled the residual scent of the girls' sweet perfume, she knew she was going to suffer dreadfully when her youngest little chick flew off out of the nest and into the big blue yonder.

5.

Tally

Tally felt like a smurf – round and blue in the face from holding her breath. All she was missing was the hook-shaped white hat and she'd fit right in at the little people's village. She'd been desperately trying to suck in her stomach so she could close her black skirt. When she'd bought it a few weeks ago, it wasn't this tight. She hadn't washed it, so she couldn't convince herself it'd shrunk. She grabbed the back and pulled out the tag, but the size hadn't changed: it was still a twenty-four. She'd hoped against hope that she'd made an awful gaff and picked up a smaller size by mistake. No, the fact of the matter was that she'd gained weight – again.

There was nothing unusual in that, of course. Being known as the fat bird in her group was the story of her life.

'Tallulah? Where are you?' her mother Greta's voice penetrated her thoughts.

'I'm in here, Ma,' Tally answered glumly.

Greta burst into the room, fizzing with energy as always. Greta was eternally in a hurry. Unlike her husband and daughter, she was a fitness fiend. Built like a greyhound, she was all sinew and muscle. She worked part-time at the local gym and the rest of her day was taken up with her constant need to exercise. She didn't cook, didn't do sitting down or watching television, didn't let sugar, fat or many carbohydrates pass her lips. She preferred to live on protein shakes and salads.

Tally might've been large, but she always dressed in pretty outfits. Greta, on the other hand, rarely wore anything that wasn't made of lycra. In her defence, she was usually training so what she wore fit with her lifestyle, but it also meant she never changed and tried out new looks.

Today, for example, she was in her mid-calf-length black running tights with a matching vest, which showed her toned abs to perfection.

Greta stood inside Tally's bedroom door, skipping from foot to foot. 'Just checking on the belle of the ball,' she said with a grin.

'Ha, ha,' Tally said sarcastically.

Greta zipped up her lightweight running jacket, and raked her fingers through her short, bleached-blonde hair. 'That hairdresser I went to last time is a total chancer, look at my roots coming through already.'

'That bright colour is difficult to keep, Mam,' Tally offered. 'Would you not consider going for a slightly toned down—'

'No, I wouldn't, thanks very much. I work hard to look like this. Just because it's a bit tricky doesn't mean I'm going to lower my standards,' Greta said sharply.

'I didn't mean it that way … Oh, forget it,' Tally trailed off.

She was talking to herself anyway, Greta had rushed to her bedroom to yank on her trainers and begin her leg stretches. As she limbered up on the landing, Tally watched her and had one of those regular moments when she marvelled at the difference in size between herself and her mother. Greta was a size eight and proud of it. She loved to point out, loudly, that some of the stores were way off the mark with their sizing. 'Look at the way this gapes on me! Size eight? I don't think so!'

Every time she said something like that, Tally winced and felt like Jabba the Hut beside her. It magnified her own body size by a thousand. All the same, Tally didn't actually wish to be the same as her mother. The fact of the matter was that Greta hadn't an ounce of flab on her body and while Tally longed to be a lot smaller than she was, she didn't find her mother's muscly, almost plastic-looking physique attractive either. If they were dogs, Tally thought, she would be a well-fed St Bernard and Greta would be a greyhound at the peak of its fitness. The only similarity Tally could see between them was their deep blue eyes. Greta and Martin were a prime example of opposites attracting, too. Martin was tall and well padded, with dark hair like his daughter. Standing at six feet tall, his mother had always said he needed plenty of fuel to keep him going – a theory he'd applied to Tally since she was young.

'I'm heading down to the gym,' Greta called out. 'I'm supposed to be on the late shift tonight, but one of the others is covering for me. I have to go for an hour to sort a few bits. You go on ahead to Auntie Mary's with your da and I'll see you there.' Greta hesitated for a moment. 'Of course, the graduation ball was the turning point in my life. That's when I first got together with your father, as you well know.' Her mother's usually hard expression softened as she remembered her own graduation party.

'Well, I think we can rule out me marrying *my* date!' Tally grinned. 'As far as I know, it's still illegal to marry you own cousin, isn't it? And it would be all kinds of wrong to marry my gay cousin!'

'That's true,' Greta smiled, 'but keep your eyes peeled for any good catches. Just because Laurence is your date doesn't mean you can't keep your options open. Sure, don't they say the right man always comes along when you least expect it?' Greta said, but Tally could see that her mind was already gone, preceding her body to the gym. 'See you later,' Greta called suddenly and darted down the stairs and out the front door.

Tally knew it was futile to argue with her mother by saying she wouldn't dream of dumping her darling cousin Laurence. Nor did she allow herself to get upset by the fact that her mother hadn't bothered to stay and help her get dressed. They'd never been close. Tally knew she had been a sore disappointment to her mother for the past eighteen years, and probably always would be.

Tallulah had introduced herself as Tally from the moment she could speak. Greta found the nickname her daughter preferred ridiculous. She didn't say anything about it for a long time, but one day she flipped after Tally had introduced herself to some new neighbours. Greta had turned on her. 'I christened you Tallulah. I thought at the time it was a beautiful name and I still do. Other people can call you what they like, but I will address you by the gorgeous name *I* picked for you.'

Tally smiled as she heard Martin, her beloved father, singing as he showered. He was nearly more excited than she was about tonight's graduation ball. Auntie Mary was Martin's sister, and Laurence's mother, and she was like a woman possessed over the whole event. After listening to the umpteenth phone call between her dad and her aunt earlier that day, Tally had teased him that perhaps he should go to the ball with Auntie Mary, they were that excited about it.

Her dad had grinned his trademark cheeky smile and winked at her. 'We just want you both to have the time of your lives,' he had retorted, clapping his hands and rubbing them together in delight. Tally thought her dad was an utter loonie, but she loved him for caring so much.

Stepping back from her mirror, she surveyed her face. Hours of experimenting with make-up had taught her how to make the most of her sapphire eyes, to accentuate her cheekbones, which was a feat in itself as they were rather well padded, and to emphasise her full lips. She was halfway there now, with her eyes done. The rest waited to be transformed.

Still, there wouldn't be a drinks reception if she couldn't squeeze herself into her skirt and bodice. Knowing her mother was gone and there was no danger of her bursting into her bedroom, Tally used a well-versed trick. Dropping to the ground, she allowed herself to relax on her back and slowly eased the zip shut. The hook and eye at the top was a struggle and made her hands sweat. Blowing all her air out and inhaling deeply, she finally made the connection. Rolling slowly and carefully on to her side, so as not to burst the entire thing, Tally eased on to her feet. All that remained was to swivel the skirt around so the zip was in the correct position at the back.

The lady in the boutique where she'd bought it, Larger than Life, had insisted the high waist and flattering shape would create a perfect hourglass shape. 'The bodice will make you look like a lady from the Moulin Rouge,' she had promised solemnly.

Trussed into her magic knickers, maximum hold slimming slip and form-reducing strapless bra, Tally felt more barbecued pig on a spit than burlesque as the shop assistant had promised.

The floor-length black taffeta skirt had been cut with enough flare to cover her amply padded hips and thighs without looking like the outer shell of a four-man tent. The matching bodice created a sculpted shape thanks to the boning, which was accentuated by rich, deep purple piping. An overall dusting of tiny violet crystals lifted the entire outfit and added a touch of glamour.

'Daddy, can you help me lace this up the back?' Tally called as she heard her father emerge from the bathroom.

Holding her corset in place at the front, Tally reversed into the narrow landing of their small two-bed terraced house. Most men might've deemed dressing their daughter to be 'women's stuff', but Martin had done the lion's share of minding Tally since the day she was born. Deftly he laced up and adjusted the back of the bodice to fit.

'That all right for you, love?'

'Yeah, I can still breathe – just about,' Tally said. 'Do I look like I'm bursting out of it all because I certainly feel like I am?' She bit her lip anxiously, feeling foolish all of a sudden. Here she was, going to a party that would be wall-to-wall with skinny girls decked out in sexy outfits, and she was actually trying to keep up with them. How stupid was she? She'd never learn.

'Turn around and let me have a look at you,' Martin said as he tucked his shirt into his trousers and patted his own ample belly. 'You look sensational, pet. Beautiful!'

'I haven't finished my face yet, and I've to put on the tulle shrug to hide my bingo arms,' Tally said as she kissed her dad on the cheek to thank him.

'Well if you're going to look even better, I might have to refuse to let you out at all,' he said sternly. 'I'll never get you back, every man from here to Timbuktu is going to want to steal you away from me.'

Tally smiled and shook her head. 'Somehow I reckon I'm safe from any male stampedes, Da.'

She saw her da's smile droop as he picked up the note of self-mocking in her voice and she forced herself to give him a big smile. He hated to hear her talk like that about herself, but you'd have thought he'd be used to it by now. Her baby photos and right through her primary school days all logged one constant: her extra padding. She'd always longed to look like one of the movie stars she admired, all toned and delicate with slender limbs, but the fact was she'd always been at least twice the size of them.

She'd promised herself a million times that she'd change her eating habits and become the butterfly she ached to be inside. It never happened. From her early teens she'd tried and failed at all the diets known to woman. The longest she'd ever lasted on any of them was three days. The cabbage soup diet ended with a gluttonous feed from the chipper. The no carbs diet had crashed and burned courtesy of a full white sliced pan, six bags of crisps and close to half a pound of butter. Any of the product-led diets with shakes and bars made her crave food so badly, she'd inevitably put on even more than she'd lost.

She looked in the mirror again, turned sideways and sighed. Why, oh, why couldn't she just stop stuffing her face with all the wrong things? She wanted to look different, so why couldn't she just stick to what she knew would work for her? The girls who would be at the grad tonight were obviously able to do it, so why not her? She sighed, picked up her blusher and started to apply it carefully.

Of course, she'd do the same thing tonight that she'd been doing since the age of eight – make jokes at her own expense, get in first before someone else could state the obvious. That was her fail-safe position and the way she'd managed to keep her head above water since early childhood. She knew it was a rotten cliché, but she'd become the jolly roly-poly girl that everyone now knew and loved. She had cast herself in that stupid role, that was the worst part of it.

On her communion day, ten whole years ago now, she'd been thrilled with herself and had believed Martin when he'd told her she looked like a princess. A snide comment from Victoria-Jane, the cool, pretty girl in her class, had almost knocked her off her feet.

'You look like a meringue with eyes,' she'd said nastily.

Tally knew even then she could bawl and sob, or suck it up and give back as good as she got, so she'd retorted, 'Thanks V-J, that's me all right, oh so sweet, I'm good enough to eat!'

The narrow-eyed nastiness had turned to mirth as the other kid giggled and told her she was a scream. Tally fixed a smile on her face, bit the inside of her cheek to stop the tears and held her head high.

Her mother, along with everyone else, assumed she was gorging her way through life in blissful ignorance, but the mask she'd assumed at that tender age was nothing but a carefully crafted disguise to hide her God-awful loneliness inside.

Fair enough, she was well able to be the witty and funny one in the group – usually at her own expense. Her tears and lack of self-confidence were locked in a box deep inside, only to be brought out at night, when she'd curl into a ball and cry herself to sleep.

Tally's weight had steadily increased over the years. The fact that she was voluptuously beautiful was totally beyond her. She wore her dark, glossy, treacle-coloured hair in full waves to below her shoulders. Her eyelashes looked like falsies and her flawless skin remained pimple-free, even through her teens. Her full-lipped smile ignited her indigo-blue eyes, never hinting at the fact that deep down she battled constantly with cripplingly low self-esteem.

Martin was the only person who had any idea how unhappy she really was.

'Tally, you are the most beautiful girl in the school,' he would say vehemently when she was sad. 'You might be a different shape to some of the others, but you're tall and broad, you should be proud of your five foot nine frame. You're big boned like myself. But you are drop-dead stunning and don't you ever let anyone tell you otherwise.'

'Thanks, Daddy,' she'd say smiling through her tears.

The problem was, Martin showed his love with chocolate bars and tried to ease her pain with cream buns. 'This will cheer us up,' he'd say excitedly, unwrapping yet another take-away for them to share while watching one of their favourite musicals on DVD.

While she loved her da dearly for showing his support, Tally truly wished the pair of them had stayed away from the fattening stuff, even for the past few weeks. She was bursting out of her outfit and no matter how much make-up she put on, it didn't make her feel good.

Turning to the side she bit down hard. This was not the image she'd had in her head for tonight. Fair enough, she had flawless skin and glossy hair, and at a distance her face was probably fine, but from the neck down she felt like a blob. This was meant to be the night that marked her passage from schoolgirl to woman. If she was being honest, all she felt was lost and scared. The anxiety was making her sweat. Lifting her arms she turned on the hairdryer, blowing cold air under each arm, praying the dark fabric of her bodice wouldn't look inked with perspiration before she even got there.

The girls in her class had been on rabbit food for the past month, determined to look even skinnier than usual. She wasn't sure if she could pull off a night of being the funny, flabby fat bird without having a nervous breakdown. She felt a lump rising in her throat as she stared at her reflection in the mirror and a sense of panic rose up in her chest. She could feel her breathing getting faster, but she couldn't stop the thoughts that were spilling through her brain. Just as she was about to grab the duvet and dive under it and text Laurence that she had a migraine, she spied a photocopy of the application she'd filled out earlier. She hadn't told Martin or Greta yet. Her dad would be like an excited puppy about it and her ma would be certain to make her feel she'd wasted her time and energy even sending it off. For now, it was her secret and just seeing the envelope sitting there on the chair gave her the calmness she needed to collect herself, take a deep breath and focus on finishing her damn make-up.

'Are you right?'

Tally looked in the mirror and mouthed the word, 'No', then she smiled at herself, pulled her wrap around her shoulders and walked out of her room and towards her father with as much conviction as she could muster.

Martin had to swallow the lump in his throat when she finally joined him in the living room.

'I know Laurence will have a corsage for you, but these are from your ma and me,' he said pulling a gorgeous bouquet of purple and pink flowers from behind the sofa.

'Da, they're so gorgeous! Thank you!' Tally could feel her eyes welling up as she took in the array of wonderful blooms. The deep-pink roses had tiny crystals studded through the middle and the over-sized organza ribbon that held the posy in place was the exact same shade of purple as her dress. The little card wished her a wonderful night and was signed with love from Ma and Da. Bless him, Martin had even made Greta sign her name on the card.

'I hope you like them, pet,' he said squeezing her arm. 'I won't give you a kiss on the cheek in case I ruin your powder.'

Tally hugged him tightly. 'Thanks, Da,' she whispered in his ear.

'Ready to go?' Martin grinned.

'Ready as I'll ever be,' Tally said taking a deep breath.

They drove towards Auntie Mary's, with Martin joking all the way to take Tally's mind off the night ahead. He could tell she was anxious. When they pulled up at the house, the front door was already open and Auntie Mary was flitting about, unable to sit still for a second. Laurence appeared at the door, grinning from ear to ear.

'M'lady! Welcome!' he called, bowing gallantly.

'Why, thank you, Lord Laurence,' Tally said out through the car window, inclining her head in regal fashion.

'Oh, Jesus, show me! Show me!' Laurence yanked open the car door and offered Tally his hand. She took it and stepped out as gracefully as she could manage. Mary gave a very unladylike wolf whistle when she saw her.

'Uh-oh, divine! Like, *hello*?' Laurence screeched, like he'd just been sent straight from central casting to play an extra in *Carry on Grad Night*.

'Isn't she stunning?' Martin said, nodding and looking proud as punch. 'You're looking pretty smooth yourself,' he said, clapping his nephew on the back.

'You like?' Laurence asked as he closed his eyes and turned in slow motion as if he were on a revolving stage.

'I love your shoes!' Tally squealed. The deep purple glittery winkle-pickers were like nothing she had ever laid eyes on.

'See – we match!' Laurence said with a grin, holding his foot towards the hem of her dress.

'I thought you were wearing the mad silver ones! You are the best, do you know that?' Tally hugged him as he caught her hand and pulled her into the house.

'I saw these and just knew they were destined to be mine. The fact that they are a totally perfect match just makes them all the more special,' Laurence said looking madly excited by the whole thing.

It took a good hour and a half to extricate themselves from Auntie Mary's house. The neighbours were in for a look and Martin and Mary were beside themselves with pride, taking photographs from every conceivable angle of the 'happy couple'. Finally, Laurence prized Tally out of their clutches and into his car and they made their way to the hotel.

When Laurence held the heavy glass door open by the long brass handle, butterflies of excitement and trepidation danced in Tally's tummy.

'Ladies first,' he said standing to attention and waiting for her to pass.

As they entered the noisy, heaving bar area, the work of the committee assaulted them. It involved a sea of silver and white ribbons and balloons that made the place look like a Christmas tree decorated by a drunk with a tinsel fetish.

'Jesus H. Christ,' Laurence hissed. '*My Big Fat Gypsy Wedding* eat your heart out! Whose idea was this? This place is usually the last word in style and effortless glam. The poor bar, I feel violated on its behalf! The nylon pussy-bow monster obviously vomited repeatedly for hours on end! Seriously! *Hello?* Call the fashion police, please!'

'Shush!' Tally giggled. 'Victoria-Jane and Samantha were in charge of the decorating and they'll be in a right strop with me if they hear you dissing their work.'

'Work? It's a travesty!' Laurence stage-whispered. 'They should hand out Motilium for the nausea. And who, pray tell, are Victoria-hyphen-Jane and Samantha when they're at home?'

Tally pulled at her wrap and tried to hide as much of herself as she could within its cover. 'They're the coolest girls in my class, Laurence, and capable of making this night a misery for me, if they feel like it.'

'Stop all that fumbling, darling,' Laurence scolded, smacking her hand gently away from her wrap. 'You look like you're trying to vacuum pack yourself with that thing. You're not a pork steak, sweetie. Now, head up, shoulders back, chest out and let's work this room!'

As she allowed him lead her from huddle to gathering, Tally wished she had even an ounce of Laurence's confidence. He was so over the top, so different, utterly flamboyant and yet beyond delighted with himself. People like Victoria-Jane, who could make Tally sweat on sight, were just a fabulous form of entertainment to him. He didn't give a toss what people thought. He was his own person and enjoyed all that life had to offer.

As she watched him making people laugh and enjoying himself, Tally suddenly realised what the real difference between them was: Auntie Mary worshipped the ground he walked on and had never made him feel like he was letting her down; he would have been a very different person if he'd had Greta as his mother.

'Ma is getting with "the gay", as she calls it,' Laurence had confided to Tally when they were fifteen. 'God bless her, I think she's hoping it's like a dose of flu and I'll get over it if she nods and smiles a lot.'

As it turned out 'having the gay' worked to her advantage. As an only child Laurence had turned out to be a wonderful son with the shopping, gossiping and closeness of a daughter all rolled into one.

'He's all the children I ever wanted in one beautiful body!' she'd said to Tally only recently.

Laurence had learned to love himself and embrace the fact he was gay. Instead of it ever being an obstacle, it was the making of him. All his potential pain or torment at being different from the other boys in his class was quite simply turned on its head and he threw his arms open to the world and all the goodness it had to offer.

Tally, on the other hand, bottled up all her fears and apprehensions, with the only solace coming in the form of food. Biscuits, buttered popcorn and buns were her buddies. Sweets were her solace. Pies her playmates. She looked down again at her big body stuffed into her dress and felt like crying. She shook her head and took a deep breath. No point ruining the night for Laurence. She'd just have to woman up and get on with it.

Laurence had escaped momentarily to get some gossip from another group and reappeared looking over the moon. 'Great news! Anna and Ben are on our table. Not sure what she's like, but he's always up for a laugh,' Laurence said. 'He's totally delicious to look at, too,' he whispered in Tally's ear. 'We like a bit of eye candy while we dine! Fun, fun and more fun, my darling girl!' Clinking his glass off Tally's, Laurence gave a mischievous smile that couldn't but make her smile too.

I can get through this, she said to herself.

Dinner was announced and the throng moved into the large dining room.

'Holy Lord above, *more* white nylon bows!' Laurence hissed. 'All I can say is that I hope they got a seriously good deal on this tat. I know you keep telling me those girls are meant to be the cool ones, but, honey, this is just tack-a-rama if you ask me.'

They took their seats at their appointed table and greeted the other students seated with them. Tally knew all the girls, of course, and they introduced their dates one by one. She could see them exchange looks as they took in the fact that she had brought her gay cousin as her date. Anna's date was sitting next to her, but Anna was too busy pushing her face into his to introduce him to anyone. He smiled warmly and nodded at Tally and Laurence. Laurence pinched Tally's thigh under the table and she shot him another warning look, but he was right – Ben was quite something to look at. Anna was a lucky cow to have landed him as her boyfriend, but then, Anna was a size eight with perfect blonde hair and a wardrobe to die for. Lucky in every way really.

There was a cheer from the front tables and Victoria-Jane took to the podium at the top of the room.

'Oh, time for the bride to speak,' Laurence joked. Their whole table peeled with laughter, causing V-J to look over in shock.

'She's like a hen on a hot griddle,' Laurence snorted.

'Shush!' Tally begged. 'She'll hear you. Please, Laurence, don't make her hate me!'

Laurence patted Tally's leg and whispered in her ear, 'But, darling, you're so out of here. This is it – end of school. Whatever you've longed to say, this is the night!'

Tally shot him a warning look as Victoria-Jane cleared her throat to speak. Laurence's eyes glinted wickedly, but he mimed zipping his mouth shut and throwing away the key.

'Good evening fellow students, and welcome to our, like, fabulous grad ball ...'

As Victoria-Jane's speech rolled on, Laurence had tears rolling down his cheeks.

'...and thanks to the committee, especially Samantha and, uh, me, I suppose. So have an amazing night, guys. This is it! The night we've waited so many years for. As a little surprise, me and the committee have organised a kind of Oscars-type ceremony,' V-J said with a dangerous smile. 'Enjoy!'

'Oh, please,' Laurence said, pretending to choke himself.

'Shush,' Tally hissed, 'one of the others might see you and tell her afterwards.'

'Ooh, I'd die of shame ... *not*,' Laurence laughed. 'She's such a twat, Tally. What do you care if she sees me? She's not your friend.'

'She actually is,' Tally argued. She changed her mind rapidly when she heard what the lovely ladies of the committee had planned.

'So, to kick off proceedings,' Samantha said snatching the microphone from V-J, 'we've got the award for the best-looking Jock to Rock the school gate!' Wolf whistles sounded as the crowd banged on the tables and whooped.

'So, the award goes to none other than ... Jordan!'

'God, she sounds like she's inhaled helium,' Laurence said shuddering. 'Oh, ahoy me hearties, who's this guy?'

'He's V-J's latest crush, of course,' Tally supplied.

Tally found the awards thing slightly uncomfortable, so she fumbled in her bag for her lipstick. She'd just discreetly applied a fresh coat when the unthinkable happened – and naturally it happened to her.

'We know she'll think this is just, like, hilarious, so we've a special award now,' Samantha said. She dissolved into a fit of giggles and waved a manicured hand in front of her face. 'Okay, yeah, I know, get it together, right? So, the very special award of "Big Mama of the Year" goes to … Ta-lu-lah!'

Tally felt like she was caught in a slowly evolving nightmare. The astonished, wild laughter that spread like wildfire around the room rooted her to the spot.

'Don't go up there. That's not remotely funny,' Laurence said, serious now and grabbing her arm to keep her seated. Tally knew there was only one thing for it. Pushing back her chair, she made her way to the podium, accepted the award and proceeded to pretend to eat it.

'Thanks, girls, you're all a hoot! This will hold pride of place alongside my burgers, pies chocolates and cakes. It's been a challenge to eat my way through the past few years, but as my ample curves are demonstrating, I've done a fine job!' Tally paused for the laughter. 'Me and all five of my chins are eternally grateful. Cheers!'

'Where's the award for the most puketastic decorations of the night, girls?' Laurence yelled out. He felt some revenge when the room erupted rowdily and napkins, swiftly followed by nylon bows, began to fly overhead.

'Ha, ha, you're *so* funny,' V-J said, looking flustered for a minute.

Tally had no idea who won the other awards or what they were even for. She was anaesthetised by misery. Plonking the trophy in the middle of the table, she waved and smiled like a robot at anyone who caught her eye. She looked at Laurence's empty place beside her and wondered where he'd gone. The rest of the people at her table looked a bit uncomfortable, but were going along with it. Anna was the only one who obviously didn't find it awkward – she clapped Tally hard on the back as she made her way back to her seat and whooped, 'Go, Big Mama.' Tally wanted the ground to just open up and swallow her, anything to get out from under those lights and those clapping hands.

'So, like, have a blast!' V-J yelled, concluding her speech. The background muzak came on and the meal began.

The crowd was clapping and laughing as Laurence reappeared with a round wooden bar tray laden with shots.

'Stupid bitches,' he said, looking furious. 'I'll be banging nails into my voodoo doll tomorrow, trust me. Right now, though, the only thing for it is tequila.'

'God, no,' Tally said, looking aghast. 'I'll puke all over myself. If there's one thing worse than a blubbing fat bird, it's a vomit-coated one.'

'The way you must feel right now, these babies are only going to ease the pain,' he said knowingly. 'Besides if you're feeling queasy, I know exactly where you can direct your spew.'

The tequila was utterly vile, but the putrid burning was oddly soothing.

'Grab the bread there and eat some, it'll help line your stomach,' Laurence instructed kindly.

'Can you pass the bread, please?' Tally asked Anna's date. 'I'm Tally by the way. Or you might know me as Big Mama,' she said, failing to keep her voice as light and casual as she'd intended.

'Ben. Nice to meet you,' he shook her hand and looked straight at her. 'I know Laurence, but I don't know anyone else here at all, bar Anna,' he said. 'So it's very nice to meet someone friendly like you.'

'I'll look after you, don't worry,' Laurence said, winking at him.

'You're all right thanks, Laurence,' he said, grinning good-naturedly.

'I'll join you and have some bread, I'm starving,' Ben said, smiling warmly at Tally and making her heart flutter.

Beside him, Anna was looking bored and pretending to pout. 'Don't forget you're here with me,' she said putting on a little girly voice and leaning forward to plant a kiss on Ben's lips. He didn't smile at her, just turned his head away as soon as she took her lips off his.

As he reached for the butter, Ben's hand brushed off the 'Big Mama' award. In one quick movement, he scooped it off the table and stashed it under his chair. Tally was so ashamed she couldn't speak. Ben held her gaze for a moment. Was she imagining it or did she sense compassion in his eyes?

When the meal was over and the music began, Laurence was like a man possessed.

'Cuz, this is where we come alive. Let's own that beat,' Laurence yelled, dragging her up to dance.

'Laurence, I can't get up on the floor after the mortification of earlier,' Tally whimpered. Contrary to what her cousin had promised, she was three sheets to the wind after the tequila.

'Fuck them and the horse they rode in on. We'll show them who's boss. Let's rock it out, baby!'

While she had a great laugh, Tally soon felt her shoes eating into the sides of her feet. She pointed at her high heels with a grimace and Laurence let her off the hook. Gratefully, she slunk back to her chair, leaving him to own the dance floor all on his own.

'Ouch! That looks sore,' Ben commented as she plonked down beside him and peeled off her shoes.

'That's what happens when you try to shove the weight of both ugly sisters into Cinderella's slippers!' Tally laughed.

'You don't look like an ugly sister from where I'm sitting,' Ben grinned. Tally looked up to see if he was taking the Mick out of her. She was amazed to find he wasn't.

'Sorry, I shouldn't be sitting here with my disgusting feet out while you're trying to have a drink!' Tally apologised, suddenly feeling shy. 'Where's Anna?'

'I've no idea where Anna went. To be honest, she's not really the person I thought she was. We've very little in common actually.'

'Oh.' Tally was at a loss. How could Ben not adore Anna? She was pretty, skinny and one of the 'cool' girls from the class. Maybe this Ben bloke was a bit of a moron.

'Listen, Tally, she was one of the vixens involved in the *hilarious* award ceremony earlier on. For the record, I wasn't laughing and I made a point of telling her what I thought of it all,' Ben admitted. 'So it would be fair to assume that we won't be seeing much of each other after tonight.'

'There I go again, causing trouble!' Tally said trying to make light of it all. She was really quite jarred, so she still wasn't sure if he was being serious or not.

'So what do you think you'd like to do next year, now that school is over?' Ben asked.

Tally looked at him sideways, wondering if she could trust him. To hell with it, she thought, I haven't said it out loud yet, but he doesn't know anyone I know, so who's he going to tell?

'I've applied to a beauty college, called Skin Deep, and I'm really hoping to get in there. It's a full-time course for a year and then I'd be ready to make other people even more beautiful!'

'No way!' Ben exclaimed. 'That's such a coincidence. My sister teaches at Skin Deep. Her name is Sinead. Actually I think you two would get on really well.'

'I haven't got a place yet or anything, I'd just love to go there,' Tally said quickly, beginning to panic and wishing she'd kept her mouth shut.

'They should let you know pretty quickly if you have a place. When is your interview?'

'Not until August, as far as I know. Apparently they allot the places taking both the interview and exam results into account, particularly the science subjects and English,' Tally explained.

'I'm sure you'll pass with flying colours. I'll ask Sinead to keep an eye out for you. A nod's as good as a wink and all that,' Ben assured her.

'Thanks a million. Sure if nothing else, you could tell your sister that I'd be great with the clients,' Tally quipped. 'All they'd have to do is pitch up to a salon and once they clap eyes on me, I'll make them feel better about themselves before I even attempt to give them a treatment!' Tally roared laughing. Ben smiled, but he didn't seem to find her comment that funny.

Tally took his reaction as a waning in interest, which she was used to with guys, so she excused herself and rejoined Laurence, who was still king of the dance floor.

It was about four in the morning when Tally, barefoot and very drunk, managed to drag Laurence away from the late-night bar.

'You stay by all means, Laurence, but I have to go home. I can't drink any more and I feel like I'm going to end up in a wheelchair my feet are so sore,' Tally slurred. 'I can't keep up with you. Your capacity for alcohol and dancing is stellar. I have to hand it to you.'

'You shall not go home alone!' Laurence announced gallantly. Reluctantly he waved and blew kisses to the remaining revellers and they fell into a taxi together.

'How're you doing, sweetie?' he said as he rested his head against Tally's shoulder in the back of the taxi.

'I'm still alive,' Tally said, kissing his head. 'You were the most admired and adored date of the evening too. So thank you for accompanying me.'

'Do me a favour, would you, love?' he turned to face her.

'What's that?'

'Keep away from those poisonous bitches. You deserve far, far more than that.'

All Tally could do was nod. She didn't trust herself to speak. A bout of ugly crying was lurking just beneath the surface of her rapidly thinning resolve.

Less than half and hour later, she was sprawled across her bed with all her make-up still on. She would've passed out in her dress except that it was digging into her in about fifteen places. After lots of fumbling and staggering around in a circle, she managed to free herself of the bodice. It had been like wearing a second ribcage and she groaned as she looked at the deep marks around her back and under each arm where the fabric had been gnawing at her flesh all night. The thoughts of having to wear it again for Laurence's grad night filled her with dread. She'd have to try and curb her eating or there was no way she'd beat herself into it again.

The zip on her skirt nearly burst as she forced it open.

'Ah, thank God,' she said to nobody and fell backwards onto her bed. Images of Victoria-Jane and her cronies swam up into her mind's eye, but she forced them back, not willing to give them any more of herself or her time. Then another image materialised, and she didn't push it aside. Her last thought as she lapsed into a drunken slumber was of Ben. God, he was gorgeous. And such a lovely guy, too. Well out of her league, of course, but nobody could stop her dreaming.

6.

Daisy

Daisy Moyes had always been self-assured. When she had started school, she'd known she preferred the red chairs to the blue ones. At the age of six, she had marched confidently into Laura Ashley with her mother and picked out the décor for her new bedroom single-handedly. She and her mother, Ava, were like two peas in a pod. Her father, Justin, used to joke to her brothers, Jake and Luke, that he'd no idea how he'd survived prior to Daisy's birth.

'Until your sister came along and showed me how to conduct myself properly, I was quite obviously a bumbling fool,' he'd tease.

Daisy was beguiling, though. She was undeniably a strong personality, but her sunny disposition meant she was adored by almost everyone who encountered her. With her halo of golden curls, eyes full of mischief and a ready laugh, it would have been hard to dislike her.

After leaving school, Daisy knew exactly what she wanted to do – become a Montessori teacher. Her superb grades and enthusiastic attitude had seen her soar into her chosen university. Now at the age of twenty-one, as she headed into her final year, she was certain she'd chosen the right career. None of her school pals had opted to go to the same place, so she'd had to start afresh socially – a new beginning Daisy had embraced with gusto. She'd made friends easily and was soon popular and sought after.

Really, up until the time she'd met Freddie, it had all been plain sailing for Daisy. College had been her focus and she'd thought she had things fairly sorted. She hadn't intended adding a relationship to her already heavily loaded schedule at that time, but Freddie had swept her off her feet. He was every parent's dream. They'd met at the Hunt Ball when Daisy was nineteen. It was late spring, just before her first-year exams. He was in his second year at UCD, studying law, and had rugged good looks to match his ambition and intelligence.

'You remind me of a porcelain doll,' Freddie had crooned into her ear as they swayed to the slow song at the ball.

'What, cold and rigid and sitting on a shelf gathering dust?' Daisy had said with a raised eyebrow, pretending to be highly insulted.

'No, delicate, pretty and someone I feel the urge to cherish,' Freddie had answered, looking serious.

Daisy had laughed off the compliment, but it got under her skin all the same. She liked that he was confident enough – personally and emotionally – to speak his mind like that.

Freddie's parents, Alfred and Ursula Prenderville, were old friends of Daisy's parents from the golf club. News travelled fast in those circles.

'Oh, my goodness, I can't believe you've hooked up with Freddie!' Ava had said when she arrived into the kitchen the morning after the ball and found Daisy perched on a high stool, eating toast.

'That didn't take long to filter through,' Daisy had muttered through a mouthful of breakfast.

'He's studying law, and quite a catch, you know?' Ava had looked smug.

'Yeah, he told me. About the law degree, not that he's a fine catch. He seemed like fun but I wouldn't go off buying a hat yet, Mum,' Daisy had said, shaking her head and grinning. 'I'm only nineteen and I'm concentrating on getting a decent career up and running once I finish college.'

Unlike some of the other guys Daisy had dated, Freddie had been very attentive from the start. He'd phoned the day after the ball and asked her if she was free for dinner that evening.

'I'm actually meeting some pals,' Daisy had fibbed. She wouldn't have minded seeing him again, but she was pretty whacked, having rolled in the door home after five in the morning. But the real reason she said no was down to 'the rules'. She and her friends, Caroline and Naomi, had learned from previous heartaches that certain steps had to be followed with men. Daisy had decided she was going to stick to the strict game plan she and the girls had devised, which basically boiled down to: don't be too eager and don't be too available.

'Well, maybe I could hook up with you and your friends later on?' Freddie had suggested, not wanting to let her slip through his fingers.

'Oh, no, that'll never work. It's a girls' night at somebody's flat. Maybe another time?' Daisy had suggested coyly. *Another rule – make him do all the running.*

'Eh, sure. What about Tuesday? I've a meeting with a tutor on Monday so I can't do then. But on Tuesday I could meet you or collect you and we could have a bite to eat?' Freddie was beginning to flounder. He wasn't used to girls making him work for a date.

'I'm totally chock-a-block next week. Sorry!' Daisy had sounded slightly apologetic, but not too bothered either way. She hadn't wanted to tell him she'd be in college or hanging out with nobody in particular. *Yet another rule – make it sound like you've a hectic schedule 24/7.*

'Well do you have plans next Saturday then?' Freddie was beginning to sound slightly tetchy.

'Yes! I'm meeting you,' Daisy had said sweetly. She could almost hear the fishing line ticking as she reeled him back in.

They'd arranged to meet for a drink and Freddie promised he'd book somewhere for dinner.

'Cool! I'll see you in Reds Bar on Saturday at seven so,' Daisy had said, sounding bright and breezy.

'Eh, sure. Listen, I'll text you on Friday to confirm,' Freddie had blurted.

'Okay then. Look forward to it, *ciao*!' Daisy had chirped.

When she'd given him her number at four the previous morning, she hadn't even expected him to remember, let alone call so swiftly.

Their first date had gone better than Daisy had imagined was possible. Freddie was actually a lot more handsome than she'd thought and he was such a gentleman. She hadn't paid for a thing and he had brought her to a really upmarket bistro, which had a waiting list as long as the River Liffey.

'The food is gorgeous, isn't it?' Daisy had said, feeling pretty tipsy. Freddie had ordered champagne and then they'd moved on to a bottle of delicious red wine.

'I love this place, but I have to say the view is extra special tonight!' Freddie had taken her hand and kissed it.

'Oh, bloody hell, you are too much!' Daisy had burst out laughing. 'What are you going to do next – dig up Barry White and have a dozen roses delivered by helicopter?'

'I'm just trying to woo you,' Freddie had answered, grinning.

'You're doing a lovely job, but take it easy there. I've two older brothers. I'm not a girl who thinks men are like Greek gods. I've grown up with the smelly socks, farts, dead arms and nose picking,' Daisy had said, putting him straight.

'I thought I'd try and control my flatulence until you at least agree to see me again. But after that I promise I'll beat you around and clean my ears with your toothbrush, how's that?'

In spite of the application of all the rules she and the girls could come up with, Daisy had fallen for Freddie. His parents welcomed her into their home with open arms. Equally, Ava and Justin accepted Freddie as a third son and Daisy's older brothers, Jake and Luke, thought he was great.

'He's well up for a good slagging and even though he's going to be a lawyer, I won't hold that against him,' Jake had teased.

All in all, everyone agreed that they were the perfect couple.

Now, a year and a half later, Daisy was coming towards the end of her third year of college. Herself and Freddie were still going strong and she was looking forward to a relaxing summer before she entered her final year of Montessori training. Freddie had phoned to finalise arrangements for their holiday. Ursula and Alfred had generously offered them the use of their holiday home in Monte Carlo.

'Just imagine, this time next year I'll be sitting my exams and starting to look for a job,' she said to him with excitement.

'Unless circumstances change meanwhile,' Freddie said.

'What do you mean?' Daisy asked him suspiciously.

'Ah, nothing,' Freddie said. 'So are you all packed and ready to go? Mum's bringing us to the airport. I hate being late, especially when it comes to flights, so we'll collect you bright and early. Make sure you're ready to go.'

'Aye-aye, Captain!' Daisy joked.

'I'll text you when we're on the way, so there's no delay,' he said sounding mildly irritated. Daisy let it drop, but sometimes she found Freddie's fussing a bit over the top. At times he needed to lighten up a bit.

Daisy ambled downstairs to spend the evening with Ava.

'Looking forward to your holiday, darling?' Ava asked.

'Sure,' Daisy said lightly. 'Although Freddie just dropped a less than subtle hint that he's planning a future together. I'm happy to go with the flow for the moment. I hope he's not jumping ahead of himself too much.'

'What if he is thinking ahead?' Ava said, patting the sofa beside her. Daisy crossed the living room and cuddled in beside her mother. 'Oh, it's just such a wonderful time in your life, darling.'

'I agree, Mum, but there's no need to get all serious. I'm twenty-one, not forty-one.'

'I know that Daisy, but look at your father and me. We married young, as did many of our friends. There's so much to be said for it,' she continued. 'We had our babies at a time when we'd the energy and vitality to enjoy you to the full. Now we've come full circle and we're still young enough to pick up on our lives as a couple again. That doesn't happen to everyone. Some people never find true love. My advice to you is to embrace it.'

'I suppose,' Daisy said, not feeling totally convinced.

'Besides, there's nothing more gorgeous than a young bride! Oh, I can barely imagine how stunning you'd be, dressed in white with a full-length veil and—'

'Mum! Hold the phone there. We're going on holiday to France, not Gretna Green!'

'I know, I know,' Ava said with a laugh. 'But remember those photos of Anne and Eamon's daughter, Sophie? She was simply out of this world. Of course, you're far more beautiful than her, so you'd be like something descended from heaven.'

'Yes, Mum, of course I would,' Daisy said grinning. She knew it was futile to argue with her mother when she was on a roll, so she sat back and only half-listened as Ava described an imaginary wedding day and dress. In her mind's eye, she was seeing the skyline of Monte Carlo and feeling the sun warming her skin.

The chalet was white-washed and rustic-looking to a point, but Ursula and Alfred had transformed the once humble farm building with a modern interior, beautiful marble flooring, air-conditioning and fresh chintzy fabrics. Outside there was a glorious swimming pool with views down the hills, framed by the backdrop of the glittering ocean and majestic Monte Carlo town.

'This place is stunning!' Daisy said, hugging Freddie. 'How lucky are we to have access to this? Your parents are so generous to allow us come here.'

'They're good people all right,' Freddie grinned. They shared a bottle of cold rosé by the pool and strolled to a small fish restaurant nearby. Daisy felt like she was in seventh heaven.

When the bill came, Freddie smiled at the waitress and winked, which annoyed Daisy slightly.

'Oh, shoot! I've forgotten my wallet. Can you get this one, babe, and I'll do the next meal?' Freddie said, clicking his fingers. Daisy noticed that he wasn't in the least bit hassled. If she'd forgotten her wallet, she'd be freaking out and embarrassed. In fact, she suddenly realised she'd been stung with more than one bill over the past few months.

'Sure, I have cash with me,' Daisy answered, putting enough money down to include a generous tip. As the waitress passed by, Freddie swiped the cash from the table and handed it to her. 'Keep the change and thanks for a lovely evening,' he said, winking again.

'You sound like you're paying a hooker,' Daisy said, unimpressed with his sleazy behaviour, not to mention his pretence that he'd paid.

'Grumpy, grumpy! Are you jealous?' Freddie jibed. 'That kind of turns me on. Let's go home and I'll show you how I really feel about you.'

Daisy allowed him to pull her close as they wandered back to the chalet. A small part of her couldn't shake the fact that she wasn't happy with his behaviour all the same. She knew she wasn't being paranoid, he'd definitely become less generous as the months had rolled by. The guy who had wined and dined her at the beginning of the relationship seemed to have slipped away, leaving a rather tight-fisted Freddie in his place.

Next morning, she was surprised when Freddie announced he was off to the golf club.

'Will I come with you?' she asked.

'If you like, but I'm playing eighteen holes, so you might be bored. Why don't you relax by the pool and I'll be back later on to take you to lunch. How does that sound?' Freddie planted a kiss on her head, swung her around, dropped her and flew off out the door before she could even think straight. As Alfred's 'France car' sped away, Daisy was left with no choice but to fix herself some breakfast and wander out to the pool.

As she luxuriated in the early morning heat and dipped her toe in the pool, a smile spread across her face. What was she perturbed for? Look where she was!

'Hey, Naomi, just thought I'd give you a quick call from Monte Carlo! Yeah, baby!' she giggled down the phone.

'Oh, I'm so jealous. It's pissing rain here and windy. Is it fabulous?' Naomi sighed.

'You've no idea! The chalet is divine and I can look out from the private pool and see the Mediterranean stretched out below.'

Feeling she'd made Naomi suitably envious and promising to keep in touch, Daisy took some pictures with her phone and posted them to her Facebook page. *Good morning one and all. Greetings from Monte Carlo, I'm living the dream!*

Daisy actually loved her morning of flitting back and forth on Twitter and Facebook, lying on the sun-lounger and kicking back. She'd just had a swim and was basking in the heat when Freddie reappeared from the golf course.

'Hi! How come you're not ready to go? We need to leave in, like, five minutes!' Freddie rubbed his forehead in obvious annoyance.

'I guess I lost track of time. It's such an amazing day, isn't it?' Daisy smiled.

'Not great for golfing, funnily enough, but I don't suppose that affects you,' Freddie snapped.

'Oh, narky!' Daisy retorted, still feeling too blissed out to rise to annoyance.

'Seriously, Daisy, we can't be late meeting Bill and Tracey. This guy is head honcho in a huge law firm back home and I need to keep in with him. I haven't sweated my bollix off all morning in the searing heat for no reason.' Striding into the house, Freddie peeled off his clothes and jumped into the shower.

'Can you grab my chinos and one of my Gant polo shirts there, honey?' he called from the open bathroom door.

'So I'm *honey* now that you need a servant, am I?' Daisy said, leaning against the frame of the door for a second. 'You didn't actually ask me if I wanted to have lunch with Bill and Tracey, whoever they are, so don't get snotty with me, Freddie.'

Freddie flicked off the power shower and rubbed his head roughly before tying a towel around his waist and pushing past her.

'Forget it, I'll find them myself. I didn't realise I was being such a nuisance, besides I just told you, Bill is an important businessman,' Freddie muttered with irritation. 'And you know how I hate dilly-dallying. Don't make us late, please.'

Daisy raised an eyebrow and decided to put his moodiness down to the heat. Rinsing herself quickly, she pulled on a little cream lacey shift dress and teamed it with pretty, sparkly flip-flops. Knowing she was pushed for time, she pulled her curls into a knot at the back of her head. A touch of tinted moisturizer and a pale lip-gloss completed her ensemble.

'Okay, I'm ready to rock and roll,' she said, grabbing her straw bag and a wide-brimmed hat. 'I've sun cream and water in here, so even if we're sitting outside we'll be fine,' she said patting her over-the-shoulder bag.

'We're going to the five-star restaurant at the golf club. It's hardly the type of place that clients end up with sunstroke, dying of dehydration,' Freddie shot back.

Daisy was a single heartbeat away from telling Freddie to shove his lunch and Mr Big Swing businessman when he planted a kiss on her lips.

'Sorry, darling, I know I'm very edgy. You look gorgeous. I'm just jumpy because this guy can potentially help me out big time with my career. I don't want to mess this up.'

They didn't speak much during the short car journey. Daisy had felt a shift in their relationship over the previous few weeks. At home she was treated with love and respect all the time. She didn't feel it was unreasonable for her boyfriend to be civil. Herself and her brothers had always had a normal sibling relationship, which involved plenty of rows and scuffles, but at the end of the day, now that they were older, Jake and Luke were courteous most of the time. That was what she expected from her boyfriend, too. If Freddie thought he could get away with behaving like a caveman, he had another thing coming.

The lunch was a total trial for Daisy.

Tracey was dressed in a linen trouser suit with a neat camisole top, professionally set hair and not a scrap of make-up. She was gentle and seemed friendly, but totally lacking in spark. Bill was pompous and loud, slightly leaning towards being weighty and he sported an unattractive, greased down comb-over. If she'd had scissors in her bag, Daisy would've loved to snip off the oily strands of hair. The chat at the table was hard going. Daisy felt like crawling under the table with embarrassment at one stage.

'Eh, hello?' Bill boomed, holding his hand in the air. One of the waitresses came over to see what he needed. 'Another bottle of the same,' he pointed to his wine glass. There were no pleasantries and a distinct lack of manners.

'Do you speak French at all, Bill?' Daisy enquired as the girl walked away to fetch the wine.

'Nope. Never bothered. They all speak English here so it's not an issue. To be honest, I come here to relax. I have a gruelling schedule work-wise back home,' he leaned back in his chair stretching his arms above his head. 'I can get by, of course. I wouldn't starve or die of thirst, put it that way!' Bill laughed heartily. Tracey tittered and stroked his arm. If he had basic French, Daisy wondered why he didn't seem to feel he should use it while engaging with the waitress.

'I love languages. I especially love the sound of the French accent and how the people use their hands so much to inject emotion into what they're saying,' Daisy said with a smile.

The waitress returned with the wine and Daisy thanked her in French and waited for Bill to do the same. He didn't even look the girl in the eye.

Excusing herself for a moment, Daisy found refuge in the bathroom. There was more marble than a graveyard and every surface shone. The golf club was as salubrious as they come, no denying that, but Daisy would've preferred to be at a tiny street café, people-watching and breathing in the warm air. She'd like to be around people her own age, who talked fast and laughed and were interested in the same things as her. In this place, she felt like she'd been sealed into a middle-aged tomb.

Running cold water over her hands, she sighed deeply. Tracey and Bill were closer to her parents' age. Obviously she knew there'd be a generation gap, and that was fine, but she'd never felt this ill-at-ease in her parents' company, or indeed that of any of their friends. Was this the sort of occasion that would make up the majority of her social life with Freddie in the future? She looked at her reflection in the mirror and felt the seeds of doubt taking root in her mind.

When she returned to the table, Bill and Freddie were in deep conversation about a high-profile case taking place back home.

'Bill tries not to talk shop when we go out, but he just can't help himself!' Tracey confided in Daisy. 'He adores his profession and it's given us a wonderful standard of living, so I can't complain.'

'Do you work yourself?' Daisy asked, sipping her wine.

'Oh, no, dear. We have two grown-up children of twenty-two and twenty-four,' Tracey said. 'I was always far too busy with them to follow my own career.'

'What would you have liked to do? There are amazing courses open to mature students these days. You could still follow your dream,' Daisy said trying to engage Tracey in a more meaningful discussion.

'All the dreams I ever had have come to pass, Daisy. All I ever wanted was to be married and have children.'

'And do you love golf, like Bill?' Daisy fixed a smile on her face.

'Can't bear it, far too much walking. I prefer to spend the time at our house. I read and most days I go to the market and pick up food for lunch or dinner if we're not dining out. I'm a stickler for my afternoon nap, too,' Tracey smiled.

'You seem very happy and contented,' Daisy said before she could stop herself. Luckily, Tracey didn't find the comment offensive.

'Yes, I certainly am. I know we're very fortunate to live the life we do. I've never wanted for anything and Bill is a wonderful husband.'

Daisy chatted about nothing in particular with Tracey until the men finally decided it was time to go home.

'We'll leave the car here, I don't want to risk driving after all the delicious wine,' Freddie announced.

'Good plan, you can collect the car tomorrow after our round of golf.' Bill clapped Freddie on the back. 'Tee off at eight, sharp. It's forecast to be a scorcher, so we're better to get going early. I think you'll enjoy Stewart when you meet him tomorrow.'

Daisy thanked Bill and Tracey for treating them to lunch and expressed how much she'd enjoyed meeting them both.

'Well, the pleasure was all ours. You're a great couple,' Bill said, pumping Daisy's hand. 'I'd stick with this man, if I were you,' Bill winked at Daisy. 'He's going to make a fine lawyer. His only vice is probably the fact that he's a little too young and fit on the golf course!'

They all laughed and said their farewells. As their taxi pulled away, Freddie waved to Bill and Tracey once more.

'That was fantastic! They really loved you, as I knew they would. Yourself and Tracey got on so brilliantly. She's a lovely woman, isn't she?' Freddie said, putting his arm around Daisy and pulling her towards him in the back seat of the taxi.

'She's a very nice lady absolutely,' Daisy answered.

Freddie caught the tone in her voice and looked at her. 'But?'

'Ah, it's nothing. We're a different generation and I suppose I just look at her life and can't help thinking it's not what I would want for myself.' Daisy didn't want to sound offensive, but even comparing Tracey to her own mother there were stark differences. Ava had a fantastically full life. She did Pilates, loved gardening, was involved in a cookery club, travelled and never seemed to be at a loose end. Perhaps it was because Justin had worked away from home a lot, but

Ava had her own life outside of her husband and children. Tracey, on the other hand, seemed to lead her entire life through Bill.

'What do you mean her life isn't what you'd want?' Freddie looked astonished. 'Bill looks after her and treats her like royalty. She seemed pretty damn happy from where I was sitting. Bill is a hugely well respected man in Dublin, I fail to see the hardship in being married to him!'

'That's my point, Freddie. *Bill* is respected. *Bill* is known. *Bill* works. *Bill* plays golf. *Bill* is a fantastic fella, if a little rude, in my humble opinion. But what does Tracey do?'

'You're in one of your moods, aren't you?' Freddie took his arm from her shoulder and turned his head to look out the window.

'So I take it from the conversation you're off to the golf club first thing tomorrow again?' Daisy said, trying not to sound as aggravated as she felt.

'Certainly am. Bill is going to introduce me to one of the partners in his place.' Freddie was totally oblivious to the fact that Daisy was fuming. This was meant to be a holiday for the two of them. If Freddie had told her before they'd come out here that it was going to be a work junket cunningly disguised as a holiday, she would at least have been prepared. This wasn't turning out at all the way she'd expected.

To top it all off, Freddie jumped out of the car when they got back to the chalet and left her to pay the driver.

That night, when she climbed into bed she immediately lay with her back to him. She just couldn't bear to go through the motions of sex with him after everything. She could hear him in the dark, listening to her breathing, she could nearly hear him deciding whether to slide over beside her or not. After a minute or two, he gave a little sigh and turned over.

The following morning Freddie sped off in a taxi and Daisy jumped in the shower and got ready as quickly as she could. Throwing some essentials in her straw bag, she headed out the door. She wasn't going to sit on her own waiting for Freddie to fit her in, so she'd gone on her iPhone the night before and figured out a route to the town of Nice.

When she eventually made it onto the bus, Daisy relaxed. She was running low on cash and hoped to find an ATM when she got there. She knew it wasn't her imagination, but any time they were alone Freddie had become increasingly talented at not paying for things. He had almost drained her cash reserves already.

The views from the bus along the way were spectacular. As she emerged at the picturesque town, Daisy's tummy rumbled. The website she'd consulted had recommended a visit to the old town, followed by a climb up the hill to Le Château. Daisy decided to follow that advice and spent the next hour rambling around the narrow, meandering streets of the pretty old town. She loved the cobbles under her feet and the sense of freedom she felt. She found an ATM and replenished her cash supply, which made her feel more secure. She hated not having any money, especially when she was on her own.

Finding a little patisserie with its outside tables bathed in sunshine, she sat down and ordered a croissant and black coffee. The pastry was buttery and deliciously light, in contrast to the rich, strong coffee. There were plenty of tourists and the summer season had well and truly kicked off, which meant it was the perfect time for people-watching.

Daisy gazed at the women more than the men. She admired their elegant and seemingly effortless style. They had gorgeous hair and skin, but their look was for the most part tailored and quite staid. While Daisy thought they were all exquisite, she decided she wouldn't like to dress in a uniform of a fitted skirt, jacket and shirt with court shoes every day. She loved frills and colour and a bit of frivolity in her wardrobe. Still, it was wonderful to sit and watch the world go by. She checked her phone, thinking she'd give Ava a call; her mother would love this place. Unfortunately, the little narrow streets didn't lend themselves to marvellous phone service and there was no coverage. Feeling a wisp of loneliness for a moment, Daisy decided to press on and climb up to Le Château and take in the view.

Although it was heading towards the middle of the day and the June sun felt very warm, the climb was worth it because the sights from the top were enchanting. Mosaic pathways led her up high above the town and she wanted to drink in everything about this stunning place. As she gazed at the beautiful waterfall and became entranced by its splashing rhythm, her thoughts turned once again to Freddie. It was like worrying at a loose tooth – she just couldn't shake free the thoughts that had begun to occur to her about him.

He was probably wondering where she was by now. She checked her phone, but she still had no network coverage. Ah well, she thought. Let him worry. He hadn't been in the least bit concerned about her as he'd sped off to play golf with the big boys that morning. She'd phone him when she was good and ready. No doubt he'd be too busy trying to impress all the right people to give her too much thought until it suited him. He could go swing – literally.

The summit was like a mini market centre, with little stalls selling delicious nibbles, drinks and trinkets. As she wandered around, looking at everything, she heard a young woman talking to an older lady.

'Ooh, look at these handmade bracelets, I'm going to buy some to bring home as gifts.' Daisy recognised the Irish accent.

'Hi, ladies, I'm Irish too,' Daisy introduced herself.

'Oh, hello!' the younger woman said. 'I'm Niamh and this is my mum, Kitty.'

'Hi there, I'm Daisy. I'm here on holiday with my boyfriend. We're staying in Monte Carlo, but I decided to come on a spur-of-the-moment trip here because he's off golfing.'

'You do right,' Kitty said. 'I'm a golf widow, too. That's why Niamh and I are here. We're from Kerry. I take it from your accent you're a Dublin lassie?'

'Certainly am!' Daisy said with a grin.

'Well, much as we love Kerry, we felt we could do with a little trip away, so we decided to have a little girly break, just for three nights,' Kitty explained.

'Gorgeous! Are you having a great time?' Daisy asked.

'Fantastic!' Niamh enthused and Kitty smiled at her.

They fell into step together and ended up spending a lovely couple of hours grazing on tasty snacks and picking up little trinkets. Daisy said she'd better make her way back down towards the bus, and Niamh and Kitty decided to accompany her.

'We're going home in the morning, so we'll pop back to our hotel and relax,' Kitty explained.

They chatted as they walked back down the hill and Daisy learned that Niamh was getting over a horrible relationship split.

'I've been moping around like a lost puppy for the past couple of months, so Mum decided I needed to snap out of it,' Niamh admitted.

'How long were you and your ex together, if you don't mind me asking?' Daisy enquired.

'Five years. It was really complicated, to be honest,' Niamh sighed. 'I knew a long time ago that Adam wasn't right for me. The signs had been there from the get-go. I just kept thinking it would all work out in the end. In fact,' Niamh looked embarrassed for a moment, 'I tried to convince myself that it would improve if we got married and had children. I didn't know that relationships weren't supposed to be stressful *all* the time.'

'Just to clarify something to you, Daisy,' Kitty interjected, 'Adam was very controlling and rather selfish. It was his way or no way. That's fine to a certain point, but there wasn't any give and take with him. It was awful for me as her mother. I was watching as my happy-go-lucky girl was drained completely by him and his moods.'

'God, that sounds awful,' Daisy sympathised. 'Have you any regrets about ending the relationship, Niamh?'

'No, no I don't. At first it was really messy because we lived together,' Niamh explained. 'I had to move back home at the age of thirty and pretty much start afresh. But now that the mist is clearing with the whole thing and I'm away from Adam, I know I'm going to be fine.'

'Good for you,' Daisy said, biting her lip so she wouldn't cry.

'Listen, you didn't come on holiday to become an agony aunt! Let's just change the subject. Have you time for a little glass of wine before you go for your bus? Our hotel is just here,' she said enticingly.

Daisy knew there were several buses going to Monte Carlo throughout the evening, so she happily accepted the invitation to have a drink with the women.

'Give me the parcels, love, and I'll put them up in the room,' Kitty offered. 'You two can order me a glass of red and I'll be back in a jiffy.'

Kitty headed off, leaving Daisy and Niamh alone.

'I'd better just phone Freddie and tell him where I am,' Daisy said. 'I was annoyed with him for dumping me, so I kind of took off this morning.' She needn't have worried, though, Freddie's phone went straight to voicemail.

'Hi Freddie, I'm in Nice, in case you were worried. I've met some Irish ladies and I'm just having a glass of wine with them. I'll be back later on.'

Daisy was actually a little embarrassed.

'The coverage all along the coast can be dodgy,' Niamh said helpfully.

'Um,' Daisy said, looking slightly distracted. Checking her own voicemail, there were no messages from Freddie. She'd been gone all day and he hadn't looked for her.

Daisy and Niamh chatted more about relationships and probably because they didn't know anything about one another, they both divulged quite a lot.

Niamh explained that Adam had been really nice to her in the beginning, but had never been overly chatty to her friends.

'It used to really bother me that he didn't seem to think he needed to make an effort with them.'

It transpired that one by one, her friends had told her they didn't get on with him. She'd become more isolated and less sociable.

'That was what Adam wanted. He was only happy when he had me to himself. I know it probably sounds endearing, but believe me it became stifling.'

'I can imagine,' Daisy said. 'I love my girlfriends, I would hate if any man forced me to choose between him and my pals.'

'It got worse, he ended up getting narky if I spoke to Mum too much,' Niamh said, shuddering at the memory.

'Oh, wow, that's a bit much! Nobody should dictate your relationship with your family,' Daisy said. Kitty reappeared and the three women chatted until the sun went down.

'I'd better head back or I'll be in real trouble,' Daisy said, standing up reluctantly. 'It was so lovely to meet you both. If you're ever in Dublin, give me a shout,' Daisy said as they exchanged phone numbers.

They waved her off as the bus doors hissed shut and she smiled and waved back. As soon as the bus had pulled away, though, the smile dropped from Daisy's face. She was awash with mixed feelings. She'd really enjoyed meeting the women. In fact, it was the most fun she'd had since arriving in France. As she sat on the bus and closed her eyes for a few minutes, she had a niggling thought: two strangers had made her feel more included than her own boyfriend. That wasn't right. Poor Niamh had waited five years and wasted so much time on a relationship she'd had doubts about. It really was food for thought. Daisy knew her parents loved Freddie but recently, and especially during this holiday, she was seeing a side to him that she really wasn't comfortable with. They hadn't discussed marriage or anything like that yet, so she knew she was being a bit presumptuous, but Daisy was certain of one thing – she had no intention of buying into a future that involved shuffling gratefully behind any man, only to be taken out of the box at dinners, lunches and convenient celebrations.

Freddie's words from the very first night they'd met rang in her ears: 'You're like a porcelain doll.'

At the time she'd teased him for saying it, but had privately thought it was quite sweet. Now she wasn't so sure. She didn't want to be a doll of any shape or form. She wanted to be the independent and educated woman she'd always expected to become. Maybe her feelings of unrest were being caused by the wine, heat and tale of woe from Niamh. But if she were honest with herself, she'd been having doubts for the past couple of months. Apart from the reluctance to put his hand in his pocket, Freddie had begun to irritate her, full stop. She bit her lip and checked her phone again. No voice messages. No texts. What did it say about them? She took a deep breath and tried to calm her racing thoughts. When I look into his eyes, she told herself, I'll see the real Freddie and everything will be okay. We are in love.

7.

Daisy

As Daisy paid the taxi driver, Freddie raced out of the chalet and launched at her. 'Where the hell have you been? I've been worried sick!'

'I went to Nice for the day. If you were so concerned, why didn't you call me? I've had my phone on and it hasn't rung once,' Daisy flared back.

'For all I knew you could've been abducted and murdered! What if your parents had called and I wasn't able to even tell them where you were?' he spat.

'If I had been abducted and murdered that would've been a terrible inconvenience for you, I can see that. But I repeat – why didn't you call me?'

'I tried a couple of hours ago and the phone went straight to voicemail, so I figured you didn't want to talk to me for some unknown reason,' he yelled.

'I was probably at Le Château at that point. I had no coverage.'

Daisy pushed past Freddie and made her way into the kitchen where she opened the fridge, looking for a bottle of chilled wine.

'Want a glass of wine?' she called out.

'What?' Freddie appeared, looking deranged.

'Wine?' She raised an eyebrow.

'What exactly is going on here, Daisy? Would you mind filling me in on what kind of a holiday this is meant to be?' Freddie boomed.

'Stop shouting, you're giving me a headache,' she sighed, pouring herself a glass of wine. '*You* are the one who buggered off and left me here without so much as a backward glance. *You* seemed to think I would sit here like a wind-up toy and wait for you to play golf and swagger around being the big man before returning and winding the key in my back when you wanted to play with me. So to answer your question, Freddie, I thought this would be a holiday holiday, not a sorry-I-have-to-go-schmooze-assholes holiday.'

She glared at him, feeling all her resentment and doubt bubbling up inside.

Freddie looked astonished. 'But I need to do some networking, Daisy. I didn't realise that was a crime.'

'Well *I* thought we were here for a holiday together, as a couple. *You* changed the rules without consulting me,' Daisy retorted. 'I'm not the type of person who sits around on my own being anybody's fool, Freddie. I went and had a day out, big deal! So sue me! Or maybe you can get one of your golf buddies to do it for you.'

Freddie was taken aback by her attitude. It was a side of Daisy he hadn't seen before. He'd come home ready to bring her out for a lovely romantic meal, with a bit of networking afterwards, only to find the place empty and not a sign of his girlfriend. Now it all seemed to be *his* fault. His mother would never behave this way towards his father. He couldn't understand it.

Daisy padded out the back and sat on a chair by the pool. She knew she had to calm herself down, but she was fuming. Freddie was acting like a throwback from the fifties. Did he honestly think she'd be sitting there like a Stepford wife, waiting for him to pay her some attention? She was going to have to rethink this whole relationship. There would be snowballs in hell before she'd end up married to such a narrow-minded person. She didn't even like who she was when she was with him anymore – all that shouting and sarcasm just wasn't her.

Freddie eventually followed her outside and sat staring at her.

'What?' she said irritably.

'I don't want to fight with you. This is supposed to be a lovely time for us, Daisy. Let's put today behind us and we'll have a great day together tomorrow. What do you say?'

Daisy played with the stem of her glass, taking deep breaths. He did look sorry and, besides, she wasn't interested in spending the next few days stuck on a hillside, albeit one in Monte Carlo, with a person who wasn't speaking to her. She took a big gulp of wine and forced a smile.

'Okay, truce,' she said quietly.

Freddie sighed in relief.

The sun beamed the following day and they rose late and lazed by the pool, reading books, making love and relaxing.

'This is the life, isn't it?' Freddie muttered as he sipped from a cold glass of lemonade.

'Yup, pretty fantastic!' Daisy agreed.

They strolled hand in hand to a fabulous restaurant where they dined on shellfish and champagne followed by tangy lemon tart.

'Just imagine, we could be here for our ten-year anniversary!' Freddie said, staring pointedly at Daisy.

'Riiight ...' Daisy wasn't sure at first what he was saying.

'I hated arguing with you yesterday. We're made for each other, Daisy. Will you marry me?'

Before she knew it, Freddie was down on one knee holding her hands in his. The look on his face was so sincere. In that moment, Daisy knew Freddie really loved her. She stared at him, down on his knees before her, gazing hopefully up at her. She was suddenly aware that the restaurant had gone quiet.

'Yes,' she heard herself say. Her head was in a spin. What the hell just happened?

The onlookers in the restaurant began to clap. Waiters appeared from every nook and cranny and began pumping Freddie's hand and clapping him on the back. Daisy was whisked from her chair and kissed on both cheeks by so many people she lost count. Champagne was summoned by an ecstatic Freddie and before she knew which end was up, she was handed both a mobile phone and a glass of bubbly.

'Darling, what wonderful news!' Ava squealed down the line.

'Mum! Oh, my goodness, I'm in a bit of a dream world here. I feel like I'm in a bubble. It's all so unexpected and ... fast!' Daisy said, suddenly feeling a rush of emotion on hearing her mother's voice.

'Hi, darling!' Justin took the phone from his wife.

'Dad!'

'We're thrilled, love. We were all dying for the phone to ring. It's been torture not telling anyone over the past couple of days,' Justin boomed.

'What? You mean you all knew?' Daisy was stunned.

'Well, Freddie being Freddie, he called in to see Ava and me before you two set off. He asked for your hand and we gladly agreed!'

'Oh, I see ...' Daisy was so confused. She seemed to be the least excited person, but she reckoned she was just in shock.

Freddie called his own parents and they had a quick word before he threw the phone on the table and pulled her into his arms.

'So how do you like the sound of Mrs Prenderville?' Freddie asked as he kissed her.

'I mightn't change my name, of course,' Daisy said without thinking.

'Oh, you are funny at times. That,' Freddie tipped her nose with his finger, 'is what I love about you. You're always joking, always a step ahead of the posse.'

Daisy didn't want to ruin the moment, but she'd just decided for certain she *wasn't* changing her name – ever.

The rest of the night was a blur of phone calls and text messages as their news spread like wildfire.

'Oh, my God! You never told us you were thinking of getting engaged!' Naomi yelled down the phone.

'That's because I had no idea. It was all a surprise, isn't it just the best!' said Daisy, biting her lip.

'Have you told Caroline yet?' Naomi wanted to know.

'No, I haven't had a chance, I'll call her now in case she feels left out.'

'I'm so excited, Daisy. Are you having bridesmaids? Count me in if you are!' Naomi sounded like she was going to burst with joy.

'Oh, God, I'll think about all that another time. But you're so gorgeous, Naomi, if you're on the altar, I'm going to make you wear a disgusting dress with an unflattering neckline and dreadful hairpiece!' Daisy giggled.

'Bitch!' Naomi laughed. 'Seriously though – I can't believe you're getting married! This is insane! We're only twenty-one, you'll be the first of all our gang. The other girls are going to be so jealous, I can tell you. Oh, my God,' she shrieked suddenly, 'that witch Katie Fields-Weston is going to have a heart attack when she hears this. She's been banging on for a year about how she's the youngest bride in our set at twenty-four, now you're going to blow her out of the water! God, I hope my turn comes soon.'

'But it is great, isn't it?' Daisy said again, not sure what answer she wanted to hear from her friend.

'Oh, God, yeah!' Naomi assured her. 'I envy you, Daisy.'

The conversation with Caroline was even more frenzied. Caroline had been in Dublin that day and just happened to pass a designer bridal store.

'I don't normally look too closely at wedding gowns, but this one was divine. In fact, now that I think about it, it's got your name written all over it. It's slinky with just the right balance between sassy and demure,' Caroline assured her. 'You don't want to shock your father and equally, you can't look like Maria from *The Sound of Music*.'

'Give me a chance! I'm only engaged and you have me dressed and ready to go!'

When she put the phone down, Freddie was staring at the bill with a look of utter shock and despair on his face.

'What's wrong?' Daisy asked, her smile fading.

'This is astronomical! I don't have that amount of cash on me. You don't mind going Dutch, do you love?' Freddie asked. 'Besides we'll be married soon, so it's all coming out of the same pot, so to speak!' he said justifying his meanness.

Daisy peeled some notes from her purse and threw them on the table. Noticing there was a third of a bottle of champagne left, she filled her glass to spilling point.

'Aren't you going to share?' Freddie asked, grinning.

'Nope! I'm drinking the whole lot myself.'

'That's not very nice!' Freddie boomed, laughing.

'No it's not, is it?' Daisy raised her eyebrows and gave him a stare that hinted at certain insanity. She glugged every drop of the champagne in record time and banged the glass down on the table.

'You're crazy!' Freddie laughed, missing her irritation.

'You're right – I'm utterly insane,' she shrilled.

By the time they got back to the chalet, Daisy was drunk as a skunk and singing Take That songs at the top of her voice.

'Shush! You'll wake the neighbours! And that's hardly ladylike behaviour for my wife-to-be!' Freddie said.

'Ah who gives a toss about being ladylike. Grab a bottle of bubbly from the fridge and let's go skinny-dipping in the pool!'

Daisy was already peeling her clothes off, although she did have a bit of a stumble as she tried to step out of her dress.

'Be careful, you're going to knock yourself out, Daisy! You're too drunk to go in the pool and you really are going to cause a disturbance,' Freddie scolded.

He scooped her up in his arms and brought her into the bedroom.

When she woke the next morning, Daisy had a dreadful taste in her mouth.

'I've inherited SpongeBob SquarePants' mouth. It's all dehydrated and parched. I'm never drinking again,' she groaned.

'You were fairly knocking it back last night, but I'll forgive you. It was all the excitement – I understand,' Freddie said with his hands on his hips.

'How are you showered and dressed already? Don't you have a hangover? Come back to bed,' Daisy said holding her hands over her eyes. 'Jeez, close the curtains, Freddie, it's so bright.'

'Well it's ten thirty, so it would be.'

'Are you annoyed with me?' Daisy sat up, squinting.

'No, not as such. I would just prefer if you didn't shout and yell at all hours of the night in the garden. This is my parents' house and the neighbours wouldn't be used to that kind of behaviour.'

Daisy burst out laughing and flung herself back on the bed. 'Oh, get a life, Freddie! I was only celebrating. If the locals find that offensive, they can have me arrested. I'm twenty-one, not eighty-one.'

Freddie stood quite still, with nothing but the slight twitch in his jaw giving away how furious he was.

'I'm off to the golf club. I really need you to back me up later on.' Freddie spoke slowly. 'Bill and Tracey are coming here for pre-dinner drinks and we'll take them to the smaller restaurant near last night's place.'

'Why are you talking to me as if I'm an errant toddler? I don't remember you asking me if *I* wanted to spend the evening with Bill and Tracey either.' Daisy sat upright as she spoke.

'We have to return their kind luncheon invitation and they're returning to Dublin tomorrow,' Freddie explained.

'Oh, well, that's the reason then! Yes, we must drop everything and make sure they don't go home starving. It would be such a travesty if we didn't see them again before we go back to the same city as them,' Daisy barked. 'I'd better remember to bring all my money and credit cards if we're paying for four tonight.' She felt like shit and she really wasn't in the mood for coaxing conversation out of Tracey.

'If you're finished having a tantrum,' Freddie said primly, 'I just wanted to mention that I didn't buy you an engagement ring as I thought you'd prefer to choose it with me.' Freddie stood looking at the floor. 'But as soon as we get back to Dublin, I'll bring you to the jewellers. I'll be back before six.'

As the front door slammed Daisy grabbed her pillow, shoved her face into it and yelled. Why did Freddie have to make her feel like this? Why did she always end up being the bad guy? He was already taking on this crazy persona of the Neanderthal man provider. It was so old-fashioned. She raised her head from the pillow as a sudden thought crossed her mind. Would Freddie want her to put her career aside now? Was he expecting her to put her own aspirations and dreams in a box and be grateful to be a kept woman like his own mother?

Gazing at the digital alarm clock on the bedside table, Daisy realised it was still only eleven in the morning. Freddie had done it again – he'd buggered off and left her by herself in the chalet, waiting for him to return with Mr and Mrs Good-for-business-contacts.

Pulling a sundress over her head, Daisy padded outside with a Diet Coke from the fridge. It was *very* glary out there. The sun, which had been a delight before, was a bit too hot and bright this morning.

She was starving, too. Whenever she was in a bad way with a hangover, she usually headed straight for McDonald's. There was no better cure as far as she was concerned: two fizzy painkillers and plenty of junk food. But here in Monte Carlo, they didn't do burgers and grease.

Grabbing the widest brimmed sun hat she could find, Daisy took her bag and mooched down the hill to the town. Figuring strong coffee and a doughy pastry with some sort of molten chocolate inside might help, she found a shaded table outside a patisserie.

Just as she'd sipped the first mouthful, her mobile phone rang.

'Hello?' she croaked.

'Darling! You sound a bit worse for wear! Did you go a bit over the top with the celebrations last night?'

'Hi, Mum. Yup. Feeling rather dodgy, if I'm honest.'

'Tell me everything! Did you guess? Had you an inkling he was going to ask you?' Ava wanted to know.

'Not a clue!' Daisy said, feeling the benefit of the caffeine and her beloved mum's voice.

'So have you had a chance to talk about the wedding? What are you thinking?' Ava sounded so delighted.

'We haven't discussed it at all, to be honest. There's plenty of time for all of that. Besides, I want to finish my Montessori course,' Daisy explained. 'If I do as well as I hope in my exams, I'll be eligible to go for the advanced AMI elementary diploma course. I've no intention of dropping my career prospects and running up the aisle to be a trophy wife.'

'That's fine, love! Nobody said you have to. Did Freddie say he wanted you to give up your studies?' Ava sounded surprised.

'No, but I'm just making sure nobody gets any ideas.'

'So you don't know if you're thinking of a wedding this year or next, then?' Ava probed, dying to be given the green light to start organising it all.

'I honestly don't know right this second, Mum.'

'Don't worry, pet, I know it's all such a whirlwind of excitement and joy. As you say, we've tons of time to get it all sorted.'

'Have you spoken to Ursula and Alfred yet?' Daisy enquired.

'Oh, yes, Justin and I had a lovely chat with them last night and we're going to the Italian beside the golf club with them this evening for a little celebration,' Ava said happily. 'We'll do a proper night when you get home, but we're all just so thrilled, we wanted to meet up to toast you two!'

'Well enjoy! I'm sorry to cut you short, Mum, but it's really hot here and I need to pay for my coffee. I'll chat to you later on,' Daisy fibbed, rubbing her forehead with her hand.

'Okay, pet, have a lovely day with Freddie and I'll chat to you later on. Love you.'

'Love you too, Mum. Bye.'

Daisy didn't bother pointing out that she was on her own and that Freddie wouldn't be back until that evening.

Feeling much more human after her breakfast, Daisy wandered around the town for a while before returning to the chalet. She'd better make an effort to look fresh-faced and happy when Freddie and their guests arrived.

A swim in the pool and a quick nap on the sun lounger made all the difference. By the time she heard the car pulling up just after six, Daisy was dressed in a cool maxi dress, glittery flip-flops and had her make-up and hair freshly done.

'Hello, everyone! How are we all this evening?' Daisy asked as she opened the front door to welcome them.

'Well, well, well. Freddie told us your wonderful news!' Tracey exclaimed, throwing her arms around Daisy. 'We're delighted for you both. I just told your fella here that he's a very lucky man!'

'And you're a lucky gal,' Bill boomed, embracing her a little too harshly. 'Apart from the fact that he just whooped my ass on the golf course, this man of yours is a great guy! I hope you'll both have as many years of wedded bliss as Tracey and I have enjoyed.'

'Thanks, Bill!' Daisy smiled sweetly.

As they took some drinks out onto the veranda beside the pool, Bill continued with advice.

'Marriage is a bit like a business, you know? You have to enjoy a good partnership. If one of you isn't pulling his or her weight, it doesn't work.' Bill sighed and shook his head. 'Both your parents got it right. So did Tracey and I. Once everyone knows where they stand, that's half the battle, you know?'

'What do you mean by that exactly?' Daisy was still smiling beautifully. Inside she felt like pushing Bill into the pool with a brick tied around his neck.

'Well, Tracey is a marvellous wife.'

'Thank you, Bill,' Tracey looked overjoyed with the compliment.

'Well, credit where it's due, darling,' Bill continued. 'She looks after me. She raised the children wonderfully. I know she'll always be there to back me up, just like you are with Freddie here.'

'I love being there for you, dear,' Tracey said, all starry-eyed.

Daisy felt a violent anger bubbling through her.

'What about *you* though, Tracey?' Daisy had to ask. 'Didn't you ever want a career or something outside of the marriage?'

'Oh, yes, I've played tennis for years and Bill has finally got me out on the golf course after many moons of begging. I'm not great, but it's fun.' Tracey giggled. 'We were young getting married and I wasn't one of those girls who knew what she wanted to do after she left school. I suppose I'm not terribly business minded, so I chose to just enjoy my life with Bill.'

Daisy nodded and said she understood and exclaimed how happy she was that Tracey had such a wonderful life. But deep down, Daisy was beginning to panic.

Her own mother had worked until she'd had children. She'd chosen to give up her career and stay at home after that, but because her father worked away in the States a lot, Ava had her own life too. Daisy could never picture her own mother sitting around waiting for her dad to come back from work. Ava was always out and about and never seemed to have a moment of boredom. So why was it that this woman was freaking Daisy out so much?

In her heart, she knew the answer: it was because Freddie thought he was getting a new, improved, younger version of Tracey.

They'd have to discuss all this when they got some alone time. She'd have to make Freddie see that she wanted to work as a Montessori teacher. She wanted to be her own person, always. Yes, she would *share* her life with Freddie, but he couldn't become her puppet master. That simply wouldn't be a good 'partnership'.

Freddie was the perfect host that night. He insisted on paying for every morsel they ate and peeled off fifty-euro notes from a wad he'd obviously been hiding.

'He's like a younger version of my Bill,' Tracey sighed in awe. 'Isn't it lovely to have a man who wants to cherish you and look after you?'

Daisy just smiled and nodded, as she'd done all night.

The remainder of the holiday in Monte Carlo slipped by quickly. None of it turned out to be what Daisy had expected. Once Bill and Tracey left, more 'friends' arrived at the golf club and yet again, Freddie was off networking.

On the return flight, Freddie suggested they move into an apartment together.

'I have a place outside Blackrock, a two-bed apartment that overlooks the sea. I had it rented out, but with the way things have gone with the economy, it'd be just as handy if we live in it,' Freddie said. Daisy loved Blackrock village. It was home to lots of boutiques and restaurants, not to mention the park and surrounding area. It was very close to Dublin city and not a million miles from her parents or her college.

'Sounds great, let's go and check it out over the next few days and make a decision then,' she agreed. 'Freddie, you know I want to finish my training. I've next year to get through, after which, results permitting, I intend doing at least one more year in college. I want to work as a Montessori teacher – you are aware of that, aren't you?'

'Right. Well finish your college by all means. Of course, I'm all on for education and you love your childcare stuff, so I'd never stop you,' he kissed her gently.

'It's not childcare – it's Montessori. There is a difference,' Daisy answered tightly.

'Yes I know, of course there is, darling,' Freddie was gazing out the window of the plane patting her leg. 'At the end of the day if you want to wipe other people's children's noses for a while before we have our own, I'm all for it. Now, I'd say our mothers are going to want a summer wedding. So will we say around this time next year? I know Mum will be delighted with the project. I can just see them now, off having lunches and meeting florists and what-not,' Freddie grinned. 'And don't worry, I wouldn't dream of turning into one of those men who interfere with all the plans. You can be bridezilla and milk every moment!'

'I'm not sure I want us to get married this time next year!' Daisy suddenly felt a bit pressurised. 'And I would really appreciate it if you don't ever refer to my course as wiping noses again.' She was feeling sick with rage at how this conversation was turning out.

'Oh, don't tell me – you've always dreamed of a winter wedding?' Freddie was only hearing what he wanted to hear – yet again. Shaking her head, Daisy tried not to blow her top.

'No,' she said very slowly and icily. 'I don't see why we should be in such a hurry, that's all. Let's just take things a little slower.' Daisy looked to him for some sort of understanding.

'I'd like to see you get my mother to think that way!' Freddie said, grinning and nodding.

'Well, it's not your mother's wedding. Nor is she in charge of what we do. So I suggest we try and focus on what we both want instead of bringing other people into the equation all the time.'

Daisy knew she was sounding snappy, but the feeling of claustrophobia was really moving in on her and she was sick of Freddie treating her like his little wifey.

Her heart nearly stopped a short while later when they emerged at arrivals to be greeted by Ursula clutching a handful of 'Congratulations on your Engagement' helium balloons.

'Hello!' she called out, rushing over to hug them.

'You must be so excited to have exchanged your usual Chanel handbag for those!' Freddie boomed. 'You're so sweet to come and meet us,' he said hugging his mother.

'Not at all, I'm just so thrilled with your news. I can't *wait* to get going on all the preparations!'

'Thank you!' Daisy shrilled as she hugged her future mother-in-law.

'No need to pay for a taxi now either, you're a star, Mum,' Freddie added.

'So how was Monte Carlo, then? Did you fall in love with the place,

Daisy?' Ursula asked as they drove home. 'I hope you did. Alfred and I have had such wonderful times there. I hope you can both make it your special place, too.'

They all chatted easily until they reached Daisy's house. Freddie said he'd go in for five minutes to shake hands with Ava and Justin.

'Congratulations, you two,' Ava called out. 'Come on in, Ursula. Let's have a toast to the gorgeous couple! Justin's just got home from the States this morning and he'd be delighted to see you, too.'

Ava led them all into the sitting room and there was a round of hugs as wine was poured and glass were clinked.

'So, dare we ask? Do you have a date in mind?' Ursula probed.

'Well, I was suggesting next summer …' Freddie began before Daisy could open her mouth.

'Oh, I think that would be super!' Ursula clapped her hands in delight.

'We could have it here if you like?' Ava added, joining in with the plans.

'Well, we said we're going to take things one step at a time and talk about all of that at a later date, remember?' Daisy said, staring at Freddie. 'I want to finish college before anything happens. I also feel strongly that I've every intention of pursuing my career as a Montessori teacher. Besides, we have all the time in the world!'

There was a slightly uneasy silence for a few seconds until Daisy smoothed things over. 'That's not to say that we can't all start buying magazines and making some suggestions!' she said, trying to keep the joviality going and not ruin the moment.

'Listen, I've a roast in the oven and there's more than enough to go around. Would you call Alfred and see if he'll come over?' Ava asked.

'Well, only if you're sure?' Ursula hesitated.

'We'd love it!' Justin said with a warm smile.

So Daisy found herself being swept along once more. Freddie did seem to be so thrilled about being engaged to her and was more than enthusiastic about them setting up the apartment together. But the doubts she'd had in France were still niggling away at the back of her mind. She didn't want to end up as a trophy wife. She couldn't deal with a life as someone's shiny keyring.

Alfred arrived and there were more hugs and backslaps and clinking of glasses. Daisy felt like she was watching a movie of someone else's life. She could see herself smiling and nodding and playing the part of happily engaged woman, but she was feeling numb and empty inside. As they all sat down to eat, she tried to shake herself up and knock away her feelings, but she couldn't seem to feel the delight everyone else so obviously shared.

'So Ava, we're going to be busy, aren't we?' Ursula smiled.

'I know,' Ava laughed, 'but I can't wait to get started on the preparations. I just can't believe I'm going to be organising Daisy's wedding! And the idea of Justin walking her proudly down the aisle …' she had to dab a tear from her eye. 'Sorry,' she smiled at them, 'I'm just so happy that our Daisy has found someone so perfect.'

Freddie grinned widely and his parents looked at him adoringly.

Justin reached over and took Ava's hand. 'I know, darling, it's just wonderful. You are so welcome to our family, Freddie.'

'And what do your other friends make of it?' Alfred asked Ava. 'I had one chap at the club tell me that our lovely children are too young to be tying the knot.'

Ava looked thoughtful. 'I've had that, too, Alfred, to be honest. One or two of my friends have commented that Daisy is very young to be getting married, and I know in this day and age very few people marry at twenty-one, but this union seems so right. Daisy is so happy. Freddie adores her. So where's the problem? A small part of me suspects my friends are slightly envious that our daughter has found such an amazing fiancé!'

The four parents and Freddie laughed loudly. Daisy managed a small smile.

Ava mistook her daughter's reaction for nervousness and reached over to squeeze her hand. 'I know it's a lot to take on board, Daisy, suddenly being the centre of attention like this, but it's going to be so wonderful. I promise you.'

As the conversation flowed on and on and on, Daisy felt like she was on an island, and everything she thought she knew about her life seemed to be receding on the horizon.

8.

Felicity

The weeks seemed to fly by that summer. Felicity took as many hours as she could get in the coffee shop. Good weather meant the tourists came in droves, ensuring tips on top of her wages. She was careful with her money and soon her bank account started to look quite healthy.

The day before the exam results were due out, Felicity and Mia decided to take a trip to Galway city together.

'I could do with a day out, we'll have our lunch and see if there's any end-of-sale bargains we must have!' Mia suggested.

'I know what'll happen now, I won't like any of the stuff that's knocked down in price. All I'll want is the new season gear that costs a fortune!' Felicity said.

'Well, you'll need some new bits and pieces for university, so it'll be good to have a look,' Mia said, trying not to sound strangled. She was bracing herself for the possibility of Felicity leaving her.

'True,' Felicity agreed. 'I can get most of the dressy fun gear from Aly's shop at discount, but I could do with a good new coat.'

It was warm and muggy, even though the sun wasn't shining, so it seemed plenty of other people had chosen to skip the beach and have a mooch around the shops, too.

'It's packed in here!' Mia commented. 'You'd swear they were giving the stuff away.'

Linking her mother's arm, Felicity had a sudden rush of excitement. 'Every time I think of the exam results I get butterflies in my tummy. I wonder if I'll get any of my choices?'

'I'm sure you'll get just what you want. You're a bright spark and you worked hard, pet,' Mia assured her.

'It'll be really weird if Aly doesn't get the same college as me. We've been together since we were tiny,' Felicity worried.

'I know, but you're so close I think the two of you will be friends for life,' Mia said with certainty. 'If you're in separate universities, it might actually do you good. It'll make you branch out a bit. That's not a bad thing, you know.'

'I suppose,' Felicity said, not sounding too sure.

She'd never been the type of girl who hung around in big gangs. Herself and Aly had always been a team. They were well liked among their peers, but everybody knew they came as a pair. Parties, holidays and events saw them arriving side by side.

Mia's mobile phone rang, causing her to root like a mad thing through her bag. 'The damn thing will stop now before I get to it,' she said sounding hassled. 'Hello? No. It's gone. I'll just wait for them to leave a message,' she said, looking annoyed.

'Here, give it to me and I'll look and see who it was, you can just call them back,' Felicity said.

'I can't see that screen without my glasses, so I just wait and hear the voicemail,' Mia admitted.

Felicity checked her mother's call log. 'It was Galway Hospital, you'd better ring back in case they need you to see someone in a hurry,' Felicity said.

Her mam had worked as a midwife all Felicity's life, so she and her brothers were well versed in dealing with their mam needing to flee the scene to tend to a mother in labour. Felicity hit redial and the hospital exchange picked up immediately. Mia gestured that she'd follow Felicity into one of the shops as she plugged her other ear with her finger.

Felicity was glad her mam still worked. She was busy most days, either with her job or the various hobbies she enjoyed. She knew Bob would still be at home – he'd probably never move out! Why would he? Having all his meals handed to him and his clothes washed and ironed, while still being able to come and go as he pleased. It gave Felicity great peace of mind to know he was there, but she knew it was going to be hard for herself and her mam to get used to not having one another to lean on.

As it turned out their shopping trip had to be cut short. Mia was needed at the hospital as they were short staffed.

'A good few of the midwives are on holiday, so I said they could call me if they were stuck. I shouldn't have opened my mouth!'

'Don't worry, Mam. We can come in again soon. Most of the stuff in the shops is sale stuff nobody wants and the autumn/winter gear is only starting to trickle in. It's not the best time to shop, in fairness,' Felicity said hugging her mam.

In order to save time, Felicity said she'd get the bus back home so Mia could drive straight in to the hospital.

As she boarded the bus, a load of lads from the Presentation College she vaguely knew waved over to her. Felicity sat just ahead of them and turned to chat.

'So who's nervous about tomorrow?' she asked.

'I don't give a toss. Once I'm away from school that's my bit done as far as study is concerned,' said Kevin.

'I've applied for Cambridge,' said Emmet.

'Seriously?' Felicity said impressed.

'Him – in Cambridge?' another one of the lads guffawed. 'If he makes it home on this bus, he'll be doing well. This dope will end up on the dole and even that'll confuse him.'

They all sniggered and punched each other in the arm, acting like five-year-olds.

Felicity smiled so they wouldn't think she was a snooty cow, but she really wanted to stand up and sit somewhere else. Having grown up with four older brothers, she attached no sense of mystery to boys. She'd had a couple of boyfriends over the previous two years, but none had lasted and she wasn't pushed either way.

Aly, on the other hand, was man-mad. She was the type of girl who loved to have at least one fella dangling on a string at any one time. She wasn't the sort who bought bridal magazines and spent hours sitting in a flower-filled meadow dreaming of the day she'd become Mrs Whoever. She just adored the chase, the flirt and the banter with the boys.

Felicity quite liked the idea of meeting someone she got on well with, but it wasn't the be all and end all of her life. There was so much she wanted to do first – study, travel, maybe do some volunteer work abroad. She stared out the bus window and dreamed about the life that might be waiting for her in the next few years – once she got the results she needed.

The following morning, Felicity was up and dressed by eight o'clock.

'Would you eat a pancake with a bit of bacon and maple syrup? That's what Bob wants,' Mia asked, shuffling past Felicity in the kitchen. 'You're dressed and all! What time have you to be at the convent?'

'Any time from nine. I'll head over once I get a cup of tea,' Felicity said distractedly.

'Will you not have a proper feed first? Bob would love you to join him for breakfast,' Mia encouraged.

'Mam, Bob wouldn't notice if you sat him with a giraffe and a family of baboons so long as you feed him,' Felicity giggled.

'Well, join *me* then,' Mia pleaded.

'I can't eat, Mam. I'd puke. Just let me drink my tea and I'll go on over to the school. I'm meeting Aly at the gate.'

'I wouldn't hold your breath, expecting that one to be there on time. She'll be late for her own funeral!' Mia said good-naturedly.

'True, but I've warned her that it's more than her life is worth to leave me pacing like a tiger on my own.'

'I'll be waiting by the phone! The best of luck, love,' Mia said as she hugged her.

'Thanks! Talk to you soon,' Felicity said, looking terrified.

'What's done is done. No sense in upsetting yourself at this point. Just go and enjoy the bit of banter with the pals this morning, lovie,' Mia advised.

Felicity fled the house like a woman on a mission.

Needless to say, there was no sign of Aly at the meeting point. Felicity was just about to call her mobile when she came clattering down the road, looking like she'd been dragged through a bush backwards.

'Sorry! Don't kill me, Flick. I only woke up ten seconds ago,' Aly said waving her arms. 'This leg isn't even working properly, look, it's still asleep, God bless it.' Aly pointed to her left leg, which did look as if it was dragging ever so slightly. 'Bad night – I'll tell you later on. Met that Joseph guy from the bar the other night. You were right – total goon. But he bought me several double gins, so it wasn't all bad.'

'Gin?' Felicity looked shocked. 'Gin turns you into a lunatic. Did he not read the safety instruction booklet that comes with you? The bit where it says – *do not mix with gin or lives could be lost. Can-can, conga and other dances requiring much pointing and clapping will ensue – with or without music.*'

'Ah, stop! I'm not that bad!' Aly laughed. 'Come on, let's go in and find out what university, if any, is going to be graced by our presence.'

The headmistress, Sister Concepta, one of the remaining nuns at the girls' convent school, was handing out the envelopes. She was wearing her best outfit – a navy dress with a tiny white polkadot detail that could easily have served as a nurse's uniform.

'Good morning, girls. The best of luck now, Lord be with you,' said Sister Concepta.

'Thanks, Sister,' the girls chorused.

'She's someone I will *never* miss,' Aly hissed. 'That woman hates my guts and I can happily say that the feeling is mutual.'

'Feck her, let's open these!' Felicity said. 'Hug first!'

The two friends embraced each other, then proceeded to rip open the envelopes.

'Oh, sweet Jesus, I'm afraid to look,' Felicity said.

'I'm not – I got 355 points!' Aly screamed. 'I thought I'd get about twenty! I'm delighted!'

'Oh, well done, honey!' Felicity hugged her.

'Go on – give us a look then.'

As Felicity peeled the page from the envelope, she felt like she was going to faint.

'Oh, my God! I got 500!' Felicity danced around in a circle as tears streaked her cheeks. Trying to do a quick tot in her head, she attempted to work out whether or not she'd be likely to get any of her top-choice universities. Of course, it all depended on the rest of the country and how high the standard was against the demand for places.

The general air at the convent was one of joviality. Most of the girls seemed to be happy enough with what they'd got. One poor soul was sobbing her heart out, saying she'd have to repeat.

'Sod that – I wouldn't repeat those exams if my life depended on it!' Aly whispered.

'I suppose if there was something in particular you wanted in life, you'd do what it takes,' Felicity said, feeling sorry for the distressed girl.

Within the hour, the bulk of the girls had left the school grounds, vowing to meet up later that night for the disco. Felicity and Aly were beside themselves with excitement. They'd wanted to go to the results party for years, but neither of them had been allowed.

'You can go when you've actually done the exams and not a minute before.' Mia had held firm on that. Aly's mother had been in agreement, so the two had been forced to wait.

'I wouldn't ever admit it to Mam, but in a way I'm sort of glad we've never been to the results disco before tonight. It makes it all the more exciting, doesn't it?' Aly said.

'You bet!'

Both girls rang home to give the good news and Felicity's phone rang non-stop for the next while as all her brothers rang to congratulate her.

Gangs of girls from their class and lads from the Presentation boys' school met up in the town and shared news.

'Let's go back to your place now,' Aly suggested early that afternoon. 'We can arse around and get ready at our leisure.'

The girls arrived at the front door just as Mia pulled up in her jeep.

'Give me a hug you two!' Mia exploded out the door, barely giving herself enough time to pull up the handbrake.

'You are just brilliant,' she squealed as Felicity pulled out the prized piece of paper with the marks printed on it.

'I've had a great day, too,' Mia exclaimed. 'Just after I put the phone down to you earlier, I got a call from Joy Green who was in swift labour, so I drove over and she delivered a healthy nine-pound baby boy at home!'

'Ah, isn't that lovely!' Felicity linked her mam's arm. 'She's three little girls at home already, hasn't she?'

'She does, and she was longing for a little boy, so I'm thrilled for her,' Mia exclaimed. 'What a wonderful day all around!'

As if on automatic pilot, Mia put the kettle on and found her cake tin. She loved her cup of tea and always had a home-baked cake or biscuit on offer to go with it.

'Especially for the occasion I have *double* chocolate fudge with a vomit-inducing amount of frosting,' Mia said with a grin.

'Bring it on! Fantastic!' the girls chorused.

As it turned out, the cake was pretty much the only thing they ate. By the time they'd danced, sang and pranced around with curlers, rollers and every kind of potion known to woman, it was time to head out for the disco.

As usual, Mia was on standby to take them to the door.

'How you two can even contemplate going out in those platforms is beyond me!' Mia marvelled as the girls waved and staggered off in their heels.

The atmosphere was electric and the girls had a blast. Rolling home after five, Mia heard them snorting with laughter as they fell into the two beds in Felicity's room. Less than twenty minutes later, silence prevailed once more.

In her room, Mia wasn't asleep. The girls were home safe, so she could relax, but she couldn't stop the whirlwind of thoughts bashing around in her brain. She was thinking about those 500 points and what they meant: Felicity would definitely get offered the course she wanted, up in UCD, in Dublin. That meant her darling daughter would be moving 130 miles away from her. Mia closed her eyes and tried to ignore the grief that was lurking, ready to swallow her up. Felicity meant the world to her, and now her world would have to be completely reordered to take account of her absence.

For so many years, Felicity had been Mia's sanity. She might not have known it, but it was true. Felicity was the glue that held Mia and the boys together. Felicity had always been a brilliant daughter and Mia loved every single thing about her. She was her mother's ally in a house inhabited by men and their ways. Her little pink babygros had added a feminine touch to washloads that would otherwise have consisted solely of rugby and GAA gear. When the older lads hit the teenage years and went around dressed all in black, Felicity's little patterned woolly tights and pretty dresses had been Mia's ray of sunshine.

Mia knew she was very lucky in the relationship she shared with her daughter. They had always been close, had never gone through an awkward or dreadful phase where they were on different wavelengths. She'd heard friends complain of that happening with their daughters, but she and Felicity had escaped it. Her sons were her princes and she loved the bones of them, but Felicity was the jewel in her crown.

She was lucky with her boys, too, as they all lived within a ten-mile radius of her house. She wondered if, in time, Felicity would find her way back again and live somewhere nearby.

Now stop that, Mia, she scolded herself. That was no way to be thinking. She might have dreaded it for years, but there was no getting away from it now: the time had come for her little girl to move on and make her own life. That was the simple truth of it and there was no way she'd be guilty of holding Felicity back from her life. It wouldn't be right.

Mia watched the rising sun slant rays of light across her bedroom wall. It's funny, she thought, how a fresh grief opens up the old ones. She could feel tears coming to her eyes as her mind ranged over the losses she had suffered.

'Amy,' she whispered softly. 'Jim … Felicity.'

9.

Tally

The summer passed in a haze of day trips with Martin and time spent alone in front of the television. Tally had taken Laurence's advice and didn't seek out her school friends, but it still hurt that they never came looking for her either. It felt like she'd finished life when she'd finished school, and all she was left with was the four walls of the little house she shared with her parents.

August and the night of Laurence's grad ball arrived all too quickly. Tally had fully intended using the summer to trim down and lose a bit of weight. Her outfit had been seriously tight in June and she'd really wanted to feel more comfortable the second time she put it on. It wasn't that easy, though. During the run-up to Laurence's big night, it was almost as if the wrong foods were jumping out at her. Just that day she'd gone out for a short walk and was passing Spar, so she figured she'd have a chicken tikka baguette. The crisps were an obligatory accompaniment, of course, and there was nothing she loved more with spicy food than fizzy orange. The larger bottle was almost the same price as the little fecky one with only a dribble inside, so she went for value. The large Cadbury bars were in a three-for-two special right beside the cash register, so she scooped those to keep for later.

The sun was shining, so she figured she'd amble to the park. Tally found a lovely spot on the park bench near the duck pond. It wasn't quite lunchtime, so the place was peaceful and quiet. Once her roll and crisps were eaten, she decided to allow herself one row of chocolate squares from a bar and leave it at that. The plain bar was nice and all that, but the picture on the front of the caramel one looked delicious. If she just had a few squares of it, she'd keep the rest for her da to have later on.

Perhaps it was the sun or maybe it was the little baby ducks, but before she knew it all the chocolate was gone.

Feeling guilty, Tally stood up and brushed the chocolate crumbs off her clothes before screwing the paper into a ball and tossing it in the bin.

She thought about going for a long bracing walk, but it was so warm she just wanted to go home. By the time she got there, she was sweating and florid in the face. Both her parents were out at work so she flopped onto the couch and flicked on the television.

Tally was so engrossed in *The Jeremy Kyle Show* that she forgot to ring Martin and tell him not to bring any dinner for her. He arrived home just after 6pm, laden down with pizza, garlic bread and wedges. She couldn't tell him she didn't want it. It would've been a waste and her da hated eating on his own.

'Your mother's working late, so it's just you and me again, kiddo,' he said.

Tea was too wet without a biscuit, so they ended up finishing off the tin.

'Are you looking forward to tomorrow night? I was speaking to Laurence earlier on and he's so excited,' Martin said.

'I know! He's phoned me at least five times this afternoon alone!' Tally said. She tried to look excited, but her outfit rose up in her mind's eye like a demon, taunting her with its hooks and eyes and promise of a humiliating squeeze into its designer fabric.

The dry cleaners had done a lovely job of cleaning her bodice and skirt, but as she tried to shoe-horn herself into it the following evening it proved to be even more of a struggle than before.

'The summer's done your waistline no favours,' Greta scoffed as she pulled at the zip on the skirt. 'How did you get into this yoke last time?'

'I put it on backwards and turned it around,' Tally said sucking in as hard as possible.

'Well there's no movement in this now, so we'll have to soldier on with the zip at the back. Get down on the floor,' Greta ordered.

Shame and misery washed over Tally as she lay face down on the pink fuzzy rug in her bedroom.

'It's moving at last, stay still while I try and get the hook and eye shut,' Greta grimaced. 'Bloody hell, Tallulah, you're lucky I do so many weights or you'd never have mastered that zip. What about the bodice? Please tell me there's only lacing in that or I'll have to call the fire brigade!' Greta burst out laughing as her daughter wrapped the top around her bust. Greta yanked it roughly into place.

'It's too tight, Ma. I can't breathe with it like that.'

'Make your mind up,' Greta said, getting really tetchy.

Even the organza wrap seemed to be more snug than the previous time. Tally felt defeated before she'd even left the house. She desperately wanted to cancel, but there was no way she could do that to Laurence. So she put a brave face on it and climbed into the car beside Martin as they retraced the journey they'd made in June, all the way to Auntie Mary's house.

'This is like Groundhog Day, isn't it?' Laurence said as he helped her out of the car and gave her a massive hug. 'Looking stunning as usual, darling,' he said as he kissed her cheeks.

'You look positively sparkling!' Tally smiled. Whether she liked it or not, this was not her night and her cousin deserved to have a date who didn't look like she was headed for death row. Still, she figured it could only be better than her own night. At least V-J and Samantha wouldn't be standing on a podium ready to rip her self-esteem to shreds.

The evening, which went on until six the following morning, was better than Tally had expected. Laurence had a great bunch of friends who all adored him and his eccentricities. None of them made rude comments about her weight and several of the girls told her she looked pretty.

Unlike at her own ball, Tally had the sense to deposit some of the shots in a pot plant when Laurence wasn't looking.

As she fell into bed after breakfast with Martin, who was off to work, the familiar feeling of loneliness flooded her once more. Would she ever meet a guy who hung on her every word? Would she ever be one half of a loving couple like some she'd spotted rocking in each other's arms the night before? Or would she end up sleeping in this very bed, with the same pink rug and matching curtains, until she was forty and firmly on the shelf?

The sound of the postman shoving a wad of letters through the creaky old letterbox woke her with a start. Gazing at her alarm clock, she realised she'd only been asleep for three hours. Yawning, she wrapped her robe around herself and padded out to the hall to retrieve the post and make herself a cup of tea.

To her surprise, one of the reasons for the postman's struggle was a large padded envelope with her name on it. Ripping it open, Tally squealed with joy. Scanning the cover letter, she bounced up and down in utter delight.

The first person she called was Martin. 'Da,' she shouted down the phone. 'I've something to tell you.'

'Jesus Christ, love, what is it?' Martin said, sounding alarmed.

'I never told you because I thought I wouldn't get it,' Tally said breathlessly, 'but I applied to Skin Deep Beauty College and … and an information pack and letter just arrived and I've got an interview tomorrow!'

'That's fantastic, love,' Martin fairly shouted down the phone. 'Sure, why did you ever think you wouldn't get it? You're only brilliant. They'll be lucky to have you there,' Martin said proudly. 'Oh, God, I'm made up, Tally, I really am. That's the best news ever.'

Tally texted her mother – she knew there was no point phoning her at work as she wouldn't take the call. *Got letter from beauty college. Interview 2moro!*

Two hours later, she got a text back from Greta: *Cool.*

As a celebration was in order, Martin brought home a Chinese take-away. Greta particularly hated Chinese food, so she decided to have one of her protein shakes and a cigarette instead.

Tally tossed and turned all that night. If she secured a place at Skin Deep, it would be amazing. There were plenty of other colleges she could try, but none of the others was only a short bus ride away, and she loved the idea of being in Dublin city centre every day.

In the morning she could hardly eat breakfast, she was that nervous. She'd tried on everything in her wardrobe in an effort to look her best. She couldn't turn up in a black-tie outfit, but at the same time she didn't want the interviewer to think she didn't care. In the end she settled on black stretchy palazzo pants and a smock-style top with a chunky silver necklace.

Martin had offered to take the morning off work and give her a lift to the college, but she told him there was no need. She was happier to go on her own, at least that way she could gather her thoughts and make sure she was there in plenty of time.

She knew the walk from the bus stop would make her look flushed and sweaty, so she'd purposely allowed herself a bit of extra time to collect herself. As a result, she was standing outside the brown wooden door to the college at 9.10am, a full twenty minutes before her interview.

She was about to pull a hankie from her bag and mop her brow and quickly check her make-up with a tiny mirror when a pretty girl walked up to the door. She had dark curly hair and the most perfectly sculpted eyebrows Tally had ever seen.

'Hello there! Are you here for an interview for a place on the course?'

'Yes. I'm Tally Keller. Are you trying for a place, too?' Tally's heart sank. This girl was slender and wouldn't look out of place at a model agency let alone a beautician college. If this place accepted the girls they thought would add to the industry, Tally was gonzoed before she even started.

'No, I'm Sinead – I'll be the big bad interviewer! Come on inside,' she said, wrestling with her key in the door. 'You're up first, Tally, so we'll grab a cuppa and get down to business, follow me!' Sinead said leading the way.

Tally was so flummoxed, she didn't have time to get herself into a total panic.

'I should've been here half an hour ago, you know yourself, but good old Murphy's law struck and my car gave up the ghost. I ended up having to call my brother Ben and he rescued me from the side of the motorway! So apologies that I'm so disorganised,' Sinead said.

'Oh, my goodness, of course! You're *that* Sinead. I met your brother at my graduation ball in June! He was there with a friend of mine and we were sitting next to one another,' Tally said, lighting up. 'He's such a nice guy.' Just as she made the comment, Tally could feel the heat rise from her toes all the way out the crown of her head. She knew she was blushing like crazy. *Why did I have to sound like a love-sick teenager talking about Justin Bieber? Now she'll think I'm stalking her brother.*

'Now I know who you are!' Sinead said brightly. 'Ben mentioned ages ago that he'd met someone who was hoping to join us here.'

Tally was stumped for a second. *Ben had mentioned her?* She'd assumed he'd only spoken to her because they were sitting next to each other and he was merely being polite.

'So, Tally, let's start with our chat. I hope you don't mind me bunging on a pot of coffee while I get going?' Sinead said beckoning for Tally to accompany her to the kitchenette.

'Not at all,' Tally said relaxing slightly. This girl was really easy-going and seemed to have a knack of making people feel at ease.

As they made their way into the more formal office with steaming mugs of coffee, Tally's nerves began to tingle again.

'Please sit down!' Instead of sitting on the opposite side of the large wooden desk, Sinead pulled her chair around to position herself beside Tally.

'Thank you.' Tally knew she sounded like she'd just inhaled helium.

'I know this is stressful for you,' Sinead said, smiling, 'and you've probably been going over questions and answers in your head before coming here, but I'll let you in on a little secret! Your exam results were amazing. Your application letter is spot on and the minute we met, I could tell you'd make a fantastic therapist.'

'Really?' Tally nearly dropped her cup of coffee.

'Due to the fact that there's a lot of study required in order to qualify as a beauty therapist, we need the students to have a certain standard points-wise,' Sinead explained. As she glanced at the photocopy of Tally's leaving certificate results, which she'd diligently faxed through the previous week, she nodded. 'Yup, your score leaves me in no doubt that you'd be well able for the course. So the interview, in your case, is to establish that you understand this isn't a year-long nail painting session or a play with make-up class. This is a tough course that demands lots of hard graft.'

'Oh, I know that and I'll do my level best, I really will. I've already bought the anatomy book, I have it here to prove it.' Tally went to root the book from her bag.

'That's not necessary, Tally,' Sinead said with a smile, putting her hand gently on her arm to stop her searching. 'You have brains to burn according to your exam results. I've no qualms there. But more than that, you've a lovely nature and I can tell already you're going to be a wonderful addition to our class!' Sinead grinned and held her hand out. 'Welcome aboard, you have a place!'

'What? Just like that? Are you serious?' Tally was shocked.

'Don't look so astonished!' Sinead giggled.

'Honestly,' Tally admitted, 'I was preparing myself for rejection. I was worried I don't have the right appearance for a beauty school.' She looked at the floor.

'Well, how a person turns themselves out has to come into it, of course. We are in an industry that focuses on looks and glamour, so it helps that you are so striking and dress so well,' Sinead said with a nod.

'No! What I meant is … I wasn't sure you'd allow hippo-sized humans in here!' Tally said, preparing to laugh heartily at herself.

Sinead looked momentarily stunned. 'All I can say to that comment, Tally, is that I've never seen a hippo that looks as good as you do. Less of that putting yourself down, Missus! At Skin Deep we like our students to hold themselves in high esteem!' Sinead's tone wasn't hard, yet she was firm.

They chatted for a few more moments before Sinead gave Tally the list of books, uniforms and kit she was required to buy.

'The uniforms are available exclusively from this shop,' Sinead pointed to the name on the sheet. 'They embroider our college name and emblem, so that's why we use them. I'd suggest popping in straight away, if you can. They usually have orders finished in a couple of days, but it's better to be organised.'

Tally's heart began to pound. She could feel sweat beginning to trickle down her back. *Ask the question. Sinead is kind, she'll be a hell of lot easier to approach than an impatient shop assistant. Ask the question, Tally.*

'This is probably a really stupid question,' Tally managed in a quiet voice, 'but do they supply out-sized uniforms, or should I get one elsewhere and bring it to these people for embroidering?'

'No, they do up to a size twenty-eight. I know that for a fact,' Sinead answered without blinking.

'Thank you.' Tally wondered briefly how Sinead knew they did such large sizes, but guessed the question must've arisen previously. There was a small comfort in that.

As Tally let herself out the door and back onto the street, she decided to take the bull by the horns and get her uniform sorted there and then. While she was still on a high from being accepted, she'd use the adrenalin rush to get the dreaded clothing purchase over with.

As it turned out, the man in the shop was very businesslike and didn't bat an eyelid when she asked for a size twenty-two uniform.

'If you can just sign the form here and give me a deposit, we'll have them ready for you this day next week. How many do you want?' he asked.

'I'm not sure,' Tally hesitated.

'Most girls going to Skin Deep get three. Because the tops are white, apparently they need plenty of washing. Probably get covered in eye shadow and all that,' the man assumed.

'Okay, I'll have three, please,' Tally said. Her hand shook as she filled in the form and wrote '22' neatly in the size box.

She'd never had to look at her dress size on a form like that before. Swallowing back the lump in her throat, she fished her wallet out of her bag. She paid the deposit, thanked the man and hurried away.

Once again she felt the familiar sense of shame wash over her. She didn't want to be large anymore. More than that, she didn't want to have to start the next chapter of her life as the Jolly Giant. But her course started in a few weeks' time. There was no way in hell she was going to lose ten stone by then.

She wasn't quite sure how she would go about it, but Tally made a promise to herself, there and then, that she was going to graduate next year as a qualified beauty therapist with a figure she could be proud of. Somehow, she'd do it.

10.

Daisy

The summer was meant to be fun. After Monte Carlo in June, Daisy had planned a couple of months of chilling out and enjoying herself before her final year of college, which was sure to be a hard slog. She would turn twenty-two in September, but instead of feeling like her life was her own and the world was her oyster, it all seemed to have spiralled out of her control.

She made plans with Ava to travel to New York, to visit Justin. While she knew August would be unbearably hot and sticky in the Big Apple, she was really excited about seeing her dad and spending some quality time with Ava. She looked forward to being out of Dublin, on her own with her mum for a while. She felt it would clear her head and help her see everything more clearly … more positively. When Ursula got wind of the planned trip, she immediately invited herself along. Once again, Daisy felt swept up in events she couldn't control. There was no way she wanted Ursula tagging along, but how could she tell her that? Ursula saw it as a chance to hang out at Vera Wang and do all manner of wedding stuff, all of which Daisy hated the very sound of. But Ava had agreed readily, so Daisy's plans were changed in a heartbeat. It was incredibly frustrating.

Freddie had been pushing for her to move into his apartment all summer, but Daisy just didn't feel ready.

'I'm a very traditional type of girl, Freddie,' she insisted. 'I'd rather stay at home until we get married.' She'd never known she was so old-fashioned, but when it came to the crunch, Daisy didn't feel ready to leave home and live with Freddie. Her parents, along with Ursula and Alfred, deemed this admirable and backed her up. Reluctantly, Freddie was forced to agree.

New York was booked for the last week in August and Ava and Ursula was so excited at the prospect. Daisy and Ava had always been close, but Daisy had always thought that when the time came to plan her wedding, it would bring them even closer. She'd never factored in the prospect of being desperately unsure about the entire idea.

She'd kept putting off buying the engagement ring, too, which had nearly driven her mother and Freddie's mother to despair. Neither of them could fathom what she was thinking. She glanced up at the clock. Ten more minutes to herself, then Freddie would arrive to take her into town. She had finally agreed to the shopping trip, and they were going to the jewellers. She rubbed her hand across her eyes and felt trapped all of a sudden. She looked down at her unadorned fingers and tried to picture a ring there – a ring that would tie her to Freddie for life. She couldn't.

She tried to shake off her ominous feelings in the few minutes left, but she was still feeling out of sorts when Freddie rang the doorbell. She let him in and he bounded into the house like an overexcited puppy.

'Ready for one of the most important moments in our lives?' he bellowed, picking her up and spinning her round.

Daisy smiled at him, but the smile didn't reach her eyes.

Freddie pushed open the door to the prestigious jewellers on Dublin's salubrious Grafton Street and ushered Daisy inside. It was cool and quiet in there, hushed like a church.

'Within reason, there's no budget,' Freddie said in her ear. 'But I will want us to agree on the choice,' he warned.

'What do you mean?' Daisy was slightly confused.

'Well, lots of people are going to look at this ring. I need to be able to hold my head up high and feel proud of what's adorning your pretty little finger,' Freddie said. 'This is going to mark the beginning of our lives together and be admired for a very long time, so let's get it right, yeah?'

'Right …' Daisy said, not entirely sure she liked his line of thinking.

'Oh, by the way, the ring is your birthday gift, too!' Freddie said, squeezing her hand and winking. 'Not many of your friends can say they were given a large rock for their twenty-second birthday, I'll bet.'

Daisy thought of the bottle of perfume he'd given her last year, which was still unopened. She was certain he'd grabbed it at the local chemist on the way to her house. It was more suited to a pensioner than a girl celebrating her twenty-first. She'd been quite disappointed that he hadn't bought her something more personal, like an identity bracelet or a thoughtful keepsake. She'd put it all down to men not having a clue about buying gifts.

But this gallant announcement that her engagement ring was to double up as her birthday present really sent shockwaves through her. Was Freddie's every action dictated by cost and reputation?

Still, what could she say? She'd sound darn right spoiled if she said she'd still love him to give her a card and a tiny, carefully chosen trinket, too.

As Freddie was greeted by the manager of the jewellers, Daisy stopped and closed her eyes for a moment. There it was again – that thing she hated. The you're-the-little-kept-wifey-person and I'm-the-big-wig-man attitude. She knew most girls would be squealing with joy and skipping around feeling lucky as hell to have all this – instead, Daisy felt suffocated.

'This is the beginning of the rest of our lives. Let's see what you can dazzle us with, my man,' Freddie said, sharing a conspiratorial chuckle with the jeweller.

Daisy couldn't help it – she hated that Freddie was so concerned about how he would look on the back of this ring purchase.

As tray after tray of glittering rings were put in front of Daisy, she found her mind drifting away to other thoughts. Freddie was accepting and declining each style on her behalf. She dutifully tried on several, with which Freddie found fault. Eventually, he decided she needed a custom design.

'I think rubies are fabulous,' Freddie announced. His mother wore a ruby ring.

'Does the lady like rubies, too?' the manager enquired politely.

'What girl doesn't want a diamond and ruby ring?' Freddie guffawed.

Daisy just smiled sweetly as Freddie gave specific instructions.

'A larger ruby than that one, with two diamonds on either side. That ought to knock the eye out of anyone who cares to scrutinise what I've provided!' Freddie said, sounding like he'd just signed off on an important business deal. Fixing his tie and yanking his suit jacket into smoothness, he shook hands with the manager and agreed a date to pick up the tailor-made ring. He held the door open for Daisy and they stepped out into the late July sunshine.

Freddie put his hand in his suit pocket and indicated that Daisy was to link his arm. That was another thing that had started to annoy her, this new requirement for linking arms. She wasn't old and feeble nor was she living in the olden days when women strolled with frilly parasols, linked to their husbands like a little pretty accessory.

'Let's go and get hammered!' she said suddenly.

'But it's lunchtime, sweetheart. I think a bowl of soup and an easy afternoon would be more apt,' Freddie answered as he walked them in the direction of one of the city's five-star hotels.

'I don't want to sit in there! It's sunny out. Let's grab a sandwich and sit on the grass in St Stephen's Green,' Daisy suggested. 'The park is lovely in the sun and we can watch the world go by!'

'This suit is Versace, Daisy dear. With all due respect, I'm not going to tell my grandchildren that the day we chose your engagement ring, we sat on soggy grass eating substandard food.'

'The sandwich shops have amazing things and it won't be soggy, it hasn't rained for over two weeks,' Daisy pouted.

'Now stop that sulking like a good girl and let's just be civilised, yeah?'

So they'd ended up having soup, which took an hour and a half by the time the stuck-up waiter went through the palaver of setting the table, offering an enormous basket of breads, changing cutlery and pouring sparkling water in painfully slow movements.

'Now isn't this pleasant?' Freddie asked smiling.

Daisy nodded mechanically. She felt like yelling. She craved fresh air. She wanted to lie on the grass and kick off her shoes. She'd give anything to be sitting in a beer garden, drinking pints of cider with lashings of ice and eating a bag of crisps. She longed to phone Naomi and Caroline and beg them to come and meet her so she could finally break cover and tell someone— *Tell them what?* she asked herself. She felt the blood run cold in her veins as she finally admitted the truth to herself: tell them that she didn't want to marry Freddie.

The realisation hit her like an electric shock.

I don't want to marry Freddie.

Oh, my God, she thought, her face going pale, her breathing getting faster. She could feel tears pricking behind her eyes and was terrified that she was going to fall to the ground, wailing, in this prim and proper restaurant. She gripped the edge of the table, trying to focus on the bowl in front of her. Freddie was rabbiting on about the wedding and wasn't paying any attention to her. She struggled to breathe normally.

The truth was staring her in the face and she couldn't deny it any longer. She'd been trying to go along with it all, hoping she would reach a point where she felt the same enthusiasm as her parents and Freddie's family, but the fact of the matter was that Freddie was just not the man for her. She'd had enough of feeling stifled. She didn't want to become another Tracey, simpering to her husband and dying of gratitude for the crumbs from his table. She wanted to be the bouncy, happy-go-lucky Daisy that she'd always been.

Freddie had moved on from wedding chatter and was telling her an anecdote from the golf course. She watched his lips moving and felt a sudden urge to slap him. Hard.

'Freddie, stop!' she yelled.

'Pardon?' He looked around as embarrassment flushed his cheeks.

Daisy couldn't believe she'd actually done that.

'Don't shout, Daisy, we're in a hotel restaurant. People will stare.'

'I can't do this anymore, I'm so sorry,' she blurted out.

'Do what? Eat soup? Are you still cross about the picnic-in-the-park thing?' Freddie grinned and put his head to the side. That was another thing Daisy couldn't abide. He did that lopsided gaze thing which showed he found her ever so entertaining and funny. She grabbed on to her anger tightly and let it guide her.

'Stop treating me like a moron, Freddie. I don't give a shit about the sandwiches. I mean us. I mean I can't do *us* a second longer. I'm so dreadfully sorry, Freddie.' Her voice dropped to a whisper. 'I don't love you the way you love me. I don't think this is going to work. I can't marry you. I'm so, so sorry.'

It was like Dr Jekyll and Mr Hyde. Freddie transformed before her eyes into a sneering, cold man.

'How dare you speak to me that way, young lady,' he began in a furious voice.

'"Young lady"? Freddie, get off the stage, we're the same age! Who do you think you are? More to the point, who do you think *I* am? A clockwork doll?'

'I've heard enough of this.' He shoved his chair back and leaned on the table, pointing violently in her face. 'Don't even consider phoning me and sobbing down the phone begging my forgiveness when you come to your senses. There'll be no sympathy from my end, I can tell you.'

'Freddie, I'm sorry for leading you on. I honestly thought I'd suddenly change my mind and want the same thing you did—'

'Don't waste your breath, Daisy. I've no interest in hearing your voice anymore,' he said, holding up his hands. 'I'm out of here. First stop is the jewellers to stop that order. I'm not wasting another cent on you. Stay out of my way, Daisy, if you know what's good for you.'

As he stomped out of the restaurant, Daisy flopped back against her chair with a thud.

The waiter approached gingerly and coughed gently. 'Is everything all right, Madam?' he asked. 'Can I help in any way?'

'Fuck me, that was crazy madness,' Daisy said. 'Oops, sorry for cursing,' she winced, looking around. As it happened, most of the rest of Dublin seemed to have had the same idea she'd had and were outside. The place was virtually deserted.

'Can you bring me a glass of pink champagne, please?' Daisy asked. 'In fact, make it two,' she said nodding firmly.

'Is your gentleman friend returning then?' the waiter asked.

'No,' Daisy said smirking slightly. 'I think we can safely say he's not coming back any time soon. I'll drink his.' The waiter maintained his composure and cleared away the remains of their meal.

When he returned with the tray, he made a big palaver of placing a little disposable drinks mat down, followed by the first glass. Hesitating, he hovered for a second with the other.

'I was serious, they're both for me,' Daisy said helpfully.

He deposited the second glass of bubbly beside the first. Daisy picked them up in both hands and clinked them together. She drained the first in two gulps.

'Sorry, bubbles up my nose,' she said in a nasally voice. 'I'll be grand in a second … Bottoms up!'

The waiter stood gawping, not sure where to put himself as she drank the second glass.

'Now,' Daisy said, banging down the glass, 'if you could bring me the bill, please, it appears my ex-fiancé has forgotten to pay *again*!'

The waiter moved backwards away from her as she began to chuckle to herself. By the time he returned, she was sitting slumped in the chair with her hands across her tummy, laughing away to herself.

'Are you sure you're all right?' the waiter asked nervously. 'Will I call someone for you?'

'I'm actually fine, but thank you so much for asking,' Daisy managed. She paid the extortionate bill for the lunch and drinks, gathered her things and left. When she stepped outside, she took a big gulp of fresh air, then stood there smiling to herself.

Standing there on the pavement, watching the people of Dublin hurrying past her, Daisy felt a long forgotten sensation – relief. She was sorry she'd hurt Freddie. She knew her parents, along with Ursula and Alfred, were going to be devastated. But then, no venue had been decided and the date hadn't been set for the wedding. She was getting out at the right time.

Daisy knew in her heart of hearts that marrying Freddie would've been the worst thing she'd ever done. Yes, people would be surprised, but she was buoyed up by the feeling that it was the right decision. Everything just felt so … right.

She headed off down Grafton Street, smiling at the world and feeling light as a feather. She thought of Freddie at the jewellers, explaining it all to the undoubtedly stunned manager, and she laughed to herself. Walking along, she made herself a promise: by the beginning of her final year in college next month, her life was going to return to the way she'd always intended it to be. She would be fully in charge of her own destiny once more. Here's to my future, she thought.

11.

Felicity

It was September, and the first day of college. The previous few weeks had been busy as Felicity had found digs, moved up most of her stuff and bought her books and other things she'd need. As predicted, UCD had offered her a place on her chosen course, a BA in International Languages with her major in Spanish. So here she was, in Dublin, miles from home, ready to become a student.

She wished for the millionth time that Aly was there beside her, but for the first September since they were three years old the two girls were pitching up at different places. It was strange, but Felicity tried to stay focused on the here and now.

Right now, she was busy trying to act as if she were as cool as a cucumber. She hoped the other students were just as nervous and wouldn't notice the shake in her hands or the sweat that was threatening to trickle down her back. She was in a gaggle of excited Freshers, all gathered at an allotted meeting point just inside the main door to UCD. The sun was beating down in true back-to-school weather style. The cloudless sky and warm early autumn air lifted the general mood higher. Felicity sighed, happy in the knowledge that she wasn't stuffed into an itchy school kilt and knitted jumper like all the previous Septembers she could recall. Glancing around swiftly, she decided she was happy enough with her chosen first-day ensemble of a floaty skirt, simple white T-shirt and denim waistcoat.

Not sure about where she should park herself, she decided to go for it and head straight for the densest part of the crowd. She'd feel like a spare part if she had to stand by herself.

Scanning the sea of new faces, she could immediately pick out the different personality types. There were the It-girls, all squeals and air-kissing with flailing limp wrists and too much bouncing. While Felicity couldn't even conceive how they afforded the highlighted hair to Louboutin-toed look, it was a scene she'd never had much time for. While she loved her nights out in Galway with Aly and her friends, she was well aware that she wasn't even at the races when it came to the style of some of this lot.

Looking at them, Felicity vowed she would stay true to herself. She wasn't going to become a person who was so consumed with how she looked that it took over her life. She was here to have fun, no doubt about it, but socialising wasn't ever going to be her career.

There was the token Goth, of course, and lots of people obviously on their own and looking very ill-at-ease. There were a few hippy types, with plaited hair and John Lennon-style shades and then there were the country girls, like herself, who looked like fish out of water. She could see some of them staring open-mouthed at the Dublin divas who looked like they already owned the place. Felicity smiled to herself and wondered what they were all making of her.

There must have been hundreds of people congregated there, but Felicity was instantly drawn to one guy. He was as tall as her brother Bob, with dark features and a relaxed confidence that made her want to stand beside him. It was just like all those mushy boy-meets-girl movies: an invisible force propelled her towards him.

'How's it going?' Felicity walked over and fell into place beside the sallow-skinned man. When he looked over at her, his eyes almost made her gasp – they were large and dark and utterly mesmerising. 'Hi.' He didn't exactly kill himself with enthusiasm nor did he remove his hands from his pocket, but the quick darting flick of his eyes up and down her svelte five-foot frame wasn't missed by Felicity.

'Arts?' Felicity asked blinking slowly, unperturbed by his noncommittal response.

'Yup, looks like we'll be rowing the same boat then,' he grinned.

He has dimples. He is totally gorgeous and I think I'm going to expire in a minute. Quick, think of some thing witty and cute to say.

He leaned against the wall and offered her a piece of gum. She waved her hand to say no thanks, and inhaled the musky scent of his aftershave. A loudspeaker announcement prompted the crowd to surge forwards inside the main entrance. He held the door open for her as they made their way into the building. The long hallway was lined either side with metal rectangular lockers. Eight or ten bright yellow doors led into what Felicity could only assume were lecture halls.

'I have to admit I'm a bit in awe of everything still. I only arrived up to Dublin yesterday,' Felicity explained. 'Fish out of water and all that, but I suppose it'll all be second nature to me by next week.'

'Where are you from with an accent like that?' Mr Gorgeous asked.

Oh, no! I sounded like a total Muppet. He's going to think I'm from a tiny thatched cottage in a place so remote we haven't even heard of the internet. Don't blow this, Felicity Byrne. Don't make this guy walk off shaking his head and thinking you're a dork.

'Just outside Galway city.' She tried to dull her accent as best she could. 'I hadn't realised until I came to Dublin how strong my accent is. You probably think I sound like something from *Darby O'Gill and the Little People*,' she joked.

'Who?' he grinned.

'Didn't you ever watch that awful Oirish movie as a kid, featuring Leprechaun-type creatures? No?' She trailed off and giggled at his confused expression.

'Thankfully, no,' he said, nudging her good-naturedly with his elbow.

'Well, you sound like Colin Farrell, for the record,' she blushed, looking straight ahead.

'Rather be like him than some Paddy's Day puppet. Will I say bleedin' this and bleedin' that then?' He chewed slowly on his gum and shoved his hands back into his grey Abercrombie hoodie.

Oh, cringe! Just don't speak again, you fool, you're blowing it big time here. Get a grip, Felicity Byrne. It's not as if this is the first boy you've ever encountered. What's wrong with you?

'I'm Shane, by the way.' He produced a hand and shook hers gently.

'That doesn't sound remotely like Colin,' Felicity said, feigning disappointment.

'I could have my name changed by deed poll if it would make you happier?'

'I'll try and get used to Shane. I'm not blonde currently, so I might just manage to remember. My name's Felicity.' She raised a single eyebrow and flashed him a wicked grin.

They both looked up as a hassled little man with frizzy sandy hair and a serious twitch in his left eye bumbled into the hall brandishing a clipboard and small megaphone. Calling out a string of names he beckoned to the list of bodies to follow. Hearing her name, Felicity looked up at Shane and smiled.

'It was nice to meet you,' she said, hating the thought of moving away from him and going into a big lecture theatre full of strangers.

'Good luck today. I'm sure we'll bump into one another at some point,' Shane said calmly.

Felicity wished she shared his confidence. This campus was enormous, she'd probably never see Shane again. She wished once more that Aly was there beside her. She'd have no problem with organising a time to hook up later at the bar. She'd a great knack of extracting phone numbers out of people, no matter how reluctant they seemed at first.

Not wanting to look like a total fool, she gave him a little wave and rushed after the retreating group.

The sandy-haired man led them into a large lecture theatre. It was decorated with dark, graduated, flip-down seating, all facing a semicircular stage area equipped with a wide screen, computer and other technical stuff. The welcome talk took over an hour. It was a general chat about the facilities and other housekeeping issues.

'I know much of what that guy is saying is probably vital, but his delivery wouldn't win him any awards, would it?' Shane said, slipping in next to Felicity. She hoped she'd managed to hide her delight at seeing him again so soon.

'He's not great with the one-liners. Don't think we'll be seeing him on *Live at the Apollo* any time soon,' Felicity agreed.

'Before I hand you over to a tutor from the Spanish Department,' the sandy-haired guy was saying, 'I'd like to encourage you all to return after the fifteen-minute interval so we can take you on an orientation walkabout.'

'God, I hope the Spanish tutor has a bit more umph than this limp squib,' Felicity whispered to Shane. He winked at her before standing up and making his way to the podium.

Felicity slid down in her chair, wanting to die on the spot as Shane took the microphone and introduced himself.

'For those of you who haven't already met me, my name is Shane Murphy. I'm a tutor with the Spanish Department here at UCD. I'd like to commend you all on your choice of course. Needless to say, I think you all have impeccable taste and I think you're all great already!'

As Shane finished his short but entertaining introduction speech, Felicity debated slipping onto the floor and crawling out on her hands and knees. She wasn't sure where she'd go after that, but she was certain she could contort herself into one of the lockers at a push, if it meant avoiding him.

Not only had she made a total idiot of herself assuming he was in the same boat as her, but she'd actually fancied him! She was only here five seconds and she was already making a total mess of things. *Agh*, she thought, *Aly, where are you?*

Her fellow students were filing out, so she tucked herself into the pack of bodies and pushed her way outside the lecture hall. Most people were either heading straight outside to light up or heading down towards the canteen. Before she could decide which path to follow, Shane came up behind her.

'Boo!' he said into her ear.

'Ha, ha!' she said, cringing inside. 'Eh, listen, I didn't realise, earlier, eh, outside that you were ... eh, are ...'

'Don't worry,' he said with a grin, 'it's my fault. I was messing with you. I should've told you, but I suppose I was flattered that you'd thought I was a student and besides, it's not every day a beautiful Fresher lands beside me and wants to chat.' He raised an eyebrow and smiled to show he was amused.

'You're really enjoying yourself watching me squirm, aren't you?' Felicity burst out laughing. 'Seeing as I've already been a total eejit, I should probably just go now ...'

'Are you going for a coffee? It's really dreadful, if that helps at all?'

'Thanks for the tip. I think I'll chance it. I guess you're going to the staff room or whatever?'

'I would be honoured to come for a coffee with you, Felicity Galway.' He grinned at her and bowed slightly, waving her ahead of him in mock gallantry.

'Oh, no, I wasn't asking you to ...' Her cheeks flamed as he began to walk towards the cafeteria. Not sure what else to do, Felicity fell in step beside him.

'It's Byrne actually, but I've been called worse. I have four older brothers so, believe me, I've learned to answer to everything from Pip-squeak to Face-ache.'

'Not many pains in the face being delivered from where I'm looking.' He paused and stared into her eyes, making her blush once more. 'As fate would have it, I grew up in a house of women. I've two sisters, Hannah and Polly, so I probably know far more about girls than any man ever should.'

'Well maybe it'll make you into a great husband,' Felicity flushed as she said it. 'Not that I'm suggesting ....' *Shut up*, she berated herself.

'Listen, Felicity, you seem like a very nice girl, and I'm not saying no as such, but maybe we should get to know each other for more than a morning before we plan our wedding? Let's aim for next week, at the very least.' He winked at her and his eyes lit up with mischief.

'Not so fast, cowboy! I don't know if you're any good at ironing or how deft you are with a frying pan. So it might have to be the week after next at the earliest. I'm not that easily marched up an aisle, I'll have you know.' Her heart was pumping to bursting level, but she was relieved to be able to engage in easy banter to hide her embarrassment. 'Besides, my brothers are sure to object to you, especially if you're not on the scene for at least ten days,' she grinned.

'I'll tell you what, I'll buy you a coffee and we can discuss the wedding another time, how's that?'

Shane walked along, seeming totally at ease with her. Felicity smiled up at him, hoping her heart wasn't actually visible through her dress.

Okay, take it easy. Stay calm, try not to say anything that makes you sound like a total spanner. Pretend you're talking to Bob or one of his rugby mates. He's just a guy. No different to any other ... oh, but he is ... he's the most divine, funny and cute creature I've ever laid eyes on. Stop it! Get a grip. You're behaving like a madwoman who's been on a desert island for ten years and he's the first man you've clapped eyes on. Oh, God, this is torture.

'Hello?' Shane was looking at her grinning.

'Sorry, I was a million miles away, what did you say?' she asked.

'Black coffee or cappuccino?'

'Oh, cappuccino, please.'

As they sat with their cappuccinos, the conversation continued to flow. A Michael Bublé song came on the radio beside the cash register, and they realised they shared a guilty pleasure in liking his music.

'Well, it's kind of acceptable for me, being a girl. At least I can get away with it by saying he's cute. What's your excuse?' Felicity asked.

'I told you, two sisters. I'm subjected to girl stuff a lot. Every now and then, I realise they must be getting to me and I actually like it!'

After drinking their coffee, which was as awful as Shane had predicted, Felicity stood up.

'I'm going to head back down to the lecture theatre and go for that walkabout. I can't even find my way to the Spar and back in this city without breaking out in a cold sweat, so I'd like to at least know how to get from one place to another while I'm on campus,' Felicity said. Lifting the hem of her maxi skirt away from the leg of the chair, she swung her tapestry bag over her shoulder.

'I'm not bothering. I think I know my way around by now. I said I'd hook up with a few of the lads,' Shane answered. 'Hey, give me your mobile number and I'll text you if there's anything fun happening later,' he said nonchalantly.

'Sure I'll see you at lectures, if not before,' she said feeling really weird again.

'I'm not a lecturer!' he corrected.

'Right,' she looked at the floor and wanted to bash her head off the wall. 'I really am determined to create a new Irish record for putting my foot in it as many times as possible in one day,' she said, looking mortified.

'Not at all, I'm totally messing with your head!' he said, cutting her some slack. 'I'll stop being so awful, I promise!'

The rest of the day passed in a blur. Felicity felt like her head was going to explode by the time she made her way back to her residence hall in Blackrock. Even though her head was filled with so much new information, there was only one thing on her mind as she thought back over her first day: Shane.

She planned to dump her bag, grab a bite to eat and a cup of tea and ring Mia to fill her in on the day's events, but Felicity's phone pinged almost as soon as she let herself into her room, letting her know she had a text message: *Great meeting u earlier. Going 4 drinks @ Duffins Bar in Blackrock, will be there in 10 mins. Wanna come? No pressure, big gang going! Shane.*

Felicity felt her cheeks heating with pleasure. When she'd swapped mobile phone numbers with Shane earlier, she *really* hadn't expected to hear from him this quickly, if at all. She could almost hear Aly's voice in her mind: '*Play it cool, girl. Don't go rushing to any man's beck and call …*'

That was all fine and well when she'd a pile of people she could hang out with, but she was a small fish in a big pond here and she needed all the friends she could get. Besides, she really liked Shane. Especially as he was forbidden fruit – well, he was staff after all. Aly was going to go ape when she told her about this. She'd call her mam first, though, because she knew she'd be waiting by the phone to hear how the day had gone. She decided she wouldn't mention meeting Shane for a drink. She didn't want her mam to worry that she was hanging around with middle-aged men or something. Thinking about him, her heart did another somersault. He was funny, despicably cute and she felt at ease with him. He obviously wanted to see her, too, or he wouldn't have bothered texting. He had a clatter of friends and yet he'd made the effort.

Sounds great c u in a while. Thanks 4 inviting me! F

As she hit the send button a ripple of excitement shimmied through her. *I can do this. I can be a college girl and cope with the unknown. I can meet all sorts of new people.*

She rang Mia, her voice bubbling with excitement. 'Mam! You won't believe the day I've just had!'

Mia listened and felt like her heart was pouring down her cheeks along with her tears.

'That sounds wonderful, darling,' she managed to say without sounding too choked.

She meant it, too. The last thing she wanted was for her precious daughter to be unhappy, but if she were totally honest, Mia would have gone for a midpoint level of elation. She felt like her youngest child was slipping away from her fast, and there wasn't a thing she could do about it.

Felicity did a quick mirror-check, applied some lip-gloss, mussed up her hair and then grabbed her bag and headed out again to make her way to the pub. As she walked, she dialled Aly's number and prayed her friend would pick up. She did, after only two rings.

'Alz, guess what?' Felicity began and proceeded to describe her meeting with Shane in great detail.

'Holy shit, no way!' Aly yelled. 'Is he all ancient with little round glasses and two spit balls at either side of his mouth and dressed in corduroys?'

'Give me a bit of credit, would ya?' Felicity giggled. 'No, he's gorgeous. You'd never in a million years think he was staff.'

'Is he one of your lecturers? God, this is kind of kinky!'

'No he's not a lecturer, he just works in the Spanish Department.'

'Oh, excuse me,' Aly teased.

The girls chatted non-stop until Felicity found herself outside the bar. Aly had enjoyed her first day, but she enviously admitted she wasn't off on a date.

'You jammy cow! You're the one who was rabbiting on to me last week about how she wasn't looking to find a man and only wanted to live her life!' Aly teased.

'I know! I know! But this guy is sooo cute. Okay, I have to go, they have those windows with lumpy coloured glass and he might be able to see me. I don't want to be overheard either. I'll call you tomorrow, okay?'

'You better! In fact, call me later on if there's any major gossip,' Aly instructed.

Felicity took a deep breath, then pushed open the door to the bar and walked inside.

12.

Tally

The first day of college came around alarmingly quickly. Although she'd honestly done her best to eat less, Tally had to admit she hadn't managed to lose any weight. Her uniforms were snug without looking like they might burst a seam at any moment, so that would have to do for now.

Greta had been pacing up and down in the kitchen dressed in her running gear when Tally had appeared that morning.

'Go on ahead, Ma. I know you've to get to work by ten. Enjoy your jog,' Tally said, releasing her mother from a stilted conversation.

'Sure, who knows, maybe you'll be able to do waxing for me at some stage soon? That'd be great,' Greta offered.

'She'll have us all looking like movie stars before we know it, won't you, love?' Martin added, hugging Tally.

He'd insisted on driving her in for the first day. She had protested, but it turned out he had swapped with someone else in work to get the day off. Martin was so proud of his daughter – if he could've gone into class with her and sat beside her, he would have.

As they drew up at the college, Martin looked eagerly at her. 'I could park and wait for your lunch break. Would you like a bit of company or would I embarrass you?' he asked.

'I don't know what way it works, Da. I didn't ask if they have a canteen or whether we go out for our lunch,' Tally said, biting her nail with nerves. 'Better leave me to my own devices for today and maybe on your next day off we could meet up for lunch. When I know the routine and all that.'

'Okay, love. I'll be pottering around anyway, so don't be by yourself if you don't feel like it. Ring me and I can be here in ten minutes. I'll collect you at half past five if I don't hear from you before,' he said, smiling as nervously as her.

'Thanks, Da.'

'Good luck, pet,' Martin called out as she slammed the car door shut. He sat and watched until he saw his daughter disappear inside the college building.

The beauty college was broken up into lecture rooms and practical-work rooms. A lady with a clipboard was waiting at the top of the stairs to direct the new students to the right place.

'Can I have your name, please?' she asked.

'Tally Keller,' she said shakily.

'Go to lecture room four and your teacher will give you your timetable and all other required information,' the pretty receptionist instructed.

Tally was shaking like a leaf as she pushed the door open. She was certain all the staff and students at Skin Deep would be like models. Relieved to see a spare seat near the back of the room, she folded herself into a chair and made sure she looked busy as she turned her phone off and rooted in her bag as if she was trying to find something important.

As the class filled up, Tally wished she had brought Martin with her for support after all. Bar three girls sitting near the front, no one else seemed to know each other. So Tally willed herself to remember that she was no different to most of the others newbies in the room.

She *was* different though. None of the other girls were shoehorned into the seat the way she was. They all had slim backs and neat shoulders. Pulling at the top of her uniform, she gazed down at her bulging tummy. The white top with short sleeves did nothing for her shape. At least the navy trousers were a kinder colour, offering a bit of a slimming illusion.

All Tally's books were neatly arranged in her new bag, a leather satchel design which she felt would only improve with use. But even that seemed clumpy and uncouth against the Juicy Couture and Guess bags that were dominating the room.

Sinead appeared, looking relaxed and happy. Tally looked enviously at the pretty petite woman's long, silky brown hair and slim figure in her navy teacher's uniform. Sinead's hair was parted in the middle and the two front fronds of hair were plaited and pulled around the back of her head and clasped with a glittery navy clip. She oozed sophistication and style. Her eye make-up was startlingly beautiful. Tally had never seen the navy shimmery smoky-effect eyes look so well applied. Sinead's deep voice and warm tone made all the girls snap to attention.

'I have a girl-crush on her, she's gorgeous, isn't she?' the lady beside Tally said, leaning towards her.

'I know, she really is beautiful, isn't she?' Tally agreed. 'Who knows, if we study really hard maybe we'll end up looking like her at the end of the course,' Tally quipped. She was delighted someone had spoken to her and that she wasn't the only one in the room who felt like a bit of a minger beside Sinead.

'You're all so welcome and I sincerely hope you're going to enjoy the course this year,' Sinead began. 'It's a tough course, but one I hope you'll all get a lot out of.'

They were given timetables and shown where they would be for each module. When they moved into one of the treatment rooms, Tally stood at the foot of one of the couches and felt a shiver of excitement. She couldn't wait to begin doing facials, waxing, massage and all the other treatments and therapies.

'So follow me back into the lecture room and we'll get going on the very beginning of the anatomy,' Sinead instructed.

Tally was captivated from the first moment. As they were brought through the names of the skin layers, the girls felt like they were starting first year medicine, rather than a beauty course. By lunchtime, they were all looking a bit overwhelmed.

'I know it's loads to take on board and the long Latin names are a bit daunting at first, but, believe me, it will all be second nature to you by the end of the course,' Sinead promised.

Tally could see that Sinead hadn't been lying when she said it would require hard graft to get through the course, but she didn't care one bit. She was in love with the college, the timetable and the vision she had of herself as a beauty therapist in years to come. She was absolutely sure she had made the right decision, and that felt really good. At the end of that first day, she floated out of the college on cloud nine, eager to tell her dad everything that she had learned.

The second and third day were passed in the theory room, where Sinead continued to glide through the ins and outs of the skin.

Each day the girls gravitated towards the seats they'd chosen on that first morning. Eventually, Tally found herself plucking up enough courage to talk to the lady beside her again.

'It's astonishing what lies beneath the surface of our skin, isn't it?' Tally ventured.

'I know, I have to say I'm a bit blown away by the detail of what we need to know. I knew there was plenty of study involved, but I wouldn't have imagined in a million years it was going to be this complex. I'm Jane, by the way,' she whispered.

'Tally, pleased to meet you.'

When they broke for lunch on day three, Jane walked out onto the street just ahead of Tally.

'Would you like to grab a sandwich together?'

'I'd love that.' Tally's face lit up as she smiled.

It turned out Jane was a single mother of three and had entered the college as a mature student.

'I married at eighteen, had the kids and never had a minute to myself. My ex-husband buggered off and left us five years ago.'

'I'm sorry,' Tally said sincerely.

'I'm not, love. He was a useless beggar. It's actually been easier since he went,' Jane explained. 'The kids are more settled and we all know where we stand. I've my routine going and we're happy out. I've a new fella and now my course. So all's well that ends well, and all that.'

'How old are your children?' Tally asked as they stood in a queue in a nearby sandwich bar.

'Fourteen, twelve and ten. Two boys and a girl. They're great kids. They trot off to school every day without any bother, so I knew the time was right to do something for myself,' said Jane.

'Good for you. You're dead right. You could always practice from home when you qualify if you wanted as well,' Tally suggested. She eyeballed the deli counter. The familiar panic began to rise from her toes. She was ahead of Jane in the queue. She didn't want to order a massive thing and feel like pig if Jane sat eating a lettuce leaf and a glass of water.

'Sorry, but I need to run to the loo, I'll be back in a jiffy,' Tally said dashing off before Jane could blink.

Waiting what she felt would be a believable amount of time, Tally emerged from the bathroom and slotted in behind Jane just as she reached the top of the queue.

'A BLT sandwich, pack of cheese and onion, large cappuccino and a slice of that coffee cake, please,' Jane said to the girl behind the counter. 'What do you feel like having, Tally?'

'I'll have a tuna, sweetcorn and mayo sandwich with a packet of crisps and a Diet Coke,' Tally said to the second assistant behind the counter.

'I'm starving. I don't know about you, but I find all the learning makes me crave food,' Jane admitted.

But you aren't obese like me. Where do all the calories go? Tally wondered.

As they sat at a small table in the corner, Jane chatted away easily, seeming totally oblivious to Tally's initial discomfort. The older woman was certainly a good size sixteen, but she was like Twiggy in comparison to Tally's size twenty-two frame.

'By the time I've fed the kids in the evening I don't feel like moving, so it's great to have the course now. I can study, which gives me a focus,' Jane explained. 'The evenings are the worst when you've no partner. The kids are asleep and there's only so much television I can bear to watch, so I won't know myself with the study to keep me going.'

'I rarely go out during the week. Myself and my da usually end up watching movies and eating all sorts of rubbish, so I'm looking forward to having the books to focus on, too,' Tally agreed.

'Isn't your mother around then?' Jane popped a crisp into her mouth.

'She is – she just works a lot,' Tally answered. 'Me and Da have always been very close.'

'That's nice,' Jane pondered for a second. 'My kids' da never gave a toss about them. He doesn't even call much. He never remembers their birthdays and we're lucky to get three selection boxes at Christmas. You're lucky to have such a caring father.'

'I know. He's a real sweetheart,' Tally said, nodding.

'I spent years trying to change myself, hoping to get my fella to show more interest in me and the kids,' Jane divulged. 'I chopped my hair, dyed it blonde, went back to brunette, lost stones in weight, piled it back on. Ah, you get the picture …'

'But none of it mattered in the end?' Tally finished for her.

'Pretty much. I was always terrified he'd leave. But now that he has, I'm happier. Funny old world, isn't it?' Jane mused.

As they finished their lunch and wandered back to the college Tally realised that that had been the first time she'd sat with a stranger and been herself. She hadn't put on any accents, tried to pretend she loved things that didn't interest her and hadn't felt under scrutiny. Jane didn't treat her like a freak and she hadn't even needed to make wisecracks.

'Hi, ladies! Nice lunch?' Sinead asked as she held the door open for them to enter the college.

'Lovely, thanks, Sinead, and you?' Jane responded smiling.

'It was pretty boring to be honest with you. I've been quite bold recently, eating junk food and whatnot. Think it's the whole settling back into routine thing,' Sinead said, rolling her eyes. 'So I sat in the park and had a salad and made myself drink a good bit of water. Back on the straight and narrow!' she said, slapping herself on the backside.

Both women laughed as they followed her into the lecture room. Tally couldn't help but feel slightly skeptical. Sinead wouldn't know cellulite if it bit her on her pert little ass. But she was so nice, Tally couldn't feel cross with her.

'Okay, girls, we're going to head into the practical room this afternoon. I'll show you how to prepare your trolleys for assessing a client's skin and we'll get going on our first attempt at facials!'

There was a ripple of excitement as the girls filed into the larger, brighter room, lined with rows of treatment couches.

'If you can just pair up, one girl lies down to be the client and the other the therapist,' Sinead explained. 'We'll swap over tomorrow, so you'll all get to have a go. The way it works at this college is that you all practise on one another. That way you know how it feels and in turn what you should be doing differently.'

'Will you be my partner?' Jane asked Tally, pretending to be shy, looking at the floor as she rotated her foot and stuck a finger in her mouth.

'Oh, okay then,' Tally said, flicking her hair the way Samantha used to. 'But don't expect me to be too nice to you!' Tally used her schoolgirl pouty voice, with the slight American twang to her words.

'Victim or murderer?' Jane offered.

'You call it, I can be either,' Tally laughed.

'Ah go on, you lie down, that way I can look forward to being pampered tomorrow,' Jane said.

Tally eased her way onto the beauty couch, which was white with metal legs. Rather spindly legs that she worried might buckle under her weight. It did creak as she settled herself into a lying down position, but thankfully it didn't collapse.

They learned how to hold the cotton wool in a certain way, lacing it through their fingers, and what direction the strokes should be for cleansing and toning the client's skin.

'If we keep up with this amount of pawing at one another, we'll all be like scabby cats by the end of the year,' Tally whispered to Jane.

'Well, I wouldn't mind having a few layers of skin scraped away. It might make me look younger,' Jane responded. 'You've amazing skin by the way. Totally flawless. I don't know if I want you looking at all my wrinkles tomorrow,' Jane said with a frown.

'Well if you can deal with my flab, believe me, I have no issue with anything that might be thrown at me! You are hardly on course for being mistaken for a prune, so I don't see why you're fretting,' Tally said, making Jane giggle.

As the days ran into weeks, Tally and the other students became more confident and knowledgeable. Most of the girls on the course were friendly and eager to learn. The three who'd sat right up the front on the first day were Tally's age and reminded her of the girls from school. They tittered and whispered and were reluctant to get to know many of the others.

Tally managed to avoid being partnered, with any of them until the final week before the Christmas exams.

'So I'm, like, waxing your legs now?' the tall blonde one said.

'Looks like it! Better make sure you have a seriously large spatula to spread enough wax on this tree trunk!' Tally said immediately, clicking into the jokey banter of old.

'I think they only come in one size. So I'll just like have to do as much as I can in the time, yeah?' the girl said, looking like she'd a bad smell under her nose.

Tally felt both humiliated and angry. She had a sudden urge to kick the dolled-up blonde bint in her pretty eyelash-batting face. To add insult to injury, the girl was useless at waxing. She kept pulling the strip off too slowly, making the wax stretch and string away from her skin like chewing gum.

'I usually don't have this problem. No offence, but I think it's, like, your skin texture. I think it's kind of like, reacting with the wax.'

Stung and mortified, Tally sat up, took a wax strip and deftly removed the clump of purple sticky gloop from her own shin.

'Sorted. Why don't we just leave the rest? I think you've done more than enough,' Tally said with an acidic tone to her voice.

'Ugh, thanks,' said Barbie.

That night, Tally eased her pain by watching one of her favourite musicals with her da. As Julie Andrews sang about the hills being alive, Tally ate an entire box of chocolate-coated mini Swiss rolls, a twin pack of Jammy Dodgers and a Mars bar. If that wasn't piggy enough, she'd put away sweet and sour chicken balls, rice, chips and a banana fritter with ice cream for tea.

'I think I feel a bit sick,' she groaned to Martin.

'You love those biscuits, don't you, love?' he said as he yawned. 'Sure you need a bit of a pick-me-up with all the college work,' he patted her leg and put his feet on the coffee table.

'The winter always makes me eat more,' Tally said.

'Me, too. I think it's just animal instinct. We need the extra fuel to keep us going through the harsh cold spell,' Martin said, justifying it all.

Tally was going to point out that they weren't mammals preparing to survive in the Arctic or camels setting off for a trek across the desert and that she already had more stored blubber than a humpback whale, but she knew remarks like that would only upset her da. His evening would be ruined and she hated to see him unsettled.

Tally sat and smiled, so her da wouldn't worry. Inside, she felt like she was balancing on the edge of a cliff. She was desperately unhappy with herself, but she hadn't the first idea of how to go about changing.

13.

Felicity

Felicity had made it through the first weeks of university. While she was coping well and largely enjoying herself, she was dying to see her family and hook up with Aly again.

As the train pulled up at Galway station, a rush of love engulfed her as she spotted her mother waiting impatiently on the platform.

'Mam!' She threw her weekend bag on the ground and hugged her mother close.

'Oh, let me have a good look at you,' Mia said, forgetting to hide her tears of joy. Once the initial emotion had subsided, the two of them chatted like old times. The hour-long journey from the train station passed in a heartbeat.

Aly was in the kitchen chatting to Bob, waiting for Felicity to arrive.

'Flick!' she launched herself at her friend amidst a flurry of squeals.

The rain and cold wind outside was no contest for the real turf fire and bottle of red wine Mia had on offer.

'I've a stew in the oven, which has been bubbling away since mid-morning. I'll have creamy mashed potatoes done in a jiffy and your favourite apple crumble is just waiting to be drowned in custard,' Mia said as her eyes crinkled at the corners in delight.

'Thanks, Mam. This is just what I need – a chilled out weekend and good feed of home cooking,' Felicity said appreciatively.

Aly was like part of the family and always had been. 'It's great to have you back,' she said to Felicity as she stretched out on the comfy sofa like a cat.

'Have you actually missed me or just Mam's cooking and lounging beside the fire?' Felicity teased.

'Both!' Aly admitted. 'You know my folks, they're not exactly the home-making type. Mam had our fireplace blocked up years ago. The only thing that goes on our hearth are bowls of potpourri.'

'Everyone's different,' Mia said diplomatically. 'If we were all the same …'

'The world would be a very boring place,' the girls finished in unison and laughed.

'So are we going drinking tomorrow night?' Aly asked with a twinkle in her eye.

'For sure,' Felicity answered immediately. 'I'm so knackered from all the new stuff, it might be nice to just go to the local for a few scoops and not go too mad?'

'Ah, we'll play it by ear,' Aly said winking. 'I know you Felicity Byrne, a couple of vodkas and you'll be flying.'

There was no sign of life from Felicity's bedroom until almost lunchtime the next day. Mia tapped on the door and negotiated her way inside with a laden tray.

'Hi, Mam, what've you got there?' Felicity said, yawning.

'I thought I'd treat you both to a bit of breakfast in bed. Bacon sarnies and mugs of tea to ease you into the day.'

As the girls munched, Mia had an opportunity to hear more of the news.

'So are you going to tell Mia about this new boyo on the scene?' Ali said, raising an eyebrow.

Felicity shot her a warning look.

'Oh, what's this? Have you met someone nice then?' Mia asked.

'He's just a fella,' Felicity said noncommittally.

'Well I gathered that,' Mia smirked. 'Who? When? What? And how long?'

'Jesus, you two are like the Spanish Inquisition,' Felicity said, feeling suddenly shy of talking about Shane. Every time she thought of him her tummy flipped.

'I met him on the first day,' she began. 'He's really cool and has a great gang of friends. We clicked immediately and he's been kind of showing me around and looking out for me ever since.'

'How does he know where everything is? What year is he in?' Mia asked.

'Well, he's not a student actually,' Felicity said, wrapping her hands around her mug of steaming tea.

'Right,' Mia said shifting on the bed. 'What is he then?'

'Ah, Mam, you sound like you're asking me if he's a bloody axe-murderer! He's staff at UCD. He works for the Spanish Department, but before you go jumping to any mad conclusions, he's my age,' Felicity fibbed. Now that she thought about it, she hadn't actually asked Shane how old he was.

Mia opened her mouth to say something, but then changed her mind. She looked at her daughter and wondered what exactly the truth of the matter was, but knew better than to pursue it right then. Felicity looked a bit uncomfortable talking about this new man of hers, so Mia would have to take it easy and draw it out of her by degrees.

'Right, you two, the day's nearly done. Are you never getting up?'

It took the girls all day to shower, get dressed and put on make-up for going to the local.

They were at the local bar by nine, and got chatting to the owner, Mike, who gave Felicity a free drink as a welcome home gesture. Felicity felt happy and relaxed, delighted to be surrounded by familiar faces.

'Oh, your phone's ringing!' Aly called, waving it at her as she returned from the bathroom. 'It's Shane! Will I answer and pretend to be you?'

'No, you will not!' Felicity said snatching it quickly. 'Hiya,' she said.

As the conversation dragged out past five minutes, Aly started to get bored and interrupt.

'Ask him if he's any hot friends,' she said, nudging Felicity.

'Did you hear that?' she said, laughing. 'He says he has a pile of them and you're to come to Dublin and meet them.'

'Tell him to come here and bring them with him,' Aly shot back.

'Of course you're invited. Yes, that is an official invitation. Would you like it in writing? Ha! Yeah, good plan. Okay cool, see you tomorrow then. Bye,' Felicity said, hanging up.

'Oooh! He really fancies you if he's calling you at nine o'clock on a Saturday night. He should be out on the pull with his mates, unless he is a cords-wearing dweeb, of course?'

'No, for the last time he's not! Hey, guess what? He suggested coming to Galway for New Year! He said Dublin is crammed and it's always messy. Himself and the lads had been planning on getting out of town and *he* would like to come here!

'Shut the front door!' Aly exclaimed. 'That'd be deadly. Is he bringing all his hot friends, too?'

'Sounds a bit like it!'

'What'll you say to Mia? Do you think she'd let them stay in your house?'

'Oh, I don't know about that,' Felicity admitted. 'It might be better if they rent a house or something. I'll think about it. I've plenty of time either way. He might've gotten bored with me at that point.'

'Somehow I doubt it,' Aly said, winking at her. 'I've never seen you like this! Felicity Byrne – you're smitten!'

Sunday afternoon came around too quickly. Felicity vowed she'd be back to Galway and Mia's care in two weeks' time.

'Well, Christmas is only around the corner, so you'll be back for a good break then, won't you?' Mia asked eyeballing her. 'You know I'd love you to come home every single night, but you need to try and make a go of it at university too, love. If you don't join in with some of the social activities, you could end up out on a limb.'

'Sure,' Felicity said evenly. 'I might see if Shane will come down for a few nights too. He was talking about a party for New Year's Eve. Maybe the lads could get a B&B and we could head into Galway.'

Mia listened as Aly made several yuletide suggestions. Thankfully, all of them involved going out in the locality.

'Shane says Dublin is a disaster on New Year's Eve so it's always better to head to the country.'

Mia was trying not to feel snappy, but Felicity had talked of nothing but this Shane lad since she'd got up. She wouldn't feel so edgy about him if he was eighteen, like Felicity, but for all she knew the man was in his forties with a wife and kids tucked away at home.

'I'm always on for meeting a bunch of eligible fellas,' Aly giggled. 'Let's try and plan that.'

'Cool. I'll see what Shane thinks. I'll text you tomorrow and let you know, okay?'

Mia knew she was probably being overly fussy as she stuffed sandwiches and a slice of cake into a bag for Felicity.

'I can't bear the thought of you eating that food on the train and, knowing you, there'll be no proper meal taken this evening,' she said.

'Thanks, Mam, you're a star,' Felicity said as she hugged her goodbye.

'Oh, look after yourself, pet, won't you?' Mia said looking sad.

'I will. I'll be back home before you know it,' Felicity said. She hated leaving her mother, especially when she knew she was fighting back tears. 'I feel so guilty leaving you. Will you be okay?' Felicity asked.

'Of course, I will. Sure, your brother will keep me busy, he eats me out of house and home and I've a load of things coming up in work. Half the county seems to be about to give birth. So don't you fret about me, love.'

Felicity knew her mother was putting on a brave face, but she felt caught between a rock and a hard place. Galway was her home and she missed it for sure, but if she was to make a go of college life, they'd both have to learn to let go a little.

An image of Shane flooded her addled thoughts. They hadn't been together that long, but Aly was right, she was utterly smitten by him. As soon as the train pulled out of the station Dublin-bound, she felt butterflies in her tummy as she thought of seeing him again.

14.

Daisy

Daisy finally made it home. The two glasses of pink champagne had given her a muzzy headache.

'I'm in here, darling!' Ava called from the living room.

'Hi, Mum,' Daisy said evenly.

Ava looked behind her in confusion. 'Where's Freddie?'

'He's … I don't know …' Daisy stood awkwardly in the doorway, jigging her foot.

'What's going on, love? Where's your ring?'

'Mum, I don't know how to say this to you, but there won't be a ring. At least not from Freddie, and possibly not ever.'

'But, sweetie, I don't understand. What's happened in the past couple of hours? You left here so full of hope and excitement? Did you have a disagreement over which ring to choose? It can all get a bit much, I suppose.'

'No, Mum, we didn't have a disagreement over the ring. It was more to do with the bride-to-be and the fact that she doesn't want to be one.'

Daisy couldn't look her mother in the eye. She knew this was the last thing she wanted to be told. But now that she'd made it through the awful scenario with Freddie, Daisy knew it was the right thing for her.

'Mum, I could've put up and shut up. It would've been easier all round to just go along with it all. I get that. But at the end of the day it's my life. I can't marry Freddie just because everyone else thinks I should.'

'But what's gone wrong?' Ava said, trying to control tears that were welling up in her eyes.

'Mum, he wasn't making me happy.'

Daisy tried to give examples, she explained about the holiday and how Tracey and Bill had freaked her out.

'I saw a flash of what my life could be like. That's not me. It's not what I want. I felt trapped and stifled. But all of that aside, I don't love Freddie, Mum. Bottom line. I don't love him.'

Ava couldn't hold it in anymore – it was just too much to take on board. Her future son-in-law was disappearing in a puff of smoke, along with the glorious wedding day she'd envisaged. She was gutted. She could see that Daisy was upset by her reaction, though, so she hugged her daughter close as she wiped away her tears. 'It'll be all right, pet. Everything will be all right.'

'I know it will, Mum. I'm sorry for putting you through all of this, but I have to listen to my heart.'

'But … you were so perfect together. I don't get it. Ursula and Alfred loved you. It would've been fantastic!' Ava said in despair.

'Mum, all of *you* thought it was perfect. You were all having a wonderful time going for lunch and dinner and celebrating our engagement,' Daisy tried to explain once again. '*I* wasn't happy, though. I don't love Freddie the way I should.'

Ava shook her head. 'Darling, we should call your father. He'll want to know about this immediately. I'll call his mobile and put him on speaker.'

Justin answered the phone cheerily. 'Hi, love. How are you?'

'I'm okay,' Ava sniffled. 'It's just that … something's … Daisy has something to say.'

'What's happened?' Justin said quickly, and Daisy could hear the alarm in his voice. She wished her mother could rein in the tears for a few minutes. It was all getting more dramatic by the minute.

'Hi, Dad. I'm just letting you know that I've … myself and Freddie have split up. I told him I couldn't go through with the wedding.'

There was a stunned silence as Justin struggled to process Daisy's confession.

'Oh, Justin, try and talk some sense into her, please,' Ava cried.

'Try and stay calm, Ava,' Justin said soothingly. 'Just listen for a minute and let's try to see this from Daisy's perspective.'

'I am,' Ava said sobbing. 'I just know this marriage would be wonderful for her. They're the nicest people and I honestly think she's just got a case of cold feet. That's normal, too. Marriage is a big change, there's no denying that, but look at how many happy couples we know.'

'Mum, please! Look at me,' Daisy implored. 'I've been miserable. I tried to do what I felt was right for everyone else. But I have to live with this marriage, not you. If I thought I could spend the rest of my life with Freddie, I'd do it. But right now that feels like a death sentence. If I'm unhappy now, what would I be like in a year or two? Suicidal? We'd end up separated one way or another. Trust me, it's better that I make a clean break now.'

'It's all right, pet, I hear you,' Justin said, coming to her defence.

'Thank you, Dad. I'm sorry for causing such upset for everyone. It wasn't a conscious decision to make such a mess of things, but I wasn't raised to compromise. He'll find someone who suits him better and he'll be happier in the long run.'

'All right, love,' Justin said, sounding tired now. 'Why don't you two talk some more, then talk to me later on. Let's just take each day as it comes with this. Nothing has to be set in stone. Perhaps your mother is right and you're balking at the thought of this change in your life. Or maybe you are making the right choice. Nothing needs to be decided this second. We've all had a bit of a shock, that's all.'

'Okay, Dad, chat to you soon,' Daisy said. She wanted to add that she wouldn't change her mind – ever. But she figured that might make her mother cry again. It was better to leave things smoothed over for the time being.

Ava's mobile lit up again with an incoming call. They both looked down at it and saw the name on the screen: Ursula.

'Oh, God, Mum. I can't,' Daisy said, with desperation in her voice.

Ava nodded wearily and Daisy escaped to her bedroom. She felt guilty for bailing on her mother, but there was no way she could take a dose of Ursula's hysteria. She decided to text Caroline and Naomi to let them know the engagement was off.

Turning her phone off, she flopped onto her bed. Now that she was alone, Daisy gazed at the ceiling and tried to figure out how she was feeling. If she was honest, she was massively relieved. Sure, she had a knot in her stomach the size of a melon, but that was immediate stress. Her inner being was calm. She knew she'd done the right thing. As far as she was concerned, there was no going back.

It would take a while for her parents and Freddie's parents to accept it, but that couldn't be helped.

The doorbell broke through her thoughts and she groaned. *Please don't let it be Freddie*, she prayed as she waited for her mother to answer.

'Girls!' Ava said, trying her best to sound cheerful. 'You're very kind to call over. Daisy is up in her room. Daisy! Naomi and Caroline are here.'

'Send them up!' Daisy called back.

'We have ice cream and vino,' Caroline announced as they piled into her room.

'Thanks, girls, you shouldn't have,' Daisy said wearily.

'You dropped your bombshell and turned off your bloody phone. We were worried you'd be hanging from one of the rafters,' Naomi said, looking at her friend with concern.

'I'll open the wine and get some spoons. Don't move,' Daisy instructed. The girls turned on music and settled themselves on the couch in Daisy's room.

'What the hell?' Naomi asked as Daisy returned. 'Are you serious about it being over or was he just being a bit of a dick and you're trying to kick him into touch early on?'

'No, it's not a threat, it's over. As in, totally,' Daisy stated firmly.

'But he's such a nice guy,' Caroline said.

'I know,' Daisy said as tears ran down her cheeks.

'His family's loaded, too. You're giving up a seriously good prospect here, Daisy,' Naomi said, calling a spade a spade as usual.

'None of it's worth it when you feel dead inside,' Daisy whispered miserably.

'Was he mean to you?' Caroline asked, suddenly worried. 'Is he one of those street angels and house devils?'

'Not exactly. It's so hard to explain, girls, but he is like something from the fifties.' Daisy tried to make them see. She told them about

Monte Carlo and how the best part of the holiday had been meeting Niamh and Kitty.

'There's something seriously wrong when you spend an afternoon with two perfect strangers and enjoy yourself more than you do with your supposed fiancé.'

'I guess.' Naomi bit her lip, wanting to understand Daisy's point of view, but the fact of the matter was that both girls would hand over their entire wardrobes, along with accessories, to bag Freddie as a husband.

'He'll be a fantastic husband, lawyer and golfer to accompany some gorgeous girl for the rest of her life. I wish him well, really I do, but I just can't be what he needs,' Daisy concluded.

'Well, we're here for you if you need us, aren't we, Caroline?' Naomi said loyally.

'Yeah, totally,' Caroline nodded.

There was a brief silence.

'Did you not go and pick the ring, then?' Naomi asked.

'We did and I guess he's going to cancel it,' Daisy said, sighing loudly. 'I know you both mean well, but I can't go over it again and again. Can we leave it?'

'Okay,' the girls looked at one another.

'In fact, I think I need to be alone right now. I know you must think I'm really ungrateful and weird, but I need space.'

Caroline and Naomi left, not looking too happy about being turfed out. Daisy put her head in her hands and let the misery wash over her. She knew the rest of the world would think that she'd lost the plot. She knew the girls thought she was crazy. In fact, she'd always had a hunch that Naomi secretly fancied Freddie. Well, maybe that could be the answer to everyone's conundrum, she figured. Whatever happened, Daisy couldn't think any more or her head would explode.

A gentle knock on the door a while later made Daisy jump.

'Yeah?'

The door pushed open and Ava put her head around. 'Sorry, pet, I know you said you want thinking space, but Freddie's on the phone. He just wants to talk to you for a minute,' Ava said, holding out the house phone.

'MUM!' Daisy mouthed silently. 'NO.'

'Hold on, Freddie, she's here now,' Ava said, handing her the phone and looking at her sternly.

Daisy felt five years old again as she took the phone.

'Freddie,' she said gently.

'Okay, Daisy, I've done a lot of soul searching and even more thinking,' he said. *What, since this afternoon?* Daisy thought with irritation.

'I've come to a conclusion,' he said. 'I'm willing to forgive you and move forward. Mum and Dad have explained that you must be feeling a little panicked, after all, getting married is a massive step for any girl. So, I'll give you the space you need. How about we go down the country at the weekend? We'll spend a night having some quiet time together and you'll see that it's all going to be fine.'

Daisy listened. Her guilt turned to anger. He was speaking to her as if she was a naughty puppy. She hadn't just peed in his slippers, she'd told him she didn't want to marry him. What sort of an egotistical asshole was he?

'Freddie,' she said evenly. 'I'm glad you feel you can forgive me because, believe me, the last thing I want is to hurt you. But we're not compatible. It's not going to work,' Daisy stated matter-of-factly.

'Let me warn you of one thing, Daisy,' he said crossly. 'I won't put up with this kind of behaviour for much longer. If I were you, I'd stop being so damn rude and get your priorities right.'

'That's just it, Freddie, I have got my priorities right. I'm not the one for you. I know that's all highly inconvenient now, but it'll seem better soon.'

She knew it wasn't polite, but Daisy hung up on him. There just wasn't anything more to be said.

A month of cajoling followed – not by Freddie, but by everyone else in her life. They all thought they could snap her out of whatever strange fancy she'd taken. As a result, Daisy retreated into herself. The previously outgoing, happy-go-lucky girl realised she offended less people when she just stayed out of their way.

The only positive constant in her life was her Montessori course. Daisy was like a sponge, soaking up all the information. Her final year at college called for her to gain some practical experience alongside her course work. She'd managed to secure several weeks of work experience in various schools and each experience left her more eager to qualify and be in a position to teach little ones. Her Christmas exams were at the beginning of December, so she had only five weeks to swat up and get the best results she could.

All the nightclubs and bars she'd frequented with Freddie before the break-up were no longer worth going to. Mutual friends, and even Naomi and Caroline, insisted on keeping up with the usual routine, insisting she'd come to her senses soon.

'Why don't you want to go out tonight?' Caroline asked for the umpteenth time. 'You never come out with us anymore. What's happened to you, Daisy?'

'I'm not in the form for it. And I don't want to run into Freddie.'

In the back of her mind, Daisy toyed with the idea of leaving Dublin when she had finished her final exams. Perhaps a fresh start somewhere else would be the best thing. For now, though, her main concern was to pass her Christmas exams, get through the festive season, preferably in the confines of her own bedroom so everyone would leave her the hell alone, and then she'd start the New Year afresh.

15.

Tally

Tally and Martin loved Christmas time. That year, like every other, they ate their way through a mammoth number of selection boxes, festive family tins of biscuits and enough bottles of fizzy orange to float a small yacht.

'Ah, sure, the world and its wife breaks out at Christmas,' Martin said as he helped himself to another roast potato.

'That's why they call it the silly season, isn't it?' Tally agreed.

Needless to say, none of that behaviour was doing anything towards helping Tally reach her goal of graduating as a *thin* beauty therapist.

She vowed to start again in the New Year and use January as the jumping-off point for a whole new lifestyle. Of course, New Year's Eve came and went and she carried on as normal, unable to break the habits of a lifetime and change her eating patterns.

One afternoon in late January, she was putting the finishing touches to a diagram of the heart when Sinead approached her desk. The rest of the class members had already gone home, but Tally had stayed back and get her diagram finished perfectly.

'How are you getting on with your study?' Sinead asked. 'Just imagine, your exams will all be done and dusted by the end of May. The months will creep up on you before you can whistle.'

'The course is great, thanks for asking,' Tally answered earnestly. 'At least I'll have the advantage of not making the clients feel intimidated. Everyone will walk into a salon, spot me and feel better about themselves immediately!' Tally grabbed her belly and wobbled it around while laughing.

'You shouldn't put yourself down all the time, Tally.' Sinead's voice was gentle. 'You're a very pretty girl. You're also above average with your grades. Your practical work is fantastic, too. You have a real flair for massage, which some students never fully grasp,' Sinead said kindly.

'It's probably all the fat on my hands, it makes the client feel like they're being massaged by warm sponges!'

'Don't do that.' Sinead wasn't being sharp, her tone was sad.

'Sorry … I was only kidding …' Tally's jaw dropped. Normally, people just giggled along when she made jokes about herself.

'I don't suppose you'd like to join me for a quick drink, would you?' Sinead asked suddenly.

Tally was totally taken by surprise. 'Well, I'd love to, but only if you're sure it wouldn't put you in an awkward position as you're my teacher and all that,' Tally stuttered.

'I don't feel remotely awkward about us having a drink together. I'd be delighted. I'm actually meeting my brother in about an hour, so you'd be doing me a favour by keeping me company until he finishes work,' Sinead said, grabbing her coat from the top of the class.

Tally felt the heat rise to her cheeks when she thought of Ben. She hadn't seen him since the night of her graduation ball. He'd been so kind to her and she had to admit, she'd thought about him more than a few times since.

'I'll make sure I'm out of your hair by the time your brother comes along,' Tally promised.

'No, I didn't mean it like that, Tally! You're so welcome to stay and have some food with us. It'll just be pub grub and I know Ben would be thrilled to have someone other than his big sister to chat to,' Sinead said.

Tally bustled off to the bathroom and did what she could with her make-up. She only had her college uniform and a coat with her, so she didn't plan to stay long. No doubt all the other women in the pub would be dolled up to the nines and she'd feel like a particularly badly dressed outcast.

'Wednesday is my only night off at the moment,' Sinead told her as they walked to the bar.

'Do you work in a salon after hours?' Tally asked, pulling her coat up around her neck to shield herself from the biting wind.

'No, I'm a Motivation Mate!' Sinead answered. 'I work with a slimming company. I'm sure you've seen the adverts on TV?'

'Yeah, I have! Wow, that's interesting. I could do with something like that myself,' Tally said flushing.

'Well, it turned my life around. I'd recommend it in a heartbeat,' Sinead said, holding the door open so Tally could walk into the warmth of the bar. 'Let's sit by the fire and I'll tell you all about it,' Sinead suggested.

Tally knew Sinead worked with people with eating disorders from time to time. She'd made reference to it once or twice in class, but they'd never discussed it in any detail. Tally had automatically assumed Sinead worked with anorexics rather than overweight people.

They ordered drinks and peeled off their coats.

'I used to be your size,' Sinead stated, holding Tally's gaze.

'*Whaaat?*' Tally narrowed her eyes and looked suspiciously at Sinead. Beautifully made-up, tiny waisted, elegant and sexy Sinead? That just didn't make sense to Tally.

'Here, I'll prove it to you.' Sinead fished a flyer from her bag. It was an advertisement for Motivation Mate's clinic. The before and after shot showed Sinead four years ago and then more recently.

'Well, blow me down with a feather,' Tally said, exhaling. 'How did you do it? You're so slim and confident. I would never have guessed ...' Tally was lost for words as she stared intently at the two images.

'I was shy, no confidence and, to be honest, I hated myself not so long ago,' Sinead said. The drinks arrived and she paid before Tally could reach for her purse.

'Thank you. I think I'm rooted to the spot with shock here,' Tally said.

'You're welcome. Now before you think I asked you here to tout for business, that's only partly true!' Sinead said, trying to keep the conversation light. 'I'd love you to join Motivation Mate, but not to get money for the company, for yourself.'

Tally looked at the floor. A rush of mixed emotions hit her. She was beyond flattered that Sinead seemed to want to help her, yet the more paranoid part of her was mortified that her teacher could see so plainly how miserable she was.

'I know it's so hard to take the first step, but I would love you to consider popping to the centre for a session,' Sinead suggested. 'You could come to me, or if you're more comfortable with a stranger, I'll recommend a colleague.'

'No!' Tally shot back. 'I'd hate to go to a stranger. I'd die of shame.'

'Would you come with me then?' Sinead was pushing her for a commitment.

'Okay.' Tally could feel tears welling up in her eyes.

'I don't want to upset you, Tally, but over the past few months, I've been observing you in class. You remind me so much of myself before I chose to change my eating habits.'

'I really want to change, Sinead,' Tally admitted. 'I'm sick of being stared at. I'm always binging and feeling guilty and awful. I hate the thought of shopping for clothes and I've no idea how to turn myself around.' Tears fell down Tally's cheeks. Sinead found a tissue and handed it to her.

'I'd like to help you, if you'll let me,' Sinead said gently.

For the first time ever, Tally felt hopeful that the life-long veil of despair that had enveloped her entire existence could possibly be lifted.

'Here's a card with directions to the centre and we'll start tomorrow. My first client is usually at seven, but we'll head over straight from college, if you're willing? That way I can show you where to come and we can get going immediately,' Sinead promised. 'I know if you think the way I used to that you'll get too scared or worried if we leave it too long. So let's do this. Let's get you motivated!' Sinead said smiling warmly. 'No time like the present, eh?'

'Thanks, Sinead. You've no idea how excited I am about this. I promise I won't let you down,' Tally vowed.

'I know you won't,' Sinead said hugging her. 'Now get yourself into the ladies and clean up your mascara before Ben gets here. All we need is a man witnessing a girl crying to make for a really cringy situation,' Sinead giggled. 'Men are as much use as an ashtray on a motorbike when it comes to sobbing girls!'

Tally burst out laughing and rushed off to the bathroom to freshen up. She'd been just in time, too. When she returned, Ben was sitting with his back to her as she approached.

'Here she is,' Sinead announced, winking at Tally.

'Hi, Tally, great to see you again,' Ben said, standing up to give her a hug and kiss on both cheeks.

'Yeah, good to see you, too, Ben. Sorry for barging in on your evening,' Tally began. 'I was just about to leave.'

'Not at all, I'm delighted to see you. Sit down there and tell me all about my mean task-master of a sister here! Come on, 'fess up now, is she a total dragon in class?' Ben said, teasing Sinead.

'Ah, she's not too bad unless you annoy her, but I'm getting used to the electric shock treatment now. That stick she has doesn't hurt that much when she beats us either,' Tally joked.

'You old boot! I'll give you an F in your exams if you don't watch it,' Sinead said, giggling.

'I'll get out of your hair,' Tally said, grabbing her coat.

'I'd really like you to stay, unless you're in a mad hurry?' Ben said.

'Really?' Tally asked before she could stop herself.

'Really,' Ben said gently. Tally was singing inside as she shrugged and said she'd just call her da to let him know she'd be a bit late.

'You hadn't bought dinner, had you?' she asked him anxiously.

'No, not yet, love. I'm delighted you're having a bit of fun there. You take your time. I'm going to head down to the local with a couple of the fellas from work. I'll see you later on,' Martin said sounding delighted.

Bless him, Tally thought. He'd have gone straight home if she'd been there. He'd never leave her by herself. But as she was occupied, she was able to have a bit of fun too. Tally felt more determined than ever to sort herself out. If she could lose some weight and gain some confidence, it would benefit her father too.

The evening flew by and Tally thoroughly enjoyed Sinead's and Ben's company. By the time they ambled out of the bar, Tally was glowing. Ben was really witty and so down-to-earth. He didn't look at her as if she disgusted him nor did he elbow her and treat her like one of the lads.

Although she barely knew the guy, Tally had a serious crush on him.

The following day, classes flew by and Sinead and Tally exchanged some knowing glances. Just before class ended, Sinead was handing out leaflets with study tips to each of the students.

'Just stay back and we'll head off together as soon as the place clears,' she whispered as she handed Tally the leaflet.

Tally felt like she was going to vomit as Sinead locked up and they prepared to head to the Motivation Mate clinic. 'I know you probably want to run and hide, but I'll be with you every second. This is it, Missus! Are you ready to rumble?' Sinead said making punching gestures.

Sinead's comment cut the tension and Tally couldn't help but laugh

The clinic was modern and bright and for all the world like an office with a couple of larger rooms added on. One room housed a fully equipped gym, the other was mirrored with what looked like Pilates things over to one side.

'Come into my lair! I'll cast a spell on you!' Sinead joked.

Tally felt instantly at ease as they shut the door and began the session.

Sinead explained her own journey from outsized to her current size. 'My diet was appalling. Every day without fail I ate four times the amount of calories required for a person of my height,' she assured Tally. 'I need you to be honest when filling out the questionnaire and we'll be able to get you going much quicker.'

Tally knew Sinead wasn't there to judge her and she believed her when she said she'd been quaking in her boots the first time she'd walked into this very building.

So Tally truthfully logged exactly how much she ate, how little she exercised and, more to the point, how desperate she felt inside.

Sinead was patient and encouraging. 'You can do this, Tally. If I could do it, anyone can. I'll help you as much as I can,' Sinead promised.

It took over an hour, a lot of sobbing and plenty of shaking for Tally to complete the two sheets of questions.

'Normal practice is that I go through all of this and we meet up here next week,' Sinead continued. 'But seeing as I know you and you've been so completely honest, I think we can just jump straight in. I'm giving you the information pack, with menu planners and beginner's exercise ideas.'

'Oh, my,' Tally said, mopping her eyes with the scrunched-up tissue she'd been holding throughout. 'This is really it, isn't it?'

'If you want it enough – yes.' Sinead took her hand and squeezed it.

Tally walked out of her first meeting feeling as if she'd lost the most important weight of all – the heavy lump of self-loathing that had been resting on her shoulders since she was a small child.

When Tally got home she suddenly felt shy about telling her da about her meeting. Greta was out, so she figured she might as well tell Martin what she was planning. What if he laughed at her or, worse, got angry? After all, they bonded over their grub. She didn't want him to feel she was abandoning him.

'Da, I've something to tell you,' she began.

When she'd shown him the leaflets Sinead had given her and talked him through the plan, Martin hugged her.

'I'll do it with you, so. It can't work if I'm sitting here with greasy food and chocolate, so we'll both eat the bars and sawdust or whatever it is they recommend,' he said.

'No, Da, that's the whole point. It's not a diet where we only eat rabbit food and go around starving for a week before breaking out and eating the leg of the table,' Tally parroted Sinead. 'This is a new way of life. A forward-thinking plan to alter the way we view food.'

'I see,' said Martin, thinking it was all as clear as mud.

'We won't be having supplements or shakes or any of that kind of mad stuff, just fresh food that nourishes our bodies and reduces the fat naturally. We'll have to start a bit of exercise too,' Tally continued. 'Just walking to begin with, nothing manic.'

And so they did.

At first, Greta didn't notice that they'd stopped eating chips, nor was she particularly mindful of the fact her husband and daughter were going for regular walks in the evening, until she arrived home from the gym one night to find the place empty.

'Hello?' she called. That was odd, usually the two of them would be starting at the television, rustling wrappers and slugging tea.

As Greta came out of the shower, towelling her hair dry and grateful to be in a cosy tracksuit, Martin and Tally arrived home saturated.

'God, it's rough out there,' Tally said. 'Are you sure you don't mind me going first in the shower, Da?'

'Go on ahead, love, just hurry up before my extremities drop off. It's Baltic out there,' he said, blowing on his frozen hands. 'Hiya, love,' he greeted an astonished Greta.

Tally made for the bathroom and Martin helped himself to a pint of water.

'I'm gobsmacked,' Greta managed. 'I thought the two of you would do this diet for two days and go right back to where you've always been – eating, sitting and more eating.'

'Thanks for the vote of confidence, you rat bag,' Martin joked. 'We're actually doing really well. We're three weeks into the programme and I feel better already. This isn't just one of those New Year's resolutions that doesn't make it past February. Tally's lost kilos, too. You should encourage her a bit, Greta, she really has thrown herself into this thing with so much commitment.'

'Good for her. Although, she'll have to shed more than a few kilos to make an impression, won't she?' Greta mused as she lit a cigarette.

Martin held her gaze and dropped his head to the side.

'What?' Greta said exhaling.

'Meet her halfway, love, please,' Martin said gently but firmly.

Greta's gaze fell to the floor. When Tally appeared, Greta made a concerted effort to compliment her. 'Your da tells me you're doing great at your slimming club, Tallulah,' Greta offered.

'Yes, both of us are making great progress,' Tally answered quietly. 'I'm heading off to bed early. Goodnight.'

Regardless of what she said, her mother had always had a knack of making Tally feel like nothing she did was of any significance.

16.

Daisy

Daisy was starting the New Year afresh, just as she'd promised herself. Christmas had been tough. Her parents had obviously been holding out some final glimmer of hope that she'd feel maudlin during the holidays and suddenly want Freddie back. When she showed no sign of it, she could see their faces dropping in disappointment. She felt like a constant letdown to everyone.

It was Saturday night, and the girls rang to see if she would be joining them. She opened her mouth to say her usual 'No', but then something made her stop. She was so tired of being cooped up in her room, not seeing anyone or having any fun. So she said yes instead and got herself ready for a night on the town.

They met up in large, popular bar and Daisy felt a huge sense of release as she mingled with a crowd of people her own age who only had one concern: partying.

'Daisy, you need to go easy on the cocktails, sweetie,' Caroline said, looking worried.

'Jeez, make up your mind, will you?' Daisy slurred. 'Last week you were whining at me because I wouldn't go to the Christmas party with you and now I'm here, dolled up and tanked up and that's wrong too! What do you want me to do?'

Daisy knew she was being a snotty bitch, but she was so bloody sick of everyone being on her case.

The Black Eyed Peas came on, so she grabbed Caroline's hand and dragged her onto the dancefloor. Daisy loved dancing and now she realised just how much she'd missed it since she'd been with Freddie. He had never liked dancing and was always happier sitting down, scoping out the competition.

'This is fantastic!' she shouted to Naomi as she joined them.

A dark, foreign-looking guy sidled up to her and put his arm around her waist. Throwing caution to the wind, she turned around to face him. Pulling him close, she kissed him there and then. They had a ball, jumping around and snogging for the next hour or so.

'Let's get a drink!' she yelled.

He motioned that he couldn't understand her over the loud music, so she mimed drinking. He grinned widely and followed her to the bar.

'What'll you have?' she asked him. He stared at her blankly again. She bought them both a bottle of beer, clinked off his bottle and smiled. He was a good-looking guy, but now that she could see him better, she wondered how old he was.

'Me,' she said pointing to herself as she held up two fingers then one, 'twenty-one,' she explained. 'You?'

He grinned and showed her with his fingers. 'Seriously?' she said feeling slightly ill. 'Sorry,' she took his beer and staggered over towards the girls.

'What's up with Romeo?' Naomi asked.

'He's bloody sixteen, that's what!' Daisy said, bursting out laughing. 'So, I took his beer away and left him for dust. Christ, I could be done for child molesting!'

Caroline and Naomi exchanged a look, but she was past caring. She was single, free to do what she wanted and that's exactly what she was going to do for a change.

A few of the girls from college rang to see if she'd like to go to a ball in Kildare on New Year's Eve.

'It's black-tie, but fairly relaxed, so you don't need to go mad buying a dress. We've eleven at the table, so it should be fun.'

She was actually thrilled to get away and agreed immediately. A weekend break was just what she needed to start the New Year with a bang.

When they sat down at their table on the night of the ball, Daisy immediately knew she had been strategically positioned beside Jack. He was a brother of one of the other girls and was quite obviously looking for a woman.

'So you're in college doing the Montessori then,' he said without looking her in the eye.

'Yeah,' she answered.

'Cool, so,' he nodded.

The meal was a bit painful. Jack seemed nice enough, but he'd the personality of a brush and clearly had about as much experience with women as breeze-block.

'So,' he said the second the plates were cleared from the table. 'Fancy an auld shift?'

'Sorry?' Daisy said, looking mildly perplexed.

'A snog'd do, or if you want a bit of how's-your-father, myself and a few of the lads have a room upstairs. I'll tell them not to come up for half an hour, like.'

Daisy looked at him in shock. 'Are you serious?'

'Huh?' He did a double-take.

'Do you honestly think you're going to get me into bed just like that?'

'Well, it worked with the last few girls,' he said, scratching his head. Daisy burst out laughing and thumped him on the top of the arm.

'Well, I hate to piss on your parade there, Jack, but it's takes a little more than a few grunts during a crap dinner to get your leg over with me.'

'But the girls said you're after splitting up with your fella and you might be on for a bit of craic.'

'Yes I am on for a bit of fun, but that doesn't mean a five-minute fumble with you!'

'Fair enough, so. There was no harm in asking, though, was there?' he deadpanned.

'I guess not,' she said, laughing hard.

Jack wasn't the only one hoping to get some alone time with her that night. Daisy was very flattered by all the male attention, but then she began to get a bit paranoid that perhaps the story of her and Freddie had done the rounds and she was being viewed as an easy target. So she decided to have a good laugh with everyone she met, but decline all offers of snogs or shifts or 'doing the beast with two backs', as one particularly persistent admirer put it. Daisy danced and joked and flirted and danced some more, but at the end of the night she went up to her room alone, laughing to herself at all the corny come-ons she'd heard in the course of the evening. For a brief moment she felt lonely, wishing she had someone there to share a pillow postmortem of the whole event, but she pushed the self-pity aside. This was the new Daisy Moyes, the one who was more than happy to be her own date and set her own rules and boundaries. She thought of the Hunt Ball, and Freddie comparing her to a doll, and she fell asleep smiling, savouring the delicious freedom of being alone.

17.

Felicity

Felicity had loved spending Christmas with Mia and her brothers and their families, but she couldn't hide her excitement at the thought of Shane's arrival for New Year. She'd found a house for him and five of the lads to rent for the weekend. Bob had kindly agreed to accompany her to the train station and ferry a couple of them in his car.

'So how old is lover boy Shane, then?' he asked as they waited on the platform for the Dublin train.

'He's twenty-eight,' Felicity said.

'Does Mam know?'

'She hasn't actually asked,' Felicity said.

'I'll take that as a no,' Bob chuckled.

'What does it matter anyway?' Felicity said, feeling irritated. 'He's dead on, you'll really like him.'

'We'll see about that,' Bob said.

As it turned out, Bob had a great chat with the lads on the way back from the station. They all loved rugby, so there was an instant connection. Felicity dropped them all to the rented house and promised to return once she'd introduced Shane to Mia.

'Good luck with that. Our mother's a scary woman,' Bob shouted.

'Shut up, Bob! No she's not,' Felicity said shooting him a glare.

Mia had been nervously waiting for Shane to arrive. She'd a chocolate cake and a tray set, ready to bring into the fire. Felicity had told her not to bother, but she wanted to make a point of welcoming him. She didn't want Felicity saying she'd made the lad feel awkward.

'Hello, Mrs Byrne,' he said politely. 'It's great to finally meet you. Felicity has told me all about you.'

'And you, Shane. It's Mia, if you don't mind. All that Mrs stuff makes me feel old,' she quipped.

The tea and cake went down a treat. Although she felt decidedly uncomfortable in her own living room, Mia was blown away by how much Felicity seemed to adore this guy.

'How old did you say you are?' Mia asked, staring straight at Shane.

'Mam!' Felicity said, choking on cake crumbs. 'You sound like you're interviewing him!'

'I'm twenty-eight,' Shane answered evenly.

'You are aware Felicity is only eighteen, aren't you?'

'Yes, she told me.'

Felicity looked like she wanted to stab her mother. 'Well, I'm going to run Shane back to the house and I'll be back to get changed for the dinner at the rugby club. Thanks for the cake.' She grabbed Shane and levered him out of the sofa.

'You don't have to leave so quickly,' Mia said, panicking.

'See you later, Mam,' Felicity said without looking at her.

'Nice to meet you, Mia, and no doubt I'll see you before we head back to Dublin,' he said.

As soon as they were in Mia's car headed towards the lads, Shane spoke. 'Why did you do that?' he asked. 'Your mother was only asking a question.'

'Yeah, one she already knows the answer to. She was going to cause a fuss. I just knew by her.'

Shane decided not to get involved with any potential rows. Mia was going out to dinner at a friend's house, so the two women didn't have time to lock horns that night.

The rugby club was jammed and the atmosphere was fantastic. Aly was in full flight. The lads all loved her and she them.

'You're right, Flick, Shane is deadly,' she said as they hugged. 'Ooh, it's nearly midnight! You'd better position yourself near his nibs.'

When the clock struck twelve, Shane pulled her into his arms and kissed her tenderly.

'Happy New Year, beautiful,' he whispered in her ear.

At that moment Felicity knew that no matter how old Shane was or what anyone else thought of him, she was head over heels in love.

18.

Daisy

Daisy was delighted to get back to college. The routine and study was a welcome distraction. She'd drunk enough alcohol over Christmas to feel pickled and fed-up with drink, so she used January to go for long walks and detox her body.

'How are you feeling about your decision now?' Ava asked as they wandered by the sea one afternoon.

'Better,' she said. 'I know you and Dad are still astonished by what I did, but I know I've made the right choice.'

'Okay love. If you say so,' Ava said. Daisy knew her mother was still upset.

'I'm not worried about meeting someone else, Mum, and I don't want you to think I never will. The right person will come along at the right time. I honestly believe things happen for a reason, you know?'

'Yes they do,' Ava agreed.

At the end of February Daisy's lecturer handed out passes to the Children's Health and Education Expo running in the local exhibition centre and Daisy decided she'd prefer to go by herself rather than with the group from her class. If she were on her own, she could potter about and suit herself.

Having walked non-stop for several hours, gathering information and advice, Daisy felt parched and her feet ached. Spotting one of the many refreshment stands, she bought a coffee and a sandwich and made her way to one of the tall round tables. To her relief, a man was just finishing and offered her one of the few high stools.

'Oh, thank you so much, it's great to take the weight off my feet for a few minutes!'

The man grunted and moved away. *Charming*, Daisy mused.

At first, Daisy paid very little attention to the stranger who wandered over and asked if he could share her table space.

'It's kind of crowded in here and they don't seem to have given the whole dining experience much thought,' the man said in a slow American drawl.

'That's true, they seem to think we all have the stamina of athletes and never want to chill out. Maybe they're just getting people like me ready for dealing with the endless energy of pre-schoolers!' Daisy suggested.

'Have you been in the industry long?' the man asked as he sipped a smoothie.

'No, I'm only starting out. I hope to graduate in May and then the world will be my PlayDoh, jigsaw and phonetic alphabet!' Daisy grinned.

'I like your way of putting things. That's real sweet. Nathan's the name, by the by. I'm honoured to meet you,' he said, holding out one of the biggest hands Daisy had ever encountered.

He must be at least six-four, Daisy mused.

'I'm Daisy,' she said as her own petite hand was encased in his.

'Pretty name for a pretty little lady.'

She looked up at him expecting him to leer at her or have a goofy grin as he acted all Jack-the-lad. Instead, he was soft and sincere, not an ounce of sleaze in sight.

He was broad and blond with tanned, immaculate skin and a wide, bright smile worthy of any toothpaste advert. But beyond his Abercrombie & Fitch tight, long-sleeved T-shirt and jeans with rips in all the right places, he emanated something Daisy hadn't come across in any man she'd met before – he was utterly genuine.

'I've seen so many stands and chatted to such an array of exhibitors here, I don't know what I want to buy now,' Daisy divulged. 'I'd intended picking up a few useful bits and pieces for my new career and now I feel a little overwhelmed.'

'Once you've been in the industry for a while, it becomes easier to spot which things are going to work and those which are merely gimmicks,' Nathan nodded. 'I don't suppose you would agree to coming on a dinner date with me?' he asked directly.

'I'd love to,' Daisy responded immediately, loving the American date-night concept.

'Would you prefer if I collect you or will we meet at the restaurant?' he enquired.

'I'll meet you there,' Daisy decided, just in case he was an axe murderer.

'Would the Four Seasons be okay with you – say seven-thirty?' he asked.

'When, tonight?' she stuttered, feeling slightly shocked.

'Unless you have a prior engagement?' He held her gaze.

'No, no I don't, I'd love that.'

He pulled a business card from the top pocket of his shirt and handed it to her. 'If for any reason you can't make it, I'll understand but would really appreciate if you could give me a call.'

'Oh, no, I'll be there.'

Daisy left the exhibition shortly afterwards, deciding she couldn't talk to any more eager-to-sell individuals. She went home, had a shower and put on a simple black cocktail dress, killer heels and applied her make-up. She decided against calling Naomi or Caroline. They'd tell her she was breaking all the 'rules' and that she shouldn't make herself so available and all the other bunkum they could come up with. It hadn't done her any good thus far, so she was happy to chuck the rules in for a night. Besides, she wasn't meeting Nathan in the registry office to get married. They were two civilised adults meeting for a dinner date.

'See you later, I'm going out to meet some friends,' Daisy called down the hall into the kitchen.

'Oh, okay, have fun. What about your dinner?' Ava called back, sounding a bit put out. 'I assumed you'd eat with me, you're only home.'

'I'm grabbing something with the gang,' Daisy shot back. 'See you later, I have my key.'

Daisy exhaled when she was out of sight of her house. She felt a little ripple of excitement as she skipped down the road to meet Nathan. The fact that their date was her little secret made the anticipation even greater.

Flagging a taxi, Daisy hopped in the back. When she'd told the driver which hotel to go to, she pulled out a small mirror and checked her make-up again. She'd have to do. Either this guy liked her the way she was or she'd move on. She wasn't getting into another relationship where she felt uncomfortable or in any way compromised. She was happy on her own, so any man she hooked up with had to enhance her life.

It didn't take Daisy long to figure out that Nathan wasn't like any guy she had encountered previously. First off, he was at the bar before her. He was dressed in a suit and greeted her with a warm smile as he kissed her on both cheeks and showed her to a small round table in the corner of the piano bar. The discreet Reserved sign and beautifully arranged silver ice bucket holding the bottle of Cristal champagne made her feel like the only girl in the world.

'Will you have a glass or would you rather drink something else?' he asked politely.

'I'd love some champagne, what a gorgeous treat! Thank you,' she said, feeling slightly shy all of a sudden.

'I'm not a champagne kind of guy, so excuse me if I don't join you,' he said pouring her drink. 'Cheers!'

He chatted easily, asking questions without being intrusive. 'I was intrigued when you told me you are about to become a Montessori teacher,' he admitted. 'My family business is all about entertainment. Focusing on kids, but so much more as well. I've moved to Europe to further our spectrum. We've done quite well with the concept Stateside, so I'm hoping it will work here too.'

Daisy sipped her bubbly and was transfixed by his smooth American tone and dashing good looks. He was like one of the models on a GAP or Abercrombie advert, she thought to herself. Some women might find him too pretty or even intimidating because of his suave demeanour, but Daisy was thoroughly enjoying both the view and the way he was spoiling her.

Realising she was staring, she shook herself up and tried to keep the conversation going. If she sat gawping like a monkfish, he'd never want to see her again.

'Will your new place be decorated in the usual primary colours with slides and ball pools?' Daisy asked.

'Yes, it'll be bright and attractive to children. But we'll also have sections with art facilities. There'll be a kitchen area where there will be half-hourly cookery lessons, a science and nature education centre with workshops, and a full Montessori programme in the entire upper level. Who knows, maybe you might consider coming to have a look? I'm currently taking CVs from prospective teachers.'

'Seriously?' Daisy's brain switched from drooling love-struck girly to being genuinely interested in the business end of the conversation.

'I gave you my card when we met earlier, so email me your CV and I'll put a good word in for you,' he said, grinning.

'Who's your boss?'

'Me.'

Nathan went on to explain that the centre would also have an area for children with special needs. He'd been in Ireland for several months and plans were well under way.

'All the art therapy and indeed most of the equipment lends itself to being used in conjunction with physical and occupational therapy. The facilities for kids with special needs are scarce in Ireland from what I can make out,' Nathan said, sipping his drink. 'This way, we can offer those kids the same amenities, but with properly trained care workers. It's all done by a strict online and telephone booking system and it's proven to be a great structure back home.'

By the time they'd finished coffee and dessert, Daisy wanted the evening to last forever.

'Can I drive you home?' Nathan offered. He'd been drinking diet soda all night.

'Well, I live in Blackrock, is that the right direction for you?'

'Sure.'

'Do you never drink or is it just because you didn't feel like it tonight?' Daisy was curious to know.

'I never drink. It just doesn't hold any interest for me anymore. I went through a phase of my life where alcohol took precedence. That doesn't rock my boat any longer. There's more to life than getting trashed.' His easy smile as he spoke meant Daisy didn't feel like a raging alcoholic beside him. 'Clearly, I don't mind others drinking, it's just that I've chosen not to partake any longer, that's all.'

'Fair enough,' Daisy said, feeling even more impressed by him.

Nathan insisted on paying for the meal.

'We could go Dutch,' Daisy offered.

'Sure we could, but no lady in my company pays for her own supper.

Thank you for the offer all the same. You're real sweet, Daisy-Duke!'
When he winked at her, Daisy felt like she was going to collapse. She'd
never felt weak at the knees with Freddie, but Nathan seemed to carry
an invisible joint-disabling anaesthetic.

She was impressed with how he insisted on paying the bill, too. He
wasn't trying to impress anyone else, he simply wanted to treat *her*.

As they approached a top of the range Lexus in the hotel car park,
Daisy couldn't help commenting. 'Wow! Gorgeous car,' she whistled,
impressed.

'Thank you, I love it.'

They continued to chat easily during the short journey to Daisy's
house. He didn't even attempt to invite himself in. He was a perfect
gentleman, getting out of the car to open her door. Taking her in his
arms, he tucked her hair behind her ear so he could see her face more
clearly.

'I really enjoyed our date. Would you come out with me again
another time?' he asked.

'I'd love to,' Daisy said, as she willed him to kiss her.

She was delighted when he obliged. As their lips met, she felt a bolt
of electricity she had never experienced with any other guy.

'I had a lot of fun with you, Daisy. You're a beautiful person. God
was smiling down on me when He led me to you this afternoon,' he
whispered.

Daisy wasn't sure if he was being sarcastic or not, but when she met
his gaze, she knew he meant every syllable.

The next morning Daisy waltzed into the kitchen, grinning like the
Cheshire cat. Ava stopped in her tracks.

'What has you looking so jolly?'

'I was on a date last night and had the most amazing time!' Daisy
said, hugging her mother.

'Oh! With who?' Ava felt her heartbeat quicken.

'He's American and his name is Nathan. You'll love him, Mum. He
is just stunning-looking and he treated me like a princess!' Daisy flew
off around the kitchen like someone from a Disney movie.

Ava was in turmoil. She was thrilled to see her happy-go-lucky daughter back to her old self, but she knew all hopes of a reunion with Freddie were well and truly scuppered.

'Tell me about him,' Ava said, wanting to feel her daughter's glee.

Daisy described each second since she'd met this stranger the day before.

'… and when he kissed me, Mum, boom! I've never felt this way about anyone. He's just amazing!'

Ava couldn't help but giggle and join in with her daughter's giddiness. 'Well, I really can't wait to meet this hunk!' she said.

Over the following weeks, Nathan was consistent and reliable in his phoning and dating habits. But, above all else, he made Daisy feel like she was the only girl in the world. Days turned to weeks and they were still together.

'Hey, Daisy-Duke! How are you this bright and sunny morning?' he chirped down the phone.

Every morning first thing, if she hadn't stayed at his apartment, Nathan would call her mobile.

'Hi, gorgeous! What are you up to?' she said, turning over onto her tummy to chat to him from her bed. Although her relationship with Nathan seemed to be getting more serious, Daisy still felt in control.

'I've a big meeting with the guys who are constructing a part of the play centre, and I'll take them to lunch. Can I swing by and collect you after six and we'll do something fun?' he offered.

'Perfect. Have a good meeting and see you later on.'

He was her other half. He viewed the world the way she did – with a smile and an expectation that the day was going to be sunny rather than dull.

A few weeks later, Justin was due home from America and Ava decided to hold a family dinner to welcome him back. She asked Daisy if Nathan would like to join them, and her daughter smiled at her delightedly and ran off to phone him. Ava still couldn't get used to the idea of Daisy being with someone other than Freddie, but she was determined to give this Nathan a chance, seeing as Daisy thought so highly of him.

'He's free, Mum,' Daisy called as she returned to the room. 'He'll be here at 7.30pm on the dot.'

When Justin arrived home at six, the house was filled with two of his darling children and his daughter-in-law, and the smell of Ava's wonderful cooking permeated every room. He was thrilled to be back among them all again, and they caught up with each other as they sipped wine.

At 7.30pm, the doorbell rang and Daisy jumped up to answer it. Ava and Justin exchanged a look – this was it.

The sitting-room door opened and Daisy stepped inside, followed by a tall, broad, blond man who was built like an American football star.

'Mum and Dad, Charlotte and Jake, I would like you all to meet Nathan.'

'Wow! Well done, Daisy,' said Jake. 'He's a good-looking one, too, he must've been the dearest at the escort agency with teeth as white as those.' Jake held his hand out to shake Nathan's, a wicked grin on his face.

'Nice to meet you, Jake. I'm not from an agency, though. Your sister and I met at a trade show.' Nathan looked slightly bewildered.

'Hello, Nathan, you're very welcome. I'm Justin. Please ignore our son, he's not really related to us, he just keeps coming back so we've chosen to accept him,' Justin joked.

'I see,' Nathan smiled and answered politely, but looked like he had no clue what was going on.

'Let me introduce my wife, Ava,' Justin tried.

'Good evening, Ma'am. Thank you for inviting me into your home. I appreciate the kind hospitality,' Nathan said.

'You haven't tried her cooking yet, I'd reserve that gratitude until you've been fed and watered,' Jake joked.

'I'm sure your food will be delicious, it certainly smells wonderful,' Nathan answered.

'This is my wife, Charlotte.' Jake pulled her up from the sofa so she could attempt to have a semi-decent conversation with the large American.

'Hi, Charlotte, very pleased to make your acquaintance,' Nathan said politely.

'Where are you from?' Charlotte asked as she shook his hand and smiled.

'California, USA, Ma'am.'

Ava rejoined them from the kitchen and Nathan smiled warmly at her. 'What a beautiful place you have here, Mrs Moyes.' He nodded as he took in the plush yet welcoming surroundings of the Moyes family home. The house was eighty years old, with original fireplaces and gorgeous ceiling moldings, but they'd chosen to make it contemporary by adding modern furniture.

'What can I get you to drink?' Jake asked politely, figuring that sarcasm wasn't going to work with this guy. 'We're having champagne if you'd like that, or perhaps you'd prefer a cold beer or glass of wine?' Jake waited for an answer.

'I don't drink alcohol, sir. Would you have a diet soda?' Nathan said.

'Sure, I'll grab you one. Well done, Daisy, cheap date!' Jake whispered to his sister as he gave her the thumbs-up.

'I'll have another drop of champagne if you're offering,' Daisy winked at Jake, who responded by sticking his tongue out at her.

The conversation flowed during dinner, and when they had settled themselves with brandy in the sitting room, Ava suggested a game of Trivial Pursuit.

'Okay, it's us crumblies against each of you two young couples,' Ava announced. 'Jake and Charlotte, pick a colour. You two as well, Daisy and Nathan, pick another.'

'You grab our piece of pie, Charlotte, and I'll make us all an Irish coffee. Nathan, sure you won't have one?' Jake offered.

'No, sir, I don't drink alcohol,' Nathan repeated.

Daisy shot her brother a dirty look.

'What? I'm only trying to be polite!' Jake defended himself.

'Just go and make the Irish coffees. Perhaps Nathan would help me move the sofas around so we can all get at the coffee table?' Justin suggested.

'Sure thing,' Nathan agreed, pleased to have something to do. Without Justin's help, he scooped up the three-seater sofa like it was toy furniture and asked where he should place it.

'Here is perfect,' Justin said sounding impressed. If nothing else, this lad is strong as an ox, he thought to himself.

Jake returned with a tray of drinks and they got down to the game.

'Excellent, prepare to have your asses whipped,' Jake exclaimed rubbing his hands together. 'Ready, Charlotte,' he said, winking at his wife.

'Excuse me, but what is this game?' Nathan asked.

'Have you never played Trivial Pursuit before?' Daisy asked as she sipped her creamy drink.

'No, I have not,' Nathan stated.

'Okay, well the object of the game is to make our way around the board by answering questions. I'll show you, it's easier to explain as we go along. Stick with me, honey, we'll beat these drunken skunks,' Daisy assured him as she slurred slightly.

'So, why do we pick a colour? Is this the preliminary question or something?' Nathan was still not getting it.

'Oh, no, there is just one of each colour so you know which counter is yours and Daisy's,' Ava tried to explain. 'If you answer certain questions correctly, you get a piece of pie to put in your counter. The first couple to fill their counter wins.' She was very aware of Justin shifting in the seat beside her. Of all the things Justin disliked, it was people who were slow on the uptake.

'Let's just get started,' he said, sounding irritated.

Some of the questions were ridiculously difficult, like asking what year certain goals were scored by random soccer players. Others were about breeds of anteaters and impossible silver screen questions that only serious movie buffs could possibly know. Thankfully, some of the questions were halfway decent and everyone managed to move around the board and collect at least some counters. When an American-based question was asked of Daisy and Nathan, she automatically assumed he would like to answer.

'Who,' Charlotte asked, 'is the former Hollywood actor turned governor?'

Silence descended on the room, as everyone presumed Nathan would know the answer.

'Go on, you say it.' Daisy put her arm around his shoulder and looked into his eyes. There was a brief pause. Nathan scratched his chin.

'Come on, then, don't keep us in suspense!' Jake chuckled.

'I will have to go with Dustin Hoffman,' Nathan deadpanned. Everyone fell around laughing, pleased that Nathan had finally loosened up and felt happy to tell a joke.

'You're so funny,' Daisy snorted. 'Don't take that as his final answer, though,' she giggled.

'Excuse me? What's so amusing?' Nathan looked genuinely confused yet again.

There was a pregnant pause as it slowly dawned on the gathering that he hadn't been joking.

'Don't mind us, too much wine with dinner. Soooo close, but the answer is actually Arnold Schwarzenegger,' Charlotte explained subtly.

'Oh, really?' Nathan nodded and clicked his fingers in an oh-shucks style. 'Sorry, babe.' He leaned over and planted a kiss on Daisy's cheek. 'Can't win 'em all, huh?' He focused back on the game, as Charlotte and Jake struggled to stifle their snorts. Ava sighed inwardly, knowing Nathan had just given himself an uphill struggle as far as Justin was concerned. He'd have to do a lot better than that to convince Daisy's father he was any sort of a decent replacement for golden boy Freddie.

At half twelve, Charlotte patted Jake on the leg. 'We'd better get going, sweetheart. I don't want to be dying of a hangover tomorrow. Thank you all for a gorgeous evening. Ava, the meal was delicious, as usual,' Charlotte said, yawning.

'Our pleasure, darling,' Ava said, peeling herself up from the sofa where she was cuddled into Justin.

When Charlotte and Jake had left, the room became slightly tense. Justin was two sheets to the wind and was glowering at Nathan. Seeing that her father was getting irritated, Daisy decided to take control.

'I'm fairly whacked myself. I'll walk you out to your car, Nathan,' she offered.

'Sure.' Nathan stood up and strode across the room and shook Justin and Ava's hands.

'I sincerely appreciate your welcoming me to your fine home. I am honoured to meet you folks,' he said. 'Daisy is very dear to my heart and I now know where she gets both her good looks and charm. Good evening to you both,' Nathan finished before exiting the room.

Justin and Ava looked at one another, and Ava shrugged. She opened her mouth to say something when they both heard Nathan speaking in the hallway.

'I don't think they liked me too much.' He sounded disappointed.

'Sure they did. It was so hard for you to walk into a house where we all know each other so well. You were fantastic! It'll just take a bit of time,' Daisy reassured him.

The front door clicked shut and Daisy returned to the sitting room and her parents.

'Well?' she asked, as she resumed her seat on the sofa. Her eyes were sparkling and she looked so blissfully happy.

'Well, he's certainly different from anyone else you've ever brought home,' Ava managed. What she wanted to say was that Nathan was unbelievably formal and quiet, that he wasn't a patch on Freddie, but she held her tongue. Nathan might be nothing like the man she'd choose for her daughter, but she wasn't going to say that now. This would require a gentle approach to show Daisy that Nathan wasn't up to her level – certainly not intellectually, judging by his performance at Trivial Pursuit.

'Isn't he just gorgeous?' Daisy sighed. 'I told you. He's just divine, isn't he?'

'Not quite the word I'd have used,' Justin grumbled.

'Justin.' Ava spun around and gave her husband the keep-your-trap-shut stare.

After Daisy had gone to bed, Ava and Justin sat up a bit longer while Justin nursed his final whiskey of the night. He was upset about Nathan and told Ava exactly what he felt on the matter of his suitability for their daughter.

'I wouldn't worry, darling,' Ava said soothingly. 'He's just not her type. My advice is to just go along with it all and wait for Daisy to come to her senses.'

'Easier said than done,' Justin said with irritation.

'We'll have to try, for her sake,' Ava continued. 'When the time's right, I'll have a word with her about it. You'll see, darling, this one will all blow over quickly. I know my Daisy.'

19.

Felicity

Felicity couldn't believe that she was approaching her first-year exams. It was March already and, come May, she'd be collecting her things and deciding what to do with her summer. College life was all that Felicity had hoped for, and more. She adored her course and had fallen in love with the buzz of Dublin. But the icing on the cake was still Shane. Growing up surrounded by brothers meant she was well able for the banter and jokes. In fact, she was more at home with the group of guys than the girls.

Perhaps it was because she and Shane were an item or maybe it was just her unwillingness to conform to the way a lot of the girls seemed to expect her to behave, but Felicity hadn't made many girl friends. She and Aly were still in constant contact, via text and email. Mia was on at least once a day, too, so Felicity never felt bereft of female contact. Last time they talked, Felicity and Aly had happily bitched about the girls on their courses.

'The girls are like a flock of sheep,' Felicity had complained to Aly. 'They all dress like clones, talk the same way and go to the same few hangouts all the time.'

'I couldn't deal with that,' Aly had agreed. 'There seem to be more alternative ones here at Galway University, but I'm happier going home for the weekends to be honest.'

'Fair enough,' Felicity said. 'But could I interest you in coming here for a couple of nights? I know you've met Shane and the lads, but only on our turf. Who knows, you might like one of them more if you come out with us in Dublin,' Felicity said, trying to coax her pal to come and stay.

Although she noticed a slight hesitation in Aly's voice, her friend did agree to come to Dublin the following weekend.

'Just you lot wait until Aly gets here to sort you out,' Felicity told the lads the following day. 'She's a wild child with a keen eye for a straight guy!'

'She was pretty cute when we met her at New Year all right,' Andrew agreed. 'Is she single?'

'Sure is. She'll give you a run for your money, I can tell you!'

Shane laughed, and not for the first time he thanked his lucky stars he'd been in the right place at the right time on the first day of college. He'd never met anyone like Felicity. Never in a million years could he have predicted that the first student he talked to, before he even got inside the university building that year, would steal his heart. Felicity had rewritten the rulebook, however. She had a magnetism that drew him towards her and he wanted the whole world to know how amazing she was. She was petite and impishly pretty, yet she'd a fire to her personality that let everyone know she was no push over. Shane loved her dry wit most of all. She could take a slagging and, by God, she could give it back.

Of course, more than a couple of people had pointed out the ten-year age gap and the fact that she was a Fresher and he was staff. But none of that mattered to Felicity or Shane.

They'd been dubbed 'the beautiful couple' by some of the more bitter girls in first year. Felicity had roared laughing when she'd got wind of that.

'What's the story with that?' she'd said to Shane. 'It's not as if I'm a total glam queen or anything. Should I be nervous now? Are we supposed to assume a new persona to keep up with this new label?'

'Yeah, I reckon you should go around with a T-shirt with my photo on it?' he'd said, pulling her into his arms.

It had taken Felicity until the end of April to convince Aly to come to Dublin for the weekend. Tonight was going to be a test of sorts. Felicity was desperate for her best mate to approve of her life in Dublin with Shane. Aly had said she liked Shane, but Felicity was nervous of her friend's reaction to her new set-up.

Shane agreed it would be better to meet Felicity and Aly at the disco later on that Friday evening.

'You two need to have few hours of yakking about hair dye and who isn't talking to whom while interspersing ten other conversations at the same time,' Shane said. 'Speaking from experience, coming from a house full of women, you'll have the whole world to put to rights before you even come up for air!'

Shane wasn't wrong. The girls hugged and squealed delighted to see each other. They went for a pizza, which didn't turn out the way the waiter had hoped. For a start, they took an hour to even place an order.'

'Sorry we haven't seen each other for a while. We're so busy chatting we haven't even looked at the menu!' Felicity apologised.

A couple of hours of gossiping, two bottles of wine and a double Sambuca each later, they finally fell into a cab.

'So, tell me who I'm meeting now,' Aly asked.

'Shane, whom you know, Andrew, Patrick, Tom and Foxy, who were in Galway for New Year, and God knows who else,' Felicity said. 'You'll love them, they're great fun!'

As predicted, the girls had a great night. The lads all loved Aly and, true to form, she had them all eating out of her hand. She was an expert flirt and always had her pick of men.

As they queued for the ladies' toilets just before the disco was due to end, Felicity pumped her friend for gossip. 'So, go on then, who've you got your eye on?'

'They're all super cool, but I'm not in the mood for a snog tonight. I'm just enjoying the bit of zazzing,' Aly flicked her hair and stuck her nose in the air dramatically.

'"Zazzing"? What in the world is that?' Felicity laughed.

'It's window shopping with a bit of sass thrown in,' Aly answered, popping a piece of gum in her mouth.

'So is there a specific gentleman who's stolen your heart back home or something? I smell a rat. You are never one to turn down a bit of a kiss,' Felicity said, narrowing her eyes.

Aly flinched slightly, but only for a split second. 'I'm just zazzing, that's all.'

Felicity knew her friend was hiding something, but decided she'd tell her when she was ready. Biting her nails distractedly, Felicity waited for Aly to come out of the cubicle.

'I know we've both had a shed load to drink and it's probably the worst time to annoy you, but I feel like you're hiding something from me, Aly. We always tell each other everything,' Felicity said. 'I know we don't get to spend all our time together now, but I'd hate to feel our closeness is slipping.'

'Not at all, you're just pissed,' Aly said quickly.

Shane was waiting for them when they returned.

'Ladies! I got your coats from the cloakroom. Ready to rock and roll?' he asked.

They were staying in Shane's that night because it was closer to the club and Felicity's room at the residence hall was so tiny.

Aly was quiet in the taxi and although she was probably exhausted after her journey, Felicity knew there was something wrong. Some of Shane's friends pulled up in a taxi at the same time, so there was enough commotion in the kitchen to give the girls a few minutes' breathing space in the living room.

'Come on, spit it out,' Felicity said, handing her friend a pint of water.

'Look, there is someone on the horizon at home. You're right about that,' Aly admitted.

'That's great! Who is he?'

'Trust me, there's a reason why I'm not saying right now, but all I ask is that you give me a little more time,' she asked.

'Okay, I'm a bit freaked I have to be honest, but if that's what you want, I'll let it drop,' Felicity held her hands up. She couldn't help feeling stung all the same. 'Anything else?'

'Eh ... no.'

'Jesus, Alz, what?'

'Okay, I'm not sure about Shane. There, I've said it.'

The words hung in the air like a bad smell. Felicity blinked in shock.

'Why? Has he been rude or offish to you?'

'No, not at all. I just don't know if I *get* him,' Aly said.

'All right, girlies?' Shane burst into the living room. 'Can I pour you a glass of wine or would you prefer a bottle of beer?' he asked, looking from one to the other.

'We're okay for the moment thanks, Shane,' Felicity said tightly.

'Is everything cool here?' he asked, looking hesitant.

'Yeah, I'm just feeling really jarred. I think I need to lie down,' Aly lied.

'Oh, poor you. Listen, you go into my room. Yourself and Felicity take my double bed tonight and I'll have a couple more beers with the guys and kip on the sofa in here,' he offered.

'Thanks, honey,' Felicity said, leading Aly into the only bedroom in the apartment.

By the time Felicity had brushed her teeth and taken off her make-up and returned to the bedroom, Aly was conked out. At least, she was pretending to be. Felicity was at a loss what to say or think. She had already fallen in love with Shane. She'd only realised that when Aly had hinted at not liking him. But it was such a horrible feeling to think her best friend wasn't cool with him.

The next morning Felicity woke before Aly and padded into the living room. Shane was on his own, panned out on the sofa. As she stared at him, Felicity knew she was way too smitten to let him go. If Aly wasn't able to accept him, they couldn't be friends any longer.

As the girls hugged and said their goodbyes at the train station a couple of hours later, the mood was still strained.

'I'll be down soon, I promise. When I get my exams out of the way, I'll be able to take stock of things,' Felicity said.

'That'd be nice. I think Mia is really missing you,' Aly said quietly.

'Have you seen much of her?' Felicity asked, feeling a stab of guilt.

'On and off, she seems great but I know she's finding it tough without you there,' Aly said simply.

Felicity made her way back to her rooms. Shane had gone to visit his folks and she was grateful for a bit of alone time. She'd give Mia a shout and tell her all about Aly's visit. That'd cheer up her Mam.

Felicity had suspected Aly was avoiding coming to Dublin and she'd been right. She wasn't sure if there really was a mystery love interest in Galway or whether Aly was simply so unimpressed with Shane that she didn't want anything to do with him – including snogging his friends. Either way, for the first time since they'd know one another, Felicity felt let down by Aly.

20.

Tally

March was unusually cold that year, or maybe it was simply that this was the first time Tally and Martin had been outdoors so much.

'That wind is biting, isn't it?' Martin said as they jogged along by the sea.

'We'll warm up soon, once we keep moving,' Tally said. 'At least it's not raining.'

Tally was being driven by the fact that they had a weigh-in with Sinead that evening. They'd really managed to turn their eating habits around and the exercise was slowly beginning to become less awful.

'Remember when we tried to run this prom back in January?' Tally said. 'People must've been on stand-by with their mobile phones ready to call the paramedics we were so unfit.'

'I'd say we were a right pair all right,' Martin agreed good-naturedly.

Sinead had been very specific about how they should start slowly and build on what they could manage. 'There's no point going out and making yourself run two kilometres on the first day, injuring yourself and never wanting to run again,' she'd explained.

'I don't think there's any danger of that happening,' Tally joked. 'If I make it to two kilometres at a snail's pace without collapsing in a heap, I'll be astonished.'

So they'd set small goals. Walking from one lamp-post to the end of the pier and back. After two days of that, they parked slightly farther away from the pier, and so on. Now, two and a half months into it, they were actually jogging. It hadn't been easy. Bars of chocolate still called out to Tally. She even found herself dreaming about doughnuts and hot squidgy pizza. She'd wake in the morning feeling guilty when she hadn't even eaten the stuff.

'I dreamed about sausage rolls with curry chips,' she'd told Martin that morning as they ate porridge with low fat yoghurt and linseeds sprinkled on top.

'Oh, stop, I'd love that now,' he'd admitted. 'One of the men in work was having a batter burger with chips yesterday. The smell of the vinegar nearly made me drool.'

Greta had appeared in her running gear, complete with her small rucksack on her back. Grabbing one of her protein shakes, she'd looked at her husband's bowl of porridge.

'Jeez, Martin, that looks like frog's spawn,' she'd said.

'It doesn't taste much better,' he'd smiled.

'See you both later on.'

'We'll be back around tea time, we're going for a weigh-in today,' Tally had reminded her.

'Right. Well enjoy that then,' Greta had said distractedly.

Tally had thought about calling her mother back and tell her she was a selfish cow for not wishing Martin good luck, but had decided not to bother. Why should she let her mother be the cause of yet another row?

'Will we go into the shopping centre before the weigh-in? It'd be nice to take advantage of being near the shops on a Saturday afternoon,' Tally had suggested. They didn't usually see Sinead on a Saturday, but Martin hadn't been able to go midweek because of his shifts at work.

'We've both lost a good bit of weight, my trousers are starting to hang off me. Maybe we could get a couple of bits,' Martin had suggested.

Tally could feel the space in her own clothes too, but instead of going and buying a whole new wardrobe, she had decided to wait a while. She didn't want to have new things just yet.

'It might sound crazy to you, but I'd prefer to hang on a while and get some things when I absolutely can't wear my old stuff any longer.'

'Fair enough, love, but I don't think the customers in the electrical store need to see the crack of my arse every time I bend over. I'll get a pair of trousers to keep me going.'

By the time they arrived at Motivation Mate late that afternoon, Martin noticed Tally was unusually quiet.

'Okay, love?'

'Yeah, I'm just really nervous that I'll have gained weight again,' Tally admitted.

'Ah, I don't see why. Did you have a few sneaky treats or something?'

'No, Da, it's just that we've both lost each time and I suppose I keep waiting for the bubble to burst. I don't trust myself to do well every time.'

Sinead appeared, looking radiant as usual. 'Come on in, you two,' she said happily. 'So, the moment of truth. How's the week been?'

'Great,' Martin answered. 'I've bought new trousers because my old ones are going to have me fired for flashing at the customers! And we ran two kilometres this morning and didn't die!'

'That's amazing news,' Sinead said, applauding them.

Martin went first, stepping on the electronic scales.

'That's amazing, Martin, you've lost six pounds this week!' Sinead said. Tally jumped up and hugged her dad. Her heart pounded and her mouth went dry as Sinead reset the scales.

'I can't do it,' Tally suddenly burst out.

'Why?' Sinead looked surprised. As tears flowed down Tally's cheeks, Sinead led her to a chair.

'Okay, let's just chat about this for a second. Why do you think you don't want to step on the scales today? Have you had a little hiccup with your eating?' Sinead's voice was soft and free of accusation.

Tally shrugged her shoulders and shook her head miserably.

'Did you have a bit of a pie-fest, love?' Martin probed. 'Nobody's going to get annoyed with you. You're doing so well.'

'I haven't eaten anything I shouldn't have. It's not that,' Tally said sighing deeply. 'I just don't believe that I'm going to be able to keep this up. It's been going so well up until now. But I'm at a point right now where I've lost a bit of weight and I'm trying all the time, but I feel like I'll never look normal. I'm exhausted by it all.'

Sinead was fantastic. She understood exactly where Tally was coming from. 'So many people doing the programme have these sorts of feelings, believe me. You've hit a wall, that's all,' she said kindly. 'You've been working so hard at being good, not to mention the study and determination you show in college, it's no wonder you feel a bit overwhelmed.'

'Ma hasn't shown any interest in what we're doing either,' Tally said quietly. 'We could've had both our jaws wired and have a permanent colonic irrigation machine attached to us and she wouldn't say anything positive. The only comments we've had have been negative.'

'Ah, she doesn't mean to come across like that,' Martin said, defending his wife.

'Then why does she do it?' Tally shouted, surprising everyone in the room.

Sinead's heart broke for Tally. She wished she could take some of her pain away. Yet she realised from experience that all this venting was a good sign. She was breaking down the barriers that had held her back in so many ways since her childhood.

'Do you want to skip the weigh-in for today? Sinead asked.

'No!' Tally looked stricken. 'No,' she said more calmly. 'Bring it on.'

As she turned the scales back on, Sinead crossed her fingers behind her back. Willing Tally to have lost as least a couple of pounds, she waited for the reading. Tally stood on the scales with her eyes closed, afraid to face the numbers.

'Tally! You've lost seven pounds! That's your best week *ever*!' Sinead pulled her off the scales and hugged her. Martin joined them and they shared a hug, with Tally laughing and crying at the same time.

'Group hug! Group madness!' Martin boomed, laughing.

'You, my girl,' Sinead said holding both her hands and facing her, 'need to start believing in yourself.'

'Thank you, Sinead. I'll try,' Tally said shakily.

As they drove home, Martin rattled on about the other people in work. Tally was only half listening. She was caught up in her own thoughts. Her father was one in a million, of that she'd no doubt. But her ma was a much more complex character. Would herself and Greta ever find a middle ground? No matter what she looked like on the outside, today's breakdown had shown Tally something. She'd lost a massive amount of weight over the past week alone, yet she'd gone into Sinead feeling heavier than ever before. So what was weighing her down?

There was absolutely no going back with regards to lifestyle, that was a given. But Tally knew she needed to address the problems she and Greta had, too. Greta's running was beginning to make sense to Tally. Her mother had spent all her adult life running away. She didn't want to do the same. Tally knew she needed to keep losing weight, but she equally needed to gain her mother's respect. From where she was standing, she honestly couldn't tell which mountain looked harder to climb.

21.

Daisy

In April, much to everybody's surprise, Daisy moved into Nathan's apartment in Donnybrook, just outside Dublin city centre.

Daisy's other brother, Luke, was home for a visit from the Lake District in England, where he worked as a vet. He was the middle child of the family and Ava thought he was the most pensive of her brood. He had a positive way of looking at life and Ava valued his opinion.

'Maybe it's like an extension of her college work when she gets home,' Luke suggested when she asked him, 'so that makes her feel comfortable?'

'Being a trainee Montessori teacher doesn't mean you should necessarily want to have a person with the intellect of a pre-schooler as your partner,' Ava had retorted, biting her lip.

'Ouch! That's a bit harsh, Mum, and, besides, it's not our choice, it's Daisy's. There's not a lot you can do about it. Just let it roll. If he's that much of a numbskull, she'll see it eventually,' Luke figured. 'There's always the possibility that Nathan is actually a good guy. Grant Daisy with a bit of good judgement here.'

Feeling rather ashamed of how she'd been behaving towards Nathan, Ava had convinced Justin to keep his cool and not say a word about Daisy moving in with her boyfriend. Left to his own devices, he would have tackled his daughter about it in no uncertain terms, but Justin allowed Ava to persuade him to bide his time.

'There's actually nothing we can do about it and, as Luke pointed out, we don't know Nathan the way Daisy does,' Ava reasoned. 'If we kick up and instigate a row, she'll just feel alienated by us. I'd hate for that to happen.'

'I know, I know, that's the last thing I want, but it's so hard to go along with something when every fibre of my being tells me it's wrong,' Justin said looking beaten.

Justin had to head back to America the following day and not for the first time, he wished he worked at home more.

'I'd imagine by the time you get home next, Daisy will be back with us,' Ava said brightly. 'Probably feeling a little blue, but we'll overcome that. She needs to make her own mistakes.'

Justin nodded and Ava worked on feeling as convinced as she sounded. They all felt sure Daisy would be like a boomerang: out the front door and right back within a few weeks.

On moving day, Ava helped Daisy to pack and move her things into the apartment Nathan had just bought. When they stepped inside the door, the two women looked around in wonder. The apartment was spacious and exquisitely decorated.

'Please tell me you had this done by a professional interior designer,' Daisy said, gasping as she took it all in. The colours were warm and calming, in hues of sea-greens and cream. Daisy knew very little about art, but even she could tell that none of the pictures on the walls was a mass-produced print from a hardware store.

'I'd love to have the balls to lie and tell you I did it all, but this is the show home. I didn't even buy the toilet paper. In fact, once that runs out I'll be at a loss,' he admitted sheepishly. 'That's the only reason I asked you to move in, actually, so you can get going with the shopping, cooking and cleaning,' he deadpanned.

'You can piss off with that notion for a start!' Daisy laughed. 'I've already tried going out with Mr 1950s and it wasn't cool, so don't go there!'

'Yes Ma'am,' Nathan said, saluting. 'Do you hear what I have to put up with?' he asked Ava.

'Believe me, she's one of the most strong-willed people I've ever met,' Ava conceded.

'Eh, I'm here and I can hear you,' Daisy commented tartly.

'I think we'll get along just fine,' Nathan said, smiling. 'I'm almost sure there's a sweeping brush in the utility room, she could always beat me with that if I misbehave.'

'Do you hear him?' Daisy said laughing.

'I'd better leave you both to it. I'm sure you don't need me hanging around,' Ava said as Daisy hugged Nathan.

'Call in any time you like, you're always welcome,' Nathan said.

'Thanks,' Ava said tightly.

As Daisy showed her to the door, Ava grabbed her daughter's arm.

'Daisy, you know you're welcome back any time you like? This doesn't have to be forever, love. If you change your mind, that's allowed. Your room will be just as it is.'

'Thanks, Mum,' Daisy said as her eyes narrowed.

'Daisy I only meant …'

'I know what you meant, Mum, and thanks for the vote of confidence.'

Ava turned and walked away, feeling miserable. When she pulled up at her empty house ten minutes later, she longed to have Justin there, too. A photograph of Daisy as a baby looking thrilled with the bunch of daisies she'd found made her fold her body against the wall and sob. This wasn't how she'd ever wanted things to go with her daughter. Damn that Nathan for getting in the way. This was all his fault, she thought bitterly.

Daisy took two deep breaths and decided she was not going to allow her mother to ruin what ought to be one of the happiest days of her life. So she busied herself unpacking her clothes into the sizeable double wardrobe in the bedroom. Fizzing with excitement, she called Naomi to tell her she'd moved in. At least she'd be pleased for her. In fact, she'd see if herself and Caroline would call over later on for a couple of drinks, to christen the place.

'Oh, Daisy, hi,' her friend answered, sounding odd.

'Hi! What's up?' she asked.

'Why?'

'Sorry?' Daisy was confused.

'No, you just seem distracted,' Naomi said, laughing awkwardly.

'Do I? Well, I was only calling to say I've just moved in with Nathan! The apartment is amazing, you'll love it. It's the showhouse, so it's like something from the telly,' Daisy enthused.

'Right.'

'Okay, listen, sorry to bother you, I just thought you might like to hear my news,' Daisy said, feeling deflated. 'Sure give me a call when you feel better or whatever …'

'No, wait. Listen. I've something to tell you … I don't really know how to say it … Well, eh, okay, here goes. Just in case you hear it from someone else, I wanted to tell you something …' Naomi trailed off, testing the water to see if Daisy was going to interrupt.

'Go on,' Daisy said steadily.

'Freddie and I were sort of with each other last night. I'm not sure if it's a once-off. Like, it wasn't planned and I don't know if it's—'

'Naomi!' Daisy interrupted. 'It's none of my business what you or Freddie get up in your spare time. So thanks for letting me know, I appreciate that as it may have been mildly awkward if we bumped into one another, but hand-on-heart, I'm cool with whatever you two decide to do.'

Daisy continued the conversation for a few more minutes, then hung up feeling furious. Naomi and Freddie were welcome to each other, but Daisy and Naomi had been friends for years and it stung to know her friend was willing to jump in and scoop Freddie up.

She took a deep breath and let the whole image of Naomi and Freddie go. If she had been in her teens, Daisy might have cared what everyone else thought, but she was twenty-two and her life was turning out to be better than she'd ever hoped. Nathan was her man and she loved him. All the other stuff paled into insignificance in comparison. All the same, she couldn't help but wish that someone apart from herself was happy about this move.

22.

Tally

Tally came on in leaps and bounds in many ways after her meltdown at Motivation Mate. Martin understood exactly how she felt and of course that was so helpful. With her final exams looming closer, she knew she needed to have a good night out to release some stress.

'Laurence? It's me, I don't suppose you'd like to go on a bit of a bender with me this evening, would you?' Tally asked.

'Well, I thought you'd never ask,' he responded. 'I'm suffering with a bruised ego as it happens, so I could do with a bit of fun.'

Tally agreed to meet her cousin outside a well-known disco bar in Dublin city at eight. She hadn't seen him for a while, but knew he wouldn't hold that against her and would click straight into fun mode.

'Tally? Where have you gone? Oh, no! What have you done with my cousin? She used to be here, but she's a shadow of her former self!' Laurence said waving his arms around before hugging her. 'You look fab, babes! How much have you lost now?'

'Over two stone,' Tally said proudly. 'I know I still have so much more to shift before I look any way normal, but I'm on the right road.'

'You certainly are. Good for you,' Laurence said, linking her arm and marching her towards the bar. 'Shot?' he asked.

'No thanks, honey, white wine spritzer for me. I've gotta watch the calories. I'll allow myself a couple of drinks, but I'm not drinking my entire week's allowance in one night.'

'Cool by me,' Laurence said, accepting her explanation. 'Wait until I tell you about this utter biatch of a guy I got myself hooked up with. Uh, I can't believe I was so blind.'

Tally grinned as Laurence proceeded to tell her yet another tale of woe concerning a man with whom he'd had a brief encounter. She found herself relaxing and laughing out loud as her cousin filled her in on the dramatic moments in his life since they'd last met up. He was like a breath of fresh air for her – a pause from calorie-counting, study, struggling to do what was right and, above all else, judgement. Not for the first time, she recognised what an amazing person her Auntie Mary was. Here was Laurence, an only child who she could easily have put massive pressure on to be the sun, moon and stars, and he couldn't be more alternative if he tried. He was skinny and kind of kookie-looking, gay as Christmas to boot and with a fashion style that would rival Lady Gaga's. If he'd been born to Greta, Tally had no doubt he'd be a quivering mess by now. Auntie Mary had accepted him and, more than that, embraced him just as he was.

'Did I tell you about Blackpool?' Laurence said, waving his hands around wildly.

'No, how did you get on?'

'Well, Da screamed like a girl on the roller-coaster, which Ma and I will never let him forget, needless to say!' Laurence told her all about the fun they'd had.

A holiday like that would never work for my family, Tally mused. Greta would immediately want to have a reccie to see how long the prom was and work out how many times she needed to sprint up and down in order to have a decent workout. She'd want to race the donkeys and would glower at anybody who dared treat themselves to a bag of chips.

Having downed several shots of vile-sounding drinks like 'snot ball' and 'vomit comit', Laurence blagged them into the adjoining disco for free.

Tally totally let loose, enjoying the seventies music no end. Needless to say, Laurence cleared the floor several times as he took his role of John Travolta in *Saturday Night Fever* very seriously.

'Kebab?' he offered as they piled out just after two in the morning.

'Hell, no! I've actually just worked my bootie in there and considering I only had two white wine spritzers, I might even have done some good tonight!' Tally said with sass.

'Wow, look at you all cocky and virtuous!' he teased.

As she cuddled into her duvet a short while later, Tally smiled. She adored Laurence. Along with her da, she knew she had two very special men in her life. Was she just being spoiled wishing she could have a good relationship with her mother, too?

23.

Felicity

After Aly had left on the train to Galway, Felicity made her way back to her rooms with the intention of ringing Mia for a catch-up chat. Before she could do that, Shane called.

'Hey,' she said. 'I won't stay on long. I really need to get a bit of study done. I've so much cramming to do, it's unreal.'

'Fair enough,' Shane said evenly. 'Do you want to tell me what was going on with Aly last night?' he asked.

'Ah, it was nothing. Too much booze, I think. You know how things can get silly, even with the best of friends.'

'Right,' Shane didn't sound convinced.

'I'll see her again soon when the exams are over and I'm sure we'll be back on track again. These things happen. We're like sisters, myself and Alz. It's not worth worrying about,' Felicity said, trying to fob him off.

'The only thing is that she told me a few home truths while you were dancing with Andrew.'

'Really?' Felicity said, sounding cross.

'It seems she's been chatting to your mother quite a bit and the royal "we" have come to the conclusion that I'm not what you need.'

'Pardon?' Felicity said quietly.

'Apparently I'm too old and we're poles apart, our relationship is inappropriate and I've stood in the way of you having any kind of normal college life. Basically that if I hadn't taken up with you, things would be better for you.'

'What?' Felicity spat. 'According to whom?'

'Well your mother and Aly it seems.'

'And you know that's a load of horse shit obviously?' she said angrily. 'Shane?'

'Yeah.'

'Oh, Jesus, don't tell me you agree with them?'

'You know I don't, but, at the same time, do they have a point? If you weren't hooked up with me, would you hang out with the Freshers more and do more stuff with people your own age?' Shane asked.

'Just back up for a second,' Felicity said. 'Do you hold a gun to my head? Are we consenting adults?'

'Look, I know all that but I have to admit it used to cross my mind when we met at first.'

'Yes but that was quite a few months ago. Surely we've moved on since then?'

'Felicity, I love you and I want to be with you, but I think you should go to Galway and sort things out with your mum and Aly. Put your anger to one side and try to sort this out constructively,' Shane suggested. 'At least Aly had the guts to say what she thinks to my face. You have to see that she's only thinking of you.'

'If she was really concerned about me, she'd see that I'm happy and be glad for me. I think this is a case of the green-eyed monster – from both Aly and my mother.'

Felicity knew that it was a bad idea to act on anger. She probably should wait until the morning to speak to her mother, but she was so pissed off with the underhanded way Aly had acted and she wanted to get to the bottom of it all.

'Hello?' Mia said answering the phone.

'Mam, it's me,' Felicity said feeling like she wanted to murder someone. 'I'm going to come straight to the point. Aly left here a while ago and Shane just told me that she had a little word with him last night, to voice both of your opinions on our relationship. Firstly, I am an adult, secondly, if you want to say something in future, say it to me yourself.' Felicity slammed the phone down and burst into tears.

Mia replaced the phone in its old-fashioned cradle and sank into a chair. She dropped her head into her hands and took a deep breath, trying to stop the tears that were threatening. She felt suffocated with desire for things to be different, to have her daughter back again.

Shane sat and thought about what might be the best thing to do. Obviously Mia and Aly wanted shot of him. He was the big bad wolf who'd tainted little Red Riding Hood and led her astray. He tried to imagine life without Felicity …

Grabbing his keys, he headed out the door.

Felicity was supposed to be cramming. Her exams were just around the corner, but she was sitting in her room, sobbing like a fool. Fresh anger towards her mother and friend kept bubbling up inside her as she replayed the different conversations in her head.

Thanks a bunch you two, she thought bitterly. Now she'd probably fail and faced the prospect of sitting, stewing, in Galway for the entire summer. Bloody marvellous. This was just fan-fucking-tastic.

A knock on the door made her jump. She brushed her hand across her eyes to wipe away the tears and opened the door. When she saw Shane standing there, she fell into his arms.

'What are we going to do?' she asked as he shut the door and came inside.

'Well, the obvious thing to do is break up. That would make your mother and your friend much happier,' he said.

'Is that what you want?' She backed away from him.

'May I finish?'

'Sorry.'

'While that might be what they'd like right now, I've decided that's not happening. I love you. Whether it suits anyone else or not, that's the fact of the matter. I've been mulling this over for a bit as I know end of term is around the corner,' he said. 'Seeing as I'm already in the shithouse with your nearest and dearest, I figure I've nothing to lose, how would you feel about moving in with me?'

'What?' Felicity stared at him.

'I know you have three more years of your course and I don't want to change that. But I'm earning enough to pay the rent. I don't want to be without you for the next four months and why should you be in rooms when you could be at my place?'

'Well, I suppose I do spend three nights a week with you as it is,' Felicity said.

'Listen, you don't have to decide this now, in fact this is probably the worst time to mention this. I had intended to wait until you had finished your exams, but I didn't want the upset from last night to make you feel I don't want to be with you.'

Knowing she wasn't going to absorb a single thing from her books, Felicity decided to go for a drink with Shane at the local pub. After she calmed down, they chatted about what they both wanted and decided to give it a shot.

'Your mother is going to really hate this plan,' he said with regret. 'It might be a better idea to drive to Galway next weekend and speak to her in a calmer fashion.'

Felicity smiled. If this was what came of being with a slightly older guy, then all she could see was the positive aspects. Her instincts were to phone her mother and yell down the phone that she was moving in with Shane and that she and Aly could go and piss off. But as Shane pointed out, that wasn't going to solve anything.

'Okay, Mr Sensible. We'll do it your way,' Felicity decided. 'I hate this awful feeling with Mam and Aly. Fingers crossed we can sort it quickly.'

As it happened, Mia was unable to sleep after their earlier conversation. Just after midnight, Felicity's phone rang. Shane had gone home and she was alone in her rooms.

'Mam,' Felicity said sounding exhausted.

'I'm so dreadfully sorry, pet,' Mia said in a strangled voice.

'Me too, Mam,' Felicity sighed. 'I don't want us to fight.'

'Believe me, love, that's the last thing I want. Aly only acted on my insecurities. I should never have conspired with her behind your back like that,' Mia said. 'When I'm wrong, I say I'm wrong. I'm sorry.'

She knew they'd planned to speak to Mia together, but Felicity became caught in the moment and blabbed her plans to move in with Shane.

'Mam?' Felicity whispered, instantly wishing she hadn't said a word.

'I'm here, love,' Mia managed. 'If that's what you both want, then I'm very happy for you.'

'Really?'

'Really.'

Mia managed to keep the conversation going for long enough to convince her daughter that she was fine.

In the space of one phone call, the tables had turned. Felicity felt infinitely better and, in truth, Mia felt like Felicity had just killed a part of her stone dead.

24.

Daisy

It was May, and Daisy had finally finished college for the last time. She'd arranged to meet Ava for lunch to celebrate. Much as she'd tried to get her to call in, Ava never seemed comfortable with calling to the apartment, so it worked better to meet on neutral territory.

'So you're done and dusted,' Ava said, looking exhausted.

'Yup, feels pretty good. I've a couple of ideas for September, but I reckon the best plan will be to get my CV into as many places as possible and hope for the best.'

Sensing her mother was barely listening, Daisy leaned forward. 'Mum?'

'Oh, sorry, Daisy, I think I'm starting the change or something. I've been feeling really odd lately, kind of clammy and dizzy. Your father keeps telling me to go and have my bloods checked. I suppose I should really.'

'How is Dad?' Daisy asked, tucking into her salad. 'I rang him the other day and he was rushing to a meeting. I feel like I haven't spoken to him properly for an age.'

'He's fine, love. He'll be home tonight. Luke, too, for a visit. Jake is in good form as well, so everyone's happy.'

'Nathan's fine too, thanks for asking,' Daisy supplied.

'Good,' Ava said. 'How are you two getting on?'

'Great, he's working really long hours trying to get his new place up and running, but he's good.'

After the conversation moved on from Nathan, Daisy saw her mother visibly relax. Daisy was getting bloody sick of this resistance to Nathan. Did every girl have this crap with her parents, she wondered? Why couldn't they just agree to go along with the fact that he made her happy? What was the big deal? They only had to see him a few times a year if they hated him that much.

As they finished their lunch, Nathan arrived.

'Hi,' Daisy said, standing up to give him a kiss.

'Hi,' he responded. 'Hello, Ava.'

Instantly, Daisy felt her mother's hackles rise. She greeted him nicely, but as soon as she could, she made her excuses and left. As they walked towards St Stephen's Green to sit and chill out for a bit, they happened to pass the jewellers she'd been to with Freddie.

'Wow,' Daisy said with a slow whistle.

'What?' Nathan said stopping.

'That's the place I nearly got my engagement ring with Freddie,' she said.

'I thought you said he was a total penny-pincher,' Nathan said, looking at the boutique-style shop.

'He was, but that was the odd thing, he wanted me to have a flashy ring so he could show all his friends what a good provider he could be,' Daisy scoffed.

'Hey, I'll tell you what we'll do,' Nathan said spontaneously. 'Follow me.'

'What are you doing?' she asked, intrigued.

'The best way to get over your demons is by facing them. Let's go inside,' he said dragging her by the hand.

'Good afternoon,' an assistant greeted them.

'Hi,' Nathan said. 'Now, we'd like to see the cheapest engagement rings you guys hold.'

'Nathan?' Daisy looked slightly mystified.

'Pardon?' the assistant asked.

'Engagement rings? Cheap ones, though. We've no money and we want something that's really good value for money, if you know what I'm saying?'

A tray of rings with stones the size of specks was produced.

'Obviously if you're looking for a stone, you get what you pay for,' the lady explained. 'This one is pretty in my opinion.'

'That's code for cheap-assed shit,' Nathan whispered as Daisy giggled.

'Which one to do you like the least?' Nathan asked her, grinning.

'Eh, I'm not sure,' Daisy quipped. 'This has the smallest little stone, it's an odd murky blue too, what is this please?' she enquired trying to keep a straight face.

'That's a semi-precious stone called a tanzanite,' the lady said holding it up to the light in an attempt to make it look some way attractive.

'Try it on,' Nathan encouraged. She did and it slipped around Daisy's finger.

'It's about two sizes too large,' the lady said helpfully.

'Daisy,' Nathan grabbed her by the shoulders and turned her towards him. 'I love you and I want to marry you. I've wanted to ask you before, but I'm terrified that other ass-wipe has put you off marriage forever. So if I buy you this horrible, ill-fitting ring and promise you can wear the trousers and even beat me on occasion with the sweeping brush if that makes you happy,' he turned to the astonished assistant, 'she hits me when I annoy her.'

'I don't! Don't mind him, please,' Daisy said, dissolving into a fit of giggles.

'If I promise to be none of the things Freddie was, would you marry me?'

'Nathan you're a total oddball,' she said shaking her head.

'Is that a no?' he asked, looking suddenly shy.

Daisy looked up at him and realised with a shock that he was serious now. Yes, he was doing it all in a very strange way, but she suddenly knew that he was, in fact, asking her to be his wife. Her pulse raced and grabbed the edge of the counter for support. *My God, do I want this?* Nathan was still looking at her hopefully.

'No it's not a no,' she said quietly, taking his hand. 'It's a yes!' He smiled broadly and she shook her head in wonder. 'Jesus, Mary and Joseph, I can't believe I'm back in this shop getting an engagement ring! This is all a bit crazy.'

'Shall I have the ring sized to fit?' the lady asked looking totally confused.

'No!' they both answered in unison.

'Will I put it in a box?'

'No, thanks, I'll wear it,' Daisy said, grinning.

Nathan handed over his credit card. When the transaction was complete, they piled out onto the street.

'Holy cow! We're engaged!' Nathan said, scooping her into his arms. Depositing her on the footpath, he grabbed her hand and pulled her over to the cluster of for-hire bicycles. Releasing two bikes from their shackles, he offered Daisy one.

'What on earth are you doing now?' she asked.

'Let's go!' he shouted, and sped off. Nathan loved the gym and was seriously fit, so he'd no problem zipping off toward the huge park at the top of Grafton Street.

'I don't think we're meant to be zooming through here on these,' Daisy called. 'It's a *pedestrian* zone.'

By the time he pulled over and stopped, she was out of breath and sweating.

'God, I'm knackered. What was that all about?' she asked.

'I wanted this moment to stick in your mind, so you'd have a fun story to tell our grandchildren,' he said, pulling her into his arms.

'Nathan, you're a spacer!'

'I wanted you to see that it's possible to be in love and even get engaged without feeling as if it's the most boring and stuffy idea on earth!'

'Okay, point taken,' she said flopping onto the grass.

'And we don't have to do the big wedding thing unless you want to,' he assured her. 'You call the shots and I'll do what I'm told.'

'Why are you being so accommodating?' she asked suspiciously.

'I've wanted to marry you from the first moment we met. But I knew it would take some serious convincing to talk you around.'

As they lay on the grass chatting, Daisy looked down at the strange ring on her finger. As she roared laughing, he swatted her.

'What now?'

'Ah, it's just that Freddie was only concerned with what other people would think of the ring he was buying me. I think we can have a bit of fun with this one! Let's say nothing and see how people react!

'I think I should phone and make an appointment with your folks,' Nathan said, serious all of a sudden. 'I should ask for your hand in marriage.'

'Ah, to hell with to that. Whether my parents want to keep my hand or give it to you makes no odds, I'm marrying you, so there's your answer,' Daisy said bluntly.

Nathan agreed to a compromise: they had been invited to dinner at Daisy's home the following night because Justin would be back from the States. He agreed that they would go along and tell her parents together.

Daisy grinned at him. 'But I warn you, if they don't like it, they can lump it.'

'I love your attitude, Daisy Moyes,' he said softly, then pulled her into a lingering embrace.

Ava prepared a fantastic four-course meal to toast Justin's return. She was delighted to have him back with her again and wanted to spoil him a bit to celebrate. Luke and Jake and Charlotte and Daisy and Nathan were going to join them, which meant it was a proper family meal, but really she was looking forward to climbing into bed that night with her husband by her side. She sang to herself as she set the table and made everything look perfect, promising that she would make this a wonderful evening.

Jake and Charlotte arrived first and were brought into the sitting room. Justin poured drinks for everyone, and they relaxed on the sofa, catching up on the week's news. They heard the sound of a key scraping in the lock.

'Ah, well-timed,' Ava beamed. 'That'll be Daisy, and the bell on the cooker is about three minutes away from telling us the food is ready.'

They all looked expectantly at the sitting-room door. It was pushed open and Daisy stepped in, holding Nathan's hand and looking flushed and excited.

'We have an announcement to make!' she said with a giggle.

'You do?' Justin had gone the colour of putty and looked like he was going to pass out.

Daisy held out her left hand and a garish little ring slipped off-centre on her finger.

Ava clapped her hand over her mouth as a single word escaped her: 'No.'

25.

Felicity

Felicity's life couldn't have been busier if she'd tried. Somehow she managed to sit her exams, pack up her room and move in with Shane all inside the space of two weeks.

'Honey, I'm home!' Shane called out as Felicity lazed in bed. He'd only gone to Spar for a pint of milk, but now he had more than cereal on his mind, knowing Felicity was still in bed.

'Nice day at the office, dear?' Felicity stood at the bedroom door, batting her eyes at him.

Over an hour later, as she lay spent in Shane's arms, Felicity stared at the curtains.

'Would you object to me changing those?'

'Why? What's wrong with my gorgeous, nylon, ready-made ones? Don't you like the cough-medicine-meets-banana colour scheme? At least the lightshade matches,' Shane mused.

'I hate even touching those curtains. I've only been here a week but already I feel like one of those plasma balls, they've given me so many electric shocks. I reckon we should devise a way of powering the cooker with them,' Felicity grinned. Shane nuzzled her neck and told her she could have whatever her heart desired. Felicity vowed she'd spend her first month's summer pay cheque on some slightly more attractive interior stuff. She'd just found out she had landed a job in the local coffee shop. The pay wouldn't be huge, but it would be enough to tide her over until college started back in October.

The only fly in the ointment was Mia. Felicity still hadn't managed to get to Galway to see her mam since she'd moved in with Shane. The guilt she felt every time she spoke to her mother was threatening to ruin her happiness.

She'd spoken to Aly and although they'd both said they hated fighting, Felicity was still worried that they'd drifted apart. Aly insisted they were cool again, but Felicity hadn't forgotten the fact that her friend was still keeping something hidden from her.

Felicity's phone rang and she moved away to Shane to look at the screen. 'It's Mia,' she said to him. 'I want to take this.'

'No problem,' he said giving her a quick kiss. 'I'll hop in the shower.'

'How are you doing, Mam?' Felicity asked.

There was a sigh from the other end of the phone. 'I'm grand, love. Don't you go worrying about me.' Mia forced a little dry laugh.

'You don't sound convincing. Are you having a sad day?' Felicity asked kindly, wishing she could give her mother a hug. All the tragedy Mia had endured in life had a habit of getting her down every now and again. Felicity knew she was the best medicine for Mia when her heart ached. 'I wish I was there with you, Mam. At times like this, I hate being away from you,' Felicity said sounding choked.

'Don't go upsetting yourself now, girl. I'll be just fine,' Mia tutted. 'In fact, I have a little surprise. No pressure now at all you understand, but how would you feel about coming on a holiday with me?'

As it turned out, two weeks previously a grateful mother who'd gone into swift labour on her second baby had phoned Mia in terror, begging for her help. Mia had raced to her house and the birth had gone beautifully. When it was all over, Mia had accompanied the newly born infant and her shell-shocked parents to the maternity unit at the hospital. They were hugely grateful, but Mia shrugged it off as just doing her job. She'd gone home and thought no more about it, until a card with a voucher had arrived in the post that morning. It turned out that the baby's father's family owned a travel agents, and they had sent Mia a voucher for a holiday that could be taken any time before July.

'Would you consider coming with me?' Mia asked Felicity.

'That sounds gorgeous, Mam! Of course,' Felicity answered instantly. 'I was going to phone later to tell you I was planning to come to Galway for a few days, but this is even better!'

'I was so excited when I opened the envelope that I took the liberty of phoning the travel agents and asking them for some suggestions about where we could go. They suggested a little fishing village in

Spain. There's a small apartment complex there that's doing good pre-high season offers,' said Mia. 'How would that grab you?'

'That will be gorgeous, and when were you thinking of?' Felicity asked.

'How does the second week in June sound?'

Felicity had a quick think and decided that would work. 'Brilliant, Mam! I can't wait. I wanted to have a bit of time before starting work, so I'd already said to the job that I'd start in mid-June, so I should be able to swing that nicely.'

'And maybe you'd come to Galway for a night or two when we get back as well?' Mia ventured.

'Good plan,' Felicity said. 'That way I can pick up the rest of my stuff and see Aly and the lads.'

'I'm counting down the days already,' Mia said, sounding delighted.

Felicity put down the phone feeling miles better about everything. She knew Shane wouldn't mind her going away for a week, and she was genuinely looking forward to spending the quality time with her mam. The move in with Shane had been so sudden and she really wanted to make sure Mia was genuinely okay with it all.

As Mia replaced the receiver she shed a few tears. But unlike the ones she'd been crying in recent times, these were joyous. She might've known things would come good. She berated herself momentarily for being so negative lately. Her theory was still correct: a door had surely opened again in her life.

26.

Daisy

Ava had honestly thought Justin was having a coronary after Nathan and Daisy made their announcement. He gulped for air while gripping the pocket of his shirt so tightly, he actually caused a rip. His sons looked at him alarm, then tried to cover for him until he had regained the power of speech.

'Let me be the first to congratulate you both,' Luke stepped forward and shook Nathan's hand, banging him on the back. 'Well done, Daisy-doo, I hope you'll be very happy together.'

'Eh, yes. Congratulations, squirt! Good man yourself, Nathan,' Jake managed.

Charlotte hugged and kissed Daisy and found herself wrapped in Nathan's ample arms. Breathing in his musky aftershave, she fleetingly got a taste of why Daisy had fallen for this gorgeous man.

Ava swallowed the large lump in her throat and held her arms out to her daughter. As they embraced she whispered, 'Are you happy, sweetheart?'

'Mum, I'm on cloud nine!' Daisy whispered back.

She wasn't sure if the tears in her mother's eyes were ones of happiness or sorrow, but Daisy hoped she would support her choice either way.

'Daddy?' Daisy looked at Justin as Ava hugged Nathan.

'If this is what you want, darling, we're all behind you!' Try as he might, Justin couldn't quite get his mouth to smile. Instead, he produced an expression that might have been more fitting to an advert for constipation relief tablets.

Daisy hugged her dad and Nathan pumped his hand up and down.

'As you are aware, I am setting up a chain of indoor play areas for children, which has worked Stateside. So, fingers crossed, we'll be okay.'

'Well, I can't ask for more than that, I suppose,' Justin answered.

Champagne was produced, dinner was eaten and the conversation was kept to small talk. Nobody stayed late, so Justin and Ava managed to hold it all together until their children departed. Luke was staying with Charlotte and Jake that night so that the brothers could head out for an early round of golf the following morning. Daisy and Nathan headed off into the night, twined around each other.

Ava and Justin waved them all off from the front door, then closed the door and stood looking at each other in dismay. Justin stalked off to the living room and Ava followed him, dreading the outburst she knew was to come. She was right, as soon as she walked into the room, Justin exploded in a rage, almost unable to articulate his emotions, he was so overcome with anger.

'*Do* something about this, Ava. You told me to trust you. You said it would all be fine,' he lashed out, pacing up and down. 'This is about as far from fine as I can imagine.'

'Justin, please calm down,' Ava said tiredly. 'I'm just as overwhelmed as you are. I can't cope with you raging at me like this.'

Justin took a deep breath and ran his hand through his hair. 'I've an idea,' he said, looking intently at her, 'why don't you take Daisy off for a break, a spa weekend, whatever. Just the two of you, so you can talk properly, mother to daughter?'

'Okay, Justin, I was wrong. I thought it was all a flash in the pan,' Ava said, sitting down heavily on the sofa. 'I don't know what we can do, though. Daisy is twenty-two. She's not a child and, by God, she knows her own mind. She's never been any different …' Ava trailed off.

'Look at the bloody ring he gave her. They're not even taking this engagement seriously. Then they're talking about having the wedding in Vegas one minute and in the fecking woods the next. It's all bananas!'

'All right, Justin, all right,' Ava sighed. 'I'll think of a break for us. If it's just the two of us, with no other distractions, I'll be able to talk to her gently and hopefully she'll see sense,' Ava said, not feeling too convinced.

Justin was right about one thing: they owed it to their daughter, and to themselves, to ensure she was making the right decision.

'I'll talk to Daisy in the morning and talk to Maureen at the travel agents, see if she has any good suggestions,' she told him.

'The sooner you get her to see sense, the better,' Justin said darkly.

Ava rubbed her temples. 'Darling, can you pour me a brandy, please. I need something to steady my nerves. '

As Justin poured her drink, Ava watched him, wondering how far he would push this. In her heart of hearts, she felt it would be like pushing against the ocean, to try to change Daisy's mind. Not for the first time, she wondered why it was always the mother who was expected to provide the oil to pour on troubled waters.

27.

Tally

Martin put his key in the door, balancing the flowers and wine he was carrying precariously. Tally's exams were over and it was time to celebrate. As the door swung open, though, he was greeted by the sound of a blazing argument – yet again.

'I was only trying to show my interest. Sorry for breathing,' Greta snapped.

Martin quietly walked down the hall and peered through the kitchen door. The two women were squared up to one another, both looking furious.

'Is that what you call it?' Tally shot back. 'We've made some huge changes around here. We cook all our meals from scratch, we haven't had a take-away for months, all the fizzy orange is gone and we drink water with lemon in it now,' Tally used her fingers to count the changes. 'We're exercising – probably not enough in your books, but we're really pushing hard, Ma. Whatever about me, I'll never put a foot right, but the least you could do is encourage Da.' Tally stormed off to her room.

'What did I do?' Greta called out.

Martin sighed and stepped into the kitchen. 'Just leave her for a while,' he said gently to his wife. 'If she's feeling the way I am, she's bloody exhausted and a bit emotional.'

'Christ almighty, I'm wrong if I don't say a thing, then I'm worse if I do!' Greta threw her arms up and marched into the living room.

Martin parked the wine and flowers on the sideboard and shook his head. He decided he could do with a hot shower to calm down.

When he came out from the shower, Tally's bedroom door was firmly shut and Greta had gone to bed too. With a heavy heart, he decided to make himself a cup of green tea before turning in for the night himself. He'd really hoped that Tally's new-found confidence would smooth her relationship with her mother, but so far it seemed to be making things worse. If Martin could keep going with the new regime and feel the way he used to when he was a younger man, he'd be thrilled. But more than anything else, he wished the two women he loved most in the world could, at least, find common ground.

After a restless night, first thing the next morning Martin phoned Sinead and requested a one-to-one meeting, saying he'd love to chat about a couple of issues.

'Sure, Martin, that's what I'm here for,' Sinead agreed immediately.

'Can you promise me something, though?' he whispered. 'Don't tell Tally I'm coming. I'll explain when I see you.'

'Okay,' Sinead said. 'What I say and do with each client is always confidential, Martin, you know that.'

'I know, but please just don't mention I'm coming this time if you can possibly avoid it,' he begged.

Martin looked petrified as he walked into Sinead's consultation room that evening.

'Hi, Martin, come on in,' Sinead said calmly.

'I feel like I'm having an affair or something, creeping in here like this,' Martin quipped.

'I should be so lucky!' Sinead giggled. 'What's up?' she said, getting straight to the point.

'I'm struggling with my women,' Martin began. 'Greta and Tally have never seen eye-to-eye, as you well know. But over the years I've managed to act as go-between and it's been manageable. But since Tally has started this programme, and indeed her college course with your good self, she's changed.'

'Isn't that a good thing?' Sinead asked.

'Of course it is, Sinead, but as she's grown in confidence, the clashes with her ma have increased ten-fold,' Martin said miserably. 'The atmosphere in the house is terrible and I feel like they'll scratch each other's eyes out at any moment. I can't handle it anymore.'

Sinead felt for the poor man. He was so sincere and desperate for a resolution to this unending feud he had to live with.

'Can I make a suggestion?' Sinead finally answered, having thought it over for a moment.

'Please do, love.'

'How about you step out of the equation for a bit?' she said. 'If you're always there to attempt to diffuse bad situations, it means they don't have to try to resolve their differences. Am I correct?'

'Yes … I suppose you are,' Martin said hesitantly.

'So if you don't do it for them, they'll have to figure it out. They're both adults now. It's not up to you to act as a referee for the rest of your days. That's not fair to anyone,' Sinead said logically.

'What do you suggest? That I go and live in a homeless shelter for a year and let them beat seven shades out of one another?'

'It's hardly going to come to that!' Sinead said gently. 'They are civilised women, don't forget.'

'Are they? You'd need to see them to know what I live with,' Martin said sadly.

'Would a holiday be possible?' Sinead asked.

'I'd hate to go away on my own,' Martin said uneasily.

'Then send them off together, just for a week. Maybe a neutral venue with a bit of sun and no Martin to step in and lead the way might do them the world of good?' Sinead sat back and smiled. 'Tally's exams are done and dusted and I've no doubt she'd appreciate a holiday. She's worked damn hard all year.'

'They mightn't thank me for it,' Martin said biting his lip.

'You can bet your ass they won't be ecstatic about the whole thing, but both of them love you, Martin. You have that power. If you organise the trip as a surprise and tell them the purpose of it, I think they'll give it a shot,' Sinead reckoned. 'If you explain how hard the tension has been for you, I'm guessing they'll at least try to change.'

Martin thanked Sinead and said he'd give it some serious consideration. By the time he walked in the door at home, tired, hungry and emotional, all he wanted was to sit and relax for the evening. He was met by Tally's retreating back, followed by a slamming door and his wife pacing up and down, puffing on her cigarettes like a madwoman.

'That girl is just getting on my wick,' Greta shouted. 'I'm not allowed to open my mouth anymore. All I asked her was how far she'd run and suggested she use a heart monitor. Well, Jesus, you'd think I'd offered her heroin!'

Tally appeared at the top of the stairs. 'It wasn't that, Ma. It was the way you sneered when I told you that I'd managed to keep jogging for twenty minutes,' Tally sobbed. 'I know that's not even a warm-up for you, but I'm trying. I'm doing my best. For me, fat lazy bitch that I am, it's a whole new concept. It was a personal best. But you just can't see that. Nothing is ever good enough for you!'

Bang. The door slammed again.

'See? Listen to the abuse I'm getting!' Greta shouted up the stairs.

Martin went into the kitchen and flicked on the kettle as his wife followed.

'She's turned into a right madam over the past while and I'm not having it, Martin,' Greta fumed. 'She can either change her tune or move out!'

Martin couldn't listen to any more. He abandoned his tea and climbed the stairs and went to bed. As he lay in the darkness of the room, all he could think about was Sinead's suggestion about the holiday. If he didn't try it, the odds were that Tally would move out or Greta would throw her out. The wedge driven between the two would be wider than ever and who knew, maybe they'd never get over it?

Martin didn't want to spend the rest of his life visiting their daughter on his own and trying to get Greta to speak to her. He could picture horrible Christmas mornings where neither would talk to the other. Birthdays where he signed Tally's card and Greta refused. He knew plenty of families who didn't speak. Then a parent would eventually die and nothing was ever resolved.

There was only the three of them. They needed each other. He didn't want to be piggy in the middle any more. Martin nodded to himself. That was it, decision made. He was going to book a surprise holiday for them. Throwing them together could go either way, he was aware of that, but the alternative looked like it was only going to end badly. Sinead was right – it was worth a shot.

A few days later, Martin arrived home from work with a definite spring in his step. When he walked into the kitchen, Greta looked at him suspiciously, but said nothing. He hugged her, then opened the door and called up the stairs for Tally to come down and join them, telling her that he had something to say.

When both women were seated at the table, looking questioningly at him, he almost bottled it. He took a deep breath and forced himself to speak cheerfully. 'I have a surprise for the two of you. You have to hear me out.'

'What have you done, Martin Keller? I know that look, you're up to something,' Greta said.

'I've booked a holiday … for the two of you. How does Spain for a week sound? I got a great deal at the beginning of June in a fantastic looking resort!'

'That's next week! I presume you're coming, too?' Tally said, looking mildly panicked.

'Ah, that's the thing. So many of the lads have been let go at the job, I can't go off this year, but I want my girls to have a holiday.'

Tally and Greta regarded one another for a moment.

'I don't think that'll work,' Tally said doubtfully. 'Why don't you and Ma go on your own?'

'That'd be nice,' Greta agreed.

'I told you I can't leave the job,' Martin was firm. 'The other thing …' He stopped and looked unsure. 'Well, the other thing, to be honest, is that I'm at the end of my tether with the fighting in this house. I can't deal with it any longer. You two need to find some way of communicating with each other that doesn't involve shouting. It's making me almost ill to be caught in the middle all the time. I need you two to try this.' He looked at them hopefully.

Tally's heart broke to see her dad looking so worried and so hopeful at the same time. Why hadn't she seen the extent of his suffering? She glanced over at Greta, who looked as upset as she felt.

'That's very kind of you, Da,' Tally said, looking pained. 'I'm sorry if it's been unpleasant for you at home.'

'Yes, you're a real trooper,' Greta said, eyes darting from her husband back to her daughter. 'I'm sorry too, you know, about the rows.'

'Good. That's settled then.' Martin kissed them both and grinned. 'You two are officially off to sunny Spain.'

28.

Daisy

Ava sat opposite Maureen in the travel agents with a fixed smile on her face.

'There are some great deals right now. It's always brilliant to get away before the schools break up,' Maureen said as her false fingernails clicked on the computer keyboard. 'My two are still at school. I can't wait to be in a position to go away with one or other of them for a grown-up holiday like this.'

'Daisy is so excited,' Ava lied. 'Your time will come, Maureen.'

'Oh, I know and I shouldn't wish the years away but it must be just fabulous to know that you're almost on a par with your daughter at this stage. More like friends? I feel like the only thing I ever say is "no" or "stop that",' Maureen laughed.

'It's exhausting when they're little, Maureen. But each stage has its disadvantages. At least you know where your two are and who they're with at all times.'

'I suppose,' Maureen replied, scanning the screen in front of her. 'Oh, now here's a stunning little development in Spain. I think you'll both love it.'

Ava sat forward as Maureen found the place in the brochure and circled it with her pen.

'It looks perfect,' Ava said after a moment. 'Let me show Daisy and I'll let you know.'

As soon as Ava got back to her car, she called Daisy. 'Hi, darling, I've a little surprise and was wondering if could I swing by?'

'Sure, Mum. We're only messing around so whenever suits,' Daisy chirped.

'Would right now be okay?'

'Of course, I'll put the kettle on.'

Half an hour later as Ava waited for Daisy to answer her buzzer, she tried to ignore her emotional turmoil.

'Ava! Come on in. Long time no see.' Nathan opened the front door to the apartment and stood aside to let Ava in to the small hall.

'Nathan, hi,' Ava replied as she passed him.

'Hey, Mum,' Daisy appeared in the hall and hugged Ava. 'Coffee?'

'Love one, thanks, honey.' Ava followed Daisy into the kitchen and sat down at the table fanning the travel brochures out in front of her. Daisy paused. 'What have you got there?'

'Oh,' Ava was momentarily stumped. She hadn't thought of how she was going to convince Daisy to come away with her. She'd been in such a hurry to organise everything, that she hadn't actually planned her strategy.

'Are youself and Justin planning a vacation?' Nathan leaned up against the kitchen counter.

'No, actually I was hoping Daisy and I might,' Ava replied hesitantly.

'Really?' Daisy turned to face her mother looking mildly surprised.

'I thought it would be lovely for the two of us to have some mother-daughter time …' Noticing her daughter's eyes narrowing momentarily, Ava felt like the walls were closing in on her.

Acutely aware of Nathan, Ava noted how relaxed and comfortable he and Daisy seemed. 'Dad and I were chatting and I was saying that I'd love a week away,' she went on. 'A girly week. You know how good he is, so he said he'd treat us. It would be kind of a—'

'A bonding week before I steal her away,' Nathan finished grinning.

'Yes, precisely,' Ava's voice wobbled.

'Why exactly do you want me to go away, Mum?' Daisy asked defensively.

'I think we need to reconnect,' Ava said simply.

'I'm not disconnected, Mum,' Daisy swiveled and put her arms around Nathan looking up at him. 'In fact I feel more stable and content than I ever thought possible.'

Nathan smiled down at her.

'Look at this gorgeous place Maureen suggested,' Ava said in a brighter tone leafing through the brochures on the table. Daisy disengaged herself from Nathan's arms and sat down opposite her mother.

'Great,' she said evenly, holding her mother's gaze.

'I think it sounds like fun,' Nathan said, surprising both women.

'You do?' Ava asked.

'Sure. I know you girls are going to go into wedding overdrive and want to talk about girly stuff so why not do it in the sunshine?'

'Exactly,' Ava said, pouncing on the shred of positivity Nathan had offered. 'We have so much to talk about and rather than me landing in on both of you all the time we could sort it this way.'

'I don't know.' Daisy looked suspicious. 'We're only engaged. I don't think I want to go anywhere at the moment.'

'Jeez, Daisy. I'll go if you don't want to!' Nathan said, banging the milk carton on the table. 'You don't mind me not finding a jug do you, Ava?' he grinned.

'Oh, no,' Ava said trying not to panic inside. 'Look at the brochure, Daisy.' She pushed it towards her daughter.

Daisy flicked to the page marked with the post it note and glanced at it for the shortest time. 'I'll think about it, Mum. Thanks for the offer but as I said I'm not sure that I want to leave this great big hunk of love,' she said, tweaking Nathan's nose. She picked up her mug of coffee and slurped it noisily.

'Daisy, you know I can't abide slurping,' Ava said automatically. As their eyes met Daisy raised an eyebrow.

Ava had never been so delighted by the diversion of a packet of biscuits.

'I'm addicted to Jaffa Cakes,' Nathan said, munching happily. 'I'd never even seen one until last week. They're so good.' He offered Ava one.

'Thanks, they are nice,' she agreed, accepting one gratefully.

'Since when do you eat biscuits, Mum?' Daisy said, refusing to cut her mother any slack. The tension in the air was reaching a point where it was fairly obvious a row was brewing.

'Show me the place you're thinking of Ava,' Nathan said, glancing at Daisy.

Ava pushed the brochures towards Daisy and Nathan. 'It seems a little off the beaten track but the travel agent assures me it's very relaxing,' she explained.

'Daisy?' Nathan said calmly.

'Yeah, I suppose it does look quite nice.' Daisy put the brochures back down on the table.

'So will you think about coming? It's just we should book as soon as we can. Before we miss out on the deal and all that.'

'I'll think about it,' Daisy said grudgingly.

'Okay.' Ava sighed and continued. 'Anyway, I don't mean to be rude but I'm going to get back to Justin. He's not home for long this time and we've a few things to do today.' Ave downed the rest of her coffee with such speed she was sure she'd burned her oesophagus. She knew if she stayed longer an argument would be inevitable.

'I'll give you a call later on and maybe we could have a chat,' she said as she stood up to leave.

'Whatever,' Daisy replied moodily.

As Ava gathered her bag and car keys she made a point of pushing the brochure towards Daisy again. 'You two finish your coffee. I'll let myself out.'

As her mother closed the front door, Daisy dipped a Jaffa Cake into her coffee.

'Well?' Nathan said, hugging her.

'Well what?' Daisy replied.

'Aren't you even going to consider your mother's offer? I think it's really nice of her. This must be sort of painful for her to have to let her little girl go. It's one thing us living together but now that she knows I'm here to stay…' He kissed her on the nose. 'Maybe you should help her out and go on this vacation? Come on, don't tell me you wouldn't enjoy a week chilling out by the pool?'

Swept along by his happiness, Daisy forgot about being stubborn and sulky with her parents. Maybe this was their way of saying sorry for being iffy about Nathan.

'You're right. It could be fun,' she conceded. 'It looks seriously enticing when I look out the window at the rain and drizzle here. Some blue skies would be pretty amazing.'

All the same, Daisy decided to wait until later that afternoon before she called her parent's house.

'Hi, Daisy,' Justin answered the phone later that evening. 'How are you?'

'Fine thanks, Dad,' she replied. 'Did you sleep last night or were you in a horrible state of jetlag?'

'I slept well, considering, love.'

'Listen, I've chatted to Nathan so I'm just calling to speak to Mum about this holiday idea.'

'Oh, right,' Justin said evenly. 'It sounds like a lovely place. Maureen has never let us down before.'

'True,' Daisy conceded. 'Anyway, I'd love to go and thanks for offering to pay.'

'Pleasure,' Justin smiled down the phone, feeling a massive relief. 'Hold on and I'll get your mother. She'll be delighted.'

Ava came on the line and promised to book the whole thing.

'I'll let you know the details as soon as I speak to Maureen.'

'Okay, thanks, Mum,' Daisy hung up the phone with mixed feelings. She desperately wanted her parents to share in her happiness and decided to view this trip as their olive branch.

29.

Tally

As the departure day got closer, Tally began to fret constantly.

'The thought of this week with Ma is terrifying,' she confessed to Sinead during a final weigh-in before flying out.

'A holiday with your mother mightn't be as bad as you're anticipating,' Sinead said, trying to calm her nerves.

'I hope you're right,' Tally sighed.

'Guess what?' Sinead said, her eyes shining.

'What?'

'I've got an offer for you!'

'What do you mean?' Tally looked stunned.

'Each year, our top five students are offered a place on an advanced course. If you choose to go for it, you'll be pretty certain of a job offer afterwards. It's a wonderful accolade, Tally, and the panel has selected you as the top choice. Do you think you'd be interested?'

Tally responded by throwing her arms around her friend and hugging her. She was speechless with excitement – to have her hard work acknowledged in this way was beyond her wildest dreams.

'How about a drink to celebrate?' Sinead suggested.

'Love to!' Tally said, smiling delightedly.

Tally had promised herself she'd use her year to change. She'd vowed to qualify as a beauty therapist and try to turn her life around. Here she was, less than twelve months later, well on her way to becoming a new woman. Filled with hope and vigour, Tally grabbed her bag and coat and left the Motivation Mate office with Sinead feeling like she was walking on air.

'Just think, this time next week, you'll be lying in the sun, basking in heat, without so much as a care for me back here freezing my ass off in an Irish summer!' Sinead teased.

'I'm still dreading the holiday, if I'm honest,' Tally admitted.

'Try and go with an open mind,' Sinead said diplomatically. The sound of Sinead's phone beeping caused her to root like a maniac in her oversized bag. 'Sometimes I wish I had a tiny handbag that just fitted my wallet, keys and phone.'

She pulled out the phone and read her message. 'It's Ben,' she said, glancing up at Tally. 'If you'd rather it was just the two of us, that's fine, but he was just wondering if I was around for a drink?'

Automatically, Tally could feel her cheeks flush at the mention of his name. She thought about him quite a lot in the privacy of her own room. It wasn't something she'd ever divulge to anyone. Besides, she knew he was out of her league and only tolerated her as she was a friend of Sinead's.

'Oh, no, I mean yes …' Tally stuttered. 'Sure, if he's around, I'd love to see him.'

As they arrived at the bar a short while later, Ben was walking towards them from the other side of the road.

'Perfect timing!' Ben said, kissing Tally on both cheeks.

'How's it going?' Sinead said, hugging him warmly.

They ordered drinks and tapas and perched on high stools at the bar.

'This place is always buzzy, I love that. Nothing worse than sitting in a place with no atmosphere and no punters. I always think the food must've been sitting there for days if they're not busy,' Ben commented as he glanced around at the gaggles of twenty-somethings standing at high tables or seated at the lower round tables. It was Spanish themed insofar as it was a tapas bar, but the style was crisp and cool with plenty of chrome against a black and white décor.

'This is pretty cool all right,' Tally smiled. Ben sat in the middle, so the girls were both able to chat to him.

'I prefer sitting up here so we can have full scanning scope,' Ben said. 'If you look in the mirrors behind the bar, you can see everyone without being caught staring!'

Tally was acutely aware of his proximity. Once or twice, the swivelled stools swung around slightly as they dipped into the bowl of olives and their legs touched.

'Sorry, I keep swinging into you I'm so eager to get at the food!' Tally apologised.

'He could do with a bit of a beating to keep him in check!' Sinead teased.

'Charming, huh?' Ben winked at Tally. 'My big sis here has always bullied me. Some things never change!'

'So Tally here is off to sunny Spain, the lucky thing,' Sinead said, putting a tasty morsel into her mouth.

'Yup, a bonding session with a mother I have about as much as common with as a tractor,' Tally said dryly.

'Well maybe you'll "find" one another,' Ben suggested.

'I'm not exactly incognito and Ma is just on her own planet. If we can spend the week tolerating each other and come home without having a massive blow-out, I'll be happy,' Tally said. 'I'm doing it for my da, to be honest. He's sick of being caught in the middle of arguments.'

'So tell Ben about your course offer, Missus,' Sinead prompted.

'What's all this?' Ben asked.

'I've been selected as one of the top five students to do an advanced year in Skin Deep in September!' Tally announced.

'Wow! That's amazing! I'm made up for you Tally,' Ben said as he hopped down off his high stool and hugged her tightly.

As he pulled away, there was a moment where the entire room froze for Tally. She felt drunk, even though she'd only had half a spritzer.

Ben climbed back onto his stool and grinned across at her.

'I'm delighted,' Sinead said. 'It'll be brilliant to have you around again.'

'Aw, thanks, Sinead,' Tally said sincerely. 'I'm just over the moon.'

The evening went by far too quickly and before they knew it, the lights were flashed on and off to signal closing time.

'I've really enjoyed seeing you both,' Tally said, hugging them outside.

'Enjoy every minute of the holiday and try to be calm. Don't rise to the jibes with Greta and I'll bet you'll see a change in her,' Sinead advised. 'You lead the way by being pleasant and, fingers crossed, she'll follow suit.'

'Aye, aye, captain!' Tally saluted. 'Thanks, Sinead. You're a star,' Tally said hugging her again.

'Oh, I think I see a taxi, I'll run and flag it,' Sinead said, running to the kerbside, leaving Ben and Tally alone.

'Have fun, and maybe we could meet up for a drink or something when you get back?' Ben suggested, looking a bit shy.

'Sure, I'd love that,' Tally felt like she was going to collapse. Her heart was thumping in her chest and she knew she was probably the colour of a boiled beetroot. 'I'll give Sinead a buzz and we can organise something.'

'I was kind of meaning just the two of us. I try to do without my chaperone at least once a year!' Ben joked. 'Can I get your number and give you call?'

'I'd really like that,' Tally managed. Her voice was very uneven and she knew she must have a face on her that looked like he'd just asked her to skydive naked in front of a crowd of ten thousand.

'You don't sound so sure …' Ben blushed. 'I'll text you and you can think about it. That way you can let me down gently if you're not into it.' He smiled and tried not to look mortified.

'No – please. You're taking my silly reaction as rejection. I'm just shocked that you want to see me, that's all,' Tally said, her heart thumping. 'It's not every day I have a guy like you asking me for my number. I'd love nothing more than to go out with you.'

Ben smiled shyly at her and nodded.

'I think we've made your sister want to disappear in a puff of smoke!' Tally giggled. They exchanged numbers and Tally prayed Ben couldn't see how much her hands were shaking as she entered his name into her contacts.

'She'll be fine!' Ben smiled over at her. 'Have a great trip and I'll call you when you get back.' He leaned over and kissed her on the lips. It was only a quick peck, but it was enough to make Tally realise that it obviously meant he was interested.

As she jumped into a passing taxi and waved to Sinead and Ben, Tally waited until the car turned the corner before she let out the loudest scream she could muster.

'Holy shit, are you trying to make us crash?' the taxi driver yelled, swerving dangerously and narrowly missing the side of a dustbin.

'Sorry,' Tally giggled. 'Ben just kissed me and said he's going to call!' she yelled.

'Fucking marvellous for Ben, but if you do that again, he'll be kissing your corpse.'

Tally was walking on air. She gave the grumpy taxi man a tip and stood waving enthusiastically at him as he drove off. Even if the sky had fallen down at that moment, nothing would have killed her spirit.

Martin was in the sitting room having a cup of herbal tea. A year ago, it would've been a hot chocolate and Lord knows how many empty wrappers would have been surrounding him on the couch.

'Hi love, good night?' he called.

'The best! I met Sinead and her brother, Ben. Great people. I'm so lucky to have found them. How was your day?' Tally asked. She decided not to mention the kiss. It was early days and she was still in such disbelief herself, she didn't want to jinx any possible future romance.

'All good my end, thank God.'

'Guess what?' said Tally.

'What?' Martin sat up straight.

'I've been offered a place on an advanced course! Starting September, you are looking at one of five people who've been hand-picked to do a further year at Skin Deep! Sinead says I'll be almost guaranteed a job at the end of it.'

'Oh, my God, that's fantastic news,' Martin said jumping up to hug her. 'Now your holiday will be even more of a celebration, won't it?' he asked dubiously.

'You bet. I'm going to make a real effort to get on with Ma while we're away,' Tally promised. 'I'll miss you, Da. Will you be all right here on your own?'

'I'll be great. I've my weigh-in at the end of the week, too, so I'll behave while you're gone,' he promised.

Martin had trimmed down incredibly. So much so, he'd fished out some old clothes from the back of his wardrobe.

'Da, I don't mean to be rude, but what in the name of God are you wearing?' Tally asked as she looked down at her father's denim-encased legs.

'What do you think? Sexy or what?' he stood up grinning from ear to ear, modelling the most God-awful pair of jeans Tally had seen in a long time.

'Oh, flaming Nora, Da. They fit you, but they're mad-looking!

You'll be arrested if you go out in them! You look like Shakin' Stevens!' Tally squealed.

'You're just jealous! I think I'm deadly. Right, let's put on a bit of music and have a quick jive around. If you do that with me, I might get the idea of wearing these out of my system,' he said with a grin. 'Come on and dance with your auld da before you go and leave me for the week!'

They pumped up the stereo and amidst roars and hoots, the two of them bopped around the room.

Feeling suddenly brave, Martin leapt off the coffee table and did an attempt at the splits in the air. The ripping noise as his jeans disintegrated from the crotch to the waist made Tally collapse in a heap on the floor.

'Stop, I'm going to be sick!' she laughed. 'That's that sorted at least. Da, I think it might be time to go shopping for new jeans.'

As he stood staring in dismay at his wrecked trousers, he grinned at his daughter. 'I think this is taking the ripped look a bit far all right!'

Greta appeared, looking very confused. 'What is going on in here? I'm trying to get some shuteye. Ah, Martin, what are you wearing, love?' Her expression changed from puzzled to a smirk.

'I found them earlier and Tally thought I looked terrible. I think I'm like a young one again!' he said, bursting out laughing. 'We were celebrating, Tally got a place on the elite team in the beauty college,' Martin explained.

'Good one, Tallulah!' Greta said smiling.

'Thanks, I'm thrilled,' Tally said. 'At least those jeans are torn now so he can't go out in public in them,' Tally said, wiping tears of laugher from her eyes.

'I actually think they're kind of sexy,' Greta said, sidling up to her husband.

'Ew! You two are mental. I'm going to bed,' Tally said, laughing.

'So are we!' Greta called back.

Tally was feeling the love after her little kiss with Ben, so she called back good-naturedly, 'Behave yourselves, you're being inappropriate!'

Mothers and Daughters ...

30.

'Ladies and gentleman, this is Captain Flynn. We are delighted to have you on board this afternoon. At present we are cruising at thirty-two thousand feet, but we will begin our descent in about twenty-five minutes. You'll all be delighted to hear that the weather in Puerto Primo, indeed across Spain, is a balmy thirty degrees, with cloudless skies. That's a lot nicer than what we just left behind in Ireland, thankfully. I hope you'll enjoy the rest of the flight and also your stay in this beautiful coastal region of southern Spain.'

Felicity and Mia were busily opening all the little packages of food on the plane.

'I'm not even hungry after that huge breakfast in the airport, but I have to say I'll never tire of the thrill airplane food gives me,' Mia said excitedly.

'Mam, how are you eating any of that? It's vile, just look at the slab of waxy cheese and the crackers look like you could break your teeth on them. The dessert thing looks like it was made ten years ago and varnished to keep it from going mouldy. What is it even supposed to be?' Felicity said, poking it with her plastic fork.

'It's not bad actually, it's some sort of custard slice,' Mia announced, wagging her foot in delight.

'Mam, you're hilarious!'

Felicity shook her head as she grinned at her mother. They'd had an emotional reunion at Dublin airport that morning. Shane had dropped Felicity off and stayed for a quick coffee before leaving the two women.

'I'm just so excited to be here, and the thought of a week in the sun with you is just the business. I'm on a high!' Mia said with smile. She looked happier than Felicity had seen her look for a long time.

'Chop, chop, shift yourself, coming through!'

Felicity and Mia glanced at one another and tried to stifle a giggle as a very skinny, über-tanned woman in a tight white jeans with peroxide cropped hair stood up from the middle seat in the row directly ahead of them.

'Tallulah, I'm bursting, get a move on there. Are you glued to the chair or what?'

A flushed-looking girl, whom Felicity would describe as curvy, pulled herself free of the seat. 'Sorry, Ma, its not the most spacious of planes. You go on ahead there.'

'Its hardly the plane's fault,' the skinny woman retorted.

As the young girl looked back and met Felicity's gaze, they shared a quick smile. The girl was voluptuous, with dark glossy hair and flawlessly smooth skin. As Felicity watched her pulling self-consciously at the smock top she was wearing, she noticed her nails were beautifully manicured and she had stunningly beautiful features. Unlike her brash mother, the girl seemed very sweet.

Tally perched on the arm rest of the aisle seat, figuring it would be easier to wait until her mother returned from the bathroom rather than shoe-horn herself into the cramped seat only to get out again five minutes later. The charter flight was filled to capacity and it was one of the older models that seemed to be designed for people with no legs who weighed as much as a gnat.

'Are you waiting to go to the toilet?' Greta called loudly as she marched back towards her.

'No, Ma, I'm just waiting to let you back into your seat. Keep your voice down, will you?' Tally said with embarrassment.

'Why? There's no shame in doing a wee. For goodness sake, Tallulah, you can be the strangest girl, do you know that? I don't know where I got you from sometimes.'

Greta pushed past her daughter and sat back down.

Ava and Daisy had heard the exchange, along with the rest of the plane. 'God I hope they're not staying near us. She's the real type who'd be over poking her nose into everything day and night,' Daisy said.

'I don't honestly care who's there as long as we have a nice relaxing week with no worries,' Ava said, lying back into her seat.

By the time the plane touched down at Malaga airport, it was lunchtime and the hottest part of the day. When the plane doors opened and the passengers stepped out onto the steps leading down to the tarmac, they were hit by a wall of heat.

The luggage carousel wasn't far from the entrance to the terminal building, and was surrounded by groups of people three deep, all jostling for a space to spot their bags.

'If we just hang back for a few minutes, we'll find it easier,' said Mia practically. 'We have our transfer organised privately, they won't leave without us, so there's no panic.'

One woman who didn't share Mia's philosophy was Greta Keller.

'Come on, Tallulah, elbow your way in there like a good girl. The quicker we get our stuff, the better. I want to get to this resort and get changed and go for a run. After sitting like a lump of lard on that flight, I feel like a caged tiger,' she huffed. 'Excuse us, sorry now. Coming through,' she said, pushing Tally by the small of her back.

'Ma, take it easy, please. This isn't helping anyone. There's a lady ahead of me with a little boy, stop pushing me, please!'

'Oh, right, you might smother the little fecker! Sorry!' Greta cackled at her own joke.

Tally's immediate instinct was to turn around and tell her ma to sod off and that if she pushed her once more, she'd box her in the face. But she remembered the promise she'd made to her dad and Sinead. She wasn't going to rise to the nasty behaviour. She was going to be calm and pleasant and hope Greta reacted nicely.

'I'll tell you what, I'll grab our bags if you want to go and find a trolley?' Tally suggested.

She owed it to the two people who were rooting for her to give this week a fair trial. Taking a deep breath, she tried to remind herself that she and her ma were just different.

'Just move on ahead there, Tallulah.' Greta was still acting like they were the front row of a rugby scrum. 'What we need to do now is dive in, snatch the bags and run. Oh, there's my bag, snatch it, Tallulah!' Greta yelled, pointing.

Why does she have to make everything sound like a race or a competition? Tally mused. All the same, she did as she was told. It was simply easier than causing an out and out row at the side of a carousel.

'Good girl, yourself. See, wasn't too difficult, was it?' Greta said patronisingly. 'I'll be out front having a ciggy.'

Tally felt herself relax as her mother bustled towards the exit. At least she could wait for her own bag in peace without being bawled at.

The crowd thinned within minutes, enabling Mia and Felicity to find their bags more easily. They too made their way into the arrivals hall.

Tally could feel her underarms beginning to soak with sweat. Grabbing a tissue from her handbag, she dabbed at her forehead and willed herself to remain calm. If her bag had got lost, she'd figure it all out. Although the nasty goblin voice in her head was trying to prick tears in her eyes. *If your bag doesn't come out, you're snookered. Nothing your mother owns is going to fit you. Odds are that there won't be an outsized shop in a tiny fishing port. You'll have to spend the week wrapped in a duvet cover inside the apartment on your own.*

As she was about to fall apart, Tally spotted her case. Flooded with relief, she grasped the handle and struggled to haul it away from the moving conveyor belt. The sweat that had built up during her moment of panic made the bag slip and whack her on the shin. Squeezing her eyes shut, she willed herself not to cry. Realising most of the rest of the passengers from her flight were well gone, she spurred herself on and dragged her bag towards the arrivals zone.

Juan Garcia, a local restaurant owner and designated driver for those booked into Bella Vista Apartments, was standing in the arrivals hall, holding aloft a sign.

Greta spotted the apartment name immediately and strode over to him.

'Hiya, Greta Keller, that's me,' she pointed at herself and poked his sign.

'I was a little confused when you come out first, you no look like Irish lady,' he stuttered, trying not to sound offensive.

'I like my sunbed sessions, you wouldn't catch me looking like a corpse like most Irish women,' she rasped. 'I don't mean to be rude, but I'm absolutely dying for a cigarette, would you mind if I wait outside?'

'Of course. My bus is just there,' he pointed. 'I wait for other passengers and then we can meet you outside, yes?'

'Cool by me.'

As she strutted away, Juan called after her to enquire if there was another person travelling with her. 'You are alone? I have here two person with name Keller on my paper,' he said.

'Ah, yeah, my daughter Tallulah is still in there waiting for her bag. She'll turn up,' Greta said, pulling a cigarette from her bag as she went.

Juan greeted Ava and Daisy next and directed them outside to his waiting bus. They were quickly followed by Mia and Felicity, giggling and clutching their duty-free gin. They headed outside to stow their bags and grab a seat on the bus. Juan consulted his clipboard again – just the skinny woman's daughter now.

The bulk of the passengers from the flight seemed to have found their various tour representatives. Juan was almost alone in the arrivals hall. Just as he was about to head outside and ask Greta if she really had a daughter, a lady who he assumed was his one remaining passenger came into view. He held up his sign again and Tally smiled and made her way towards him. 'Sorry! I'm coming! Apologies for holding you up!'

'You are Keller lady?' Juan asked.

'Yes, Tally Keller. So sorry I've kept you waiting,' she said.

'It's no problem, you take your time, lady,' Juan answered graciously, then introduced himself.

Juan realised Tally was actually only young. The extra weight she was carrying made her look older from a distance. She was so unlike her mother – curvaceous, with glossy hair and the warmest smile Juan had been treated to in years.

'Wow, it's like stepping into an enormous hair dryer, isn't it?' Tally exclaimed as they walked outside.

'Beautiful, no?' Juan said proudly.

'Oh, it's gorgeous,' Tally answered as she made it to the bus, continuously wrestling with her suitcase, which was a wheeled one with a mind of its own.

'Sorry, Juan, I nearly skinned your heel there, this case is like a dodgy supermarket trolley,' Tally said, gritting her teeth as she struggled. 'It doesn't go in the direction I want it to. It just shoots off of its own accord.'

'Don't worry, lady, you leave there. I take it for you.'

Ava and Daisy had just settled themselves into their seats as Tally hauled herself up the steps onto the minibus, where she was greeted by the others.

'Hello, everyone! Sorry if I held you all up. I had an awful moment back there. My bag was one of the last to come out,' she explained. 'I actually thought it had gone astray. Luckily, it turned up.'

'Jesus, Tallulah, you're blessed. As you can easily see,' Greta continued, 'I could possibly make do with some of her stuff, but she wouldn't get her big toe into my gear,' she chuckled.

Mia and Felicity, who had already taken their seats on the bus, stared at Greta in astonishment.

Ava and Daisy didn't even dare glance across at one another.

Suck it up and ignore her, Tally told herself. If she so much as opened her mouth, Tally knew she'd start an unmerciful row with Greta. So instead she mopped her brow with a tissue and sat with as much of her back to Greta as she could.

'Wow, it's seriously hot in here, isn't it?' Tally commented in a jovial voice to the others. *I'm going to be very pleasant and Ma will follow suit.*

'Hopefully some air-conditioning will come on when the bus starts,' the pretty brunette answered. 'I'm Felicity by the way and this is my mam, Mia.'

'Hi, pleased to meet you both. If you haven't already met, my mother's name is Greta and I'm Tally,' she said.

'Your name is Tallulah,' Greta snapped, shaking her head in annoyance.

'But everyone I know bar you calls me Tally,' she said through gritted teeth. 'Tally will do just fine,' she said, turning back to the others.

'I call you that because that's what you were christened. I picked your name and I happen to like it,' Greta snapped. 'Just because you decided you don't 'feel' like a Tallulah, you insist on being called Tally. Bloody kids, huh?' Greta said to nobody in particular.

'Tally it is,' Felicity smiled. Tally smiled back, grateful for the support.

'If it makes you feel any better, Tally,' Mia interjected, 'at least your bag didn't look to be as enormous as Miss Felicity's bag. We ended up being stung in Dublin airport for extra weight,' Mia said, rolling her eyes.

'Oh, they can be real sticklers with that, can't they?' Tally said. She regarded the mother and daughter. Both had sallow skin and glossy dark hair, which the younger woman wore loose. As she turned to face Tally so she could chat more freely, Felicity flicked her hair back off her face.

'You actually look really familiar, have we met before?' Tally asked as she took in Felicity's sparkling chestnut eyes and the dimples in her cheeks when she smiled.

'I don't think so,' Felicity answered shyly.

'Some of her pals say she's the spit of Cheryl Cole. Of course, I don't see it, but what would I know, I'm only her mother,' Mia said, smiling.

'That's it!' Tally nodded. 'You really do look like Cheryl Cole!'

'I wish I had her money,' Felicity giggled.

'You and me both,' Daisy said, turning around to join in. 'I'm Daisy and this is my mum, Ava.'

The bus coughed into life and Juan leaned behind to tell them that they would reach Bella Vista in just over an hour. 'It's just you lovely ladies, so we can go now, yes?'

'Jesus, it's like sitting in a kiln in here. I hope to God there's air-conditioning on this thing. It's not exactly a luxury vehicle, is it?' Greta said, fanning herself dramatically.

'I'm sure the cool air will kick in once we get going,' Mia assured her.

'Have you been here before Tally?' Felicity asked.

'No, I've been to other parts of Spain, but never Puerto Prima. Have you?'

'No, we got a gift of a holiday voucher and this place just seemed really special,' Mia answered. 'The travel agent said it'd be right up our alley.'

'Well as long as there's a gym nearby, I'll be happy,' Greta said, jigging her leg up and down repeatedly.

'Are you a gym bunny then, Greta?' Felicity asked.

'Sure am. What about yourself?'

'I try and stay trim, but I'm not great at going to the gym if I'm honest,' Felicity answered.

Greta looked like she lived on her own nervous energy and would burn off a thousand calories a day just existing. As she grasped the back of the driver's headrest in front of her, Felicity couldn't help but gaze at her hands and arms. In her tight T-shirt and equally unforgiving white skinny jeans, Greta displayed a body that quite obviously didn't know the meaning of the world cellulite. To say that there'd be more fat on a rindless rasher was putting it mildly. Her neck and even her face were like a single solid block of muscles, with the only concession being her tight mouth and pert nose. Her skin was so tanned, she could have been turned into a handbag without too much difficulty.

Juan looked in his rear-view mirror as they made their way onto the motorway. Whatever about the others, Señora Keller was a tough cookie.

'Oh, look at the sea, girls! I just know this is going to be the most fantastic week,' Mia said, hugging Felicity excitedly.

31.

Ava and Daisy were settling into their apartment. A whoosh of cool air had hit them as soon as they bundled in the door.

'Wow, this is gorgeous!' Ava exclaimed as the heavy wooden door slammed behind them.

The open-plan apartment was floored with a pale cream marble throughout. The décor was fresh and contemporary, yet there were lovely touches. Someone had taken the time to dot vases of fresh flowers in pink hues on the side table and kitchen counter. The lovely blue and white tiles lining the kitchen walls picked up the cornflower tones of the sofa cushions. Instead of the usual fold-out, futon-style sofa they'd seen so many times in previous rented accommodation, this place boasted squidgy over-stuffed cream sofas and furniture that anyone would love in their own home. The blackout material was cleverly concealed behind pretty, vintage looking lace drapes, all held back by a large blue bow.

'I love the throw on the back of the couch, it matches the blinds in the kitchen,' said Daisy. 'Mum?'

'I'm in the master bedroom, it's fantastic. Look at the lamp shades, they're glittery in the sunlight. I'd never have thought of putting silver in a bedroom like this. It's gorgeous, isn't it?'

'You take this room. Oh, look at the en suite, it's even got a big shower with one of those massage heads.' Daisy rushed into the second bedroom, which was almost as large and had sea-green colours throughout.

'Daisy, you have to see this view!' Ava called from the balcony.

The gardens and pool area were just below, but a few feet beyond lay the most perfect little beach. With white sand and picture postcard blue and white striped parasols with matching loungers, it looked so inviting.

'If I died this minute, I can't imagine heaven would be much better than this!' Daisy squealed as she hugged her mother. 'I'm going to text Nathan and tell him we're here. After that, I reckon we should just grab our swimming things and get into that ocean.'

'Sounds perfect!' Ava agreed. Luckily, her daughter was too busy to see her face fall. At the mention of Nathan's name, Ava had felt instantly stressed all over again. Ava could understand why her husband was so protective of their only daughter. They wanted the very best for her, including a gem of a partner. They thought they'd struck gold with Freddie.

If she was totally honest, she and Justin had relaxed in the knowledge that Daisy would be loved and cherished. Then the whole dream had become a living nightmare. Daisy's u-turn had come without any warning.

In the beginning, Ava really hadn't seen Nathan as anything but a rebound relationship. But the whole situation had grown wings and now, they were being catapulted into this new wedding plan with a guy they couldn't connect with, from Lord knew where. She knew Justin was beside himself at the idea that Daisy might lock herself into a situation she hated, with a man who proved to be all they feared he was. Justin was jumping the gun, of course, but she knew he just saw a long line of worst-case scenarios every time he thought of Daisy married to Nathan. She also knew he was relying on her to make Daisy see things from their point of view before this week was out.

Juan had directed the others to building two, so Tally, Greta, Mia and Felicity all made their way around the pool and through a garden gate to the steps leading up to their apartments.

'This looks great,' Mia said, smiling delightedly.

They reached the entrance to the apartment block and were greeted by a lift.

'You go on ahead and send the lift back down, we'll never all fit in there,' Felicity said to Greta and Tally.

Greta didn't need to be asked twice and promptly piled all her stuff into the lift. Tally was going to point out that they should've offered it to Daisy and Mia first, but they were chatting away happily and didn't seem put out, so Tally kept quiet. She knew that if she made a scene her mother would probably fly off the handle and call her a stick-in-the-mud or something worse. That would fill her with rage and resentment and the mood in their apartment would be savage.

'Catch you later, ladies,' Tally said, waving as the lift doors closed.

'See you,' Felicity said, waving back.

'Do you think the apartment is going to be as pretty as the brochure? I have to admit to feeling a little nervous after the state of that bus,' Mia said to Felicity as they waited for the lift to return.

'I'm sure it'll be lovely. They can't show a photo of gorgeous rooms and have a sad dump as the actual place,' Felicity said, sounding distracted.

When she turned around, Mia realised her daughter was busily texting.

'I'm just sending … sorry, give me a minute … and there … sorry, I was just texting Shane to let him know we're here. He said to call him from the airport but it was all a bit hassley in the bus and I didn't want to talk to him in front of the others. I've just let him know I'll call in a while,' Felicity said, failing to notice Mia's changed expression.

As Ava looked at the tiny pink flowers dotted through the creeper that was winding its way up the side of the balcony and inhaled the warm soft sea air, she convinced herself that everything was going to be just fine. She was going to talk to Daisy, Daisy was going to listen and realise how much sense Ava and Justin were making. It would all work out in the end.

In Apartment 220, Greta Keller was standing out on the balcony, and she could see Ava across the way looking out to sea.

'Find me an ashtray would you, love?' she called to Tally. 'The plants don't look like they'd survive my shoving butts into them.'

'Ma, did you see the bedrooms? This place is pure class. Lovely big beds and the shower is like something from the *Starship Enterprise*,' Tally called from inside.

'I'll look now once I've finished my fag. All this blue and white stuff is so clichéd and Spanishy, isn't it? Could they not come up with a more original theme?' Greta grumped.

'Eh, we're in Spain, Ma. That'd be a good reason for the place to look Spanish. What did you want? A tricolour draped over the balcony with shamrocks stenciled around a turf fireplace?' Tally answered as she dumped an ashtray (blue and white pottery) on the wrought-iron balcony table.

'I'm only saying,' Greta said, exhaling and looking affronted. 'I'll keep my opinions to myself in future. Maybe you can buy me a big zip and I can glue it on to my gob and you can open it when I'm allowed speak?' Greta called in.

She's looking for a row. Just ignore her, Tally told herself. Although the option of a large zip would be fantastic, she thought with a smile!

'I'm starving. I might put on a cooler dress and head off in search of the supermarket. I love going shopping in foreign countries,' Tally looked excited. 'I can just hear the shops calling out to me, *Tally come and visit us!*'

Greta smarted. That sounded like her idea of hell. Martin and Tallulah loved trotting around the local centre at home. If that rocked their boat, good for them, but she really didn't relish the thought of having to do that here.

'Why do you want to go to a shop while you're on holiday?' Greta asked crossly.

'I just want to grab a few basics. Da and I always look forward to mooching around a new place,' Tally's eyes lit up when she spoke of her father. 'Can I get you anything?'

'I have a particular loathing for Spanish food,' Greta said defensively. 'It's all sugar-loaded carbs or swimming in oil. I've my protein mix with me, so I just need the water.'

'Whatever,' Tally said, walking into her room.

She figured there would be no point in pressing her mother to join her after that comment.

'I'll put my gear on and go for a swim. It's a bit hot to go running yet, so I'll be down by the pool,' Greta decided. 'There are two keys, so let's take one each and you can join me when you get back,' she called to her daughter.

Greta loved the heat and she'd definitely enjoy getting even more of a tan, but she'd have to make sure to find a suitable gym. She was damned if she was going to end up the size of an elephant by the end of the week. Striding into the master bedroom, she stood with her hands on her hips staring at the décor – far too glittery and sugar-plum fairy for her liking. She preferred clean lines and less of this fussy effect.

She'd sort her training gear, get it all neatly put away and press on with getting herself motivated. She'd learned the hard way that being slow and slovenly made her miserable.

In her room, Tally upended her suitcase and flung her clothes haphazardly into the wardrobe. Grabbing a floaty sundress, she took off the leggings and smock top she'd travelled in. Rotating her foot while leaning against the wardrobe door, she noticed her feet were quite puffy from the flight. She'd brought mostly black clothes, knowing she'd feel more comfortable if she could hide some of her worst bits. Padding into the bathroom, she gently applied some waterproof make-up. She slid her manicured feet into flip flops, then grabbed her beach bag, stuffed her phone and wallet inside and set off.

She could hear her mother stomping around the master bedroom, flinging drawers open and shut. Knowing her, she'd have all her training gear and clothes stacked perfectly. Greta was a stickler for order. Martin used to say he'd never be able to leave Greta as nobody else would iron his boxer shorts the way she did.

'See ya!' Tally called out, forcing herself to be cheery.

'Cheers!' Greta yelled back. Coming from the air-conditioned apartment into the midday heat, Tally felt like she could barely breathe. She made her way down the steps and back to the gate, then stepped through into the pool area. She turned her face up to the sun, feeling the hot rays washing over her.

'Fabulous, isn't it?' a voice called.

Tally opened her eyes and squinted against her sun blindness. It was Daisy, in her bikini.

Now this was what Tally would look like, if she was given a choice. Daisy was small and petite, with not an ounce of flab in sight.

'Oh, hi again,' Tally stuttered, remembering her manners. 'Are you heading for a quick dip?'

'You bet. Are you coming down? I'd say you could do with cooling down too,' Daisy said. 'An Irish June is nothing like this! The colour of that sky is amazing, isn't it? It's like looking at an enormous aquamarine.'

'I know, it's gorgeous. I'm going to grab a few bits in the supermarket,' Tally explained. 'I might see you down there in a while.'

'Cool,' said Daisy. 'Catch you later then. I've got a pile of magazines with me, so if you feel like chilling out and flicking through some celebrity gossip, I'm your woman!'

'Thanks,' Tally answered with a smile.

Contrary to what her ma expected, Tally was on the hunt for rice cakes and fresh fruit. She was determined to do herself proud on this holiday. She hadn't eaten a bar of chocolate or a packet of crisps (her crippling weakness) in over four months. She wasn't going to let her hard work go to waste – or waist, more to the point.

Besides, she thought with a grin of excitement, she was meeting up with Ben when she returned. She absolutely had to look her best.

32.

By four o'clock in the afternoon, the Spanish sun was still heating the air to a delicious twenty-six degrees. Although the complex was almost fully occupied, the spacious pool area meant it never felt crowded.

Greta decided against swimming after all. All the sitting on the plane and bus had left her feeling claustrophobic. She needed to run and feel free. Dressed in her shorts, singlet and lightweight trainers, she filled a large water bottle with electrolytes. Throwing cigarettes, goggles and oil into a neat nylon backpack, she headed off for a jog.

Ava had followed Daisy to the poolside loungers, where she found her daughter chatting to two other women from their flight.

'Hello again,' Ava smiled at Mia and Felicity. 'Isn't this place just so relaxing?'

As Ava peeled off her navy splashed with acid green beach wrap to reveal a matching strapless one-piece suit, Mia couldn't help but feel slightly envious. Like her daughter, Ava had a neat and slender figure with smooth, honey-toned skin. Her pale golden curls were tucked into a wide-brimmed straw hat, which boasted tiny hints of navy twinkles. As Ava arranged herself on the sunbed beside Daisy, Mia couldn't help but marvel at the fact that she didn't seem to have an ounce of cellulite.

While Mia wasn't exactly like a Jaffa-fruit on a bad day herself, she still had the odd patch of orange peel here and there. But Ava and Daisy were so chatty and friendly, Mia soon forgot about feeling jealous and, with Felicity, began to enjoy the company of their new friends.

'I worked as an airline hostess for a few years before the children were born,' Ava divulged. 'It never ceases to amaze me how us Irish always seem to gravitate towards one another,' she noted cheerfully.

'That heat would have to be beneficial, wouldn't it?' Daisy commented as she lay back down, drinking in the afternoon rays.

'Gosh, yes, it's so relaxing. Once I know I have my factor thirty on,

I'm happy. I really don't want to get burned,' Felicity said, examining her shins to make sure they weren't turning pink.

'Hello all, I'd recommend a dip in the sea, if you have the energy,' Tally appeared by the side of the pool from the direction of the beach. 'The waves are fairly high, but it's gorgeously refreshing. I was only walking along the edge of the water, but even that is amazing. I feel like I've had a pedicure. The sand isn't stony, but it's not that fine dusty stuff either. It's just perfect.'

'I admire your energy!' Ava laughed. 'I think I'm doing well making it as far as here with my beach bag and a book.'

Tally felt more confident than she had for years as she arranged herself on a lounger near Felicity. For the first time ever, she felt slim and comfortable with her own body.

As Tally was sitting in a reclining position in her dark, billowing sundress, with iPod earphones poked into her ears beneath a huge straw hat, Ava glanced at the girl and thought she looked Rubenesque against the navy and white-striped fabric of the cushion on the chair. She seemed like a lovely-natured girl and the type of person she'd enjoy getting to know over the next week.

Greta broke the air of calm a short while later. Like a fireball, she jogged up to where the ladies were relaxing and flicked the sole of Tally's foot to get her attention.

'Cock-a-doodle-do! Wakey-wakey, shakey-shakey!' she called.

Ava sat up to say hello, and was struck by how like a two-legged greyhound Greta looked – she was in tiny shorts and a tight singlet and was dripping wet.

'All right.' Greta nodded at Ava.

'Hi, nice to see you again,' Ava said in a friendly tone.

'Greetings, ladies!' Greta called out and saluted the others. They all mumbled a very chilled, semiconscious response.

'How was your run, Ma?' Tally answered as she pulled her earphones free.

'Ah, dodgy enough. It's bloody roasting here. Doesn't really lend itself to any kind of decent speed. I'll have to find a gym first thing in the morning. I'll have a quick swim and join you all in a while. This is obviously the lizard-lounging spot,' she cackled at her own joke as she pulled her running shorts and vest off to reveal a string bikini.

All the women, apart from Tally, stared as discreetly as they could. She had a body-builder's physique, with a full six-pack and protruding muscles in her upper thighs more suited to an Action Man doll. There was no doubting she had a finely tuned body without an ounce of flab, let alone a scrap of cellulite, but whether or not they would want to look quite so masculine was the question all the women were asking themselves.

Greta had a slightly different definition of 'a quick swim' from the rest of the group. She waded into the water, oblivious to the cute chubby babies with puffy swim nappies and fluffy hair, or indeed the frolicking teenagers. Pulling her goggles into place, she found the widest part of the oddly shaped pool. Starting off quite slowly and steadily, she built up speed until she was slicing through the water at a rate of knots.

'Your mum is an amazing swimmer, isn't she?' Daisy said to Tally, breaking the awkward silence that had settled since Greta had appeared.

'Oh, yeah, Ma lives for her exercise. She works part-time in a gym and puts in a lot of time personally with her training,' Tally said gently.

'Is she a professional athlete?' Mia asked, trying to make sense of it all.

'Oh, no, she just believes in pushing herself to the extreme. She doesn't do anything by half measures. As you can see, I'm her polar opposite. I take after my da. Obviously!' Tally giggled as she placed her hands on her belly and wobbled it like jelly.

'Don't you be putting yourself down, girl,' Mia said immediately. 'You look absolutely gorgeous. I'd kill for your curves and beautiful skin.'

Tally smiled shyly at her, but felt like a million dollars.

When the fervent swim session ended, Greta emerged and patted herself dry with a small towel from the end of Tally's sunbed. Not bothering with a towel or wrap to lie on, she flung herself on a lounger, snatched her rucksack and proceeded to lather what appeared to be oil on her skin.

'Ma, please don't tell me you're putting oil with no protection factor on your skin,' Tally said.

'I use a sunbed most days on my way out of the gym. It's not as if I need to get any kind of a base colour. Relax! Besides, it's late afternoon, once you don't go out in the midday sun you don't burn, everyone knows that, Tallulah,' Greta scoffed. 'This one thinks because she goes to beauty school that she's the sunscreen police! If you saw the number of bottles of this and sprays of that in her bag, it'd make you laugh.'

'Ma, the sunbed is lethal for your skin, as you well know. But it burns a different layer of skin. It doesn't matter what time of the day it is, you need protection factor to stop the harmful rays from causing any further damage,' Tally worried.

'I love your "further damage", making out I'm a burns victim. You sit and listen to your music or go off and don't annoy me,' Greta said, looking over at Mia and rolling her eyes. 'Kids, huh?'

'Your daughter is actually correct,' Mia pointed out. 'I'm not as well versed in matters of the skin as Tally, but I am a healthcare worker so I do know enough to realise that pouring oil on, especially in this kind of heat, is dangerous.'

'Ah, you all need to live a little. Besides, I'm not going to be lying here. I'm going for a walk along the shore in a few minutes. All this lolling around makes me edgy,' Greta retorted defensively. 'I'm just not a person who enjoys being lazy.'

'Yeah, Ma does enough exercise for the lot of us. You go and enjoy your walk and I'll catch you later,' Tally said, eager to diffuse the uncomfortable atmosphere that was creeping in. 'Do you want to go out for dinner earlyish tonight, seeing as we've been on the go for so long? I don't know about you, but I'm wrecked. Getting up so early this morning to get our flight has knocked the stuffing out of me,' Tally yawned.

'You and your food! You're a gas woman altogether. Don't fret, you won't starve to death, not that you'd ever allow that happen! But, no worries, we'll go when I get back. I'll only be an hour or so,' Greta said while bending to touch her toes and rising again and flinging her arms high above her head. Knocking her head from one side to the other in jerky motions, she finished by weaving her fingers together and yanking her arms forward causing her knuckles to crack.

'Ladies – later,' Greta stated.

'Will your mother actually go walking for a whole hour after running and swimming?' Ava leaned out from under a brolly to ask.

'Oh, God, yeah. She'd often run for four hours at a time,' Tally explained. 'She'd think nothing of spending an entire morning in the gym. She moves from the weights to treadmill and sometimes she likes the cross-trainer. It puts her in better form, and she loves it. It's just her thing, I guess.' Tally shrugged.

A short while later, Felicity rolled onto her back and sat up feeling a bit disorientated.

'Morning all!' she said. 'I was totally clapped out. I hope I wasn't snoring and dribbling. I just couldn't stay awake, lightweight that I am! I'm ravenous. What time is it?'

'It's nearly five o'clock.' Tally looked at her watch. 'I have some fruit here if you'd like a banana or an apple? They look lovely, I'll join you in fact.' Tally pulled the supermarket bag from under her chair and went around the small group sharing.

'Thanks a million, that'll keep me going until dinner time,' Felicity said, choosing a banana.

'Anyone else?'

'I'd love an apple actually,' Daisy said standing up and pulling her bikini bottoms out of her bum. 'This is the worst bikini, if I so much as attempt to swim wearing it, I'll end up flashing. Thanks, Tally, I haven't had an apple for ages. I'm really bad at eating fruit actually,' Daisy admitted.

'Well you don't look it! I wish I had your figure,' Tally said.

Ava and Mia both declined a piece of fruit. Both women were engrossed in their books and seemed to be enjoying the relaxation.

The three younger women meandered towards the shallow end of the pool. A tiny Spanish toddler with dark curls and chocolate-coloured skin was splashing delightedly with a plastic Hello Kitty watering can.

'Isn't she like a little doll?' Daisy said, lowering herself to say *hola* to the baby. 'I'd love to have at least four children,' Daisy admitted.

'Are you married?' Felicity asked.

'Not yet, I actually just got engaged to my boyfriend, Nathan. I'm just finished my training as a Montessori teacher as well, so it's all go in my life!'

'That sounds really exciting! Have you any wedding plans yet?' Felicity asked. 'Oh, wow, your ring is … different.' Felicity reached down and scooped Daisy's hand in hers.

'I have to say, I nearly passed out when Nathan gave it to me. You see I was engaged once before,' Daisy giggled. She filled the girls in on a brief version of the Freddie fiasco and the subsequent alternative proposal from Nathan.

'Well I'd settle for a fleck of cubic zirconium on a tin ring from the Hallowe'en brack just so long as I knew I'd found the right fella!' Tally said, taking Daisy's point.

Daisy grinned. 'To answer your question, I'm not sure exactly when the wedding will be. I hope to chat to my mum about it this week, in fact. I honestly don't want to leave it too long, we know we want to be together, so what's the point in waiting for years? My parents were hung up on the Freddie plan, so it's taking a bit of adjustment for them to come on board with liking Nathan.'

'You're dead right. If I met the man of my dreams, I'd have him whisked up the aisle quick smart,' Tally said. 'If Nathan loves you and you're happy, I'm sure your parents will come around to your way of thinking sooner or later.'

'Do you have a boyfriend at the moment?' Felicity asked Tally.

'No, not me,' Tally said, looking down at the ground. 'When you're a woman mountain, you don't get too many offers.' She looked up and realised that she had embarrassed the two girls. She mentally kicked herself – she was doing exactly what Sinead had asked her to stop doing: making a joke of herself. Felicity and Daisy were so friendly, and here she was acting like an idiot. 'Although …' she went on with a smile, '…there is someone I have my eye on.'

'Ooh, tell us everything,' Daisy said smiling.

Tally told them all about Sinead and how she'd met Ben. It didn't matter – this was a holiday friendship, so she could be honest about it.

'I'm a bit nervous though because I *really* like Ben. And I don't want to mess things up with Sinead or make a fool of myself,' she finished.

'I don't think you'll do anything of the sort,' Felicity said. 'Obviously I haven't met Ben, but it sounds to me as if he's very keen!'

'What about you Felicity, do you have a beau?' Daisy said, crunching her apple.

Felicity finished her banana and walked out of the pool for a moment so she could bin the skin.

'Yeah, I'm actually seeing a Dublin fella called Shane. I met him in university and we got together pretty early on – well, the first day of college to be exact! He's a dote. We recently moved in together and my mam is finding it really hard to come to terms with the fact that I've no plans to return to Galway in the near future. He's also ten years older than me and works in UCD, so you can imagine that I haven't exactly picked an easy option for my poor mam to accept.'

'Doesn't your mother like Shane, then?' Tally asked.

'Well, both herself and my best mate Aly thought he was unsuitable. Aly kind of took it upon herself to tell me so a while back. So things haven't been that straight forward where Shane is concerned,' Felicity answered sadly. 'The main reason it's all so hard for both of us is that my father died when Mam was pregnant with me. So we've always been seriously close. I'd hate to think that I'm hurting her.'

'I'm sure she only wants you to be happy,' Daisy said gently.

'She seems just lovely,' Tally said, glancing over at Mia. 'Daisy's right, I'll bet all your mother needs is a bit of time to adjust.'

'I hope you're right, girls,' Felicity said, looking troubled for a moment.

'We sound like we've a similar pitch to put forward over the next week,' Daisy said to Felicity. 'Let's hope the magic of the Spanish sunshine can help our mothers see that we're happy with our fellas!'

'I don't know about you two, but I feel like I'm about to fry like a piece of bacon!' Tally said fanning herself. 'I'm going to plunge in and have a swim.'

'Good plan!' Daisy agreed.

The water felt silky and soft against their hot skin. The cloudless blue sky and delicious sunshine made for a wonderfully relaxing swim.

Daisy and Felicity emerged before Tally. Waving to let her know they were getting out, Tally waved back to indicate she would follow.

As Daisy patted herself dry and pulled her sodden curls into a clip, she watched Tally in the water. There was no denying the girl was on the larger side, but she could glide through the water with an ease and grace that she couldn't manage in a fit herself.

Felicity approached Daisy with a soft flowing sarong knotted around her. 'Tally's a really lovely girl, isn't she?' she said.

'Gorgeous,' Daisy agreed, 'even if she doesn't realise it herself. I'm not so sure about Greta, though. She's a bit of a Scary Mary.'

'I know,' Felicity said with a laugh. 'I think I'd be living away from home 24/7 if she was my mother!'

Tally waded out of the pool and scuttled past the others, who were all assuming their terrapin positions again, basking in the early evening glow.

'Nice swim?' Daisy said lazily.

'I feel so much better after it,' Tally said happily.

'You're showing us all up!' Felicity said, flopping onto her side to join in the conversation.

'Not at all, you two skinny minnies hardly need to spend your time thrashing around in the pool,' Tally said, gathering up her things. 'I'll see you all later or tomorrow. My ma will be back soon and we're going to head off for an early bite to eat. It was great to chat to you earlier on, girls. Have a lovely evening whatever you decide to do.'

'I've a pile of magazines here if you'd like to lounge for a bit?' Ava said gently.

'Oh, thank you, but I'll go and get myself organised,' Tally replied. 'I might have a look tomorrow, if that's okay?'

'Of course, we might see you later on!' Ava answered. 'Enjoy if we don't.'

'Bye everyone!' Tally waved briefly and ventured off towards her apartment.

'She's so easy to chat to. Really bubbly and friendly,' Felicity said, 'which I would doubt comes from her mother's side of the family.'

'I think you're right,' Ava agreed. 'Her mother doesn't exactly embody gentle acceptance of her daughter's sweet nature.'

'Ha! A sledgehammer hurtling towards you at fifty miles an hour would be more gentle than that woman,' Daisy scoffed.

'Daisy!' Ava glowered at her daughter.

'Well! It's true,' Daisy defended herself.

'Come on you,' Ava said, swatting her daughter's arm playfully, 'enough gossiping. Let's go get ready for dinner.'

'See you two later or tomorrow,' Daisy called as they walked off.

'I think I'll head up for a shower,' Felicity said to her mother.

'Grand. I'll let you go ahead, give you time to get showered. I'll be up in ten minutes.'

Mia settled herself back on the lounger, happy to have the whole pool area to herself for a few quiet moments.

33.

Mia was just thinking about packing up and heading to the apartment when Greta came charging back to the pool area, sweat dripping from her face.

'Still here?' she called out cheerfully.

'Trying to get the energy to move,' Mia called back with a smile.

Greta walked over and dropped down onto the lounger beside Mia's. 'I feel much better now,' she announced. 'A bit of exercise just puts me to rights.'

Mia looked at her curiously, wondering what drove this woman to move constantly. 'Don't you like relaxing at all?' she ventured.

Greta looked at her. 'I know you've probably all decided that I'm nuts,' she said in a quieter voice, 'but it's just what I need to do. It's my way of dealing with stress.'

'I hate to think what kinds of stress you have,' Mia said with a grin.

Greta looked over at her and found herself laughing. Mia was so warm and direct – she was Greta's kind of woman.

'Do you go away with your daughter often?' she asked.

Mia shook her head. 'No, never. My husband died when I was pregnant with Felicity, so there was never enough money for luxuries. I'm a midwife and I've always worked, but I had five children to raise on my own, so holidays didn't feature. And now,' Mia looked down at her hands and sighed, 'well, you know yourself, Greta, it's empty nest time for me. Felicity's studying up in Dublin and has a young man, so this was really my only chance to get a bit of time with her.'

Greta regarded her thoughtfully. 'Empty nest doesn't bother me at all,' she said honestly. 'Once Tallulah is doing okay, I'm happy to do my own thing.' She glanced over at Mia, who was trying to hide her shock. 'I sound like a crap mother, don't I?' she said. Mia realised that Greta's voice was tinged with sadness.

'No, you don't,' she said gently. 'Different strokes for different folks and all that. You're obviously an excellent mother because Tally is a wonderful person.'

'Thanks, Mia,' Greta said, 'but that's down to her da, my husband Martin. He's an angel and he pretty much raised her. Myself and Tallulah … well, we don't really see eye to eye. It drives poor Martin mad. That's why we're here, in fact.'

'I don't follow you,' Mia said.

Greta sighed. 'We've been fighting non-stop lately. Tallulah is on a health kick and she's doing well, but Martin thinks I'm not supportive enough. I honestly don't know where I went wrong. I've set the best example I know how. I'm fit, healthy and driven, but all my good intentions are always taken the wrong way. It kills Martin that Tallulah and I aren't best mates. I know he'd love it if we spent hours in the shopping centre together and sat around swapping tips on eye shadow, but that's just not my thing. Even if I forced myself to do it, I know it would all end in tears. Tallulah and I are like oil and water. It makes me sad, but I can't say that to her. I loved my mammy and miss her so badly at times it makes me cry. If I dropped dead tomorrow morning, I reckon Tallulah would be relieved.'

'Oh, Greta,' Mia said, 'you don't realise how much she needs you. Mothers and daughters can be a strange one, but that's because the love they have is so intense. You two might fight, but that's the flipside of love, isn't it?'

Greta didn't look convinced.

'This week in Spain is meant to fix everything. At least, that's what this woman Sinead thinks – she's this counsellor type who Tallulah thinks the world of. She has poor Martin and even Tallulah convinced that throwing us together in an apartment miles away from anywhere with nobody else to talk to is going to make everything great. In fact, the pressure it's putting us both under to make a dramatic transformation inside seven days is awful. I feel like I'm on one of those reality shows where you're watched by cameras and a loud voice booms through speakers telling us what task we have to complete.'

Mia looked at her sympathetically. She had thought this woman had no feelings at all – how wrong she'd been. She was just like every other mother she knew, fretting over her relationship with her children.

'I can definitely understand that you feel pressure, but you just never know how it'll go. If you give it your best shot, perhaps you and Tally will go home next week feeling more at ease with each other. Your husband probably just wants you two to get to like one another again. He doesn't expect you to be like two peas in a pod.'

'Well,' Greta said, looking over at Mia, 'fingers crossed a bit of sun, sea and sangria will make things easier between us. It would mean the world to Martin. I wouldn't mind it if we could be bit more compatible too, if I'm honest. I'm getting weary of all the tension.'

Mia reached over and patted her hand, making Greta jump. She wasn't one for physical displays of affection. Suddenly, she felt embarrassed. She leapt up from the lounger.

'Anyway, Jesus, listen to me, banging on and on like an oul one in confession! Sorry, Mia, you're here to relax, not have parenthood discussions.'

Mia smiled warmly at her. 'Not a bit of it. I love talking about children and the joys and sorrows of being a mother, it's always interesting.' She knew that Greta was feeling awkward after saying so much, so she quickly changed the subject.

'Come on, our daughters will think we've fallen in the sea – or run off with a waiter!'

'Chance would be a fine thing,' Greta said with a grin, and they headed towards the gate leading to the apartments.

34.

Ava and Daisy pushed open the door to Casa Blanca, Juan's restaurant, and smiled as he came across to greet them.

'Moyes by two, no?' Juan stated and grinned.

'Hello, Juan, nice to see you again. It's Ava and Daisy,' the older woman said smiling. They were still in their beachwear, dressed in floaty Egyptian cotton kaftan-style dresses and flip-flops. Ava had her silvery blonde curls swept off her face with a wide cotton stretchy headband, while Daisy's was caught up in a twinkling scrunchie. Glancing around the small beach-front eatery, they noticed the night lights dotted around and the salmon-pink accents in the bows on the wicker chairs and the cloth napkins picked up the colour of the walls. The floor was stone with rush matting, creating a little pathway to the beach. If they'd been any closer to the ocean, they would've been floating.

'I love your restaurant, it's so inviting and pretty,' Daisy said looking around.

'*Adelante*, come in. You are very welcome. I present Yvette, my wife,' Juan boomed cheerfully.

'*Hola*, hello ladies,' Yvette said kissing them on both cheeks. 'Come and sit, I have a lovely table for you both on the veranda. You can look at our beautiful Mediterranean Ocean and relax.'

'You speak perfect English. It puts me to shame, my Spanish is so poor,' Ava cringed. 'Every time I come to your country I vow to learn Spanish when I get home. Of course, I've never got around to it.'

In the end, Daisy and Ava had decided they hadn't the energy to go back to the apartment and go through all the showering and changing palaver. So they'd simply scooped up their things and gone straight down the boardwalk, to Casa Blanca.

'What would you ladies like to drink?' Yvette asked. 'I recommend my husband's sangria. Nobody on the costa makes one quiet as good as Juan's.'

'Oh, that sounds delicious. What do you think, Daisy?' Ava asked.

'Bring it on,' Daisy said, clapping excitedly.

Laughter and chatter filled the air along with the mouth-watering aroma of garlic and fresh fish. As they clinked glasses moments later and sipped the chilled fruity drink, both of them felt their shoulders relax. 'Ah, this is what holidays should always taste like!' Ava exclaimed.

Not only was Juan's sangria tasty, it was also deceptively potent. Having devoured a bowl of gazpacho and gambas al pil-pil, both ordered swordfish, which was fresh and light.

'Can I get you ladies some *postre* or dessert?' Yvette asked.

'Oh, no, thank you, that hit the spot for me, do you want something, Daisy?' Ava offered.

'No, thank you. I'm very happy, too.'

Yvette retreated with the dessert menus and continued to serve the rapidly expanding crowd in the restaurant.

In spite of their best intentions, Daisy and Ava were seduced by the aroma of warm, sweet waffles being presented to a neighbouring table.

'Oh, Mum, they have melted chocolate stuff on them too. We could share a portion,' Daisy suggested.

'Share the guilt more like it,' Ava laughed. 'Go on then, we're on holiday after all.'

As they were tucking into the divine dessert and sipping the rest of their sangria, Greta and Tally walked in.

'Hiya, ladies,' Greta called. 'What's the food like?' she bellowed for all to hear.

'Superb, we'd recommend it,' Daisy called back. 'Not that we could've said it's poisonous, go some where else,' she whispered out the side of her mouth to her mother.

Only one table remained and it happened to be alongside Daisy and Ava.

'We'll join you,' Greta said, without checking if anybody objected. 'You've got a dribble of chocolate on your chin there, Ava.' Greta stabbed at her own chin for emphasis. Blushing, Ava thanked Greta and dabbed herself clean with her napkin. Tally hung back, hesitating momentarily before walking over to sit opposite her mother.

'Hi, Tally,' Ava and Daisy said, smiling warmly at the girl. She looked gorgeous in a black maxi dress with pretty lace trimming along the neckline and hem. Her glossy hair was caught up in a glittery clip to one side and she was perfectly made up. Her skin was dewy and flawless. She looked strikingly attractive yet heartbreakingly unsure of herself.

Greta lit a cigarette immediately, flinging the box and lighter on to the table. Leaning onto the two back legs of her chair, she hung her head backwards, exhaling loudly.

'Eh, pardone, Señora, no smoking here,' Yvette rushed over to say.

'No smoking? In Spain? Are you having me on?' Greta guffawed.

'Yes, the law changed and we can have huge fines if we allow the smoking in public places,' Yvette said apologetically.

'Oh, don't be ridiculous, we're nearly in the sea as it is. Surely this doesn't count?' Greta snapped.

'I'm afraid it does. Please, I beg you not to smoke here.' Yvette answered with a cool smile, but all the women knew she meant business.

'Great. I might as well finish this one now I've lit it. I've started so I'll finish, huh!'

Standing up to stride onto the beach, Greta headed towards the sea. The daylight was fading and the colours were spectacular as the blushing sun was being absorbed by the inky seawater.

'All right with you if I stand over here?' Greta yelled back, seeming oblivious to the rest of the diners. 'They haven't made it illegal to walk near the Mediterranean, have they?'

Yvette gave her a thumbs-up sign and a fleeting smile.

Tally wanted to die of shame.

'How was your meal, ladies?' Tally enquired quietly.

'Gorgeous. I'd recommend the swordfish, it was simple but really delicious,' Daisy answered.

Yvette appeared to see if she could sell the second couple of ladies a jug of Juan's famous sangria.

'It sounds lovely, but I'm going to have a white wine spritzer if you don't mind,' Tally was slightly apologetic. 'I think my mother would love the sangria. Do you serve smaller jugs? I don't think she'd drink the larger size.'

'Yes, of course, we do a small carafe that is perfect for one person. Do you want lemonade or sparkling water for the spritzer?' Yvette asked.

'Sparkling water, please,' Tally said smiling.

By the time Greta returned, the drinks had arrived.

'Do you mind if we order, Ma? I'm starving,' said Tally.

'Yeah, whatever. Just get me a salad. Nothing weird in it mind you, just a lettuce-and-tomato type of thing,' Greta said, sipping the sangria suspiciously. 'Has an appetite like an ox this one,' she said, winking at Ava. 'No doubt she was munching on God knows what by the pool all afternoon, and now she'll be ready to go again. I don't know where she puts it all. Well, I do, but you know what I mean?' Greta threw her head back and bellowed.

'Ma, too much,' Tally whispered, shaking her head.

Greta fiddled with her lighter, mildly baffled at how people continuously took offence. She was only trying to break the ice. The two women were kind of hard work and she thought she'd help things along. She should've known better, she'd just keep her trap shut for a while.

Yvette's arrival lifted the awkward moment as Tally ordered her mother's ensalada de la casa, along with the swordfish for herself as recommended by the others.

'Can I bring you chips or side salad or rustic potatoes with that?' Yvette enquired as she took the menus back and tucked her pen into her hair.

'Just a side salad, please,' Tally replied politely.

'How do you like my husband's sangria, Señora?' Yvette asked Greta, trying to win her over.

'Yeah, it's not bad. Wouldn't drink too much of it, mind you. It probably has the same amount of calories as a wedge of chocolate cake,' Greta said, pulling a face.

Yvette opened her mouth to say something and decided not to bother. Besides, the loud woman was totally uninterested in chatting and was busy bending down, massaging her calf muscles under the table.

'I always get stiff after flying, all the fluid retention I reckon. I'm going to have to source a proper gym, the heat here is a curse for jogging,' Greta sighed, speaking to nobody in particular.

'Why don't you just try to relax a bit for the week, Ma?' Tally suggested.

'I'm not like you and your da, Tally. I don't get a buzz out of sitting around staring at the box. I need to keep myself moving. My body is a temple. It's just the way I am. I care about how I look, so have me shot!' she said, as she held her hands up in mock-surrender.

Daisy felt a surge of anger and frustration on Tally's behalf. This woman who claimed to be the healthiest person on the planet was a chain smoking, tan-orexic foghorn from where she was sitting. The way she dismissed her daughter was shocking.

Sensing the building anger in her daughter, Ava stretched and yawned exaggeratedly. 'Sorry for being such a killjoy, but I really need to hit the sack. I'm not as young as I like to believe. Would you mind if we hop off?' Ava asked a relieved Daisy.

'I'm tired too, Mum, it's been a long day. Hope you enjoy your dinner, ladies. No doubt I'll see you around tomorrow, Tally.'

'Of course. I'm sure we'll catch you at some point. Sleep well,' Tally said.

Without waiting for the bill to be brought, Ava and Daisy went up to the small counter and paid on the way out.

'That woman Greta is vile! Tally is so ladylike. How on earth could she be the product of that loud-mouth?' Daisy hissed.

'She's pretty forward all right. I reckon she has a lot of personal issues. We shouldn't judge people we don't know, but, having said that, she seems to have an unfortunate habit of putting her foot in it, especially with poor Tally.'

Daisy and Ava linked arms and strolled in the balmy evening air along the small stretch of path to their complex.

'It's such a compact little resort, I'm a bit worried we're going to be inundated with that woman's relentless commentary for the week. I'm beginning to wonder whether or not this is going to be a relaxing holiday at all,' Daisy worried.

'We can avoid her if we want to. The pool area is actually quite big and we can be a little bit strategic about where we perch ourselves,'

Ava yawned. 'Don't worry about Greta. We could always set up camp on the beach if she's posing a problem. Casa Blanca isn't the only restaurant either. We'll venture farther along the coastline tomorrow evening when we're more rested. Apparently the port area is full of eateries, so I wouldn't stress about her.'

Within half an hour, Daisy and Ava were tucked up in their separate bedrooms. Ava phoned Justin.

'Hi darling, how are you?' Ava asked.

'I'm great, what's the place like?'

'It's lovely so far, and I think we'll have a relaxing week here. We miss you, though. How are the boys? Any news?' Ava yawned again. 'Oh, excuse me, I'm bushed after the flight and the heat this afternoon.'

'No news, everyone's fine as far as I know. You go to sleep and let me know how you get on with your persuasive powers with Miss Daisy-doo.'

Ava was so tired she couldn't even read a magazine, let alone any of the four books she'd brought along. Turning the light off, she sighed and vowed to think about the mission of making Daisy see sense when she had the energy.

In her room, Daisy was chatting on the phone to Nathan. Eagerly she filled him in on everything from the colour of the apartment floors to all the other Irish people they'd met.

'That Greta lady sounds like a total shipwreck. She should be living in the States and she could spend half her life in therapy sorting out all her personal issues. Oh, honey, I miss you,' said Nathan.

'I miss you, too,' Daisy said feeling a bit overcome with emotion all of a sudden.

'I hope you're caring for your stunningly beautiful engagement ring!'

'I am and, as a matter of fact, the girls noticed it today by the pool. It's certainly a great talking point!'

Twenty minutes later, they hung up and Daisy nodded off to sleep, smiling. Nathan was the sweetest and most caring man she'd encountered after her beloved dad. The difference between Nathan's manner and Freddie's was so stark. She would never have considered attempting to chat to Freddie the way she did with Nathan. Besides, it always had to be about who it was good to be involved with and what they could do to further Freddie's fledgling career. Mundane things like feelings and sharing each other's day would never have been on the radar for Freddie.

Daisy was certain that Nathan would never crowd her or try to take control of her the way Freddie had. Daisy was in no doubt she'd found her perfect partner. She couldn't wait to chat to her mum about wedding plans this week. The more she thought about it, the more she was shifting towards having a big, traditional day. She felt giddy at the idea of planning it and arranging it – and then actually doing it. A wedding day with Nathan would be amazing.

As Daisy drifted off to sleep, she hoped herself and Ava could come to an understanding about the whole thing. Daisy felt it was time for her parents to accept Nathan, or face driving a permanent wedge between them.

35.

As it was their first full day in Spain, the Irish women were eager to prevent themselves from burning. It was ten in the morning and the ladies had gravitated towards their previous spot from the day before, relaxing poolside.

'I get a tan easily enough, but I really haven't been exposed to this kind of heat for such a long time,' Mia said, lathering more sunscreen on her arms.

'I'm the same,' Ava agreed, 'being burned and sore is no fun. I think I'll hide under an umbrella for a while. It's just so lovely to allow the heat seep into your bones, though. It's so relaxing.'

By early afternoon, Felicity, Mia, Daisy, Ava and Tally sat together to the pool's edge, letting their feet dangle in the cool water.

'We're like one of those Richard Attenborough documentaries – "and by the time the heat hits their bones, the girlies migrate towards the wallowing hole!"' Felicity commented putting on an attempted voiceover.

'Ha! We are a bit like wildebeest cooling ourselves!' Daisy giggled.

'Speak for yourself, I'm going to be a gazelle and leap into the water nymph-like and nimble,' Felicity shot back, plunging into the pool.

'Not exactly the most deft and splash-free dunking there, lovie!' Mia called after her. 'I think you're still in the wildebeest category for now!'

'Cheeky!' she waved back, lying on her back and enjoying the water.

'Is your mum taking it easy with the sunbathing today?' Daisy asked Tally diplomatically. The others leaned in, dying to know where the older woman had gone.

'She found a gym in the next town. She was up at the crack of dawn and went off in her running gear and sent me a text just after eight to say the gym at the main port have agreed to let her pay to use their facilities for the week. So, she'll be happy. At least I'll be able to relax now,' Tally tried to look nonchalant as she spoke. 'Sure, I'll only be sitting here like a slug for the week and we'd end up getting on one another's nerves so – happy days!'

Both Mia and Ava regarded the girl with sadness. She was gentle and sweet and craved to be loved. Any fool could see that her issues with weight were as a direct result of her mother's self-obsession.

'Does your mum ever *not* work out?' Daisy asked.

'No.' Tally sounded less upbeat than before. 'I think I'll join Felicity, this wallowing wildebeest needs to get swimming!' Tally joked as she dove into the water. This time there was barely so much as a splash as Tally began to slice through the water with the grace of a swan. Felicity climbed out and left her to it.

Daisy wasn't in the mood for a full on swim, so instead she dunked herself in and out a couple of times and padded back to her sunbed. She didn't mean to be nosey, but she noticed that the only food Tally had brought to the poolside was a bag of green grapes and large bottle of still water.

Daisy had little tiny cakes, a bag of crisps big enough to satisfy King Kong and a can of Diet Coke.

Felicity was also eating junk food and offered everyone a handful of bright orange cheesy curls.

'I don't normally eat this kind of stuff, but when I'm on holiday I turn into a dustbin,' Felicity mumbled through a mouthful of crisps.

'Me too,' Daisy agreed, grabbing a big handful. 'You know the way some people say they can't manage to eat in the heat? Well, I'm like I have worms when I'm on holiday. I spend my time wondering what to eat next. Perhaps it's the too-much-time-and-too-little-to-do syndrome, but I will spend this entire week scoffing, let me warn you!'

When Tally finished her swim, she perched on the edge of her sun bed and drank a third of her bottle of still water.

'God, it's hot, isn't it?' she gasped.

'Yup, especially when you're pounding up and down the pool. You're a fab swimmer,' Felicity said, still posting crisps into her own mouth. 'Want some?' she leaned across to offer Tally what was left of the super-sized bag.

'No, thanks, I have some grapes I'll munch on when I'm hungry,' Tally answered, smiling.

Only a few months ago, Tally would've eaten the whole lot. She wouldn't have given it a second thought. But now that she had learned to rethink her attitude to food, she was surprised at how little appeal fattening stuff held for her.

'Oh, try one of these. They're to die for. I'm not usually a cake fan, but they have a lovely almond taste, want one?' Felicity offered the bag to Tally.

'How do you girls eat that stuff and stay so trim?' Tally asked. She'd never for a minute have brought up a conversation with *thin* people before, but these girls seemed genuinely nice.

'I honestly don't eat junk food as a rule. I'll probably put on a few kilos this week, but I'll be good when I go home and make sure I lose it again,' Daisy admitted.

'Me too, I often go for the whole day in college without eating. I know that's so bad for me, but I've never struggled with my weight either,' Felicity admitted.

'I've actually been trying really hard for the past few months. I know you'd never know it to look at me, lard arse that I am, but believe it or not, I'm smaller now than I've been for years.' Tally pulled at the wrap she'd encased herself in, making sure she wasn't bulging out anywhere.

'That's amazing, good for you,' said Felicity straight off.

'How are you going about it?' Daisy asked, sounding genuinely interested. 'I don't want you to think I'm a stalker or anything, but I have to admit I noticed you only seem to eat fruit and even last night when we left you at the restaurant, you'd ordered really healthy food.'

'I guess it's probably a shock seeing as I'm so enormous, but I'm determined to turn myself around,' Tally divulged.

'Does your mum help you with exercise advice? Has she told you to do the swimming?' Daisy asked.

'God, no! Ma doesn't really take much interest in what I do. I'm not sure she even notices I'm doing any of this stuff. I did tell her, but she won't believe me until I'm a size eight! So, I won't hold my breath. God knows I've a fair way to go before I look even remotely normal!'

There it was again – the mask of self-deprecation that she was so used to hiding behind. It was hard to break the habit of a lifetime.

'My da is great. He and I are a similar shape. We've got into bad habits over the years and we're working together to try and change.' Tally's face lit up when she mentioned her father.

'That's great you have a bit of support. It's always easier to do any new venture alongside another person, isn't it?' Felicity said.

'For sure! Da's brilliant, we've even started a vegetable garden at home. He texted me this morning to say he ate some of our carrots last night in front of the telly. He's so proud, he actually sent me a photo of the carrot!'

'No way!' Daisy smiled. 'Good for you, I really admire you. I know loads of people who are doing this grow-your-own thing too. People are paying for allotments now, aren't they? I think it's fantastic. Nathan and I live in an apartment so unless I start some window boxes, it's not going to happen.'

Tally felt quite overcome with emotion. She was glad of her large sunglasses so the other two couldn't see the tears in her eyes. These girls were young, pretty, friendly and, above all else, thin, yet they genuinely seemed to like her. They actually appeared to want to talk to her. They listened when she spoke and didn't make her feel like a freak. Then there was her date with Ben when she returned.

For the first time ever, Tally felt like she was beginning to fit in. She didn't need to call herself a whale or behave like a circus act to be accepted.

Sinead was right. Her life was heading in a new direction. There was light at the end of the long, long tunnel she'd been crawling through for so long. Popping a grape into her mouth, Tally felt a rush of hope. Maybe she and her ma would find a common ground at some stage, too. She knew she needed to park all the hurt her mother had caused her as a child and try to forge a new adult relationship with Greta. Maybe this week was a good idea after all.

36.

Greta appeared at the poolside later in the afternoon with a face like a turnip, all purple and knobbly.

'Good workout?' Tally asked, squinting up at her mother.

'Yup, pretty good. Hello all,' Greta called out, doing a saluting movement with her veiny hand.

She was dressed in a sports swimsuit and was shifting her weight from one foot to the other constantly.

'Why don't you sit down and read a magazine for a while? It's so relaxing here,' Tally suggested calmly.

'Ah, no, I'll leave the beached whale behaviour to you lot,' she said, winking at Daisy and laughing.

Nobody reacted.

Jesus, thought Greta, this lot are a right shower of drips. Not so much as a grin out of the whole lot of them. What on earth have I said now?

'Ma, what would you think about going for a meal with the others tonight? We were thinking of strolling towards the port and sussing it out,' Tally filled her in. 'Mia was talking to the lifeguard and he's recommended a couple of restaurants. It'd be fun, what d'you reckon?'

'Well, I can hardly say no with five pairs of eyes boring into me, can I?' Greta snorted. 'Ah come on, girls, I'm only kidding. Joke? Never heard of sarcasm, no?'

'Will we take it that you'll join us then?' Mia interjected, trying to lighten the atmosphere. It was so unfortunate, but any time Greta appeared, she seemed to rub everyone up the wrong way.

'Yeah, sure! That'll be deadly. Just let me know what time. So, then ...' Greta looked uncomfortable. 'I think I'll have a dip in the pool. Why not, eh? That's what it's there for, what?' She padded over to the edge and flung herself into the pool, and started a fast-paced front crawl.

'I'm sorry, she doesn't mean to come across as rude. I'm sure she's really pleased about us all going out,' Tally said, mortified by her mother's brash behaviour.

'Listen, there's no pressure at all,' Daisy said, trying to smooth things over. 'Have a chat with your mum when you go back up to your apartment and if you'd rather do your own thing, that's totally fine.'

'Absolutely,' the others confirmed.

'Thanks, all of you, but I'd really like to join you, if I may. If my ma doesn't want to, that's her lookout.'

They all went back to reading their books or listening to music.

Greta emerged from the pool surprisingly quickly. 'I'm heading to the beach. This pool is like a bath. It's full of old people and toddlers on massive floating giraffes. Who ever heard of bloody African animals in swimming pools? Ridiculous,' she scoffed.

'I'll join you at the beach,' Tally said, rolling off her sunbed.

'You'll have to walk there, do you think you'll manage?' Greta guffawed. 'Will I run over the road to the supermarket and get a trolley so I can push you?'

Tally strode past her, bashing her with her shoulder as she passed. She continued to march until she hit the edge of the rolling waves. Dumping her towel and bag at a lounger on the beach, Greta came up beside her daughter.

'What's your hurry? I was just thinking you—'

'*Shut up!*' Tally screamed.

'Don't you dare talk to me like that,' Greta yelled back.

'Why not? All you ever do is put me down. Since I was a baby you've spent your days making me feel like I'm nothing.'

'Whoa, there, my girl! Hang on for one second. I spent years banging my head against the wall over you. I simply gave up trying to help because I thought you were happy the way you are,' Greta said with her hands on her hips.

'Happy? Any shred of happiness I've had in my life was in spite of you, Ma. If it wasn't for Da and Sinead, I would *believe* that I am nothing more than a pie with eyes because that's what you conditioned me into thinking.'

'I never held you down and made you eat, Tallulah! You don't catch me gorging myself on chips and pouring fizzy crap and beer down my gullet constantly, do you?'

'No, of course not. You wouldn't have time. You're too busy running and doing step aerobics and downing thick pink shakes rather than spending time with me or Da. When did you ever cook a proper dinner? Everything is always about you. More to the point, 'skinny you'. Guess what, Ma? There's more to life than resembling an orange pork steak.'

'What do you mean an orange pork steak? How dare you, I look amazing for my age!'

'According to whom? I think you look starved and unhappy,' Tally yelled. Now that she'd started, she couldn't stop. 'I've lost a huge amount of weight already. I'm turning my life around, and Da is helping me.'

'I'd be happy to help you, but you've never wanted my advice. You and your da are like that,' Greta shot back, her body stiff with anger.

'Has it never occurred to you that I might like to have a relationship with *both* my parents?' Tally cried.

'There's never been any room for me in your relationship. You two have a little clique where you sit and eat. You watch your movies. You go shopping. You don't need me or want me there,' Greta said, sounding like a wounded child.

'No, Ma, that's all you choose to see. The fact of the matter is that I've stopped all that, but you're so self-obsessed you haven't even noticed. I came away with you because I wanted us to try and build a relationship. I wanted to see if it was possible for me to actually know what it feels like to have a mother who cares about me. Or one who even knows the first thing about me. But obviously I over-shot myself there. I should've known not to expect any love from you. You hate yourself, so why on earth would you want to love anyone else?'

Tally didn't wait for any further comment.

'Tallulah,' Greta yelled. 'Wait, this isn't how I want it to be. I want us to have some sort of connection, too. Really I do.'

'My name is Tally,' the young girl shouted over her shoulder as she ran towards the apartment complex. Spinning around she hollered again. '*Tally!* Got that? Everyone else can manage to call me what I prefer. So if you say you want to change things between us, which I very much doubt, begin by calling me Tally.'

Bloody hell, Greta mused in astonishment as she watched her daughter race off in the direction of the apartments, she's not as unfit as I thought.

Tally gulped in air as she stood in the freezing cold shower moments later. She needed to cool down on every level. She wasn't guilty or upset, though. Instead of the usual sinking feeling that engulfed her after an altercation with her mother, she felt lighter than any weighing scales could ever show. As she was wrapping herself in a towel, her mobile phone rang.

'Hi, Sinead! You did remember I'm in Spain, didn't you? I'd hate to run up a huge bill for you,' Tally greeted her.

'I'm only on for a minute, I was just thinking about you and wanted to give you a quick buzz to check in. How are you getting on?'

'God, you must be psychic! I just had a showdown with my mother.'

'Oh, no, Tally, I'm sorry to hear that. Are you okay?'

'Do you know what? I'm better than I've been in years – possibly ever. I vented so much pent-up emotion and it feels amazing.'

'Good for you, but how is it all going to pan out for the rest of the week now? I hope it doesn't set you back,' Sinead worried.

'Not at all, I've met a couple of other Irish girls over here. They're so easy to chat to. They don't make me feel like a freak of nature!' Tally gushed.

'Oh, darling girl, that's because you're not a freak. I'm so pleased you've met some decent people.'

'They really are, so far it's been positive in all quarters bar my mother. We're all going out for a meal this evening and I'm honestly looking forward to it. I've decided whether or not Ma comes is her lookout. I'm going to join the others and she can like it or lump it.'

'That's so mature of you. Enjoy every second of your holiday. You deserve it, you've worked so hard over the past few months. How's the food? Are you managing eating in restaurants or has it been difficult?' Sinead probed gently.

'It's not difficult at all, there's so much fresh fish and salad available, it's actually easier than I could've hoped.'

'I'm so proud of you, Tally. You're some woman, do you know that?' Sinead shrilled.

'I'm aaaall woman, every bit of me,' Tally joked.

'Ah-ah. No putting yourself down, not even in jest! You are coming out of your shell, my girl. This is only the beginning. Listen I'm going to fly, but text me if you want or call me any time, okay?'

'I will. And Sinead?'

'Yes Tally?'

'Thanks for caring.'

'My pleasure, you're not difficult to care for. Mind yourself, and don't forget to have fun!'

Tally felt as light as Kate Moss after a week with vomiting bug. She'd managed to stand up to Greta and show that she was above her bullying. As she flicked through her holiday wardrobe, she decided tonight demanded something that wasn't black. The ankle-length, fuchsia pink maxi dress, with a large rose in turquoise beads adorning the side, caught her eye. She'd bought the dress because she loved the pretty colours and the fact that it was girly and glamorous, but she'd never honestly thought she'd have the nerve to go out in it.

By the time Greta strode into the apartment an hour later, Tally was applying the second coat of 'pink power' nail polish.

'I'm meeting the others at seven at the gate leading to the beach. We're walking to the port for a drink, then dinner. If you think you can be pleasant, come along; if not, I have my own key,' Tally said without even looking up. Blowing on her nails to make sure they dried evenly, she found herself humming her favourite Take That song.

'Have you gone mental?' Greta came right over to stand in front of her daughter.

'You're invading my space, Ma. Take a step back, will you?' Tally looked up and met her mother's gaze head on.

'I repeat, have you gone mental?'

'No, quite the opposite. I'm returning,' Tally said, smiling.

'What?' Greta demanded, looking perplexed.

'I'm *returning* after a long spell of being *mental*, as you put it. Well, mentally tortured and made to feel like a second-class citizen. I'm not allowing you to do that anymore. I've a long way to go with my weight and in here,' Tally knocked her own head with her knuckles. 'But I think I can do it. I have support and I'm going to use it.'

Greta opened her pursed lips to say something, but she suddenly found herself at a loss. She couldn't find a fitting comment to come back at her daughter with.

'I'm going to have a shower,' she said quietly. She'd never been aware that the banter she and Tallulah shared had hurt the girl so deeply. When she'd accused her of putting her down all the time, Greta had felt like she'd been winded. As she'd pounded up and down the coastline in dismay, she'd comforted herself by thinking that Tallulah was just going off on a mad one. That perhaps the heat was getting to her.

Wandering into the master bedroom, she pushed away the feelings of guilt that were spiking her conscience. She never intended to hurt Tallulah. She'd always assumed the girl simply didn't want to have a relationship with her.

Greta felt cheated and ashamed in equal measure. All these years, it now seemed to be transpiring, both women had been yearning for the same thing. *But you're the adult here. She's only a kid. You should've known. It's all your fault,* the voice in Greta's head taunted. Right at that moment in time, Greta felt worse than she'd ever thought possible. Even at her heaviest and most self-loathing stage, she hadn't been this miserable. She looked at herself in the mirror and her jaw set in a determined line. 'I'll come with you all for dinner, so don't go without me,' she called back to Tally.

'Suit yourself,' Tally answered calmly.

In the shower, Greta scrubbed her skin until it stung. She needed to try and work out how she could take the first step towards making amends with her daughter. This was a mess that couldn't be sorted by running away.

Tally put the finishing touches to her nails. Unlike her mother, she was actually feeling better by the minute. The tables were turning in the two women's lives. The question was whether or not there could ever be a midway point where each could understand the other.

37.

In Apartment 230, Ava was applying aftersun using disposable gloves. She always liked the one with the tan enhancer in it, which roughly translated as fake tan with the added advantage that it didn't make her skin so dry that it felt like it had been sanded.

Daisy had painted her nails with a coat of clear nail varnish to enhance her quirky engagement ring, which she had now fallen in love with. She was delighted at the thought of meeting the other girls tonight. Daisy knew they were going to have a lovely night this evening, but she also desperately wanted to get Ava alone to talk about the possibility of a Christmas wedding.

There was a knock on the apartment door and Daisy jumped up to answer it.

'Tally, Greta! Hi, come in! Mum's just ready now,' Daisy greeted them.

'I hope you don't mind us barging in on you, but I thought we'd collect you on the way,' Tally smiled.

'You look gorgeous,' Daisy exclaimed to Tally.

'Thanks, I love my white jeans,' Greta answered as she pushed past Daisy to nose around the apartment. 'Ah, yeah, it's the same as ours, isn't it, Tallul— eh, Tally?' she corrected herself.

'Some of the accessories are a bit different, but it's pretty much identical,' Tally answered without smiling at her mother.

Daisy could tell the atmosphere still wasn't brilliant between the two women, but Tally seemed less stressed than before.

'You look stunning,' Daisy repeated, making sure everyone in the room knew the compliment was aimed at Tally.

'Yes you do, what a beautiful dress,' Ava added as she wafted into the living room, bringing a scent of Chanel No. 5 with her.

'Thanks, girls,' Tally smiled. 'You both look great, too. Isn't it amazing how even one day of holidays can make all the difference? We'll all be glowing and looking ten years younger by the end of the week.'

'Amen to that notion!' Ava laughed. 'Ready to go?' she asked.

Mia and Felicity were just beyond the gate where they'd arranged to meet up. The sun was still shining and the temperature was just perfect for an early evening stroll.

'Hi, ladies,' Mia waved. 'Isn't this just glorious? I love balmy evenings when you don't need so much as a cardigan, yet there's that gentle breeze. I love Ireland and couldn't live anywhere else in the world, but by God I'd love it even more if we had this for even a bit of the year. Wouldn't that just make it perfect?'

The group ambled happily along by the seaside pathway, enjoying the gentle sound of waves lapping at the shore as the sun began to set. Following the coast to their right, the ladies passed a number of small complexes similar to their own. All the buildings were low rise and compact, with pretty gardens and well-tended shrubs lining the walkway. The small port, which certainly didn't house enormous yachts or look as if it would attract rock stars and racing car drivers, was picturesque and quaint. Built in a semi-circular shape, the open-fronted buildings boasted boutiques and every type of eatery, from Chinese to typically Spanish.

As she inhaled the warm air, Mia fell into step with Ava.

'So are you enjoying yourself so far?' Ava asked.

'Oh, tremendously,' Mia nodded. 'It's such a treat to get time like this with Felicity.'

'Do you get to see much of each other at home?' Ava asked, wondering about their set-up.

'Not anymore,' Mia said, and Ava caught the tone of regret. Mia looked over at Ava with a sad smile. 'She headed off to college last September, up in Dublin. I'm in Galway, of course, so there's a fair distant between us now.'

'I know that feeling,' Ava said with a sigh. 'Is it purely geographical distance?'

Mia stopped walking and looked at her. 'You're a canny one,' she said. 'We must have more in common than we knew.'

Ava looked at the figures of Daisy and Felicity walking on ahead and nodded slowly. 'I'd say we do, Mia, I'd say we do. Tell me, how has her moving out been for you? Daisy moved in with her boyfriend just a few weeks ago, but I already feel like a part of me is dead.'

Mia looked almost scared to admit her true feelings, but she knew Ava was a kindred spirit. 'That's exactly how I feel, you've hit the nail on the head,' she said quietly. 'Felicity moved to Dublin for college, of course, but then she met a chap called Shane and now she's living in his apartment. He's ten years older than her, Ava, and I don't know what to say or do about it. I know she has to grow up and move on from me, but I never thought it'd be so hard to let go. That's the only reason I haven't curled up and a ball and given up is that I know she's happy right now.'

'Oh, I'm with you on that one, Mia,' Ava agreed. 'There's something very special about the mother-daughter bond, isn't there? But it's also very difficult, you have to keep trying to maintain the boundaries, don't you? There's such an urge to step in and make everything better, but it just doesn't work when they're young women themselves.'

The two women shared a battle-weary smile, acknowledging the years of hope and heartache that constituted motherhood. They understood each other perfectly, even without words.

'Well, from past experience I've learned that the best cure for heartache is to keep myself busy. I need to shake myself and look to the future, join a class or somesuch. And then there's retail therapy, of course, which many women will agree can be a wonderful help. I indulged in a bit of that before we came away,' Mia said with a laugh.

'I have to say, I'm your sister when it comes to shopping. I have friends who loathe it. I often wish I was like that, then I'd be rich!' Ava laughed. 'Did you have any luck on your expedition?'

'Indeed I did, girl,' Mia nodded. 'My swimsuit hadn't been updated for years and although I'm fierce thrifty, even I knew I needed a new one. No matter who you are, the arse-hanging-down-to-the-back-of-the-knees look just isn't attractive in a swimsuit!'

'Ha! I certainly need a good solid one piece at my age!' Ava agreed.

'Well, Ava, I struck gold. I stumbled upon a little boutique with an entire stock that I loved.'

'Oh, it's great when that happens. I do find it hard to get clothes at my age, I don't want to look like mutton dressed as lamb, but at the same time I'm not ready for tweed skirts and boring twin-sets topped off with a house coat.'

'This place I found was just the ticket, and the girls were lovely too, which was half the battle. They knew what to mix and match and what would suit me. There was none of the loud thumping music and skimpy clothes that make me like an ageing walrus trying to squeeze into narrow, uncomfortable stuff that's too young for me anyway.'

'Oh, there's nothing worse,' Ava agreed. 'I thought it was just me, but some of the shops play such loud music and are so dimly lit that I almost panic and have to leave. I know they're probably aiming at the younger market, but we're the ones with the money, let's face it!'

'It's true for you, girl,' Mia agreed. 'Well, now, if you're ever in Galway, I'll bring you to this place. If I won the lotto tomorrow morning, I'd go and buy one of each thing they had in the shop. I was there for ages, trying one outfit after another. I've found a lot of the assistants make me feel as if my curves are a dreadful affliction devised by the devil in a bad mood, but these girls were friendly and open.'

'Sounds like a shop made in heaven,' Ava said, smiling. 'You'll have to give me the name of it.'

Mia stared out towards the horizon, then turned back to Ava again. 'Actually, between you and me, I'm a bit embarrassed now by what I said to the girls in the shop that day,' Mia admitted.

'Why, what happened?' Ava asked.

'Ah, I just told them how much I appreciated their advice and guidance as I was used to having my daughter with me for help and I missed her input, that she's a great eye for colours and knows instantly what suits me. I said that without her, I thought I'd be too vulnerable to go to the city on my own. I obviously looked very forlorn and depressed,' Mia said, cringing at the memory of the conversation.

'And what did they say?'

'Ah, Lord above,' Mia sighed, 'one of the girls asked with glistening eyes if poor Felicity was dead.'

'Oh, no! I don't believe you,' Ava said sympathetically.

'So I had to quickly say it was nothing like that. That she's only gone to live in Dublin. I felt so silly.'

Ava put her hand gently on Mia's arm. 'Look, Mia, I totally understand where you're coming from. I'm struggling with letting Daisy go right now and she's only living around the corner. So believe me, your reaction isn't out of the ordinary.'

'I've no doubt it's not, but I actually lost my firstborn child, another little girl, Amy, to cot death a long time ago. So I know first-hand the difference between a child moving on and a death,' Mia said, struggling to keep the emotion out of her voice. 'Do you know what, Ava? Now that I'm saying it all out loud to you, it's really driving home the fact that I should concentrate on being more positive about this next phase in Felicity's life.'

'Easier said than done though,' Ava pointed out. 'I wouldn't be too harsh on yourself, Mia.'

'Ah, thanks girl. God forgive me, but I wonder whether I'm turning into a bit of a sour auld one. I seem to have it in my head I don't like this fella she's moved in with,' Mia continued. 'He's older than her and works at UCD. I keep thinking I'd like him more if he were the same age and lived within a two-mile radius of our house, but, do you know, I'd probably find something wrong with him at that!'

'Well if you're beating yourself up, you should pass the stick to me,' Ava admitted. 'Daisy and I are in danger of being torn apart just at the minute, too. Justin, my husband, and I are against her engagement to this Nathan fellow.'

'Why, doesn't he treat her well then?'

'No, nothing like that. She was engaged before to another boy and we all adored him. But Daisy wasn't happy, so she called it off,' Ava explained.

'And now you don't want her marrying the man she actually loves instead?' Mia raised an eyebrow and smiled.

'Okay, point taken,' Ava grinned.

'Ah, listen, people in glass houses and all that,' Mia said, linking

Ava's arm. 'It's very easy to see the wood for the trees when you're on the outside looking in. It's not quite so simple when it's your little girl involved, is it?'

As they reached their destination, the younger girls were delighted to find a little row of typically Spanish boutiques.

'I love the late opening hours in these countries,' Daisy exclaimed. 'That shop might be tiny, but I can already see at least two pairs of shoes that could be coming home in my suitcase,' she said.

'Why don't we have a drink and bite to eat and we could always have a quick retail therapy session afterwards?' Felicity suggested.

They settled on a place that boasted the best paella at the port, courtesy of a small chalkboard at the entrance.

Tally stuck to her white wine spritzer while all the others opted to share jugs of sangria.

'Why aren't you having what everyone else is having?' Greta asked. She figured she needed to start making a huge effort to notice what her daughter was doing.

'It's too sugary and high in calories. I'd rather have my two glasses of white wine, watered down with sparkling water. I'm going to have fresh fish, too, if that's okay with all of you. I'd eat the entire sharing dish of paella on my own given half the chance, but it's too much of a carb overload. I'd prefer to go for the fish option and that way I can have wine,' Tally explained.

'You do whatever suits you, darling,' Ava said, smiling.

'What sort of a system is it?' Mia asked. 'Or would you rather we didn't discuss it?'

'Oh, I'm totally happy to talk about it. It's a motivation therapy, Mia. Basically, unlike the usual weight-loss programmes where there might be points or a certain amount of food allowed, this works on the mind and body,' Tally explained. 'The clinic looks to the emotional reasons why people overeat and they have amazing back-up tools to help,' Tally continued.

'What, like, milk shakes and that sort of thing?' Daisy asked.

'No, they don't go for products, it's more about building self-confidence and training yourself to feel and act in a positive manner, while simultaneously tackling the nutritional element. They have CDs and DVDs with positive thinking strategies, as well as meal and recipe suggestions. But for me the biggest difference is that I have a lady called Sinead as my 'motivation mate'. She's like a constant back-up counsellor whom I can speak to and meet with. She's also been through the same journey I'm on.'

'What, she was a blimp?' Greta said, unable to stop herself. She spluttered with laughter at the thought of Tally's up-on-a-pedestal counsellor being a fattie.

'Well, that's not the kindest way of putting it,' Mia said, shooting the woman an icy stare. Greta blanched. She'd done it again, said the wrong thing.

'I was only messing, I didn't mean to come across as rude, honestly,' Greta said, looking edgy.

Mia was surprised – that was the first time she'd heard Greta apologise for putting her foot in it. She wondered if something had happened earlier to lead to this change of heart. Having chatted to her the day before, Mia was well aware that Greta genuinely didn't set out to upset Tally, but hearing her voice an actual apology was a massively positive step.

'What Sinead does,' Tally continued, choosing to ignore Greta's rudeness, 'is help change my perception of myself. She's encouraging me to become the person I long to be on the inside as well as the outside.' Tally was amazed at how calm she was discussing all this. Normally she'd be beading with sweat, terrified of what the others thought of her mother. But something had clicked in Tally's head during her outburst that afternoon. It wasn't a reflection on her if Greta landed herself in hot water. She wasn't going to feel responsible for her mother's blunders any longer.

The waiter came and took their order. Felicity and Tally ordered fish and all the others agreed to try the paella.

When the food came, Greta put some on her plate and spent the next few minutes shoving it around with a slightly disgusted expression on her face.

'Don't you like it?' Tally asked her mother.

'No, too heavy and fishy,' Greta said, looking at the food as if it was going to poison her.

'I've a protein shake in my bag and I'll drink that instead. I'll catch you all later.' She excused herself hurriedly and left Tally and the others to eat their food.

'I'm sorry, everybody, Ma doesn't mean to be rude. She's just not a restaurant type of person. She's not used to sitting over food for long periods, and she's happier with a shake and a fag for her dinner,' Tally explained. 'She's kind of complex, to be honest.'

'You don't need to apologise for her, love,' Mia said, patting the girl's hand. 'Let's all just enjoy our meal. Once your mother is happy having a little walk around, sure isn't that what it's all about? We're on holiday after all!'

'Indeed,' Ava agreed. 'We should all do as we please while we're here. I'm sure your mother wasn't planning to spend her week with strangers, so there's no pressure at all from our end, is there, Daisy?'

'No,' agreed the younger girl through a mouthful of food.

'I can't speak for Ma, but I'm thrilled to have met you all. You're all really easy to chat to and I feel like I can be myself. As long as I'm not intruding, Ma can go and swing.' There was silence for a moment as nobody knew what to say.

'Cheers!' Felicity shouted, holding up her glass.

They all saluted and the awkwardness passed. They ended up chatting until the staff politely asked them to leave. They looked around in surprise, realising they were the only ones left in the restaurant.

'Let's go back to our apartment and have a couple of drinks. We bought a ton of white wine in the supermarket.' Felicity suggested.

'Good thinking, Bat-Woman,' Mia agreed.

They paid the bill, strode back towards the complex and headed for Apartment 210.

'I'll just check on Ma and see if she'd like to join us, if you don't mind?' Tally asked. With her new-found inner peace, Tally decided she didn't want to fight with Greta anymore. She didn't want to live with the negative energy constantly. She was going to make the move to try and be adult-like and hope to God that her mother had the wherewithal to follow suit.

'Of course, love. Tell her she's more than welcome, sure it's only over the corridor,' Mia assured her.

Greta was out on the balcony smoking when Tally let herself into the apartment.

'Do you want to come and join us for a drink? They're really nice women, if you give them a chance you might think the same,' Tally encouraged.

'Ah, sure, I'll come over for a while then.'

As they both arrived at the apartment, it was as if the other women had made a silent pact to try and keep the mood positive. They all smiled a little wider and giggled at the slightest things. But Greta just didn't lend herself to being pliable. She was what Mia classed as 'tricky'.

Unlike earlier, Greta was flooring the wine. 'I think there's a hole in my glass, I'll have another drop if it's going,' she said, helping herself to the bottle. 'Give me five minutes and I'll grab some wine from our place.' Greta had leapt up and returned before anyone could blink. The wine seemed to have loosened her tongue. 'You see the way all of you love sitting around all the time doing nothing? I can't do that. I would be insane.' Greta banged the two syllables out on the table. 'Totally doo-lally.'

'Well, believe it or not, the way you can't relax or concentrate on a book for five minutes, *that* would drive me to drink,' Mia commented as she took a sip of wine.

'Looks like it has already,' Greta pointed out. They all burst out laughing and the conversation turned to other things.

Once she relaxed a bit, the other ladies saw a different side to Greta. She was actually dreadfully unsure of herself. The rushing around and outward bravado was obviously masking years of uncertainty.

'I wasn't always this driven, you know,' Greta confessed, waving her fifth glass of wine about. 'In fact, if any of you saw my wedding photos, you'd laugh. I looked like one of those caricature hippos in a tutu.'

'I can't imagine you ever looked like that,' Ava said.

'Believe me, I could've crushed you by sitting on your lap,' Greta confirmed. 'But, bless him, Martin still fell in love with me. He's seen me go through the transformation from *huge* to this!'

'He sounds like a good man,' Daisy commented.

'Oh, God, he is, love,' Greta said, banging the table again for emphasis and swigging her wine. 'Isn't he, Tally?'

'That's one thing we can always agree on for sure,' Tally smiled.

'When you've found the right man, there's a sense of knowing, isn't there?' Ava offered.

'You bet,' Felicity said, staring at Mia.

'Amen to that!' Daisy said, making eye contact with Ava.

'Listen, ladies, I'm beat. I'll have to love you and leave you. Thanks for having us over,' Greta said, standing up and staggering a bit. 'Oops, I think I'm langered!' she said, bursting out laughing.

Her laughter was infectious and as the stood holding the back of the chair cackling away, the others dissolved into giggles along with her.

'See you all tomorrow,' Tally said, waving as she guided her mother out the door.

'We could have a bit of a sing-song tomorrow night,' Greta said. 'I can do a bit of Adele for you.' As the hiccups took over, Tally led her towards their apartment.

'That was a bit of fun, wasn't it?' Tally said yawning.

'Tally,' Greta grabbed her arm as they shut and locked their door for the night. 'I'm sorry ...'

'For what, Ma?' she asked, looking confused.

'For everything. You're a great kid. Well you're a lay-dee now I suppose,' she said in a posh voice starting to giggle again. 'Give your old ma a hug.'

Tally almost had to pinch herself as she felt her mother's arms embracing her. It was the first motherly gesture she could remember receiving for a very long time.

38.

Although it was only June, the temperature had hit thirty-four degrees by mid-afternoon. Ava and Daisy had a quick bite of lunch in their apartment before making their way to the pool.

'Hi girls,' Tally greeted them. 'I'm just grabbing a bottle of water from our apartment. I'd recommend the beach today. It's stifling at the pool. The beach isn't a whole lot better, but at least there's a gentle wisp of a breeze by the sea.'

'Thanks, Tally, we'll take your advice on that,' Ava said gratefully. 'See you shortly.'

The twosome arrived to find Greta pelting up and down along the shoreline in bare feet, running shorts and a singlet vest. She waved as she grimaced and kept jogging.

'How does that woman have the energy to run in this heat?' Daisy said quietly to her mother.

'Search me. Mind you, I wouldn't have the inclination, let alone the vigour,' Ava said, waving back. 'Do you want to join the others or sit on our own?'

'I'm easy, although I do want to chat to you about the wedding. If you'd rather we do that in private, then maybe we should sit down the other end a small bit,' Daisy said.

Ava felt rooted to the spot. This was the moment she'd been dreading. She'd been thinking long and hard about the conversation she'd had with Mia. Ave knew she had to try and see things from her daughter's perspective a little, but she was being torn in two directions. Justin had been on the phone again, as strong as ever in his opinion that Daisy had taken leave of her senses and it was their duty as parents to save her from herself.

'Her snap decision to dump Freddie was totally out of character. She's just not herself. All this defiant behaviour is a cry for help,' he had insisted.

The thing was, Ava didn't think she agreed with her husband

anymore. Daisy had always known her own mind. The thing was, Daisy knowing her own mind had quite simply never posed as a problem for herself and Justin before. But that didn't mean they were right and she was wrong. If parenthood had taught Ava anything at all, it was the fact that children could be totally unpredictable. None of them came with a guidebook and what might suit one child wouldn't necessarily suit another.

Luckily, Tally arrived back and they fell into step with her and ended up at a neighbouring sunbed, which meant there could be no private wedding talk. Ava knew she was putting off the inevitable, but she just couldn't face it, not yet.

Mia and Felicity were both tucked under a shade, reading books and listening to iPods.

'Hiya, girls!' Mia yelled.

'Jesus, Mam, keep your voice down, I think there's a deaf woman in Morocco who didn't hear you.'

'Sorry,' Mia apologised as she released her earphones. 'I got a gift of this thing from my sons and I'm always forgetting to pull the bits out of my ears before I talk.'

'Well, I'm impressed you know how to use it at all,' Ava said.

'It's not bad once you get the hang of it. One of the lads puts the music on for me and I know which buttons to press after that. I've everything from classical stuff to Elvis.'

As Mia and Ava sat and talked about the wonders of technology, Daisy told Felicity and Tally about the Flamenco dress she'd bought that morning in the nearby market.

'Oh, you mad thing! I saw those when I was out for a walk earlier,' Tally laughed. 'I wouldn't get my big toe into one at the moment, but I have to admit I did think they were gorgeous.'

'So are you going all Flamenco for your wedding, then?' Felicity asked.

'Oh, I never thought of that! But, then, it wouldn't be seasonal. I still have to talk to Mum about it, but Nathan was on the phone last night and he's looking to do the wedding just before Christmas! His family will be over from the States and he'd love for it all to happen then.'

The girls chatted about themes and styles and their ideas of how they'd always dreamed they'd look on their wedding day.

'I was never big into the whole wedding thing,' Daisy admitted. 'Quite frankly, I don't mind if we get married up a tree by a squirrel just so long as it happens.'

'Seriously?' Tally said with interest. 'I think I'd be off buying every magazine going and doing up rotas of which shop I should visit next so I could totally lap up every moment of it all. It's so romantic!'

'You really are an awful soppy git!' Daisy teased.

'Yup, I admit it, I'm a true romantic. I love old movies and chick flicks and all that goes with it,' Tally stated.

'I'm probably somewhere in between,' Felicity mused. 'I wouldn't be satisfied with the squirrel ceremony, but I wouldn't be on for *My Big Fat Gypsy Wedding* either.'

'Can you imagine my mother if I suggested that kind of an over-the-top do?' Daisy giggled. 'Then she'd really have something to complain about!'

All the ladies, bar Greta, had a relaxing time whiling away the afternoon, dipping in and out of the sea and lolling under umbrellas. Greta was simply incapable of sitting still and headed off to the gym.

'I'm going to pop back to the apartment and have a shower and wash my hair. I've had enough of the heat for the moment,' Ava announced.

'I'll come with you, Mum,' Daisy agreed.

All the chat with the girls earlier had made Daisy feel really excited about the wedding. She wanted to sit and run through the plans with Ava.

'Let's have a glass of chilled white,' Daisy suggested as they trooped up the stairway to their apartment.

'That sounds delicious. I'm not usually an afternoon drinker, but I can't think of anything I'd prefer right at this moment. We can sit in the shade of the balcony and have a natter.'

Daisy bundled enthusiastically out onto the balcony with the wine and some crisps.

'So, I don't know if you overheard my conversation with the girls earlier, Mum, but Nathan wants to do the wedding at Christmas time. What do you think?' Daisy's eyes were shining.

Ava had, of course, heard the girls talking. Her mind had been racing as she'd tried to think of a way to stall this whole wedding.

'I'm not sure Christmas is a brilliant time, darling. Don't people have enough on? It'd be a shame for the wedding to be lost in the hubbub of Christmas.'

'Oh, no, I think if we had it on the twenty-third, everyone would be in top form and ready to celebrate. The other reason is that Nathan's family are coming to Ireland and they'd love to work it all into their trip,' she reasoned. 'Besides, Dad will be home from New York for definite too, so it works for us all.'

Ava kept hearing Justin's anxious voice in her head, instructing her to get Daisy to change her mind. That was all fine and well and she could understand that her husband didn't want their daughter to marry Nathan, but at the end of the day, what was most important? Daisy's happiness, that's what.

'Do you really love this guy?' Ava asked after a few large gulps of wine.

'Steady on, Mum, you're going to be hammered by six o'clock if you're not careful.'

The normally mischievous Ava didn't crack a smile. 'Do you honestly see yourself spending the rest of your life with this guy?' Ava needed to get a serious handle on what she was dealing with here before she voiced any kind of opinion.

'Why is he "this guy" all of a sudden. His name is Nathan, as you well know, and what's with the shuddering innuendo that he's some sort of second-rate option?' Daisy looked stung.

'Daisy, Daddy and I aren't sure about him. I have to be honest with you. In fact, we're worried that he mightn't be, how shall I put it, right for you,' Ava admitted, her voice wobbling.

'Yes, but don't forget you and Dad thought Freddie was the perfect man for me and he was a total ass. What's your problem with Nathan? Spell it out, Mum.' Daisy was quite clearly fuming.

'We're terrified he's too different, he's grown up on a different continent.'

'Thanks for your "concern" and all, but since when do either of you live with him? You actually don't know the first thing about him. You're so bloody busy comparing him to Freddie the Freak that you haven't bothered to see that he makes me happy,' Daisy practically yelled.

Daisy jumped up from her chair, stomped off and slammed the door behind her as she disappeared into her room.

Ava's head fell forward and she squeezed her eyes shut. *Well done, Ava, you handled that really well.*

In her room, a sobbing Daisy was dialling Nathan's number.

'Hey, Daisy-Darlin', how's your day going?' he answered in his usual sunny way. Daisy wanted to bawl down the phone and tell him that her mother was being a witch. Right at that moment, all she wanted was Nathan's arms around her. But on hearing Nathan's kind and gentle tones, she bit her tongue. He'd be crushed to know that her parents wished he'd evaporate from her life forever.

'Hi, honey,' she managed to croak through her sobs.

'Hey, what's up?'

'Ah, nothing much, I think I've a bit of a sniffle from the air-con. It happens to me sometimes,' she lied.

Nathan told her all about the sites his company had secured. So far they were on target for building four indoor centres in Ireland.

'My father is real happy that we're managing to acquire these places so readily. I guess it's kind of harsh, as we're making hay while some poor people are struggling financially. But the truth of the matter is that we could never have afforded to take on so many places if the Celtic Tiger was still roaring.'

Daisy lay on the bed and listened to Nathan's Californian lilt as he filled her in on his plans. Finally, she said her goodbyes and hung up. She lay on her bed, feeling foolish for her earlier behaviour. She sighed heavily, pulled herself up and padded over to open the door. She went out and found Ava still sitting on the balcony, her eyes betraying the tears she'd cried.

'Mum,' Daisy said gently, 'I'm sorry I behaved like a teenager. It wasn't helpful.'

'Can we talk?' Ava looked about as stricken as Daisy felt.

'Let's go into the living room.' Daisy flung herself on one of the plump sofas, looking miserable.

'I'm sorry, love. I'd no right to tell you Dad and I don't approve of Nathan. It's not up to us who you marry,' Ava hung her head.

'That's all very well, Mum, but now I know how you both feel it actually changes a lot. I will marry Nathan. You can be sure of that, but I need time to think about how I should go about it. I'm not having you and Dad ruining our day, so we might change plan and go abroad and have an intimate beach ceremony or something. To be perfectly honest, the thought of it being just the two of us in the Caribbean or somewhere similar, with no stress, is extremely appealing.'

'Daisy, please! Your father and I would die if we couldn't be at your wedding. Daddy has always dreamed of walking you down the aisle. It'd crush us both if you exclude us,' Ava pleaded.

'Mum, I'm not going to allow you and Dad make me feel like Princess Fiona marrying Shrek. I'm happy with Nathan, and if you can't bring yourselves to stop with the control thing, then I'll be forced to make a choice. This is killing me, but you've now cornered me and the moment of truth has arrived,' Daisy stated firmly. 'I'm a grown woman and I'm entitled to make my own decision.'

'I'm sorry, love. Dad and I had no idea how unhappy you've been,' Ava said sounding choked. 'There is one other reason why I personally have been opposed to your marrying Nathan and I haven't even voiced it to your father,' Ava hesitated.

'What?' Daisy sounded like she was all out of sympathy for her mother.

'Daisy, I've lived through my entire marriage balancing my time with your father. I know his job has given us a comfortable lifestyle and that he can't do what he does in Ireland,' Ava took a deep breath. 'I didn't want to raise three children in New York, so Daddy's commuting has been our compromise.'

'Go on,' Daisy encouraged.

'You and your brothers are my most amazing accomplishments in life. It's hard enough having Luke in the UK, but at least he comes home regularly and I can visit him any time I like. But I'm terrified Nathan is going to want to move back to America and take you with him.'

'Oh, Mum,' Daisy said sadly.

'What if you have children, which I sincerely hope you do, and they're taken away from Dad and me? I honestly don't know if I could deal with it.'

'You should've told me all this before, Mum. You've skirted around the issue since the day Nathan and I got engaged. Right now, I'm so hurt that I'm not sure I believe what you're saying. I need to think,' Daisy said, grabbing her sunglasses and storming out.

Not quite sure where she was going, she found herself stomping along the coastline towards the port. It was almost seven in the evening and she groaned as she spotted Greta jogging towards her. Florid in the face and bathed in sweat, the other woman waved.

'Hello, Greta,' Daisy managed, forcing herself to be mannerly.

'Hi, Daisy, off to the port for a mooch around, are you?'

'Sort of.'

'Are you all right?' Greta stopped jogging on the spot and stared at Daisy.

'I've had a bit of a blow-up with Mum. I came out to cool off. I'm not sure where I'm going, to be honest.' Daisy sat on a low brick wall and stared across the little pathway out to sea.

Greta plonked down beside her and exhaled loudly. 'Jesus, it's hot here, isn't it?'

'Sure is.' Daisy really wasn't in a lets-talk-about-the-weather mood. 'Especially if you're doing frantic exercise. You're like the Road Runner, do you know that? Don't you ever get sick of booting around like everyday is an Olympic race?' Daisy asked. She knew she was being more than a little forward, but she didn't really care.

'Ah, I suppose I'm used to it. I don't quite know what to do with myself if I'm not bopping around, you know?' If she was meant to take offence, Greta certainly didn't. 'So what have you got to be glum about? Pretty little thing like you, with a man waiting to marry you at home and a new career about to take off.'

'Yeah, you'd wonder how I've a worry in the world when you put it like that. But guess what, Greta? Just because I'm slim and have a boyfriend doesn't mean I'm exempt from any negative feelings. Imagine, I'm a size eight and yet I still get angry and sad. Astonishing, isn't it?' Daisy scowled at the ground as she shuffled her toe in the small scattering of sand that had been thrust onto the pathway from the beach.

'Ooh, pa-ding! That'll level me, won't it?' Greta nudged the younger girl with her shoulder. 'Want to tell me what's going on, or would you rather I said *meep-meep* and buggered off like the Road Runner, as you so delicately called me?'

'Sorry, Greta, that was rude. I'm just really hurt.' Tears began to course down Daisy's cheeks as she spoke. 'Mum has just told me that neither she nor Dad want me to marry Nathan. They're hung up on an ex-boyfriend who they deemed to be my Prince Charming. The only problem with that plan was that I didn't love him. The other thing which my mum has only just admitted is that she's scared I'll run off to America with Nathan.'

'You and your ma are very close. I don't know Ava that well, but I have eyes. I can see that she adores you. She probably *is* afraid you're going to take off with this American hunk of yours and leave her broken-hearted,' Greta mused. 'You've a special bond, you and your ma. Not like Tallulah and me. We don't have the mother and daughter thing. She's just a daddy's girl and I've had to accept that.'

Greta shrugged as she dropped her gaze to the ground, too. 'Give your ma a break, love. When Martin and I got engaged, I think my ma was so relieved that someone wanted me, she didn't think twice. It helped that Martin was Auntie Marie's son. She was my ma's best friend. You're different though. You have it all going for you, love. I'd say they also feel nobody's good enough for you. That's nice, though. They mean it in the best possible way, I reckon.'

Daisy sat in silence for a few moments. 'Why did you, or your mother for that matter, think you wouldn't get anyone else?'

'Because I was fat and useless in those days. But Martin, God bless him, liked me the way I was.'

'And does he still like you as much now that you spend your entire existence running away from the fat person you quite obviously still see in your mind's eye?' Daisy looked at Greta's sunken cheeks and her prune-like, sun-damaged skin.

Greta looked a bit startled for a moment, but then recovered herself. 'Martin is one of life's gentlemen. He has always loved me, no matter what way I've looked. He loves his daughter, too. The only one who's had trouble loving me is myself,' Greta said honestly. 'As you have summarised after knowing me only jig time, I spend my time running away. I need to slow down. I want to try and be the mother my daughter deserves,' Greta said quietly. For that moment, she was tender and reserved. The brashness faded. 'Tell me about your fella, this Nathan,' she said to Daisy.

Daisy spoke about Nathan. She told Greta how much he made her laugh and explained that he was different from any other guy she's ever known.

'He has this new business, a lovely flat, a flash car, he's stunning looking, works out in the gym, even *you'd* approve of him!' Daisy sighed. 'But for me, the most important thing is that he doesn't view me as a possession or someone he can control. He lets me be myself.'

Greta didn't move or even attempt to speak. She too stared out to sea and tried to take in what Daisy had just said. She'd never viewed herself the way this girl had just described. She'd never in a million years have thought that anyone on the planet would have thought she was anything but fit and über-healthy.

This young girl was right about one thing, though. Greta still looked in the mirror and saw a fat, lazy slob. No matter how many kilometres she ran or how many strokes she swam, the image in her mind never lost weight.

'Your parents sound like decent people. Do yourself a favour and give them a break,' Greta said, still looking ahead.

'Well if it's lets-all-dole-out-advice hour, you should give your daughter a chance. She's struggled all her life having been labelled as the fat and slovenly one by you. She's changing and she's trying so hard. If you don't give her a break, she's going to pass you by in a jiffy. Then, not only will you be running on your own, but she won't be there waiting when you return.'

Both women sat unspeaking for the longest time. The light faded as the sun melted into the sea.

'Do you know what's weird?' Greta broke the silence.

'What's that?'

'If Tally had tried to say what you just said there, I'd go off on a mad one. I wouldn't even listen to her.'

'Why not?' Daisy looked at the older woman. 'Or am I being too forward?'

'No, it's a fair question. I'm ashamed to admit, but I always think I'm right and she's wrong.'

'She knows that. Even I can see it and I've only just met you,' Daisy said.

'Do you think it's too late to try and change our relationship?' Greta asked.

'It's never too late to tell someone you're sorry,' Daisy said. Instinctively, she reached her arms out and hugged Greta.

'You're a beautiful girl – and not just on the outside,' Greta said warmly. 'Do me a favour, will you?'

'What's that?'

'Take your own advice. Tell Ava you're sorry for having a freak attack just because she gave her opinion. She's also opened up her heart to you about your da being away so often. That can't have been easy. I've no doubt she's feeling pretty rotten right now.'

Daisy knew Greta was making sense. She knew her parents would walk over hot coals for her. But a small part of her still felt undeniably hurt on Nathan's behalf.

'Will you do *me* a favour, then?' Daisy asked in return.

'Go on then.'

'Will you ease up on Tally? Your daughter is a wonderful person. She's doing so much to try and change herself at the moment. She wants to be happier and feel better about herself, but no matter how much weight she sheds, the one thing that would make her feel as light as a feather is your love and understanding.' Daisy looked directly into Greta's eyes. 'She's not hard to like, Greta. She's funny, sweet and such a caring girl. Yes she's quite obviously close to her dad, but that doesn't mean you can't join in too.'

Greta pulled a box of cigarettes from the back pocket of her running top. As she inhaled the smoke, Daisy giggled.

'What?' Greta looked her up and down with a slight grin.

'I could barely drive the distance you seem to run and swim each day, and yet you smoke. Has it never occurred to you that cigarettes aren't great for your health?' Daisy bit her lip hoping she hadn't gone too far.

'Ah, sure, I can't be perfect! Otherwise I'd be irritating!' Greta burst out laughing. 'I know I should give up. I know it's an antisocial habit, but one step at a time with the whole change theme.'

'Will we go back and face the music?' Daisy asked.

'Yeah, come on then. I'll go and see if I can start to make amends with my daughter.'

'And I'll try and understand my parents more.'

The two women strolled back to the apartments together, ready to face whatever lay in store for them.

39.

The following morning Greta went for her usual early morning jog. As she picked up a bottle of cool water at a small store, the owner approached her.

'You like go to typical Spanish trip? Is very happy and so much for you to see. I have only few seats left in my bus, so I give you good price,' the man said.

'Where is it to?' Greta shouted. She figured if she spoke slowly and loudly, he might know what she was on about.

'Ronda. Very beautiful. Usually price sixty euro, I do you nice price.'

'How much for six?' Greta said narrowing in on him.

'I do you forty euro each,' he said, eyeballing her right back.

'No, thirty-five. There's six of us, so that's a lot of cash for you, my friend,' she bargained. He acted as if she'd just suggested hacking his own leg off with a shovel.

'Ah, no, lovely lady, it's too little for me.'

'Suit yourself then,' she said, grabbing her bottle of water. 'See you so.'

As she was about to run back her señor reappeared.

'Okay, we do thirty-five euro each.' Spitting on his hand to seal the deal, he held it out for her to shake. 'You come here,' he pointed at the small car park behind his shop, 'three o'clock this afternoon.'

'Deadly, see you then,' she shook his hand. As she ran back towards the complex and rubbed her hand off her jogging shorts, she sincerely hoped the others would go along with the idea. Still, she figured if they didn't want to she'd just avoid the man the following day. There were plenty of places she could buy water instead.

Tip-toeing to the door of Ava and Daisy's apartment, she listened outside for a minute to hear if they were awake. She could hear mumbled talking, so she knocked.

They were delighted with the idea and agreed immediately.

'Thanks for thinking of us, Greta,' Ava said. 'We'll really look forward to that. It's lovely to see the surroundings rather than confine ourselves here all week.'

Mia and Felicity were just as enthusiastic and agreed to meet at the bus later on.

By the time three o'clock rolled around, the ladies were really excited about the excursion. Meeting at the gate to the complex, they wandered towards the bus.

'We'd better keep it to ourselves that we only paid thirty-five each for the tour,' Greta mused. 'We don't want to start a riot!'

They were surprised to see a large crowd at the buses.

'Wow, there must be seventy or eighty people going,' Ava said looking impressed. 'It makes me think it's going to be really good.'

Just under an hour later, they finally pulled in at the foot of the village. The view of the costa below was spectacular.

'It was worth coming all the way up here just to see that,' Greta said as she stretched her legs. 'This is real old-style Spanish stuff, isn't it?' she grinned.

The tour guide called them all over, announcing that she would take one busload and her colleague would take the other.

'I will bring you to the spectacular Feria Goyesca now. This is the original birthplace of bull fighting in Spain.'

'Gosh, I hope they don't still hold bullfights here,' Daisy said, looking nervous. 'I really wouldn't be into that.'

'No, me neither,' Tally agreed. 'I know it's their tradition and all that, but it looks barbaric on TV.'

'It's actually really interesting as the tradition is so old,' Felicity explained. 'I've learned quite a bit about it in my Spanish course in UCD. The matadors are seen as real heroes. Just the way lots of football fans would worship David Beckham, the Spanish adore the really talented bullfighters.'

'I'd rather look at Becks than a bull being tortured any day,' Daisy said.

When they'd seen the museum where the bullring used to be, the tour was led to the cobbled alley towards the Mondragón Palace and Ronda's stunning, leafy Plaza Duquesa de Parcent.

'Here you can observe the convent, churches and the toytown bell tower of the Iglesia Santa Maria de Mayor.'

'I'm parched. I don't know about you lot, but I'm ready to sit down and have a drink,' Greta said. It was particularly hot that afternoon and the six agreed to wander towards the plaza, which was surrounded with pretty restaurants and bars.

'We need to keep an eye on the time, to make sure we make it back to the bus for home time,' Mia said.

A jug of sangria was on the cards. Tally had her usual spritzer and they all settled into the basket-weave chairs. Kicking off their flip-flops, they relaxed happily.

'This was a great idea, Greta, thanks for taking the initiative,' Ava said.

'Ah, no worries, it wouldn't have entered my head if I'm honest, it was just because yer man said it to me. It's nice to do something different though, isn't it?'

When they'd eaten lunch and paid for the drinks, the group decided to meander back toward the bus.

'Does anyone want to look in the souvenir shop?' Tally asked.

'Not really,' Ava said, looking around to see what the others thought.

'It's only crap, isn't it?' Greta said. 'Ashtrays with bulls on them for a tenner. No thanks.'

As they came down the hill to where the buses would be waiting for them, they stopped in their tracks. The parking spot was empty.

'Were we meant to meet in a different spot?' Mia wondered.

'No, they definitely said to come back here,' Ava said, looking worried.

'What time is it again?' Tally asked.

'It's only a quarter to six. They said six on the dot,' Felicity said. 'Oh, Jesus,' she said suddenly, as her hand flew up to her mouth. 'I never changed my watch when we landed! I'm still on Irish time. The bus left an hour ago!'

'You're not serious?' Greta said, looking stricken.

'How are we going to get back from here?' Mia said, trying to remain calm.

The braying of a nearby donkey made them all turn.

Greta started to cackle first. Her throaty smoker's laugh was impossible to resist. Tally was so relieved her mother wasn't flying into a fit of rage that she began to giggle too. Within seconds, all six of them were falling around laughing.

'I'll go and speak to some of the locals,' Felicity said. 'What's the point in me going to UCD to learn Spanish if I can't get us out of a tight spot like this?'

Perhaps it was the sangria or maybe the sun had finally got to her, but Greta flopped onto the dusty ground and sat with her back against an old stone wall. 'Feck it, I'm sitting here until we decide what to do.'

The remaining ladies looked at one another in shock.

'Greta! You're sitting down when you could be marching up and down ranting!' Mia said in jest.

'Yeah! I am, amn't I?' she grinned. 'Listen, I won't freak you out totally. I'll have a fag and at least you won't have me carted off by the men in white coats.'

'It'd have to be a donkey in a white coat, I'm afraid,' Felicity said returning. 'Do you want the good news or the bad news, girls?'

'Give us the bad news first,' Tally said lightheartedly.

'Well, there isn't a bus out of here until eight o'clock tomorrow morning. There are taxis, but we'd need two and it'd cost us a fortune to get back to the port.'

'Oh, God, what'll we do?' Ava asked looking a bit panicked.

'Well, we could throw caution to the wind and go back to the square. As it happens there's a local festival on tonight. It's not a tourist thing at all but more for the locals. But I've managed to blag us a table at one of the little tavernas. I'd say the food will be cheap as chips and it should be a bit of craic.'

'That's all fine and well, but where are we going to stay?' Ava still wasn't convinced.

'Why don't we go and have a few scoops and see where we end up?' Greta said, standing up and brushing the dust from herself. 'We're on holiday. There's six of us, so we won't be murdered. Sod it!'

Greta stomped off back towards the square, so the others followed obediently.

The whole atmosphere had changed when they rounded the corner. Locals of all ages, from babies to wizened elderly people with missing teeth leaning on walking sticks, had come out to enjoy the evening. Tapas were on offer, with no choice and certainly no menu.

'This could be anything,' Greta said as she poked the latest dish. 'All I can recognise is what used to be a tomato at one point in its life. What do you think the purplish meat is?'

Felicity had a quick chat with the waiter to confirm her suspicion. 'It's bull's testicles,' she said laughing out loud as Greta retched and spat it out.

'Ah, fecking hell, girls, this is seriously bogus. I rarely eat meat or big dinners as it is and the one time I do I end up eating, it's a bloody bull's arse.'

'Well not his arse, strictly speaking,' Tally laughed.

'There's only one thing for it, we'll have to get rat-arsed,' Greta announced with a glint in her eye.

'As opposed to bulls-ballsed,' Mia giggled. The unpredictableness of their situation was making her feel eighteen again – it was like backpacking or interrailing. She felt like anything could happen, and she really didn't mind if it did.

Vats of local wine were the cheapest option, so they went for that. By the time the flamenco dancing and live music began, they were flying high on vino and life. The chairs and tables were moved to the walls and musicians seemed to emerge from the woodwork. The freedom and passion the locals displayed as they clapped and danced entranced the women.

'It's wonderful the way they totally lose themselves in the music, isn't it?' Ava said, clasping her hands in delight.

Felicity was impressing them no end with the fluency of her Spanish.

'Come on, girls,' she said, suddenly beckoning to the five. 'They want to hear us sing now. I've been talking us up and they're expecting U2 meets Riverdance!'

'I can't sing a note,' Ava said, looking petrified.

'Come on, Tally, and we'll give them a few bars,' Greta instructed.

'Do you both sing?' Felicity asked in delight.

'Ah, Mammy always loved a bit of music, in our house growing up, so everyone had to do a party piece when there was a get-together.'

'What are you thinking of?' Felicity asked. 'I can play a few chords on the guitar if they'll let me borrow one.'

Mia felt like her heart would burst with emotion as, moments later, Tally and Greta sang a moving version of 'With or Without You' accompanied by Felicity on a Spanish guitar.

As the song progressed, Greta was struck by the pureness of Tally's voice. Stepping to the side, she figured this was Tally's moment to shine.

'My smokey auld voice isn't adding to the song,' she whispered to Ava. The other woman responded by patting Greta on the leg in support.

All Tally's inhibitions seemed to melt away as she accepted the raptured applause from the locals.

After several more duets, it was clear that Tally and Felicity were the people of Ronda's answer to *The X-Factor*.

'It's so bittersweet to hear her play some of these tunes,' Mia whispered to Ava. 'Her father was a wonderful musician in his day. None of the boys are that into playing and until now, I never realised just how talented Felicity is.'

'Maybe you assumed the boys would follow the male role and play,' Ava said.

'I think so,' Mia agreed. 'I'd say Jim is so proud of her right now.'

They needn't have worried about finding a place to stay. By the time the music came to an end, the sun was beginning to rise.

'Well look at us herd of mad mares,' Greta slurred. 'Up all night drinking and singing goodo!'

'Seeing as we're here, we should go and see the sunrise properly,' Ava suggested. So they bade farewell to the locals who'd managed the all-nighter with them and made their way to the edge of the village. The low stone wall of the old town was the perfect perching post to watch the wonderful display of colour Mother Nature was providing.

Drunk as skunks but unbelievably relaxed and happy, they sat in a row sagging slightly sideways and put their arms around each other's backs.

'Beautiful,' Mia stated.

'Stunning,' Ava added.

'Gorgeous,' Tally sighed.

'*Bonita*,' Felicity said.

'Magnificent,' Daisy whispered.

'Fan-fucking-tastic,' Greta said, before cackling and knocking them all sideways like floppy dominoes.

They all slept on the bus back down to the port. Luckily, there were very few other passengers so nobody had to breathe the fumes of drink as they all snored.

'I'll see you all later,' Tally said, looking shaky and pale as the bus deposited them near their complex.

'I reckon a few hours of sleep and then a bit of lolling by the pool will be the extent of my plans today,' Mia agreed.

'I'm not as young as I used to be,' Greta said. 'Even I can't move a muscle today.'

Waving to each other and promising to hook up later, they all wandered towards their respective apartments. It had been a night of girly bonding that none of them would ever forget.

40.

It was after three that afternoon by the time Daisy appeared by the poolside.

'Good afternoon!' Ava said, smiling warmly at her.

'Hi,' Daisy yawned. 'I can't manage to motivate myself at any decent time here. I think it's those blackout blinds. When there's no daylight, I don't know if it's the middle of the night or halfway through the day.'

Tally and Felicity strolled up behind her.

'Morning!' Felicity said squinting.

'Hi, girls,' Daisy greeted them.

'Hi, everybody,' Tally said, dumping her bag on a sunbed.

Ava and Mia were stretched out, having enjoyed a swim.

'Does anyone feel like going for a bit of brunch to one of the beach bars?' Felicity asked.

'I'll go with you,' Tally said. 'I've a ton of fruit and porridge upstairs, but I couldn't be bothered cooking, so I ended up wandering straight down here – holiday brain has well and truly kicked in for me and I'm starving now!'

'Me too, I'm always hungry, mind you,' Daisy agreed. 'Mum? Mia? Do you want to come?' Felicity offered.

'I'm happy here, love, thanks all the same,' Ava answered. 'I'm feeling a bit worse for wear after last night.'

'Me too, you young ones go on ahead and we'll see you later,' Mia answered.

Pulling on sunhats, the girls waved as they ambled slowly towards the sea and the line of traditional Spanish *chiringuito* beach bars.

'Is your mother off training?' Daisy asked as they settled at a shaded table perched on the edge of the beach.

'Naturally,' Tally said. 'Ah, listen, she'd be like a daddy-long-legs on speed if she didn't go and use up all her energy. She said she was only going for a gentle jog after last night, but I'll believe that when I see it.'

'Will we order some sangria?' Felicity said. 'Hair of the dog and all that? I don't know about you two, but I'm feeling pretty ropey.'

'Yup, not feeling great myself,' Daisy agreed. 'The sangria can only help at this point.'

'I think I'll stick to a spritzer,' Tally said, looking green. 'Although when I got up a while ago, I swore I'd never drink again!'

'Ah, sure, we're on holiday,' Felicity said, justifying it all.

Moments later, Tally Daisy and Felicity clinked glasses.

'To holidays,' Felicity said.

'To finding new friends,' Daisy said.

'To the future and all the wonderful things it's going to bring to each of us!' Tally said.

The girls chatted easily. Their tongues were well and truly loosened an hour and a half later.

'I'm getting pretty pie-eyed,' Daisy said with a hiccup. 'I need a large bottle of water and some food.'

Each time the waiter had approached to take a food order, they'd asked him for five more minutes, explaining they hadn't had time to look at the menu. In the end, he'd given up and simply brought the drinks they kept requesting.

'Good plan,' Tally said. 'Although right now, after two glasses of wine, I'm not even hungry. I just want more wine!' she giggled.

'Eh, honey, that's your third glass!' Daisy pointed out.

'Oh, so it is!'

They ordered some salads and bowls of gaspacho soup and a bottle of cava.

'Bubbles go with everything and I can't drink any more sangria,' Felicity said.

'No, me neither,' Daisy agreed.

'So, we'll go with the sensible option of adding bubbles,' Tally sniggered.

'I'm at a really strange place with my mum,' Daisy suddenly sighed. Leaning her elbow on the table, she rested her chin in her hand.

'Me, too,' Felicity agreed.

'Me three, mind you, it's nothing new in my case,' Tally said. 'Last night was so much fun though, wasn't it? No arguments and no talk of weddings, moving in with people or diets.'

'Maybe that was just what we all needed,' Felicity said, shrugging her shoulders. 'A bit of uncomplicated quality time?'

'Hiya, ladies!'

All three turned to see Greta jogging towards them, waving happily.

'Having a bit of a liquid lunch then?' she asked.

'It wasn't meant to be,' Daisy giggled, 'but sometimes things just evolve, isn't that right, girls?'

'Yup!' Tally was grinning like cat.

'Well, enjoy. I'll see you later.' Greta turned to walk away.

'Do you want to sit and have a drink with us, Ma?' Tally offered.

Greta looked momentarily stunned. 'Ah, no, I'd only bring the average age to an uncool level. I'll leave you to it,' she said softly. 'But thanks for asking.'

'She's not a bad old skin,' Daisy said as Greta left.

'She's great as long as she's not *your* mother,' Tally said pointedly. 'Try growing up in the same house as her when you look and feel like a space-hopper with legs.'

'Was she that bad?' Felicity asked.

'Worse,' Tally said, looking sad. 'I've got my da though, so I'm lucky about that.'

'I never knew mine,' Felicity stated. 'He died before I was born.'

'Do you feel you missed out?' Daisy asked.

'Honestly – no. I can't miss something I never had. Besides, Mam was amazing,' she said. 'I have the opposite problem to you and Greta, I guess. Myself and Mam are so unbelievably close, I feel like I'm crushing her heart like a grape now that I've moved in with Shane.' Felicity became gloomy, too, and tears sprang up in her eyes. 'Ah, sorry girls, you'll think I'm such an eejit, but every time I think of my mother on her own in the house, I feel like I've abandoned her.'

A bit like a domino effect, when Felicity started to cry, so too did Tally, followed by Daisy.

'Sorry,' Tally sobbed. 'I hate seeing anyone cry. I always have to join in. I'm such a softie, I even cry during movies I've seen fifty times before,' she admitted.

'I don't usually cry much at all, so I wholeheartedly blame both of you,' Daisy said as she tried to stop blubbing. 'It must be contagious.'

'Let's blame it on no sleep last night and far too much alcohol,' Tally said, wiping her eyes with the napkin.

As the waiter came bumbling over with their food, he stopped in his tracks looking puzzled. Daisy cracked up laughing at his reaction.

'He really thinks we've all lost the plot here, girls. We've gone from laugh a minute to howling like three widows at a funeral.'

'I need some stodge,' Felicity announced. 'I'm ordering some chips and garlic bread to go with my salad. Any other takers?'

'Defo,' Daisy nodded.

'Not for me,' Tally said, feeling empowered. 'I've passed the point of no return. I can't afford to eat that kind of stuff anymore. The new me is now in charge. I'll have a tuna salad, please,' Tally said to the waiter.

As the other two tucked into their carb-laden feast a short time later, Tally felt an enormous sense of pride as she enjoyed her salad. Amazingly enough, she really was enjoying it too. Her newly trained taste buds could appreciate the gorgeously sweet flavour of the Spanish beefsteak tomatoes and the aromatic olive oil dressing. Just wait until she told Martin and Sinead about this show of willpower!

'So do you reckon you'll hook up with Ben when you return?' Daisy asked, eating another few fries.

'Every time I think of him, I feel like my stomach is filled with butterflies,' Tally said. 'I can't believe he really wants to see me.'

'Sure, why wouldn't he?' Daisy demanded.

'Ah, this is all very new for me, Daisy,' Tally said shyly. 'I wouldn't expect you two to understand. I'm sure you've both had your pick of men, but I'm kind of mortified to admit this ...'

'Go on,' Felicity encouraged.

Tally took a deep breath and spoke in a fast whisper. 'I'm a virgin and Ben is the first guy who's ever wanted to get to know me, as such.' She blushed liked crazy and put her hands over her face. 'Oh, God, you both probably think I'm such a dork now.'

'We don't at all.' Daisy glanced up at Felicity.

'Absolutely not,' Felicity agreed immediately. 'We all do things in our own time. Besides, your love life is nobody else's business.'

'I think I only told you both because I know we won't see each other again!' Tally admitted.

'Well, on that note, I'd love to hook up with you both after we get back,' Felicity said. 'Sorry, Tally,' she said with a smile, 'you'll have to face us again.'

'Great plan,' Daisy answered. 'I'm dying for you both to meet Nathan. If we have a big wedding, I hope you'll both come, but either way I'd love it if you could have a proper look at him before the big event!'

'Please don't think you have to invite us to your wedding,' Felicity said quickly.

'Totally,' Tally agreed, but she was touched Daisy would think of them like that.

'I know I don't have to, I want to. I'd love you girls to be there.' Daisy looked sad again. 'I'd like some happy faces there, people who are glad for me on the big day.'

'I think it's going to be fine, Daisy, try not to worry,' Tally said, reaching over to stroke her arm. 'Your parents adore you and when push comes to shove, I bet they'll put their preconceived ideas aside. Your happiness is the most important thing to them.'

'I agree,' Felicity said firmly. 'Now who's for some of those chocolate brownies that I spied on a passing plate earlier?'

'Oh, I think I've done enough damage for one sitting,' Tally said, holding her hands up in surrender.

'You're so good!' Daisy said. 'I'm the opposite to you, I feel once I'm on the slippery slope, I might as well keep going!'

'Me too,' Felicity agreed. 'Once I start being naughty, I can't stop!'

'How about we order one portion and we'll all have a little bit?' Tally suggested. 'They did look seriously good and now that you've mentioned them, I'll be dreaming about them. This way I can have a taste and get it over with!'

'Deal!' the other two chorused.

They enjoyed their dessert, paid the bill and staggered back to the complex.

'That was a long lunch!' Ava said, squinting up at the girls.

'Sure was,' Daisy answered her mother.

'World put to rights then?' Greta asked.

'Somewhat,' Tally grinned.

'Well we had a lovely picnic, courtesy of Greta,' Ava said.

'Really?' Tally looked shocked – both at the notion that her mother had produced food and that she'd been that sociable.

'I figured what was good for you young ones was good for the mammies,' Greta said. 'So I rustled through our fridge and was most impressed with the salad stuff you had tucked away there.'

'Your mother is a great cook, we had a very tasty lunch,' Mia said.

'That's good, so there were a few of the world's problems sorted poolside too by the sounds of it,' Daisy said, grinning.

'You got it,' Ava smiled.

Within minutes, the six of them were out for the count. Even Greta had succumbed to the heat and allowed herself to have a snooze. The warm, soft breeze and gentle background swishing of the sea made for a perfectly relaxing afternoon. By early evening all the ladies had woken, taken a dip in the pool and returned to the loungers for a flick through the pile of magazines they'd accumulated between them.

The swim woke Greta and they were almost less unnerved when she said she had to go for a proper splash in the sea.

'Ma, I was beginning to wonder if I should phone for an air ambulance for a moment there?' Tally teased her.

'What do you mean?' Greta asked, gazing down at her daughter.

'Lunch, napping and bobbing in the pool, I was wondering if there'd been an alien abduction in Ronda last night!'

'Ah, I think the sun's getting to me,' Greta said. 'I'll do a couple of kilometres in the sea now and blast away the lazy cobwebs,' she finished.

'Enjoy,' Ava said as they all waved.

'I think in spite of herself, Ma is enjoying the break away,' Tally remarked to the ladies as her mother strode towards the beach.

'She certainly seems less on edge,' Mia agreed.

Tally had never felt so comfortable with herself. For once she was able to sit there and feel like she was joining in rather than fitting in.

Daisy looked over at her mum as she chatted to the others. She adored her mum and could plainly see how the others had warmed to her. She was a wonderful mother and lady over all. She really hoped Tally and Daisy were right about her parents coming around to accepting Nathan. She hated the awful atmosphere that had crept into their lives.

For her part, Felicity was also mulling everything over and starting to feel better about it all. She knew her mam loved her – just like Ava loved Daisy – and wanted the best for her. One thing the holiday had taught Felicity was that Mia was well capable of socialising and making friends. When she got into the swing of that back home, Felicity was sure she'd forge a new life for herself and not feel her absence so keenly.

By the end of the holiday the mood in each apartment had shifted massively.

'Have you enjoyed yourself?' Felicity asked Mia.

'Oh, more than I ever expected,' Mia answered honestly. 'Not only have we been able to spend some time together but I've met two lovely friends in Ava and Greta. We've swapped numbers and I honestly think we'll make the effort to meet up at some point soon.'

'That's brilliant, Mam,' Felicity said, looking relieved. 'I've loved getting to know the girls, too. We're going to stay in touch, especially as I'll be in Dublin.'

Mia looked up at her daughter. There was still sadness in her eyes at the mention of her living in the capital, but Felicity saw acceptance all the same.

Greta was helping Tally close the zip on her suitcase.

'That was a great week, wasn't it?' Greta ventured.

'It really was, Ma. I think Da is going to be thrilled when we tell him all about it.'

'Let's try and keep the effort going when we get back home, yeah?'

Tally smiled, her mother was trying so hard. She had to hand it to her, when she got an idea into her head, she went with it full throttle.

Daisy hung up from chatting to Nathan.

'I'd say he's dying to have you back,' Ava said as she walked over to her daughter.

'Yeah he really misses me,' she said simply.

'And why wouldn't he?' Ava tucked a curly strand of hair behind her daughter's ear. 'It'll all be fine sweetheart. I'll talk to your father and we'll get over this bump in the road. Can we try for a fresh start when we get back?'

'I'd love that,' Daisy said hugging her tightly.

As the plane departed from Malaga airport later that evening, all six women felt a major shift had occurred in their lives. None of them would ever forget the week they'd spent in Spain.

Women ...

41.

Felicity

Felicity had the most delicious sleep in her childhood bed and didn't stir until well after ten the following morning. Grabbing her phone, she called Shane before she'd even rolled out of her bed.

'Hello.'

'Jesus, you sound as rough as a bear's arse. Were you drinking petrol last night?' she asked, laughing.

'Oh, my God, it's not funny. Foxy and Andrew decided to make mojitos. But I don't think there was any soda water used after the first three. I feel like I've been savaged by a Rottweiler. So when are you coming back to mind your poor ill boyfriend?' he asked. 'I've had enough of being abandoned by you. We're supposed to be living together. I need you here. My liver can't keep up with it all, let alone my other vital organs,' he said suggestively.

'So you had a terrible evening from start to end, is that what you're expecting me to believe?' Felicity grinned into her pillow.

'You're so heartless. It might have been a tiny bit of fun. It would've been better if you'd been here, though,' he said.

'Oh, you do say all the right things,' she giggled. 'Even if you don't mean it, it's nice to hear,' she yawned.

'I take exception to that. I just can't wait to see you.'

'I can't wait to see you, too. But this is my final step away from Mam. I know this has all been really hard for her and seeing me clear the rest of my stuff from my room is going to be like a smack in the face for her,' Felicity said sadly. 'Ugh … I wish today was over and done with. I hate having to upset her.'

'I know,' Shane said quietly. 'I promise all this will be worthwhile. We'll visit Galway often and make sure to tell Mia she's to come up to us, too.'

'Thanks, honey, I will,' Felicity said. 'I'll call you in a while. Now go and take some paracetemol,' she instructed.

'Yes, Ma'am!' he said. 'Later!'

'Morning, sleepy head.' Mia was crunching toast and pouring herself a mug of coffee.

'Hi, Mam. That coffee smells good. How are you? You look like you've been up and out already,' Felicity said looking at her mother's coat slung over the back of the kitchen chair.

'I was just over at the graveyard. It's a horrible day outside. Come and sit with me so I can look at you.'

'Mam, you've been looking at me non-stop for the past week. I haven't morphed into someone else overnight, you goon!' Felicity laughed.

'I know you haven't. What I mean is, let me savour you.'

Felicity shook her head and gave her mother a hug. 'You're a crazy woman, you know that?'

'Felicity, love, sit down for a minute and let me have my say. I went to the grave early this morning and I have it all set in my head now.' Mia paused and gathered herself. 'I went to the grave today to talk to Amy and Jim. When I lost my baby girl, the world caved in on me, Felicity. I hope you never feel anything like it. But then you came along and the sun came out again, and you've been my sunshine ever since. I've held you close because I love you, and because I needed to. But that has to change now. I know you're feeling torn about the fact you've moved in with Shane in Dublin.' In spite of all her best intentions, tell-tale tears began to slip down Mia's cheeks.

'Mam!' Felicity reached over and took her mother's shaking hands. 'Please don't cry.' Felicity was sobbing, too.

'Let me finish, pet.' Mia took a quivering deep breath and continued. 'Believe me, if I could lock you up in a box and never leave your side I would gladly do it. But you'd be miserable. All I ever wanted for you was happiness. So, much as it breaks my heart, I know I have to set you free. You and Shane need to give your relationship your very best shot. Never hesitate to call me or come home for a bit of comfort and please, my darling girl, promise me one thing?'

Felicity's tears were blurring her vision and she knew she was sniffing uncontrollably. 'What's that?' the young girl managed.

'Be happy, pet. But don't ever be afraid to come home. Don't stay away if you're not content and above all, don't be a stranger. As we know only too well in this house, life is short. Life is ever so precious. You only get one go, one shot at living, so make the most of it, my darling. Don't hesitate and don't, for God's sake, feel guilty for following your heart, ya hear?'

Felicity stood up from her seat and threw her arms around her mother, nearly knocking her backwards off the chair.

'Thank you, Mam. Thank you for putting my happiness first and for telling me it's okay to move on. I know you would rather I stayed with you until I'm old and wrinkled, and I can see it in your face that it took so much selflessness to say all that to me,' Felicity wiped her tears with her hand and tried to steady herself. 'I love you all the more for being so strong. You've given me the most amazing grounding and you've ensured I've started off with a heart filled with love and a head full of confidence. I won't let you down, and I will never be a stranger. I promise,' Felicity vowed.

'Shane is welcome here any time,' Mia said. 'So don't think you have to leave him behind. You don't have to choose. Lord rest him, your daddy would probably turn in his grave, but I've decided you and Shane can share a room if you come to stay. So let there be no reason why you don't come and spend a day or two here, if the mood takes you.' Mia sighed as she finished saying her piece.

'Thanks, Mam. For everything. You're a star, do you know that? I know you have your reservations because Shane is a bit older, but look at it this way, he'll look after me.' Felicity kissed her mother's cheeks and hugged her tightly.

'Go and ring your boyfriend and tell him you'll see him tomorrow. I'm sure he's sick of waiting and wondering when he can have you back.'

Felicity abandoned all attempts at eating her breakfast and bolted to her room to phone Shane.

'... so I'll see you tomorrow afternoon!' she exclaimed.

'That's so cool, I can't wait.' Shane was doing his best to sound exhilarated, but his voice kept cracking and his eyes burned.

'Get some sleep and make sure you don't look like a drunkard when I get there tomorrow,' she warned.

'Jeez, you're not even back yet and you're nagging me,' he sighed.

By the time she'd finished chatting to Shane, and had showered and dressed, Mia had organised to call over to Terry, Felicity's eldest brother.

'Would you like to come with me?' Mia asked. 'I was going to meet your sister-in-law, Carrie, for a bit of lunch and maybe take the boys to a movie. God knows they're little live wires and Carrie always loves to get a couple of hours on her own. I'm dying to give the boys the little pressies we got them in Spain, too.'

'Sounds great. I love seeing my nephews and I haven't had a chat with Carrie for ages,' Felicity agreed.

'You two look so healthy!' Carrie exclaimed as she hugged them an hour later. 'We all look so pasty and white in comparison. You picked a damn good week to elope, I can tell you. All we were missing at one stage was the ark. The rain literally never let up for the entire time you were gone,' she said, biting into a burger.

For ease and by request of the boys, the women had ended up in a burger joint. The boys were thrilled as they played with the toy they'd got in the box of food. The noise level was a few octaves above relaxing and the sound of screeching children was mixed in with the piped music, but at least they could all have a quick catch-up.

'I need a wee,' Kyle announced.

'Quick then, love, we don't need any accidents,' Mia leapt to her feet and winked at Carrie, indicating she'd take care of the bathroom visit.

'How was the break? Mia looks ten years younger. She was so excited about spending time with you,' Carrie said, looking fondly at her mother-in-law's retreating back.

'It was gorgeous, Carrie, really relaxing and we met some lovely people, which was an added bonus. I had a terrible feeling of guilt in the pit of my stomach, though,' Felicity admitted.

'How so?' Carrie asked.

'Both Mam and I have been skirting around the fact that I've moved in with Shane up in Dublin. It has been really hard on both of us. I knew I'd done the right thing insofar as I love Shane and want to be with him, but I hate the fact that I have to hurt Mam in the process,' Felicity explained. 'But Mam and I chatted about it only an hour ago. I didn't know how to broach it with her and she came out with it herself,' Felicity explained. 'She said she wants me to be happy and that Shane can even stay in my room any time we want to come home for a visit,' Felicity said.

'That's great, girl. So where's the problem?'

'I'm having the time of my life up in Dublin, Carrie, but I suppose I have to learn to park the dreadful feelings of guilt when I think of Mam on her own down here,' Felicity admitted.

'She's not on her own, you silly thing. Bob is still in the house. We're always around and she's still working as often as she wants. She misses you like crazy, don't get me wrong, but don't spend your time thinking you're doing something bad. Every girl has to leave her mother at some point. What would you prefer? To still be at home when you're fifty? To be wheeling your eighty-year-old mother to mass every morning and using a trip to the local tea shop as your outlet? Get a grip, Felicity!' Carrie said gently yet firmly. 'Life is for living. You only get one bite of the cherry. You studied hard to get into that college, not every girl gets the opportunity you've created for yourself. Some people never find love in their lifetime either. Don't ruin it with a dose of the guilties,' Carrie warned. 'Grab your well-deserved happiness with both hands and enjoy your life, girl!'

'Yes, Ma'am!' Felicity saluted in jest.

'Ah, you know what I mean! Another thing – once you have kids you'll be grounded enough. I wouldn't change the lads for any money, but, holy God, let me tell you, it's damn hard work. Take pleasure in the here and now, Felicity. It'll fly by and you don't want to harbour regrets later in life.'

'I just worry about Mam, that's all. I can't help it.' Felicity shrugged her shoulders.

'I'll keep an extra eye on Mia and if I think she needs a fix of her darling daughter, I give you my word I'll call you and summon you home, how's that?' Carrie asked.

'Thanks, Carrie, that's a deal.'

'One condition, however ...'

'Go on,' Felicity smiled.

'You take the boys for an hour now. They've new season stuff in my favourite shop and I'm dying to go into the dressing room with twenty things and try them on in peace. Even if I don't buy so much as a sock, I just want to go and play and pretend I still have an identity outside being a mammy, even for an hour!'

'You're on!'

That night, after Felicity had finished another mountain of home-cooked food, Aly arrived.

'It's so good to see you, girl.' They hugged and kissed each other warmly.

'I'm really sorry about all the weirdness to do with Shane and   all ...' Aly trailed off.

'It's okay,' Felicity said, feeling relieved. 'I think you'll really like him if you give him a chance.'

'I'm sure he's brilliant or you wouldn't want to bugger off and leave us all!' Aly slagged. 'Now tell me all about your holiday, was it really relaxing?'

'Not entirely,' Felicity laughed. 'We did an all-nighter in a village in the middle of nowhere.'

'Stop!' Aly said. 'With Mia, too?'

As they shared a glass of wine with Mia, she couldn't hide her joy at witnessing the familiar giggling and banter. 'God, I've missed all the gossip since Felicity and you don't sit here filling me in all the time. Boys tell you nothing. Half the town could be murdered in their beds and the lads would say "everything's grand".' Mia raised her eyes to heaven. 'How's your mother doing since her hip operation, Aly?'

'She's not too bad now, Mia. I'll tell her you were asking for her. She's back doing the basics, but it knocked the stuffing out of her. It's made her shed a couple of pounds in weight, which isn't a bad thing. She says she's determined to keep it off now she's had a head start.'

'Well, I've started Pilates,' Mia continued, 'Niamh Prendergast, who was a couple of years ahead of you girls at school, is teaching it in the church hall. I love it anyway. There's always someone to go for a coffee with afterwards, which is probably the best part, if I'm honest.'

'I'll tell Mam, thanks Mia. Maybe she'd go along with you next week,' Aly said nodding.

As the conversation moved to Shane and how Felicity was dying to see him again, Mia said a silent prayer to herself. *Surround me and mind me, Amy and Jim.* Raising her glass of wine, she saluted her angels above. Felicity wasn't dying, she was doing the exact opposite, she was just beginning to live. Mia knew she'd survive and the world would keep on turning. Sure, hadn't she done pretty well so far, all things considered?

42.

Daisy

Justin was delighted to welcome his girls back home. He had arranged his work schedule so he could pick them up from the airport. After a round of bear hugs, he dropped Daisy to her and Nathan's apartment, then he and Ava had driven home. He wanted more than anything for Daisy to say she was coming with them, but it was obvious she couldn't wait to see Nathan again.

As they shared a glass of wine before dinner, Justin and Ava talked about the holiday. Finally, Justin broached the subject that was the elephant in the room.

'So, sweetheart, how did Operation Nathan go?' he said lightly, but anxious to hear her reply.

Ava grew quiet and her face clouded over.

'What's wrong?' Justin looked nervous.

'She really loves him, Justin. I broached the fact that we have our reservations about him and she was devastated. She reacted really badly and was deeply hurt,' Ava continued. 'Look, I know you mean the best, but it's not up to us who she marries, love. We can't tell her what to do. Her eyes light up when she talks to him. During the past week, I knew when she'd spoken to him on the phone because she'd be glowing. She's so happy. Isn't that all that matters?'

Justin sighed deeply. His legs were crossed and he began to jig his foot up and down, the way he did when he was agitated.

'I honestly thought you'd have this sorted, Ava. This is serious, this guy is looking to marry our daughter and if what you're saying is right, he'd be the father of our grandchildren some day.'

'Eh, sooner rather than later if they have their way. They want a minibus as their family car. They want as many children as possible,' Ava said, shaking her head at the thought.

'I don't get it,' Justin said, looking upset.

'I know all that, Justin but the guy is obviously smart. He's organising this business and seems to have won our daughter's heart. He's not nasty, he's gentle and kind. He doesn't even drink, let alone spend all his time and money in a bar. Just because he can't answer all the questions in Trivial Pursuit doesn't mean he's unworthy.'

'I know, I know,' Justin said in exasperation.

'Nathan's family are coming to Ireland for Christmas and they want to have the wedding then,' Ava spoke as casually as she could.

Justin sighed and rubbed his head. He could see he was beaten. If Ava had decided to take Daisy's side, then he was well and truly out of the game. 'Well if that's the final answer, I guess we'll have to learn to accept Daisy's choice,' he said uncertainly.

Ava smiled at him, silently thanking him for taking the high road.

Back in their apartment, Daisy and Nathan were curled up on the sofa, talking to his parents on speakerphone.

'We cannot believe our son has fallen in love with an Irish girl. We're so excited about meeting you and your family,' his mom was saying. 'Now you can call me Brea or Mom, which ever you're more comfortable with Daisy.'

'And equally I am Pete or Dad, you can decide.'

'Thank you, I think I'll go with Brea and Pete for now, if that's okay with you guys,' Daisy said grinning happily.

'Sure, sweetie!' Brea giggled. 'We wish we could make it over to meet with your parents before the wedding, but Pete and I are so busy with our business, it just isn't going to be possible. I would like to speak with your parents though and exchange email addresses,' Brea continued. 'We would love to share the cost of the wedding. In these modern times we don't feel it's right to leave the entire cost to one party. Also, if we could contribute, we would feel more comfortable about inviting some of our own friends,' Brea explained.

'Well, I'll give you my parents' home number, but why don't we drop over to them tomorrow and we can phone you from there and have a little conference call?' Daisy suggested.

'Perfect, sweetie, we look forward to that,' Brea concluded.

Daisy phoned her parents to tell them the great news.

'That just sounds super. That'll make my day so much brighter,' Justin slurred.

'Are you pissed, Daddy?' Daisy giggled.

'Nope, just a tiny bit tipsy. But this news has spurred me on. I was dithering as to whether or not I'd open another bottle of wine, and you've just made my mind up for me,' he answered.

Daisy decided to ignore the acidic tone to her father's voice, she simply wasn't going to allow him to dull her spirits. So she ignored the loaded comment and happily agreed that herself and Nathan would call over for dinner the following evening, when they would also speak with Brea and Pete.

Daisy was so excited she could barely contain herself.

'Your parents are so friendly. They seem genuinely delighted about the wedding, too,' Daisy commented. She hoped her own parents would come around. She knew her mother had got used to the idea of her impending marriage, but knowing her father, it would take a little persuading to change his mind. Besides, Daisy thought, sighing, she hadn't licked her determined personality off the ground!

Justin woke the following morning with a vicious hangover. He hadn't drunk so much for ages. 'That young man is to blame for my sickness today,' he grumbled as he staggered into the en suite bathroom at ten thirty.

'That's the longest you've stayed in bed for years. You're like a naughty teenager. I've no sympathy for you, drinking half a bottle of whiskey after all that wine. What did you expect, Justin? You snored like a walrus, too. I had to move into the spare room,' Ava said crossly.

'That's Nathan's fault, too,' he barked.

'How is that? He might be big and tall, but he's not the bionic man. He didn't stretch his arm across from their apartment and pour the booze down your neck. You sat and muttered like a loony as you splashed that muck into a glass and drowned your sorrows last night. You were dreadful company.'

'That was fifty-year-old *muck*, that should be savoured and enjoyed for special occasions. I *had* to drink it for medicinal purposes. Being forced to change my mind doesn't come easily to me, Ava.'

Ava decided to leave the room and go for a walk. Justin wasn't going to come around to the idea of Nathan overnight. But the pressure was now on her to keep Daisy and Justin from coming to blows over the whole thing. One was as stubborn as the other.

By that evening, Justin was feeling a little less raw. The combination of Solpadeine and a day spent watching old John Wayne movies had soothed him enough to remove the scowl from his face.

It was lashing out of the heavens with rumbling skies when Daisy and Nathan pulled up in the driveway.

'They're here, now promise me you'll be open-minded, Justin,' Ava begged. 'We don't want to make Daisy feel she has to choose between us and Nathan.'

Ava pulled open the front door and turned on her most welcoming smile. She'd prepared Justin's favourite dinner – home-made soup, roast beef with all the trimmings and crème brulée for dessert.

'Hi, Mum, you look pretty. Isn't this rain so depressing after Spain?' Daisy said scurrying in the door. She looked gorgeous in a simple white linen dress. The natural blonde highlights in her hair were like spun gold through her curls, her skin was evenly glowing and dewy-looking. Nathan strode in and kissed Ava on both cheeks.

'You look so beautiful after your holiday, Ava. It's good to see you again. I missed you,' Nathan stated, smiling.

His direct talking about his inner feelings was so American and so un-Irish, Ava wasn't quite sure how to answer.

'Oh, thank you. It's, eh, great to see you again too, dear,' she managed, feeling like an emotionless fish.

'Daddy!' Daisy ran to hug Justin.

'Hello sweetheart, you look fantastic after your holiday. Great to see you, love,' he hugged and kissed his daughter. 'Nathan.' Justin shuffled forwards and reluctantly offered his hand to be shaken.

Nathan not only took his hand, but pulled it towards him and yanked Justin into a full man-hug.

'Isn't it great to have the loves of our lives back again? I'm sure I speak for both of us when I say it's just a pleasure to see our beautiful women back home where they belong. Don't they both look stunning?' Nathan looked from mother to daughter and winked at Daisy.

'Shut up, Nathan!' she said grinning.

'I'm allowed to be enthusiastic,' Nathan said, defending himself as Daisy tried to swat him.

'I need a drink,' Justin muttered, stomping from the living room.

As if on cue, Nathan's phone rang.

'Hey! Good timing, I'm just here with the Moyes and unless Justin and Ava would rather you call back, this seems to be a good time. That okay with you folks?' Nathan asked.

'Perfect!' Daisy answered. 'Put them on speakerphone. Hi, Pete and Brea, I'd like to introduce you to Ava and Justin, my parents.'

'Hi there, it's so great to finally talk to you guys.' Pete sounded really happy.

'Hello there,' Ava said, forcing joviality.

'Hello,' Justin said, sounding as cheerful as a man on death row.

'Hi, you two, I am so excited,' a woman's voice shrilled down the line. You have no idea how much we're looking forward to getting to know you. We are so happy that our babies have fallen in love. Isn't this just the best?'

'Hi, Brea!' Daisy called.

'Hey, Daisy, sweetheart. I'm so animated here, Pete is telling me I'm like a kid going to Disneyland for the first time!'

Justin drained his glass and marched towards the spirits cabinet located at the end of the living room. As Ava tried not to sound negative, she watched Justin pour a large whiskey.

'We would ideally prefer to meet with you both face to face, but sadly we are very much tied into business commitments currently,' Pete began. 'So we are hoping you'll excuse our not coming to see you guys. But Brea and I would very much like to contribute to this wedding.'

Justin was back beside Nathan's phone and attempting not to choke on his whiskey. 'We have every intention of paying for our only daughter's wedding, Pete. Thank you all the same, but I won't hear of you funding this venture,' Justin snapped.

'With all due respect, Justin, this is a family occasion and we would be more comfortable knowing we could share this day in every way, including the financing,' Pete shot back.

'We would love to be involved, please let us,' Brea said brightly.

'Why don't we exchange numbers and email information and we can discuss all the money matters as we go along?' Ava interjected, before an out and out row erupted.

'Sure thing,' Brea answered.

'Listen, we haven't even decided what we're doing yet,' Daisy said, trying to quell the rising storm.

'So, Mom and Dad, we are proposing doing this on December twenty-third. Daisy and I discussed it last night and we think it would be the easiest for everyone,' Nathan boomed.

'What do you all think?' Daisy's voice took over.

'Oh, that sounds wonderful, you guys,' Brea said, sounding very emotional.

Daisy looked to Ava and Justin. Her father looked like he'd been smacked in the face with a frying pan, and Ava looked like she was about to pass a kidney stone. Her face had gone a lurid shade of pink and she appeared to be reeling. Sitting down on the edge of the sofa, she took a big swig of wine.

'Is it okay with you folks if I email your details to my parents?' Nathan asked.

'Eh, yes, go ahead,' Justin said quietly. Nathan ran into the kitchen so he could call out the details in peace while Daisy, Ava and Justin shouted their goodbyes to Nathan's retreating phone.

'So, what do you reckon?' Daisy asked, biting her lip nervously.

Justin closed his eyes and swallowed hard. Maybe Ava was right. It wouldn't matter if it was Nathan or Jack the Ripper, nobody would ever seem good enough for his only daughter.

'Okay, love. Let's organise this wedding if that's what you really want,' Justin managed to force himself to speak. 'If you're happy, we're happy,' he said with shining eyes as he exchanged a look with his wife.

For the first time in weeks, Ava looked like the gorgeous woman he'd fallen in love with so many years ago. Justin felt a stab of guilt as he realised the pressure he'd been putting her under. Daisy wasn't a doll they could keep locked in her room, they'd raised her to speak her mind and to make her own choices.

'If it all goes pear-shaped, never think the door is shut here. I'll always be your daddy, remember that,' Justin said, sounding strangled.

'Oh, thank you, Daddy, you've no idea how happy that makes me feel.' Kissing both her parents swiftly, Daisy bounded from the room to find Nathan.

'Well done you,' Ava joined her husband from the sofa across the room. 'That took a lot of guts and I know this is killing a small part of you that will never recover, but she's determined to go through with this. You're doing the right thing, love. Let's just hope they'll make a go of it,' Ava said, kissing her husband tenderly. 'You stink of whiskey. Please don't get blotto again. You snored like a drain last night, and, besides, we have to eat dinner. It mightn't look great if you're passed out on the floor in front of your son-in-law to be.' Ava smiled at him.

'I'll lay off the whiskey as long as you lay off the son-in-law references for the moment.' Justin looked stricken again. 'Baby steps, please,' he said, looking exhausted.

'I hear you,' Ava said.

'And I'm not having those people paying for this. We will pay for this wedding. I'm not even discussing that matter,' Justin warned.

'Fine, whatever you say!' Ava held her hands up in acceptance. 'You can discuss those details with your new best friend, Pete.'

'Don't push it,' Justin said, looking cross again.

'Joke?' Ava had the twinkle in her eye that melted Justin's heart every time she wanted her own way.

43.

Tally

Tally returned from Spain feeling more positive than she'd ever thought possible. She spent a day with Sinead and the other teachers having a full briefing on how the advanced course would run. Then she went home to fill her father in on everything.

'It'll be over by the end of April, so I can look for a job before the summer rush of new graduates,' Tally told him.

'That's brilliant news, love,' Martin said, hugging her. 'You deserve it, you worked so hard to get your exams and anyone who knows you can see that you'll be fantastic as a therapist.'

When Greta got back from her run that evening, Tally couldn't wait to tell her.

'Good for you, Tally. It sounds like you have a great plan set in place now.' Have you and your da eaten yet?' Greta enquired.

'No, we were waiting for you. I've fresh fish with brown rice and veggies,' Tally said, trying to sell the meal to her mother.

'I'm going to have a slim-shake, I think,' Greta said, walking towards the bathroom.

'Ma, you're doing it again,' Tally said gently.

'What?'

'Refusing to participate and resorting to your gloopy shakes. The dinner I've made is healthy and low in fat. Come and join us, please,' Tally begged.

'Eh, right. I'll be there in a minute,' Greta said, hesitating. She honestly did want to be more family orientated, but old habits died hard. She had become so unused to eating proper food, she simply never thought of food as a social thing. But if Tally and Martin had waited for her to come back, the least she could do was join them.

She hadn't gained any weight since she'd been eating dinners with them more often. Tally was right, the food they were eating these days was healthy and good for her. Given the choice, Greta would honestly go for the shake because it was just less hassle – the calories, fibre, fat content and nutrients were all measured out. But she needed to make the effort.

Dinner was pleasant. They chatted normally and Greta actually managed to eat most of what was on her plate before she excused herself and went out the back for a cigarette.

The sliding patio door opened and Tally joined her.

'What've you done? Why are you looking at me like that?' Greta narrowed her eyes suspiciously.

'Can I ask you something and will you promise not to go off on a mad one?'

'I can't promise anything, but go on, try me,' Greta said, folding her arms.

'Well, Sinead and I were wondering if you and Da would come to the clinic with me next week for a family session?'

'What, like some wacko Americanised therapy type of thing?' Greta asked. 'Ah, Tally, it's not really my thing. I see all that kind of thing in the same light as laying on the floor beside a monk with a shaved head clanging mini bells as we all chant. The thought of sitting in a room chatting really doesn't appeal to me.'

Tally didn't answer. Nor did she stomp off in a huff looking all weepy the way she used to. Instead, she looked her mother in the eye and waited patiently for a slightly less knee-jerk reaction.

'Are you serious? You want me and your da to go and sit in a room with this stranger and talk about fatness?'

Tally didn't flinch. She didn't make a smart comment nor did she make any attempt to shift the feeling of unease that had descended between them.

'Sorry. Old habits and all that,' Greta had the grace to blush and avert her eyes to the ground. As she plucked up the cigarette butt she'd just crushed, she found herself alone in the garden. Tally had walked calmly back into the house.

'So when's this yolky-ma-jig happening then?' Greta asked when she stepped back inside.

'Provisionally tomorrow night, if that suits you? Da says he'll come any time,' Tally said.

'Right, well I suppose I could go for a run afterwards, couldn't I? How long will it all take?'

'An hour, two at the most.'

'For what? Are we writing a proposal for world peace? What in the name of God are you thinking of doing for all that time?'

'It's a session for us all to talk about how we feel, and then Sinead responds with what she thinks might help going forward,' Tally explained.

'But we have mouths, why can't we just talk here and now, and you can go in and tell yer one what we said and she can write down what she wants us to do?'

Martin had joined them in the kitchen. 'Greta, Tally has just outlined the reason she wants us to sit together and talk properly. You don't listen, you don't let the girl express herself and, besides, it can't do any harm,' he said gently.

'Right! Tell me what time and where and I'll be there,' Greta promised.

Tally went off into her room to listen to some music. As she lay there, musing over her mother's reaction and how the session might go, her phone rang.

'Hi it's me, Ben.' His voice sounded friendly yet oddly nervous.

'Hi, Ben! How's it going?' Tally was so glad he couldn't see her face. She was instantly sweating and felt like she might drop the phone she was so excited.

'Good, thanks. How was your holiday?' Ben asked.

'Oh, it was fantastic, but I'm glad to be home,' Tally said, willing herself to relax and not come across like a crazy woman.

'Sinead tells me you had your meeting in the college about your course!' Ben said cheerfully.

'Sure did, it sounds like it's going to be fantastic. I feel really lucky to have been picked.'

'So do you reckon you could find the time to meet up for a bite to eat?' Ben asked.

'I think I could possibly fit you in at some stage!' Tally tried to sound nonchalant, as she jumped up and down waving her arms in silence.

'Cool, shall we say tomorrow night then? Maybe the tapas bar again and if you're not up early next day, we could go on to a club? But – only if you feel like it,' Ben suggested.

'I'd love that, and clubbing sounds brilliant.'

Tally hung up and screamed exactly like a crazy woman. Both Greta and Martin rushed into the room, expecting to find her lying under a collapsed wardrobe or pumping blood.

'What?' Martin yelled. 'What happened, love?'

'I'm going on a date! A very important date!' Tally sang.

'With who?' Greta said, grinning.

'Ben.'

'Who's he when he's at home?' Martin asked, looking slightly edgy all of a sudden. 'He'd better treat you right.'

'We're going for dinner and some dancing, Da, we're not eloping to Australia! He's Sinead's brother and he's really decent,' Tally said, squealing again.

'That's great news, Tally.' Greta looked very impressed.

After she'd shooed her parents out of her bedroom, Tally began to try on every item of clothing she owned. She wanted to look well for the meeting with Sinead and her parents, but, above all, she wanted to look her best for her date.

She couldn't believe she was actually going on a date with Ben! She was so relieved he'd actually phoned. He had said he would, but Tally had been fighting a niggling feeling of doubt in the back of her mind that he'd change his mind and not bother. The memory of their brief passing kiss just before she went on holiday came flooding back. She'd thought about it so many times since, but had almost convinced herself she'd imagined it. Now she knew she hadn't.

Tally and Martin were sitting waiting outside Sinead's office the following evening. They were twenty minutes early.

'Hi, Tally, why don't you both come in? Hello, Martin, good to see you again,' Sinead said, shaking his hand. 'Thanks for coming, make yourselves at home. Is your mother still on target for five o'clock?'

'So she said,' Tally answered nervously. They'd all agreed to meet earlier to accommodate Tally's evening plans.

Sinead squeezed Tally's hand as they waited for Greta. 'Heard you and my little bro are off out later. Just for the record, he's a bag of nerves and can't wait to see you.'

Tally could barely believe her ears. Ben was nervous about meeting her? He was gorgeous and cool and could have any girl he wanted. She found it difficult to fathom that a date with her would even register on his radar.

There was no time for Tally to ponder any further as Greta appeared, looking as nervous as Tally felt.

'Ma, thanks for coming.'

'I said I would, didn't I? Hello there,' Greta nodded and smiled at Sinead, wasting no time in checking her out with a drink-it-all-in look.

After the slightly awkward greeting, Greta perched on a chair and shifted around uncomfortably as Sinead brought them all a cup of tea.

'Not for me thanks, love, I've water here.' Greta brandished a bottle from her bag.

'I'd love a cup,' Martin said, smiling as he tried to make the atmosphere less edgy.

Sinead explained that there was no right or wrong way to conduct the session. That it was simply an organised conversation where Tally could express her feelings and ensure that her parents understood how and why she was trying to change her lifestyle.

Greta jigged her leg constantly as her eyes darted around the room.

'So the whole ethos behind our programme here is to get to the root of problems, so we can all learn and move on,' Sinead said as she looked at Greta. 'Tally can you put your finger on how you feel at home and most importantly how each of your parents makes you feel?' Sinead prompted.

'Okay.' Tally's hands began to shake.

'Go on, love, tell us how you feel,' Martin said, urging her to open up.

'Well …' Tally faltered for a moment. 'Da has always made me feel comfortable and good about myself. Ma, you've never given the impression you're interested in anything I do. The only flicker I've had was when we were in Spain. I know you've been trying since and I appreciate that, really I do, but we've a long way to go. In my opinion ...' Tally trailed off.

There was a brief silence.

'Okay, would anyone like to comment?' Sinead asked.

'I know everything is my fault. I'm trying, that's all I can say,' Greta said, as her leg continued to jig up and down.

'Nobody said it was all your fault, Ma.'

'Didn't you? Why does your father get to be the hero, when he's the one who fed you all the crap since the day you were tiny? You and he are like a little clique and I'm the outsider in all of this.'

'If you feel like an outsider, the only person who's put you there is yourself,' Tally retorted.

'How do you figure that, then?'

'Ma, all that matters to you is being skinny. We all know that I used have a bad relationship with food. As you've never been shy of pointing out, I used to eat too much. But, your own relationship with food is just as destructive. You *hate* food. You spend your time looking at other people's plates in disgust. When was the last time you sat down, relaxed and enjoyed a meal?' Tally asked.

'I enjoyed last night's dinner. I ate that, didn't I?' Greta asked, looking stung.

'You did, fair play to you,' Martin said, patting her leg.

'Hold on a second though, Ma. I had to practically beg you to eat with us. You wanted to have a shake instead,' Tally shot back.

'It's just habit.' Greta looked at the floor, unable to meet her daughter's accusing eyes.

'But you don't demonstrate healthy eating philosophies,' Tally said. 'Even in Spain, any time you did join myself and the other women, you commented on how vile the food looked.'

'Is there any grain of truth in what your daughter has just said?' Sinead's face was neutral as she spoke.

'Listen, I just prefer to feel like my body's a well-oiled machine. It's my thing,' Greta said, sounding less sure by the minute.

'Well, that might true in your own head, love,' Martin interjected. 'But, Greta, you are a bit obsessed with being thin.'

'You're saying that like it's not a good thing?' she said defensively, feeling a bit brow-beaten.

'It's not the most important thing in the world, Ma. At least, it shouldn't be.'

'Then what are we all doing here if being thin isn't important? That's a bit pot, kettle and black.'

'Ma, I don't want to be obese anymore. I want to be healthy and I want to feel better about myself. The difference is that Da and me are trying to live a balanced and healthy lifestyle. What you do is verging on torture,' Tally whispered.

'I don't see it that way. Jeez, who's the odd one out in this room?' Greta sighed. 'Is the main aim of this entire exercise to point out that I'm the big bad wolf?'

Sinead took the conversation to a calmer level by acknowledging that each person in the room was entitled to his or her own opinion.

Before the session became too negative, she directed Tally into saying what she was hoping to achieve by continuing with the Motivation Mate programme and how her parents might help.

'I have always been the fat, unattractive child. I have never walked into a room and thought I was noticed for positive reasons. I've learned through speaking to Sinead that I have many positive qualities to my personality. I know I have friends. But I need to build up my self-esteem.' Tally's voice wavered and she simply allowed the tears to roll down her cheeks. 'In order for me to do that, I need you to continue to try and meet me halfway, Ma. I know we discussed this in Spain and you promised to try and think before you comment on my size.'

'I'm doing my best,' Greta said.

'We both know you are,' Martin interjected. 'I can see a change in you already,' he said kindly.

'I know I'm not perfect, but I'm really beginning to wonder, do you even love me, Martin? If I'm such a wicked witch, why are you still married to me?' Greta turned to her husband with raw fear in her eyes.

'Nobody in the world is perfect, Greta. I do love you, of course I do. I think all three of us have quite a lot to work out.' Martin stood up and pulled his wife into his embrace. 'I'd love it if you would give yourself a break every now and again. If you could find it in yourself to relax enough to go for a dinner out and sit and enjoy just chatting and letting it all hang out. Who knows, you might like it. We never do that.'

'Since the smoking ban, I've no interest in sitting in bars or restaurants. I spend the time putting my coat on to go out and stand in the pissings of rain while I wave in the window at you and Tally eating. I've just got into a rut where I'd rather be at home,' Greta admitted.

'But what about Da and me?' Tally asked. 'Don't we count?'

'Of course you do,' Greta sighed.

'I think you've all done exceptionally well tonight. Bravo!' Sinead interjected.

'Is the time up?' Tally asked surprised.

'We've gone way over time actually,' Sinead said, glancing at her watch and winking at Tally. 'Things to do and people to see!'

So the group dispersed and Tally said goodbye to her parents.

'I'm just going to fix my make-up and I'll go off and meet Ben,' Tally said.

'Have a great time, love,' Martin hugged her.

'I hope this brother of yours is all right,' Greta said to Sinead.

'Ma!' Tally burst out laughing.

'Sorry! I'm saying the wrong thing again. Me and my big mouth. See you tomorrow,' Greta said to Tally as she left with Martin.

Sinead smiled at Tally. 'You can call and let me know, Tally, but I would urge you to come even once more as a group of three. I think you've made real progress here tonight.' She gave her a quick hug. 'Now go and fix your mascara and get around to the tapas bar and put my poor brother out of his misery!'

'That wasn't too bad, was it?' Martin said, putting his arm around Greta as they walked out.

'You think?' Greta said sarcastically.

Martin kept quiet until they reached the car and sat inside. He put the key in the ignition, but didn't turn it on. He turned to his wife. 'Talk to me, Greta,' he said gently. 'Please tell me what's going on in that head of yours.'

Greta stared fixedly out the window, her fingers tapping incessantly on her cigarette pack. 'I don't know, Martin,' she finally said. 'I was ready to put on a smile and say it was all a deadly idea and that I'd hug Tally and we'd all feel better. I'd no idea it was going to go like that.'

Martin reached over and held her hand. Greta took a deep breath, and suddenly the floodgates opened.

'I really didn't think the reason I was going there today was to hear that *I'm* the one who has a problem, too. I've honestly never thought my lifestyle was so negative. I didn't think my choices were damaging to me or anyone else. But then … when Tally pointed out that I make disgusted faces at other people as they eat, that struck a chord with me. I had no idea I do that.'

'Didn't you?' said Martin gently. 'But you're so focused on food, everything about it.'

Greta looked at him. 'To be totally honest, I feel like I've had a trough of iced water dumped on my head. I'm gob-smacked that you two find my indifference to food off-putting. In my head, it's all healthy and positive and makes complete sense.'

'Does it still make complete sense?' Martin asked, rubbing her hand softly.

Greta looked like she might cry. 'I suppose that's the most shocking part of this,' she said in a near whisper. 'Now that I've had my eyes opened to the way you perceive me, I don't like it. I want to change it.'

'That's wonderful, lovie,' Martin said with huge feeling in his voice. He was close to tears, too. This was an absolute breakthrough.

'From the time I lost my baby weight after I had Tallulah, I've been like a hamster on a wheel. What began as a healthy habit has rocketed into full-on hell. I *know* I have a constant feeling of guilt if I don't exercise every day. I *would* love to learn to relax every now and then.'

'I'll help you,' Martin said. 'I'll do anything you need.'

Greta smiled at her husband through eyes brimming with tears.

'Thank you. You're a wonderful man, Martin, do you know that? I want to change for you. I want to quit the fags, for starters, then work on my attitude to food and exercise. And I really, really want to mend things with Tally. I can't believe I've passed on my food hell to her. I didn't know I was doing it, Martin, honestly.'

Martin held her face in his hands. 'You're a wonderful woman, Greta my love, and you have everything it takes to be a wonderful mother. You can make yourself, and us, happier. And I know it'll be hard, but I know you can do it.'

Both crying now, Martin leaned over and kissed his wife full on the lips. In the darkness of the car, they clung to each like life rafts in a storm.

44.

Daisy

It was the end of June and Justin was back in his office in New York. The amount of the time he spent over there was slowly reducing, but Ava had to admit she was relieved to have a week of concentrated wedding organisation time.

Daisy was buzzing. Not only was she ecstatic about all the plans, but Nathan had also asked her to set up and manage the Montessori school in the new flagship store of his business. The young couple had dropped in to show Ava the samples of wedding invitations and share their good news about the Montessori idea.

'My dad is so excited about Daisy getting involved in the business,' Nathan explained to Ava.

All of a sudden, Ava knew she needed to take more notice of what this guy was doing. Not only was Daisy adamant about marrying him, but he now planned to employ her, too. If this went pear-shaped, Daisy stood to lose everything. She sincerely hoped her daughter was right in deciding this man was her knight in shining armour.

'Sorry to sound so vacant, Nathan, but can you please explain about the business in more detail?' Ava asked.

'Our franchise is called Infants 2 Elders and we're going to do the exact same package for Europe as we've done in the States. We've got a couple of hundred sites across the US, so it's high time we conquered Europe, too,' he said with a grin.

'It all sounds very promising,' Ava managed.

'There is nowhere in Ireland like our centres to date. We'll do state-of-the-art bowling, laser guns, inflatable sumo-wrestling rings, movie theatres, soft-floor zones and much more. Not to mention disco zones with specialised dance workshops for all ages. Coupled with ice cream and soda bars, it offers a whole world of indoor family entertainment. We can't believe it hasn't been done properly in this country so far. Especially when the weather is so mixed,' Nathan continued, pitching the idea like a pro. 'Seeing as your government have made the move to provide pre-school education to all children going forward, the Montessori element is going to be one of the most important cogs of our wheel. Once the kids are finished with their morning of education, we have a ready-made client base on site. It's proved to be a resounding success back home and I know it'll work here too,' Nathan said earnestly.

'Can you imagine how fabulous this is going to be, Mum?' Daisy threw her arms around Nathan as he pulled her close and kissed her on the top of her head.

Ava was quite simply blown away by it all. She and Justin had been concentrating on the fact that Nathan wasn't Freddie, but she realised with a bang that they'd totally missed the fact that Nathan was equally as driven and eager to secure a great future for their daughter.

'It all sounds fantastic,' Ava admitted. 'I really hope it all works out the way you hope,' she said, feeling ashamed of how she had misjudged Nathan.

'Oh, it *will* work out, Ava. We have this business down to a tee Stateside. I've no qualms about it ticking along nicely here, too,' Nathan assured her.

'I don't want to sound like a total bimbo here, but we have to sort this invitation card and get it off to the printer, so let's focus for five minutes,' Daisy said, interrupting the talk.

'See, she's already the boss of me, aren't you, darling sugar plum, light of my life?' Nathan teased her.

'Once you know that, we'll be happy forever!' Daisy laughed.

'I'll go along with whatever you ladies want, but might I say I love this one?' Nathan's hand rested on the card that Ava liked more than all the others.

It was a crisp white card with a large embossed heart in a pearlised finish in the centre. The envelope was plain apart from the same pearlised lining. To Ava it represented pure elegance. No bells and whistles, just gorgeous.

'I love that one too. What do you think, Mum?' Daisy giggled and clapped her hands in excitement.

'It's gorgeous, guys!' Ava said, feeling excited suddenly.

'Let's do a cream and pearls theme!' Daisy exclaimed. 'So basically it'll all be crisp and clean with a slightly vintage edge. I can see the function room now, all antique lace with pearl details. We could even have a Christmas tree decorated with strands of pearls and white lights,' she squealed.

'Speaking of the function room, where did you have in mind? I know your father had always said he'd like you get married here at home. We could have a marquee and do the place whatever way you want,' Ava raised an eyebrow suggestively.

Daisy and Nathan glanced at one another.

'Well, we chatted last night, and we think The Four Seasons would be perfect,' Daisy bit her lip.

'So you're going for it big time then?' Ava commented.

'My family will be so glad to help out with the cost,' Nathan interjected.

'Oh, no, I think Justin would have a conniption if he thought he couldn't pay for his little girl's wedding. So thank you for that, but we'll see to it ourselves,' Ava answered firmly.

Daisy rooted in her handbag and produced a folder with the Four Seasons emblem on the front. 'We're a step ahead of you!' she giggled. 'We dropped in on the way over here, and guess what?'

'What?'

'They have availability on the twenty-third of December!' Nathan and Daisy grinned at her.

'Yay!' Ava said, hoping she could talk Justin around. He'd always assumed Daisy would have her wedding at home.

She accepted the folder graciously and thumbed through the pages. 'This all looks super. Why don't you leave this with me, and Justin and I will meet with the co-ordinator when he returns next week?'

'Weeeell …' Daisy giggled again. 'We paid a deposit. The room is booked! Nathan paid!'

'Wha— Oh, right.' Ava didn't quite know what to say. She longed to have Justin beside her. At least if he was hyperventilating and looking like he was going to have heart failure, she could be the calm, mollifying one. But right at that moment, she was on her own and she had to stifle a scream. This was happening so quickly, Ava could barely keep up.

Nathan's phone rang. 'Excuse me, ladies, that's my foreman. He's meticulous with detail and we're at a crucial stage with the ground preparation. Some of the ready-made units are arriving by ship in two weeks.'

Feeling even more confused, Ava just waved limply at his retreating back and sat there, feeling numbed and lost.

'Nathan's Infants 2 Elders venues are all pre-fabricated units, so they can ship them anywhere in the world. All that needs to be done here is to prepare the foundation. The module is dropped into place and ready to function within weeks,' Daisy nodded. 'Mum, I feel like I'm in a bubble! I feel if you pinch me, it'll all be a dream!'

'I'm a little confused, Daisy,' Ava said. 'How come you're so on for the white wedding stuff now? What's changed?'

'Nathan is letting me choose, he's not ordering me around the way Freddie did. I never thought I'd be into the whole girly thing, but now that it's happening, I'm realising I like this whole traditional thing.'

As it turned out, Nathan had to hurry off and be on site with his foreman.

'You gals gonna be okay without me for a few hours?'

'Of course, darling. You go and Mum and I will order the invitations we picked and maybe I could persuade her to accompany me to that bridal shop I was telling you about earlier.' Daisy and Nathan kissed for slightly longer than Ava felt at ease witnessing.

'So, I'm not going to be in trouble later on when I get back, am I?' Nathan asked.

'No, why?' Daisy asked, smiling.

'Well there's only so much of this wedding lark I can take. I think I'm better off doing my work and leaving it to you two. I just didn't want Daisy to have to do it all on her own.' Nathan looked at Ava.

'She won't have to, Nathan,' Ava said pointedly. 'I'll take it from here.'

'Cool, because I'm quite frankly not the best person I know at the whole colour scheme and theme stuff.'

Ava was having a bit of an out of body experience. Her baby girl was getting married! For Christ's sake, this was one of the moments she'd dreamed about since the day she'd been born. But she hadn't envisaged the scene this way. She wished again that Justin was there beside her.

Daisy had probably buffered those feelings of loneliness since she was born. Now Ava realised she was feeling quite alone.

'So, what do you say, Mum? Mum?'

Ava realised Daisy was staring at her. 'Sorry, love?'

'Will you come with me in to try on wedding gowns?' Daisy stared at her mother. Her sun-kissed face with her round sapphire eyes and pale golden hair evoked such love in Ava's heart. She loved everything about her beautiful daughter.

'Of course I will! Just try and stop me!'

'Cool! You go and get your bag and I'll phone ahead to make sure someone is there to help us.' Daisy clapped her hands together in delight, just like she'd always done as a little girl.

45.

Tally

Tally was left feeling a bit raw after the session with Sinead and her parents, but as she retouched her make-up, she talked to herself sternly in the mirror. This is your first date with Ben and you are not going to blow it or waste it by being self-absorbed. Tonight was difficult, but you got through it and now you're out the other side and free to enjoy yourself. A final comb through of her glossy hair, and she was ready.

As she walked to the bar, Tally gripped her mobile in her hand, full sure Ben would send her a text at the last minute to say he couldn't make it. The text never came and when she pushed open the door of the bar, he was there waiting for her.

'Hi,' she said, hoping her voice would actually work.

'Hi, yourself.' Ben took control of the moment and stepped forwards to kiss her. Instead of doing the polite acquaintance thing of air-kissing her cheeks, he went straight for her lips. Tally tried not to behave like a cartoon character and lie on the floor with imaginary birdies tweeting around her head – but that was exactly what she felt like doing!

'What'll you have to drink?' she asked, taking out her wallet.

'Oh, no you don't,' Ben scolded. 'It's on me. White wine spritzer?' he suggested.

'Thank you, and I'm most impressed you remembered what I drink,' she said, smiling widely.

After the initial few minutes, they were chatting ninety to the dozen like old friends. After they'd gone through her holiday and Tally had told him about the other girls she'd met, Ben had an outburst that astonished her.

'Daisy and Felicity sound dead-on,' he said. 'Unlike those bad bitches you were in school with.'

'What do you mean?' she said, laughing in shock.

'Oh, seriously! Come on, Tally, I think your graduation ball was one of the worst in memory,' he admitted.

'Why? You were with Anna?' Tally gasped.

'Precisely. She's the most selfish, vacant girl I've ever come across. She takes the words high maintenance to a whole new level!' Ben said. 'God, she was such a pain in the ass that night.'

'I thought all the guys fell at her feet! She always had a knack of making me feel like a swamp creature,' Tally said honestly.

'That just makes me laugh! Have you looked in the mirror lately?' Ben asked.

'Eh, yeah! And I know full well that I'm not a patch on Amy. I'll never be like her, but, do you know what – I'm getting to accept that now,' Tally said.

'Jesus, I hope you never end up like Amy. You're dead right, you're not a patch on her. She's a moaning, annoying pain in the butt. You, on the other hand, are fun, caring and stunningly beautiful! Tally, you need to realise how amazing you really are,' Ben said tenderly.

'I … don't know what to say …' Tally was utterly transfixed. To her, Ben was the most gorgeous and cool guy she'd ever met. She couldn't believe he actually fancied her. She was so full of self-doubt, she half expected him to say he was only teasing and he'd come to meet her for a dare.

'Why are you looking at me with such disbelief?' he asked.

Tally blushed with embarrassment, but decided honesty was the best policy. 'I don't understand why you seem to want to be with me. You could have any girl you—'

'I don't want just any girl, Tally. I want you.' He blushed as he leaned forward to kiss her. Tally felt herself tingling from head to toe. She'd had the odd fumbled kiss with teenage boys, but never anything real. Certainly never anything like this! She felt like she'd been asleep until now, like Sleeping Beauty, and Ben was kissing her into life again.

The rest of the night was like a blur of bliss. They went to a club and spent the night dancing and laughing and, best of all, kissing.

'I'll call you in the morning,' Ben said in her ear as she got out of the taxi at her house.

'Okay, talk to you then. I had the best night ever!' Tally said honestly before she slammed the car door. She was dying to tell him she dreamed about him and thought he was the bees knees, but she figured that might be a bit full on. The poor guy would probably think she had a wedding dress stowed in the wardrobe ready to march him up the nearest aisle. No, she needed to at least *try* and be cool!

Tally was awake bright and early the next morning. She'd planned to go on a tour of a local garden with Martin. Her phone rang.

'Good morning!' Ben shouted above the city traffic noises. 'I'm on my way into work and I'll be stuck in meetings pretty much all day. I just wanted to check in with you. How's it going?' he asked.

'Great, thanks! I'm going to a garden with my father, just for a little day trip.' Tally suddenly thought Ben would think she was a bit of a dweeb.

'That sounds really nice, it looks like the rain's going to hold off too,' he said.

'I had so much fun last night. Thanks for sticking to your word and phoning me too,' Tally said hurriedly.

'Hey, the pleasure is all mine! So do you want to meet up later on? 'Tell me to back off if I'm being too forward,' he added.

'Not at all! I'd love to. How about I give you a call after work and we can make some plans?' Tally said beginning to believe Ben really did like her.

'Cool! I better go, talk to you later on, okay?'

'Okay, have a good day!' Tally said.

Martin was singing in the kitchen. Tally rushed in and gave him a big hug.

'Good morning! You're in a good mood. How was your date?' asked Martin.

'Brilliant! I had the best time. Ben is dead on. And he just called!' Tally danced around in a circle.

'What's all the madness in aid of?' Greta said as she marched into the kitchen dressed in her running gear.

'I just had the best date of my life with Ben, that's all,' Tally said, smiling like the lovesick teenager she was.

'Good for you,' Greta grinned. 'Did you take a bag of speed while you were with him? You're making me nervous. You're like a crazy lady!' she teased her daughter.

'No, Ma, I'm just high on life!'

'Are you too high to go to this garden today?' Martin asked with a wide smile.

'No, but I can't promise not to squeal from time to time,' Tally answered.

'Bloody heck, I think she's finally lost it,' Greta said to Martin. 'Right, people, I'm off for a jog and I'll meet you both later on for lunch, cool?'

'I thought you were coming, too,' Tally said, looking slightly deflated.

'I'm trying, love. But meet me halfway, can't you? I hate plants. I'd only ruin it all for you,' Greta reasoned.

'Ma, this is something Da is interested in. Remember what Sinead said about broadening your horizons and thinking outside of what *you* want all the time?' Tally said.

'I know, and I said I'll meet you after. I'll do the Brady Bunch thing, just not in a garden. I'm not a gnome or a fish on a plinth with water spouting out my mouth.'

'You could be the grumpy goblin in the corner,' Tally suggested, laughing.

'It's fine, Tally. We'll meet up for lunch,' Martin said, smoothing the situation.

Tally was on too much of a high to argue with her mother and besides, Martin seemed to be perfectly happy with the arrangement.

A while later, Tally and Martin arrived at the stately home, which had only recently been opened to the public. Linking arms, the father and daughter took a little leaflet and followed the garden walk. Some of the more rare species were labelled and numbered, with information presented on a wooden plaque.

As they rounded the corner, a pretty pond dotted with plants and a centrepiece of a stone mermaid water feature came into view.

'Oh, look, Da, isn't that gorgeous. Imagine waking up in that room and being able to see this every day,' Tally said as she looked back towards the big house.

'It'd do your heart good, all right,' Martin agreed.

'Listen, Da,' Tally began. 'It says here that this particular type of pond lily has been here for generations. The family who own the garden have carefully taken it indoors when the pond freezes over and kept it in peat moss in a shed, before submerging it again once the weather improved. Although this is not the original plant, it is a direct cutting that has been cultivated over the years. Isn't that lovely?' Tally sighed.

'Sure is, pet. Just shows how dedicated some folk are when they want to keep a tradition alive.'

Tally couldn't help feeling a bit emotional as they walked on.

'What's wrong, love?' Martin stopped and stared at his daughter.

'Ah, don't mind me, I'm just being silly,' Tally grinned with glassy eyes.

'Try me,' Martin said, picking up her hand and patting it.

'I just think it's lovely that a family would care so much about keeping a little pond plant going, and obviously doing so for generations. It's real team work and a shared common interest.'

'Yes, I suppose it is a great thing. Why does it upset you?'

'Ma promised on holiday and during our session with Sinead that she'd try to change. Now she won't even come and walk around with us. I know she's trying and she's got better, but I can't help feeling she's still stuck in her own self-obsessed world. I'm not even sad for *me* any more, it's more for *you*, Da.'

'Don't be sad for me, love. I'm as happy as can be. Haven't I got you here with me? Your ma just doesn't really see the point in doing stuff she hates. She's probably right. You don't catch me jogging for two hours or flinging myself around a gym dressed in lycra, looking like one of those cyclists with the skinny arses peddling up the motorway in the rain! I know she loves me, let's face it, if she didn't, she'd be gone. I love her too, warts and all.'

'Don't you ever wish she'd consider you more?' Tally asked.

'If she changed totally, she wouldn't be my Greta. I know you and her have your differences. I know you're on a journey at the moment to try and find happiness and all that. I applaud you for it and I'll help you any way I can, but maybe you need to accept that your happiness shouldn't depend on changing your mammy,' Martin suggested. 'I hate to sound negative here, love, but I don't think Greta is ever going to turn into the person you seem to think she should be. Would it be impossible for you to try and build on the relationship you already have?'

'Maybe you're right,' Tally said, thinking it over. 'Last night, Ben told me I'm gorgeous.' Tally looked shy and delighted.

'Well he's right there, you are gorgeous,' Martin stated.

'It's made me think differently about Ma. I can get the softness and tenderness from you. And if Ben and I keep going the way we've begun, he'll fill in even more blanks going forward.'

'You're playing a blinder, love. Your life is moving at such a fast pace now. You've your whole life ahead of you. Why don't you just try to take each day as it comes?' Martin suggested. He began to whistle the tune of Monty Python's 'Always look on the bright side of life', bopping his head from side to side comically as he did so.

'Da, you're a madman, do you know that?' Tally burst out laughing.

As they were about to leave the garden and get the bus to meet Greta, Tally's mobile phone pinged.

'Oh, text message from this new fella, is it?' Martin jibed.

'No, it's Daisy, one of the girls we met in Spain. She's wondering if I'll meet herself and Felicity for a drink,' Tally smiled.

'Text back and tell her to sod off. Tell her you're not interested in any fun or chats. That she's mistaken if she thinks that you might be able to go anywhere that's a bit of craic,' Martin assumed a cross face.

'Okay, Da, point taken! I'll stop with the wound-licking act and get on with it.'

'Atta girl,' Martin said, shoving his chin in the air as he marched them towards the walled garden.

46.

Felicity

Felicity was standing in her bedroom, attempting to pack the stuff she thought she'd actually need. After Mia had broken the ice and talked about her heartache at dealing with Felicity's change of life, the two of them had had brilliant chats the previous night. Felicity had promised to look to the future and embrace her life with Shane. Mia had promised to tell Felicity if she was feeling blue.

This morning all tender moments had been well and truly put to one side as Felicity and Aly had turned the room into what looked like the aftermath of a large bomb.

'If you're not taking this, can I borrow it?' Aly asked, holding up a prom-style dress in apple green.

'Oh, God that's so vile on me, have it,' Felicity said, nodding.

'What on earth are you two doing in here?' Mia appeared and leaned against the doorway cradling a cup of coffee.

'Packing!' both girls chorused.

From where Mia was standing, there were very few items being put in any kind of order. The girls were simply emptying any drawers that might have previously held clothing and adding it to the jungle of stuff on the floor, bed and chair.

'Any word back from Shane?' Mia asked.

'Yes! Sorry, I forgot to shout down to you, he's borrowing his mum's jeep and he's on the way. So at least I don't have to lug everything on the train.'

'I told you I'd drive you there,' Mia said gently.

'I know, Mam, but our apartment is pretty basic and until I sort a folding bed, you'd have to stay on the sofa. You'd be too exhausted driving to Dublin and back in one day,' Felicity reasoned.

'This way, Shane can do all the donkey work too, make himself useful!' Aly giggled.

'We'll stay for lunch and head off while it's still bright, if that's okay?' Felicity asked, looking teary-eyed again.

'Perfect, love. Whatever suits you,' Mia managed. 'I'll just go down and boil the kettle. Come down when you're ready, girls.'

Between herself, Felicity and Aly, they'd been going from floods of tears to raucous laughter since the night before. Now Aly looked set to have another round of tears. She suddenly hugged Felicity tightly to her, unable to speak the emotions she was feeling.

'Ah, stop making me cry, you wagon,' Felicity said. 'I've been in Dublin since September and living with Shane for a couple of weeks, nothing's changing really.'

'Yes it is,' Aly sobbed. 'You're moving the rest of your stuff. You're not coming back.'

'Aren't you happy for me?' Felicity asked.

'Of course I am, you goose!' Aly said. 'It's *me* I feel sorry for. I just miss you, that's all!'

'You know where I am, come and stay more often,' Felicity suggested.

'Deal,' Aly said and hugged her.

As they bundled some boxes into the room, Aly began to fold things and place them inside. When a small amount of order had been reached, they got into the swing of it.

'Wow, that looks great and, look, you have a pink carpet, Felicity. Fancy that?' Aly giggled.

'Yeah, it hasn't seen the light of day for at least ten years!' Felicity marvelled. 'Just imagine how clean this house is going to be now?'

The sound of tyres on the gravel outside made them all stop and look out the window.

'Shane!' Felicity said, flinging a shoe onto her bed and dashing down to greet him.

Aly followed her down the stairs and met Mia at the bottom. 'We'll be okay,' she said tenderly to Mia. 'We're going to miss her like hell, but we'll look out for each other, right?'

'Thanks, pet, I appreciate that,' Mia said, hugging the girl gratefully. 'Go on out and say hello, I'll just run to the bathroom.' Mia leaned against the wall in the bathroom, feeling numb. She'd been awake for most of the night and had got herself into a pragmatic frame of mind.

She was not going to be a dribbling mess when Felicity and Shane left. She would not glower at the young man or say anything snappy. She did genuinely like him, but today she was going to put on an Oscar-winning performance. Willing herself to go back out to the kitchen, Mia braced herself and plastered a smile on her lips. The wind was totally taken from her sails when Shane greeted her with a rectangular box, carefully wrapped and decorated with a large floppy white satin bow.

'This is a little gift from me to you,' Shane said, offering Mia the present.

'Ah, Shane, you didn't have to do that,' Mia was totally flummoxed. Assuming it was a large box of chocolates, she was surprised by the weight of it.

'What is it?' She stared at Shane, who was grinning from ear to ear.

'Open it and see,' he said, looking excited.

'What did you do?' Felicity asked, putting her arms around him.

As Mia pulled the wrapping away, a silver laptop was revealed.

'Oh, Shane, this is too expensive. It'd be wasted on me, love. I can barely use the computer we have. These things cost a fortune, I can't accept it,' Mia stuttered.

'You can and you will. It's my small way of sharing Felicity with you. I know it's not easy for you two to be separated, so this little beauty has Skype. I'll set it up for you now and it means that you can see one another and chat for free any time you feel like it,' Shane concluded, pulling the laptop free of its box. 'I got a really good deal on it, too,' he added. 'My colleague, who's in charge of IT in UCD, was buying in some new equipment for next term and I got this for a song!'

Mia plopped down onto a kitchen chair and shook her head. 'Well, you are the most thoughtful and generous man, Shane. I can't believe you've done this for me.' She was genuinely blown away.

'Shane this is amazing, thank you,' Felicity joined in.

'Well, if I'm being completely honest, there's a bit of selfishness on my part. If Felicity can see you and chat to you, I know she'll be happier. That way, I have more chance of keeping her with me! I know she's found it hard to move away from you, so I figured this might help.'

'Where's mine?' Aly asked, nudging Shane. He turned and smiled at her.

'So am I forgiven for stealing her?' he asked.

'Yeah,' Aly had the grace to blush. 'Can we start afresh?'

'Of course,' he said genuinely. 'Please do come and stay when ever you like.'

'Cheers,' she said.

As Shane busied himself with setting up the laptop, making sure it was fully operational, Bob burst through the back door.

'Yo!' Bob called, shaking Shane's hand and clapping him on the back. 'How's it going? What's happening here?'

'Shane just brought me this new laptop so I can go on this Skype system and see Felicity while she's in Dublin,' Mia said, still overwhelmed by the gesture.

'Cool! That'll be amazing, nice one Shane,' Bob smiled. 'Right, before you two head off into the distance, it's rasher sarnies and mugs of tea all around. I've the batch loaf and the packets of bacon here. I'll make it while you have a quick Skype lesson, Mam,' Bob announced.

'*What?*' both Mia and Felicity yelled at the same time. Bob had never made as much as a cup of tea without a struggle, and now he was offering to make lunch for everyone in the room.

'I'll just have a tomato sandwich, love, I'll make it myself in a while,' Mia said. 'I'm trying to be good and things like rasher sandwiches aren't on my agenda anymore. I'm going to be a new woman, I've started my Pilates and I'm going to be as trim as can be,' Mia announced proudly.

'Ah, me arse. How the hell did generations of people survive to ripe old ages without all this nonsense? It's a rasher sandwich, not a bag of crack cocaine,' Bob huffed.

'Well, if you look at the statistics, people *didn't* live as long before we had all this knowledge. Look at your father. He didn't make it to his fortieth birthday. It's no joke, we all need to be more aware of what we're eating,' Mia said sagely. 'Tally, she's one of the girls we met in Spain, was telling us all about the new way of eating she's taken on board. It makes sense and, besides, you lot are all in the high risk category seeing as your daddy died from his dickey heart.'

'Will I go out and start digging graves now then?' Bob grinned. 'I'll just put the bacon on the pan, and then you can come out and let me know where you'd like me to plant you, if you want?'

'Cheeky git.' Mia had to laugh. Bob would die with a smile on his face, of that she was sure. He never took himself or anyone else too seriously.

'Well I'll have a rasher sandwich, just so long as you have brown sauce,' Shane joined in.

'That can be arranged, my man,' Bob bashed him on the back. 'Felicity? Aly? Bowl of air, glass of water or killer rasher sandwich from hell?'

'That's not funny, Bob!' Felicity tried to sound cross, but in spite of herself she began to giggle. 'Mam is only trying to be sensible about her diet, and she's dead right.'

'I've just had an idea,' Bob said, scratching his chin. 'This new job I got is supposed to involve making kitchens. Why don't I tell the boss to forget that and we'll just make coffins instead? I'll set up a truck in the town selling sandwiches and while people hand over the money, I'll have another lad there with a tape measure, so we can have them fitted for a casket at the same time. I'll be a millionaire!'

'Oh, my God stop it, that's enough,' Mia said, trying to stop herself from giggling too. Bob was on a roll now. When he got giddy, he was dreadful.

'Do you know what?' he continued. 'If I'm going to be dead soon anyway, I reckon I might as well enjoy myself even more. I think I'll start on the Elvis diet and eat burgers for breakfast and battered Mars bars for lunch. If I mix it all with enough pills, I could kill myself by next Wednesday. That way I won't be cluttering up the morgue over the weekend and the funeral could be done and dusted by Friday.'

'Enough!' Mia scolded.

'So, I've a little bit of news myself,' Aly interjected as Bob clattered about with frying pans and the toaster.

'Oh, go on, tell us.' Felicity turned her attention from Shane to her friend. 'Is it about your mystery man? Are you finally going to spill the beans? Will we all approve? Why didn't you tell me last night?' Felicity fired questions at her friend.

'Jeez, give her a chance, will you?' Shane said, smiling at Felicity.

Aly's cheeks flushed and she looked hesitant. 'Well, the answer to the first part of the question is yes – it is about the mystery man I mentioned back in Dublin, but whether or not you'll approve is another thing.'

'Ooh, tell me! Who is he? Has Prince Charming trotted into NUIG in his silver Porsche and swept you off your Jimmy Choos?' Felicity teased. 'I can't believe you stayed here last night and never mentioned this. Come on, who is he?'

'He's not quite Prince Charming, but a pretty cool guy has got me into his VW Polo and swept me off my Primark 100 per cent plastic platform Mary-Janes!' Aly giggled.

'Who? Who? Do I know him?' Felicity was dying to find out.

'You could say that all right,' Aly said shyly.

'Oh, Jesus, give me a hint,' Felicity was trying not to shout as she bounced up and down in the chair.

'Well, you've known him for a long time and although your relationship can be tumultuous, you generally get on well,' Aly said, squeezing her eyes shut and screwing up her face.

'Not that goon Jack that I went out with last year. Please tell me it's not?' Felicity squealed.

'God, no, give me a bit of credit, will you?' Aly exploded.

'Go on then, I haven't a clue.'

Aly took a very deep breath. 'Bob,' she said.

'Who?' Felicity was confused.

'Bob,' Aly repeated, a little more clearly.

'Ah, stop, seriously, who is it?' Felicity was giggling at first, but then realised Aly was being serious. 'My Bob? Our Bob? As in Bobbert? Him?' Felicity pointed at her brother.

'Yup, the very one. It is I – her knight in shining armour!' Bob sidled over and put his arm around Aly's waist.

'Wow,' was all Felicity could manage.

'I can't believe I didn't cop it,' Mia said as the smile spread across her face.

'Well, if you'd given me a year I wouldn't have guessed that one. So how long has this been a 'thing'?' Felicity tried not to sound like a cross teacher, but she knew that was exactly how she was coming across.

'You remember the last time you were home and we went on to the party when you decided to pull a boring biddy on it?' Aly tried to keep it all sweetness and light.

'Yeah.' Felicity wasn't sure about being labelled a boring biddy, but what could she say?

'Well, you drove me into your brother's arms,' Aly finished, laughing dryly. 'When you two were away last week, we spent the whole time together and, so far, so good,' Aly smirked.

'"Good"? Is that all I get?' Bob grabbed Aly and tickled her.

'Okay, you're amazing then!' she squealed.

'That's more like it,' Bob said, planting a kiss on her head.

'And is this serious or another one of your fly-by-night jobs? I know you, Aly. You get bored swiftly and move on. I just don't want this to come between you and me. If you and Bob decide to call it a day, I don't want a situation where I can't get you to call over or end up that I can't mention my brother without you going off on one,' Felicity said honestly.

'I hope it won't come to that.' Aly didn't do her usual, telling Felicity to stop being a drama queen, nor did she do her usual 'college is a code name for shag-fest' speech.

'Ooh, do I sense a serious tone in your voice, Miss Alyson?' Mia teased gently.

'We *really* like each other, and we've kept our relationship quiet for a couple of months for all the reasons you've just mentioned. But seeing as you're heading back to Dublin and we mightn't see you for a while, we thought the time had come to let the cat out of the bag, so to speak,' Aly admitted.

'I think it's great news. Good for you guys,' Shane called over his shoulder.

'You sound different this time, do you know that?' Felicity dropped the teasing tone and pulled her fingers through her hair. Aly had always been the one to flit about and avoid taking life too seriously. She'd even given Felicity a bit of grief about settling down with Shane so soon. It really was a shock to her that her mad brother and her best friend were an item.

'It *is* different. Oh, God, I'm so glad to be able to talk to you all about it. I've been dreading telling you. Neither of us planned it. It just came about, but it feels right.' Aly bit her lip.

'Hey, what do you mean you've been dreading telling them about me?' Bob swatted her on the back of the head with the tea towel. 'I'm a damn fine catch, you should be over the moon to formally announce to my mother and sister that I am allowing you to date me,' he said in mock disgust.

'Leave the girl alone for a minute, you messer,' Mia scolded gently. 'I know why it's hard for you, love,' Mia said, turning to Aly, 'but all I can say is that I couldn't think of a better girl for my Bob. You're already like a second daughter to me, and, what's more, you've known this lunatic most of your life, so you'll have a fair idea of how to handle him! I'm delighted for you both,' Mia hugged her.

'Thanks, Mia, I'm so glad you approve,' Aly admitted. 'Flick? What about you? Are you weird with it or do you think it's okay?'

'I'm actually stunned, if I'm totally honest!' Felicity burst out laughing. 'But it's fantastic news. As Mam says, you know Bob a long time and if you think you can cope with him, more power to you.' Felicity hugged her friend and they exchanged a silent look that said all they needed to say.

'Excuse me. I'm not exactly ecstatic about you two acting as if Aly has agreed to take on a deaf, dumb and blind puppy here. I'm in the room, I have ears and I can hear you all talking. Where's the loyalty? Why aren't you all saying, "God love Bob, having to put up with Aly?" Since when is she Mother Teresa? That one's as mad as a brush. I'm the one who should be getting hugs and support,' Bob said, grinning like a man in love.

'You don't need support Bob, you'll be in the morgue next Wednesday, remember – death by rasher sandwich,' Shane deadpanned.

They finished their lunch and Shane and Bob moved the last of Felicity's things into the car.

Aly hugged her friend. 'Don't be a stranger. I hope it all continues to go well for you, honey. Shane's a dote and he's quite clearly mad about you. Oh, give me another hug, stay in touch, girl, won't you?' Aly began to cry, despite her best intentions.

'Stop, you're making me cry now, too.' Felicity began to shake. 'Make sure that brother of mine is good to you. I'm truly delighted you two seem so happy. I know we fight at times, but he's a good man and I know he'll look after you. He bloody well better, or he'll have me to answer to!' Felicity added.

'Thanks for not being annoyed about it,' Aly said, taking Felicity's two hands.

'Why would I be annoyed, you silly thing?' Felicity asked.

'Well, I wasn't sure if you'd be all odd about it. I can't predict the future, but I hope Bob and I will make a go of it together.'

'I hope so, too.' Felicity grinned. 'I bloody knew you were up to something. That weekend when you came to Dublin you were acting totally weird. I knew you were annoyed with me about Shane, but I couldn't for the life of me figure out why you were turning down the chance of a shift!'

'Am I that transparent?' Aly asked.

'No, only to me because we're like that.' Felicity entwined her fingers to prove her point. 'Take care, girl. Oh, and Aly?'

'Yes?'

'Mind Mam for me, will you?'

'You don't even need to ask. You know it'll be my pleasure to keep her posted on all the gossip!' Aly promised, wiping her eyes.

Felicity said goodbye to Bob and went to find her mother. Mia was avidly wiping the already spotless kitchen table.

'Thank you, Mam, for making it easy for me to make this final move. For not making me choose and for loving me this much,' Felicity sobbed through her words. 'I know I could never replace Amy. She will always be your little angel looking down on us all, but I've always known that what we have is extra special. You've been my mam and my dad,' Felicity said, biting her lip.

'And you and your brothers have been my world,' Mia finished.

'But none of the fundamentals need change, Mam. I'm only up

the country, I'm on the other end of the phone, and now Skype. Shane knows he'll be spending lots of time in Galway, too.'

'I'll be grand. Just grand. My new computer will make all the difference. I can't believe we'll be able to see one another, isn't it marvellous? And what about Bob and Aly? Sure I'm tickled pink by that news. She's a great girl,' Mia mused. 'She's no substitute for you, my pet, but she's a grand young one and I'll be thrilled to have her knocking about the place. We'll be great, you and I,' Mia said as she tucked a strand of Felicity's hair behind her ear. 'Take care, my sweet baby girl. Come back any time you like and never forget where your home is,' Mia said.

Astonishingly, neither of them cried as they hugged that time. It was as if the time for tears had passed. Both knew they loved one another and both held lots of hope for the future.

As they drove off, amid lots of waving and beeping, Felicity and Shane glanced across the car and their eyes met.

'Okay?' Shane asked as his hand rested on her leg gently.

'Better than that, I'm delighted,' Felicity answered, picking up his hand and kissing it. 'Let's go home.'

47.

Daisy

Daisy felt like she was going expire with excitement as she allowed the lady to help her into the champagne-coloured gown at Bridal Bliss. It was named by all the magazines as *the* place to buy that special dress. The moment herself and Ava had walked in, Daisy had felt like she'd stepped onto a cloud of fluffy and gorgeous wonderment.

'Oh, Mum, just look at the headpieces,' Daisy said, exhaling as she pressed her face against the cool glass of the show stand. Lit beautifully, the cabinet contained decorated combs, tiaras and brooches.

'Hello there, ladies, you're so welcome today. Can I take your name, please?' A small lady with treacle-coloured hair swept up in an elegant chignon approached them.

'I'm Daisy Moyes, we spoke on the phone earlier, and this is my mum, Ava.'

'Ah, *oui*. You are so welcome. I am Estelle and I will be happy to show you some ideas today,' the petite French girl said. 'So, firstly, are you looking for a dress or headpiece or shoes?'

'Yes, yes and yes. All of the above!' Daisy's eyes were flashing with glee.

'Okay, so we are your first port of call, or you have already seen a style you like?' asked Estelle.

'No, this is the first outing,' Ava interjected. 'We've both heard a lot about your shop and of course we've seen photos of celebrities wearing your dresses.'

'Okay, that's *fantastique*. So you may be familiar with the knowledge that all our dresses come from Paris. They are all unique and although we have some samples, each one can be adapted and designed to suit the bride. No two are the same and we aim to create something that will make you feel like you are the only bride in the world! Would you like to browse first or do you prefer to describe your own personal image of how you would like to look and I can suggest some samples for you to try?'

Both women looked at one another in delight. This was just the most fantastic thing they could imagine. It all sounded so chic and beautiful, especially presented in a throaty French accent by the lovely Estelle.

'Why don't we let Estelle make some suggestions? Seeing as she knows exactly what's here, otherwise I'm worried we'll still be here in a month's time petting dresses and veils and getting nowhere,' Ava said.

'Good plan, Mum,' Daisy agreed. 'First off, the wedding is set for December twenty-third, so it'll be a winter style dress. I wanted to have pearls as my theme, so perhaps a slightly vintage style?'

'*Bon*. You are not giving me too much time, young lady! We will need to work quickly if you are to choose one of my dresses. Usually we ask at least six months to fit and style the bride, but of course, we can work with speed for you,' Estelle smiled.

Daisy went to the plush fitting room and Ava was shown to a pale-coloured chaise longue and given a frothy cappuccino by Estelle's assistant, Lucy. Before she could contemplate for long, Daisy reappeared.

Ava felt a lump rise in her throat instantly. As Estelle helped Daisy stand on a satin-covered plinth, the sun shone through the window and picked up the tiny seed pearl detail around the Grecian-style plunging back of the dress. The front had a V-shaped detail, which was studded with the same tiny pearls at the back. The chiffon was so fine and wispy, it looked as if it'd been constructed using fairy's wings. Although that exact dress was too long for Daisy, the flow of the floor-length fabric skimmed her neat frame beautifully.

'Might I suggest the accompanying head wear?' Estelle asked.

'Sure,' Daisy said with a slightly wobbly voice. 'Where's the mirror? There was none in the dressing room either. I want to see how it looks! It feels amazing, but I need to see it,' she said, feeling a little frustrated.

'All in good time, my dear. I will reveal when I think you are ready to see yourself.'

Within minutes Estelle and Lucy had attached a sheer veil on a comb to the back of Daisy's head.

'If you like the style of veil I will have it worked into the band, the comb is purely to achieve the effect, you understand.'

Lucy, who had disappeared momentarily, came back wheeling a square metal unit with several drawers.

'I want to see the headbands please, Lucy. The ones that just slot over the hair and fall into place, skimming the forehead and hugging the back of Daisy's curls.'

Opening the third drawer down, Lucy revealed a selection of hoops made of silver and gold.

'I think gold will compliment the hair best,' Estelle ordered.

'This one came in yesterday. I think it's like something from *The Little Mermaid*,' Lucy said, smiling.

The circular hoop was crafted in a dull gold-coloured metal, with hundreds of dot-sized pearls interspersed with crystals. As Estelle slid it on to her head, Daisy's blonde curls were contained yet the simple hairband didn't swamp her.

'Personally I don't like too much glitter on brides, but I think the simplicity of this gown and Daisy's gorgeous pale curls allow us to play a little with the crystals, *non*? For me, a simple mule shoe with a mid-sized kitten heel, accentuating the pearls once more, would finish this look. I have a sample here from the latest Jimmy Choo collection. There is no problem with ordering this pair should you love it. I think you will.' Estelle nodded confidently as she bustled behind a heavy curtain returning with the shoes.

As she lifted the lid, the smell of leather filled Daisy's senses. The shoes that lay nestled in a bed of cream tissue paper looked like they'd been hand-crafted by elves.

'Oh, Mum, just look at them!'

Ava was rooted to the spot as Daisy fitted on the slippers.

'Are you thinking of a church ceremony or will you have the wedding at the reception venue?' Estelle asked. 'There are matching coats for most of the gowns. This particular one has a particularly stunning full-length cape, which is fitted at the bodice and falls to the floor with a slight train to the rear.'

'We haven't discussed where we'll do the ceremony yet,' Daisy admitted. 'We have the reception venue organised for the Four Seasons, but I guess I always imagined myself walking down the aisle with my dad,' she said wistfully.

'I think he would be gutted if you deny him the chance to do that, love,' Ava added.

'Okay, so we will need the cape. But firstly, I will reveal this first look. Don't be polite, I need your first gut reaction. If you don't love, love, love it, that's not a problem. We have many, many dresses. This is just the first one that came to me when I lay eyes on you!' Estelle strode forwards and with one swift pull, she opened the curtains on what the ladies had thought was another dressing room opposite the plinth Daisy was standing on.

Three huge mirrors with gentle, primrose-coloured lighting revealed an image that made Daisy cry out and pull her hands to her mouth.

'Love or hate? Tell me, my darling,' Estelle asked dramatically.

'Oh,' Daisy whispered. 'It's just perfect. What do you think, Mum?'

'I can barely speak,' Ava managed. 'I never imagined you'd look so elegant and beautiful, yet it's delicate and young at the same time. I think Daddy would be as proud as a peacock to walk you down the aisle in that dress. You're simply stunning, sweetheart.' Ava wanted to stand up and hug her daughter, but her legs seemed to have lost all power. She was blown away by her daughter's loveliness.

'Mum, do you think I'd be utterly mad to say that I don't even want to try on any more dresses?' Daisy bit her lip. 'I feel like this is mine already. I know anything else I try on will pale in comparison. It's comfortable, too, which is a bonus!'

'Oh, darling, darling, darling!' Estelle exclaimed. 'The bride must be comfortable on the day. Gone are the days when we go around feeling like we are going to pass out with tight fabrics and rough bits poking into the flesh. Oh, no, we are most concerned that you are able to relax and enjoy every moment of your romantic day, *non*?'

As Lucy helped Daisy off the plinth and back towards the changing room, Ava waited until her daughter was out of earshot before she got down to brass tacks with Estelle.

'Okay, what's the bad news? What kind of money are we talking for the whole lot?' Ava asked. 'Put it this way, should I have the cardiac ambulance on standby when my husband gets the credit card bill?'

'Ah, ha! I like your sense of humour, Madame!' Estelle's eyes twinkled as she spoke. 'I will not lie, the shoes are not cheap. The particular veil we chose is the least expensive in the entire collection, and the dress is mid-price range. For the entire look, including the cape, we would be looking at this.' As she typed a figure into a calculator, Ava was almost afraid to look. With one eye shut, she peered forward.

Never one for driving a hard bargain, Justin had often told her she was a total pushover. Swallowing hard, she took a deep breath.

'Would you throw in a crochet corsage for me?' Ava said, chancing her arm.

'I think that would be fair. Also we don't charge extra for fitting the dress, which will be customised to Daisy's shape,' Estelle replied.

'Okay. You've got yourself a deal.' Ava shook hands formally with Estelle.

Right at that moment in time, Ava would've sold the house from under them to pay for the dress, if that was Daisy's heart's desire. But contrary to her husband's assumption, Ava wasn't *that* much of a pushover. She'd come away with a total bargain when the flower for her own yet-to-be-purchased outfit was taken into account. Well, applying her own unique shopping logic to the situation it was a bargain!

'I just can't wait for Nathan to see me in this dress,' Daisy said, her face a picture of delight as they walked up the steps from the shop and back into the shopping crowds on the street outside.

'Let's phone Dad and tell him all about it, seeing as he's just paid for it all,' Ava said, fishing her phone out of her bag.

'Oh, I meant to say that to you, Mum,' Daisy said nonchalantly. 'I promised Nathan he could pay for my dress. He feels really strongly that you and Dad aren't letting him or his family join in with the wedding, so I agreed he could pay for the dress. I'll tell him the amount this evening and he'll give you the cash.'

'Pardon?' Ava whispered, feeling like she'd been winded.

'I told Nathan he could pay for my—'

'I heard what you said, and there's no way on earth Nathan is paying for your wedding gown.'

'What now, Mum?' Daisy said, throwing her hands up in exasperation. 'Why can't you just give Nathan a break?'

'Why can't you give your father and me a break?' Ava shouted.

'Let's start now, shall we?' Daisy spun around to walk away. 'Let's just keep away from each other for a few days, Mum. You get your head together and I'll do the same. I'm not spending the rest of my life walking on egg-shells with you.'

As Daisy disappeared into the city centre crowds, Ava was left fuming on the pavement.

48.

Felicity

As Shane and Felicity pulled up outside the apartment, she sighed with relief.

'It's great to know I've sorted my thoughts and I know I'm here to stay,' Felicity said.

'So, when you moved in with me last month I was only on trial, is that it?' Shane poked his tongue out at her to show he wasn't being serious.

'Ah, you know what I mean,' Felicity said. 'It was one thing saying it to my mother and everyone on the phone, but it's different now that I'm officially here with all my belongings.'

'I know,' Shane agreed. 'I'm so relieved. A tiny part of me worried that you might come home from Spain and tell me you'd changed your mind. That you wanted to go back to Galway after all.'

'Not on your life!' Felicity said as she leaned over to kiss him.

Dialling her mother on Skype, she was delighted when Mia answered instantly.

'Were you sitting on the laptop?' Felicity giggled.

'Nearly! I was just on Facebook organising a date!' Mia shouted.

'Mam, you don't have to yell into the screen! My volume is right down low in case you blast me across the room!' Felicity laughed.

Mia did the same with her mobile phone, she seemed to have it drummed into her head that all technology required slightly slower, much louder than usual speech.

'So tell me all about this date, is it someone I know?' Felicity had never heard her mother mention going on a date, so this was utterly groundbreaking news.

'I don't know if you ever remember me telling you about a lady called Aoife? I met her when we stayed with your late Auntie Rita while I was pregnant with you.'

'Yes, you've told me about her over the years. So have you decided to explore a muffled lesbian tendency you've been harbouring over the years or is this just a friendship thing?' Felicity asked.

'Ah, stop that, you cheeky pup. She's a person I connected with at time when my life was seriously bleak and I'm so thrilled to have found her again,' Mia said.

'So I don't have to introduce you to my friends as Mam and her life partner Aoife then?' Felicity teased.

'Stop now and listen, will you?' Mia grinned into the camera. 'She's been living in London for years and moved back to Ireland just six months ago. Would you believe, she's settled less than an hour's drive from this very house, and we're meeting for lunch next weekend.'

'That's brilliant, Mam, I'm delighted for you.'

'Yeah, I'm really looking forward to catching up with her.'

Although the screen could sometimes become slightly blurry because of Mia's constant moving around while she was on Skype, there was no denying the wide smile Felicity could see at that moment.

'Well, I'm off to meet some friends for a drink, catch up. I'd better get going actually,' Felicity said, glancing at her watch.

'I'll chat to you tomorrow,' Mia said, waving enthusiastically.

Mia shut down the Skype and returned to Facebook. Aoife had just got back to her again, suggesting a café in town for their reunion. Mia smiled to herself at the idea of seeing her friend again – how old would the two of them look!

She hugged herself in anticipation, feeling like this was a really important step in so many ways. This was the first event of her new life – she'd taken the plunge now. She was going to join another class, master the computer and say yes to every invitation that came her way. There were so many things she'd like to do and now that her children were reared, she could finally indulge herself. She had her head fixed firmly to the future. She wasn't going to sit around moping, causing her children to worry about her. No, she was made of sterner stuff. She was going to get out there and embrace life and see where it would take her.

49.

Tally, Felicity, Daisy

It took until the end of July, a few weeks later, for the three girls to finally hook up. Felicity pitched up at the bar on time. It was one of those massive stone buildings in Dublin city centre, with impressive pillars and enormous wooden doors and vast expanses of buffed original floorboards. Although the building was protected and dated back to the 1900s, the modern furniture and over-sized lamp lighting created a trendy and funky atmosphere. The place was buzzing outside with smokers huddled around patio-heaters, swaying to the beat emanating from the bar inside.

She wasn't a smoker, so she knew she couldn't really comment, but Felicity always found it baffling how girls in skimpy dresses could stand outside in all weathers. As she pulled open the large heavy wooden door, she spotted Tally just ahead of her, scanning the room for a familiar face.

'Boo!' Felicity said, tipping her on the back.

'Felicity, hi! Great to see you, you're looking fantastic, how are you?' Tally said warmly, giving her a big hug.

'Wow, you look absolutely stunning, Tally! Check you out!'

Tally was wearing a pair of loose-fitting charcoal grey trousers with a black fitted jacket and a white camisole top. Her hair was glossy, her skin as flawless as ever and she was meticulously made up. Pillar-box red lipstick added the final glam factor to her look.

'I'm feeling great, I have to say. Let's see if we can grab a table. I arrived literally seconds ahead of you, so I'm not sure if Daisy is here. Let's have a quick scope around and try to shoehorn ourselves into a little space,' Tally suggested, navigating the growing crowd.

Seeing a high round table with four high stools, the girls made a beeline for the spot. As there were lounge girls circulating, they perched up on the chairs and flung their bags onto one of the stools to keep it for Daisy.

'So tell me everything! Have you made your final move to Dublin yet?' Tally asked.

'I sure have. It's going so well, Tally. I'm delighted with myself. I'm doing bits and pieces of work and getting ready to go back to college. I'm delighted with life, I have to say. What about yourself?'

'Well,' Tally said, flagging down a lounge girl and ordering them a drink each. 'My new course kicks off properly in September. I've my books all sorted already and I'm ready to rock and roll,' Tally sipped her drink. 'I'm really buzzed up about it all,' she grinned.

'So I can see! You look utterly stunning too. You've lost so much weight since I saw you in Spain!' Felicity complimented her.

'Ah, thanks, Felicity, I've dropped a further two dress sizes actually. I'm a very proud size fourteen now!'

'Hi, girls, so sorry I'm late! It's been a mental day!' Daisy bustled in looking slightly hassled.

'Daisy!' Tally exclaimed, hopping off her high stool to hug the girl.

'How's it going?' Felicity said warmly, kissing her cheek.

'Jezz, look at you, hot bod!' Daisy whistled as she looked Tally up and down slowly. 'You are looking *hot*!'

'Ah, stop it,' Tally said, flushing.

'What did I tell you?' Felicity said, nodding.

'You're looking mighty fine, too, my pet, but this siren beside you is just smokin',' Daisy said to Felicity.

They ordered a round of drinks and when they'd all clinked glasses, the chat turned to weddings.

'So, we're all set for December twenty-third!' Daisy said. 'Oh, listen to me gushing away here. I'll shut up now. I was *so* not like this before I met Nathan,' she admitted.

'Well I'm one of the most romantic fools you could ever meet, so you can gush away about it all and I'll lap it up!' Tally giggled.

Daisy filled them in on what her dress was like – avoiding the awful argument she and Ava had started outside the shop.

'Oh, it sounds like some thing from a fairy tale,' Felicity said, clasping her hands in delight.

'Well, you'll see it for yourself, please God. I hope you'll both come? I'm dying to meet Shane, and Mia must come, too. And I want to meet your dad, Tally. Having heard so much about him in Spain, I feel like I know him already,' Daisy added. 'Of course, your own invite is plus one, if you so chose,' Daisy winked at Tally.

'Weeeelll,' Tally raised an eyebrow and grinned. 'I will take you up on that! As it happens, myself and Ben are getting on really well,' Tally's eyes sparkled as she spoke.

'Fantastic! Tell us everything!' Daisy said, leaning in for all the details. 'I knew you were meeting him when we returned from Spain, but I wasn't sure if I should ask in case he'd turned out to be a tosser!'

'Girls,' Tally began, 'I can't believe it. He's just the most amazing boyfriend, but more than that, he just gets me. We have such a giggle together and he's utterly divine to look at.' Tally produced her phone and showed the girls pictures of him.

'Bloody hell, you don't do things by halves, do you?' Daisy whistled. 'He's gorgeous!'

'I think so, too! My life is just so, so different to this time last year. I feel like I'm in a dream!' Tally said, sounding completely lovestruck. 'Oh, and by the way,' she beckoned for them to lean in and whispered, 'I'm no longer a virgin.'

'I knew you looked different,' Daisy teased. 'There was I thinking it was all down to weight loss. There's a lot to be said for a good old-fashioned shag to bring out the colour in a girl's cheeks.'

'Jesus, Daisy!' Tally said looking stunned. 'Although I have to say, if I'd known just how amazing the whole thing is, I reckon I'd have started when I was sixteen!'

'So, he's good in bed, I take it?' Felicity grinned.

'Well, obviously I've nothing to compare him to, but to say he takes me to a place that I never guess existed is putting it mildly!'

'Oooh, brilliant!' Daisy giggled.

'Well you deserve the very best,' Felicity said warmly.

'Hear, hear!' Daisy said, raising a glass.

'To love, marriage and a damn good shag!' Tally said, winking.

By ten thirty, the bar was bursting at the seams. The music had been pumped up and the punters' voices had done the same.

'Free passes for the disco bar upstairs, girls?' An oiled topless male model sidled past and flicked three passes onto the table. 'Be there or be square, that's the scene jelly-bean, see ya soon I presume,' he finished off by doing a double pirouette.

'Sod it, I was really enjoying him until he did the Billy Elliot move at the end there. Why are all the most divine guys gay?' Tally sighed.

The girls decided to have one more drink and see if they felt like going dancing, but as the tunes from the disco bar and the flashing coloured lights beckoned, the trio found themselves migrating towards the dance floor.

The music was fantastic, incorporating eighties hits, nineties classics and all the current floor-fillers. They hardly sat down for the next three hours.

It was Daisy's round, so she rooted in her bag for some cash. 'Damn,' she said, realising she'd a missed call from Ava. *She's probably calling to say sorry for being a total bitch earlier at the wedding shop.*

Just then an unknown number rang through.

'Hello?' Daisy put her finger in her free ear to try and hear.

'Daisy?' the man's voice shouted. 'This is Mark Shaw, from the golf club. Your mother has just been taken to hospital in an ambulance. I thought you should know.'

'What?' Daisy shrieked in terror.

Running outside so she could hear properly, Daisy got the details. Phoning her dad, his phone instantly went to voicemail. She knew Justin was en route from New York, but his flight obviously hadn't landed yet. She left him a breathless message.

'Dad, meet me in Dublin Central Hospital. Mum's been taken there. I'm on my way now. I don't have any more details. I'll call you when I do.' Dialling Nathan's number, she quickly explained what was going on.

'Grab a cab and I'll meet you there. Try not to panic,' he said as she hung up.

Contrary to Nathan's advice, Daisy chose to go totally bananas. Running back into the club, she found the two girls.

'It's Mum,' she said, grabbing hold of them, tears spilling down her cheeks. 'She's been taken to Dublin Central Hospital. The man from the golf club doesn't know any further details. Oh, Jesus, we had a massive row earlier on. What if she dies and I never said sorry?' Daisy was weeping openly now.

'Daisy, you've got to calm down. Look at me. Felicity and I will go with you to the hospital right now. I'm sure Ava will be fine,' Tally sounded a lot calmer than she felt.

Ten minutes later they bundled out of a taxi outside the hospital. While Tally paid the driver, Daisy raced ahead inside, with Felicity hard on her heels. Tally ran after them. Inside, they found Nathan talking to a doctor.

'Nathan,' Daisy cried, throwing herself into his arms. 'What's going on?'

'Hi, love,' he said, giving her a quick kiss. 'I'm trying to get some information about Ava's condition.'

'Are you family?' the doctor asked.

'Yes,' Daisy said, catching her breath. 'I'm her daughter.'

'It seems your mother has a ruptured appendix. She's going to require surgery. We're just waiting for a team to scrub in and she'll be taken down to theatre.'

'Will she get a private room afterwards?' Nathan asked.

'I'll see,' the doctor said, fobbing him off. 'Just sign this form, please, and we'll work out the rest later.'

'Hold on one minute,' Nathan said crossly. 'Ava has insurance and I want you to assure me that she will have a private room. Also, who will be operating on her?'

'Pardon?' the doctor said, looked slightly miffed.

'I want to know who her surgeon will be,' Nathan demanded.

Flicking through a file, the doctor moved his pen along the list. 'Well there are two surgeons on tonight.'

'What's the difference between them?' Nathan asked directly.

'Well one, Mr McDermott, has been operating for slightly longer.'

'How much longer?' Nathan wasn't letting it drop.

'He's our senior general surgeon,' the doctor finally admitted.

'Good, we'll have him then.'

The doctor looked like he wanted to deck Nathan, but the large American wasn't remotely phased.

'As you may have guessed from my accent, I'm not from around here. Where I come from we believe in good customer relations. Now I know it's not PC to think of a hospital as a business, but the baseline fact is this: Ava has paid for her health insurance, so I want her to be well looked after. Daisy here is very distressed about her mother and I want you to assure us that the care she receives will be the best this hospital has to offer.'

'Okay!' the doctor said, throwing his eyes to heaven.

'So glad we understand one another,' Nathan said, clapping the doctor on the back. 'I'll be here waiting, so if there are any issues, of any kind, come and let me know, yes?'

'Right.' The doctor went to the nurses' station. 'Mrs Moyes is going to be operated on my Mr McDermott now.'

'She'll be fine, Daisy, come on and sit down and we can call your father to fill him in,' Nathan said, turning her around.

'I'm right here,' Justin said. 'I arrived a few moments ago. Nathan, I have to hand it to you, that was pretty direct trouble-shooting, son.'

'Dad,' Daisy hugged him, fresh tears spilling over again.

'I appreciate your care and most of all how you took control of that situation just now,' Justin admitted. Holding his hand out, Nathan took it and they shook solemnly.

Daisy looked up at her father as they walked to the waiting area to fill the girls in on the latest events.

'Daisy,' Justin said, holding her back as Nathan introduced himself and spoke to Felicity and Tally. 'I was wrong about Nathan. He's a good guy.' Her father looked choked up with emotion.

'I know that,' Daisy said, not giving him an inch.

'I should've trusted your judgement more. I apologise,' he said.

'That's okay, Dad. Don't worry, you have about forty years to make it up to us.'

50.

Tally

Greta was just out of bed, padding around the kitchen and lighting her first cigarette of the day, when Tally arrived in the door.

'Jesus, Tally, you nearly scared the life out of me. Have you been out dancing till this hour?' Greta said, looking her daughter up and down. 'You look fairly whacked, if you don't mind me saying.'

Things had been improving slowly but surely between Tally and Greta. They both made an effort to include one another in general chit-chat.

'Oh, God, I was at the hospital,' Tally said wearily.

'What? With who?'

Tally filled her in on the events.

'That's terrible,' Greta said. Her brow furrowed as she pictured Ava. She was such a lovely woman.

'It was looking good when myself and Felicity left, though. She was in the recovery room after her surgery and they seemed pleased with her progress. Daisy promised to text us later, to let us know how she is.'

Tally left her mother and showered quickly before hopping into bed for a couple of hours.

Greta was on a mission. She too had to be in work, so she'd only a couple of hours' running time available before she had to open the gym at seven.

The cool early morning air filled her lungs as she stretched out her leg muscles at the side of the curb. She started off at a measured canter, then gradually picked up the pace, enjoying the feeling of her body easing into the run and soaking up the benefits of it. The rhythm of the beat from her earphones and her pounding steps worked their usual magic. When she'd completed her first couple of kilometres, she felt herself slipping into her comfort zone.

Greta felt she was making an enormous effort to go along with all the therapy stuff. She bit her tongue any time a funny comment sprang to mind. At one point she had felt like she needed to go around with a sock in her mouth and muzzle strapped to her face, just to avoid saying the first thing that came to her mind. Slowly, she'd learned to count to five and think about what it was she was going to say, then decide whether or not to say it.

She had also made a concerted effort to cut out her evening shake and was now 'partaking in family meal times'. They sat together at six thirty most nights and had a low-fat dinner, like a piece of fish and salad. That was fine by Greta, it was just the whole charade of the thing. For the first few times she'd felt like a right spanner, sitting and making cheerful conversation with her own daughter and husband. But after three days of it, Tally had made a big speech about how much it all meant to her and that they were a real family now, and Martin did the slow nod thing and smiled. He'd squeezed Tally's hand and reached for hers. Before she knew it, they were all holding hands.

'Are we having a séance or a salad?' Greta had asked, feeling uncomfortable.

'No, Ma, we're just having a lovely moment,' Tally had beamed.

Martin was grinning like a Labrador and even winked at them both in glee. Greta couldn't take it and began to giggle.

'What?' Tally asked, surprised.

'I'm sorry, I find this all a bit staged, but it's very pleasant I have to admit,' Greta said, smiling. Her husband and daughter smiled back at her.

Tally and Martin had become so concerned about her smoking that she'd taken to puffing when they weren't around. She'd had to take one cigarette and a lighter in her sock the day before, so Martin wouldn't see the packet as she left for work. Maybe one day she'd stop smoking, but, for the moment, the happy-clappy stuff was more than enough to deal with.

By the time she returned from jogging, Martin had gone to work and there was no sound coming from Tally's room. Poking her head around her daughter's bedroom door, she paused for a moment. Tally was out cold, lying on her back, with her hair tossed to one side and draped down the pillow.

She'd her nana's cheekbones. Greta had always thought her own mother was beautiful, and Tally was actually the spitting image of her. As she turned to leave the bedroom, Greta caught sight of a jacket slung over the back of a chair. Flicking the label over she saw that it was a size fourteen.

Well I'll be damned, Greta thought. She had to admit she felt an odd sensation deep in her chest. It bubbled all the way to her throat and formed a lump there. Her eyes threatened to water. *Get a grip and stop being such an eejit.* Before she could leave the room, Tally's eyes fluttered open.

'Ma?' she said, sitting up and rubbing her face. 'Is everything okay?' Tally asked looking slightly confused.

'I … eh …' To her horror, Greta couldn't stop the tears that were rolling down her cheeks.

'Ma? What's happened? Is Da all right?' Tally sat up abruptly.

'Your daddy's fine,' Greta managed. Lunging forward, she wrapped her arms around Tally, pulling her into her embrace. Years of pent-up emotion poured from Greta's inner core.

'It's okay, Ma, just let it go,' Tally whispered.

Tally fully expected her mother to pull away and either flee the room or apologise and make a smart comment. But Greta surprised herself and her daughter by sitting up straight and taking a long, deep breath.

'Well done, love. I just saw your jacket there. You've come such a long way, I had no idea you were down to a size fourteen. I was staring at you while you were asleep just now. You're the image of your nana, do you know that?' Greta smiled sadly. 'I always wanted to be like her. When herself and Auntie Marie, your daddy's mother, used to dance in the kitchen to the radio, I used to look at Mammy and wish I had her looks.'

'Really?' Tally was barely able to breathe. Was her mother actually suggesting that she, Tallulah, the fat useless embarrassment of a child, might be beautiful?

'You're like her in more ways than one. You have her personality, too. She was always calm. She didn't make a fuss of anything. When I was fat, she just made me dresses that were larger,' Greta said.

'Did she ever suggest you should lose weight? Was that why you took up the exercising?' Tally ventured gently. It was so strange that her mother was even sitting on her bed, let alone crying and now bearing her heart. Tally was afraid if she moved suddenly or said too much, the bubble of emotion might burst and the moment would be gone forever.

'No, Mammy never made me feel bad. She just accepted whatever made me happy. When your daddy and I got married, Auntie Marie did say that she couldn't believe the difference in the size of the pattern in comparison to my graduation dress. They made both my dresses, you see. I remember it like yesterday, the two of them sewing and drinking tea in the kitchen. Mammy gave Auntie Marie the look. Just a flicker with her eyes, but it spoke volumes.'

'What did the look say?' Tally asked.

'It said, let it go, don't make an issue of what size she is either way.' There was a long pause in the room as Greta allowed the tears to fall.

'Why are you so sad, Ma?' Tally pressed her gently.

'Because I know I've done you wrong, love. If Mammy were still alive, she'd never have allowed me to criticise you the way I did. She hadn't a nasty bone in her body. She had a wonderful way of accepting people. She used to turn heads, she was so pretty. She'd push the pram down the main street and I'd hold the handle at the side. She'd wear a slick of lipstick as the only nod to glamour and yet she emanated such beauty, people would stare. I used to long for someone to look at me like that.'

'But Da does,' Tally interjected.

'Does he? I always wondered if he just married me because it was easy. You know him, he's the sweetest man alive and would do anything to avoid offending a soul. It's occurred to me more than once over the years that he simply did what he knew Mammy and Auntie Marie wanted.'

'Ma, that's insane! Da adores you! He might be all the things you say, but he's not stupid nor is he a liar. He married you and stayed with you all these years because he loves you. I'd be the first to say he's a prince among men, but he's not a saint!'

Tally felt like the wind had been knocked out of her. She couldn't believe that beneath the gruff exterior, her Ma was so frightened and unsure.

'I don't think I've ever even realised how much I've been running away from emotionally,' Greta said sadly.

'You've been running physically and emotionally,' Tally stated.

'I love my jogging though,' Greta affirmed.

'Do you?' Tally questioned.

'Yeah, honestly. I know it's not your buzz, but I feel free when I'm running. I listen to my music and each step I take jollies me along. I don't have to think too much, I can just escape.'

'Maybe you should try to stop escaping. Would it be so awful to join in some more? I'd really like you to,' Tally added.

Fresh tears made Tally lunge forward. 'I'm sorry, Ma. I was only trying to make you feel better.'

'You're so like your nana, it's astonishing. I can't believe I never saw it until now. I've behaved abominably for so long and now I'm scared it's gone too far, that we'll never click.'

'I've always loved you, Ma. You just mightn't have been ready to accept my love.'

'I thought you didn't need me. When you were a baby, your nana was your hero. When she died, you became your daddy's girl. I suppose I never felt needed.'

'I always needed you, Ma. Why do you think I've worked so hard to change? Yes it's for myself, I needed to lose the weight and change my lifestyle, that's obvious. But most of all I want you to be proud of me. I want you to love me.'

'I do, pet. But, I need you to try and understand me a little, too,' Greta reasoned. 'I feel like I'm walking on eggshells all the time with you and your da. I honestly feel like an outsider most of the time,' Greta admitted.

Greta and Tally heard the front door slam.

'Only me! Head like a sieve, forgot a thing for work,' they heard Martin call out as he flew in the front door.

'We're in my room, Da!' Tally yelled back. She sounded really upset. Spotting Greta's trainers beside the door, Martin's heart sank. He really hoped the girls hadn't been arguing again.

'Hi, girls,' he said, looking anxious. 'Hey! What's happened? Did someone die?' He rushed to the bed and dropped onto his knees between his wife and daughter. Pulling them both into his arms, he rocked and hushed them as they both sniffled. 'What's happened?' he ventured a second time.

'Someone has died, as a matter of fact,' Greta said, standing up and pacing up and down with her hands on her hips. Her face was all mottled and blotchy.

'Oh, God, who?' Martin asked.

'The nasty gremlin that's stood between Tally and me for a long time,' Greta stated.

'Everything all right, love?' Martin whispered to Tally

'Do you know what, Da? I really think it will be.'

51.

Daisy

Ava recovered well from her surgery, although it knocked the stuffing out of her for a while. Her family let her have as long a convalescence as she needed. Daisy didn't mention Nathan or weddings or arguments for some weeks after that awful night at the hospital, but she knew her silence couldn't last forever.

Finally, she visited home one day and found Ava looking well and rested, sitting on the couch with a recipe book, planning a dinner for Justin. Her energy levels were returning to normal and she felt able to contemplate housework and cooking again. Daisy came in and sat beside and they held helds in silence for a couple of minutes.

'Mum, I'm so sorry for what happened that day,' Daisy said quietly.

'I know, and it's in the past. We both regret it, but it's over and forgotten,' Ava said immediately.

'I know things are so much better between Dad and Nathan now and that it all paled into insignificance once you were rushed to hospital, but I want to clear the air about the dress.'

'Okay,' Ava said, looking hopeful.

'I've been thinking long and hard about the future. I'm not going to work for Nathan when Infants 2 Elders opens the Montessori.'

'But I thought it was what you always wanted to do?' Ava said, surprised by this turn in Daisy's thinking.

'It is,' Daisy assured her. 'I just want to do things on my own. I'd only be getting the job because I'm Nathan's wife. I need some experience and I need to make my own way in the world.'

'I see,' Ava said, looking impressed.

'And with regards to my wedding dress,' Daisy continued. 'I have some savings from the money Gran left me in her will.'

'What? That was years ago!' Ava was astonished.

'That may be, but I never had anything special to spend it on, so it's been sitting in an account. So I hope you can be happy if I tell you that Gran is buying my wedding dress.'

Ava gazed lovingly at her daughter. 'That's a lovely idea, pet, she'd be so pleased.'

October came and went and, before she knew it, Daisy was looking at the box of wedding invitations the printer had just delivered.

'Nathan?' she called excitedly into the bedroom. 'Come and open the parcel with me.'

Striding into the living room of their apartment, Nathan kissed her on the lips and stood with his hands on his hips.

'You do the honours,' he offered.

Ripping the box open, Daisy jumped up and down with excitement as she gazed at the cards.

'They're so beautiful, look at the pearlised paper and the matching lining of the envelopes, I love them.'

'Me too. I'm so glad you're happy with them,' Nathan said nodding. 'I've printed off all the address labels for you, so we can get all the ones to the States immediately. My folks are so excited about coming to Ireland, this is just going to make Mom insane with joy,' said Nathan. 'Would you give her a call and do the girly-screechy thing down the phone to her, just so she feels like she's part of it all?'

Brea had been on the phone so regularly that Daisy had almost forgotten they'd never actually met.

'Sure,' she said to Nathan with a smile. 'I can do girly-screechy for Brea. I can't wait to finally meet them in the flesh.'

'Well, only two weeks and they'll be here. I'm so glad you asked them to come and help out with the final arrangements. It means so much to them that your family are welcoming them like this. It makes it all even more special for me,' Nathan said, kissing her again.

Since the night at the hospital, Daisy and Nathan had grown even closer. The fact that the atmosphere between Daisy and her parents had relaxed so much had added to the euphoric build-up, too. Ava had thrown herself into all the wedding preparations with gusto. Daisy was adamant that Brea should be included in all the conversations. So they ended up doing conference calls regularly.

When the invitations had been posted, Daisy and Ava were like excited children waiting for the postman to arrive every day. Work on Nathan's Infants 2 Elders flagship store was in its final stages and it was due to open the second week in January, with the other regional stores to be finished by June.

Brea and Peter were due to arrive from California three weeks before the wedding. Nathan had organised an apartment in the same building as Daisy and himself, so his parents could be close by without invading anyone's space.

The day they arrived, he and Daisy made their way out to the airport to collect them. As they stood in the arrivals area, Daisy pulled at her coat and patted her hair to make sure she looked presentable.

'Relax! Mom and Dad are gonna love you. You already know them from all the girly talks you guys have been having over the phone. So chillax!' Nathan assured her.

Brea was not at all what Daisy had expected. For some reason, she'd had an image of a brash-looking, slightly over the top character. Instead, a tall, blonde, slim and very attractive woman came striding through the arrivals gate. Dressed in skinny jeans, leather jacket and high leather boots, this lady was more Ralph Lauren supermodel than footballer's wife.

'Sweetie!' Brea spotted Nathan and ran open-armed towards her son. With tears rolling down her totally line-free face, she embraced her son.

'Daisy! Oh, my goodness, it's so amazing to finally meet you.' Brea turned and hugged her close. Daisy felt slightly overwhelmed by the time Pete arrived with the luggage trolley. As they bear-hugged and banged each other on the back, Daisy smiled at the two men. Nathan had his mother's blonde hair and blue eyes, and his father's sallow skin and manly physique. Just like his son, Pete was a big man by any one's standards. But beside Daisy's petite five foot two inch frame, the man was like a giant.

'Well, aren't you the cutest little thing I've ever laid eyes on?' Pete said, stooping and hugging Daisy gently. 'I'm afraid if I squeeze you too tightly, you'll break. My son told me the day he met you that you reminded him of Tinker Bell the fairy, and you know, he was right!'

'Hello,' Daisy said, meekly looking up at Pete's six-foot four frame.

There was no denying it, Brea and Pete were a gorgeous-looking couple. Pete had thinning hair, but his dark tanned skin against his greying temples made for a distinguished and dashing look.

Brea, Daisy assumed, had had some help in the facial department. She looked almost younger than Daisy and as fit as an Olympian.

As Ava pointed out the following day in the privacy of the kitchen when Nathan brought his parents for an introductory lunch, whoever Brea had found to do her 'work' was a genius.

'She *has* to have had stuff done. She has the complexion of a teenager, yet she doesn't look like a canvas – all stretched and frozen. She's beautiful, isn't she?' Ava said in awe.

'Completely,' Daisy agreed. 'And she's so nice. It's an unusual combination. Women who look like her are meant to be utter cows!'

Both Daisy and Ava found that the more they got to know Brea on the run-up to the wedding, the more they liked her. She was ladylike, funny and always positive and complimentary towards them.

Justin was thrilled to realise that Pete was easy company, too. The three men went for a long lunch two weeks before the wedding, dropping in on the way to see the final touches being put in place at the Infants 2 Elders flagship store.

'It's some set-up you've got going here,' Justin said, openly impressed.

'It's a great success back home, so I'm hoping we'll take the market share across Ireland and Europe too, Justin. You know yourself, once a concept works and is tried and tested, and once the focus remains the same, it can pretty much work anywhere. I've great faith in Nathan here, and he's one of life's steady sorts. Brea and I are awful proud of him, and I hope he and your little girl will be very happy together.'

'We hope so, too,' Justin said, feeling like a rat for having such doubts about Nathan initially.

'Oh, while I have you both here,' Nathan said, 'I may as well update you on Daisy's decision. She has decided she doesn't want to come and work here after all.'

'What? Why?' Pete said, looking flustered.

'She figures she wants some experience first. She also said she's not prepared to be the boss' little wifey, sitting in a cushy job!' Nathan smirked.

'Jesus, that girl is as stubborn as a mule at times,' Justin said, shaking his head.

'I wonder where she gets that from?' Nathan asked him with a smile.

52.

December: Daisy... I do...

On the morning of 23 December, there was enough frost on the ground to make the garden look sugar-coated. The sky was clear and bright blue and the sun was shining through the branches of the fir tree that had been growing just opposite her bedroom window for decades. As Daisy looked out from the comfort of her old bed, she rested her chin on her hands and sighed happily. By three o'clock today, she'd be Mrs Nathan Taylor.

A faint rapping on her door made Daisy jump.

'Hi, honey,' Ava padded into the room with her hair wrapped in a towel turban. 'The hair and make-up girls will be here soon. How are you feeling?'

'I'm so excited, Mum, but I feel really calm in another way. I always thought I'd be a bundle of nerves on my wedding day, that I'd turn into a bridezilla and spend the morning yelling at people and bursting into tears!'

'Well, there's still plenty of time to do that, if you feel the need,' Ava said smiling.

'No, it's okay, thanks. I just want to bottle the way I feel right now and hope it lasts for a very long time.'

'I hope so too, sweetheart,' Ava said, sitting down on the side of the bed. 'Your brothers will be here shortly, I've arranged for them to come and share breakfast with us. Just the five of us, like old times. Not that I feel like eating a bite!' Ava giggled.

'Oh, Mum, that's such a gorgeous idea, thank you,' Daisy said, hugging her mum. Justin appeared in the room and nodded at Ava. They looked nervous and Daisy immediately wondered what was coming next.

'Daisy, we wanted to give you this,' Justin said, producing a little red velvet box and an envelope. Daisy was already welling up as she opened the envelope.

Inside was a wedding card with a slip of yellowed paper inside. It was a piece of headed paper from a clinic in New York, dating back to 1985. It was an appointment card with one Dr Macintosh for a PGD procedure.

'What's this?' Daisy asked, looking puzzled.

'It's the day that you were conceived,' Ava said, holding her gaze.

'What does PGD mean?' asked Daisy.

'It's a special type of IVF,' Ava answered. 'We went to a special clinic in the States that offered the possibility of choosing the sex of your baby. We already had your two brothers, but I was desperate for a girl. So we took the necessary steps in order to have a girl. We chose you, Daisy.'

'You're our designer baby,' Justin added, looking slightly ill at ease and embarrassed.

Daisy was astounded. This was the first time she'd ever heard any of this and it was a lot ot take on board. 'Do the boys know about this?' was her first question.

'No. The only people we ever told were another couple who went through the same thing at the time, but we don't see them any longer,' Ava explained.

Daisy sat in stunned silence as her parents explained the story of how she'd come into existence. She never had any inkling of what her parents had gone through to have her. She sat on her bad, shaking her head, trying to grasp it all.

'And why did you choose to tell me now?' she asked them.

'We wanted you to start your new life, your married life, without any secrets from your old one,' Justin answered. 'It just seemed the right time to let you know this. We hope you're not angry that we didn't discuss this with you before, but we never wanted Jake and Luke to feel that they weren't enough for us. We love all of you equally, the only difference is that you came into our lives in a slightly different way.'

'Wow,' Daisy said, whistling.

'Aren't you going to open your gift?' Justin asked.

Daisy popped open the square box and revealed a chubby gold heart pendant on a sleek chain.

'Oh, it's beautiful,' Daisy whispered.

'It's a heart of gold for our most precious girl,' Ava said as her voice cracked. Daisy turned it over and the inscription read: PGD – Precious Girl Daisy

'Thank you both,' Daisy said as tears fell down her cheeks. 'I'll always be your little girl, no matter how long I'm married or how old I get,' she added firmly.

They embraced each other and Justin and Ava looked at each other happily, glad they'd made the right decision.

'All right, Daisy Moyes,' Ava said eventually, 'I think it's time we got you ready for your wedding.'

As Justin walked his beautiful daughter down the aisle later that day and handed her over to Nathan, he felt a huge rush of love for her. He was so delighted that he and Ava had mended their relationship with Daisy. As Ava took his arm when he stood beside her in the front pew of the church, he kissed her and closed his eyes momentarily, praying Daisy and Nathan would be as happy as he and Ava had been.

At the end of the ceremony, Nathan broke with tradition by scooping Daisy into his arms and running back down the aisle with her. The congregation burst into spontaneous applause and everyone piled out into the church courtyard to embrace the newly married couple.

For Daisy, it was all a bit of a blur as people came up to them to congratulate them. There were so many new face to get acquainted with, all the relatives and friends of Nathan's from America, that it was all a bit overwhelming. But at the centre of it all stood Nathan, calm and solid – her husband.

At the Four Seasons later that day, the mood was buzzy and relaxed as the two hundred-strong crowd chatted and enjoyed a pre-dinner drink.

'Felicity!' Tally called out as she entered the reception area and accepted a glass of bubbly from the waiter.

'Tally! Wow, look at you! Oh, my God, you look even more stunning than usual!' she exclaimed as she stared at Tally's long, midnight blue dress.

'Thanks. *Size twelve*,' she whispered with delight before turning to introduce her plus one. 'Felicity, this is Ben,' she said proudly.

'Hi, Ben, it's lovely to meet you. I'll introduce you to Shane in a minute, he's just parking the car,' she said, kissing him on both cheeks. 'You look dashing, too!'

'Well, thank you, it's great to finally put a face to the name! Tally's told me all about you,' Ben said with a smile. 'This is a great way to kick off the festive season, isn't it?' As they gazed around the room, the attention to detail was spectacular. Daisy had gone all out with the pearls and cream theme, but it had been executed so prettily. White poinsettia plants dotted the room, set into simple cream pots. The stamen had been carefully studded with tiny pearls, making a subtle yet gorgeous decoration. Several real Christmas trees scented the room beautifully, while their white lights and strings of pearls added understated elegance.

'Are you staying the night or is Shane designated driver?' Ben asked.

'We're actually staying over, which is a real treat.'

'Us, too,' Tally said, eyes sparkling. 'The deal was so good for wedding guests, so we figured it'd be rude not to stay!'

'Not to mention the idea of waking up in the Four Seasons on Christmas Eve!' Felicity added.

Mia, Greta, Martin and another lady made their way over to the group.

'Hiya, Felicity love,' Greta said hugging her. 'This hunk of manhood must be Shane,' she said as he came up behind Felicity with the car keys in his hand.

'Yes it is and don't give him a big head, please,' Felicity giggled.

'How're ya, Ben,' Greta said, chucking him on the cheek. 'This is great, being surrounded by gorgeous young men in monkey suits. God, I love a nice tux on a fella,' Greta said with delight.

'Eh, what about me?' Martin said, puffing his chest out.

'Ah, sure, you're a lovely boy, too,' she cackled.

They all shook hands and clinked glasses.

'This is my friend, Aoife,' Mia said. 'We were pals many moons ago and met up on Facebook again recently.'

'They're not 'life partners' either,' Felicity pointed out.

'Thanks for pointing that out, darling daughter,' Mia said. 'Cheeky mare. She seems to think she needs to constantly assure the world that I'm not gay.'

'The best way to cure her of that is to raise an eyebrow and say this is my special friend Aoife and elbow Felicity next time you're out,' Greta said, winking.

'True for you, girl,' Mia laughed.

The gong sounded, indicating they should all take their seats, and the crowd shuffled towards the dining tables.

'Any one had a chance to look at the table plan?' Martin asked over his shoulder as they moved towards the double doors of the dining room.

'Yes, I did,' Tally said. 'We're all on table seven! That's my lucky number!'

'It's certainly my lucky table today, with my two ladies by my side,' Martin said, kissing Greta on the cheek and winking at Tally.

'Did you all recognise Tally today?' Greta asked. 'My amazing disappearing daughter!' she said.

Tally flushed with joy as her mother swatted her with her pashmina.

'I already told Tally how brilliant she looks,' Felicity commented. 'But Greta I have to say, you're looking very chic yourself.'

'You like?' she asked. 'It's not my usual clobber admittedly, but Tally and I went on a shopping trip the other week. I've knocked the fags on the head and decided to treat us both to a special outfit with the stash I'd accumulated.'

'Well I never thought I'd see you in a pink cocktail dress,' Mia said warmly.

'I know!' Greta grinned. 'There's even a bit of glitter on it! I'm in danger of looking like a lady, God help us all!' Martin pulled out her chair to allow her sit and patted her hand as he joined her at the table.

'It's strange to see Greta with Martin actually,' Felicity whispered to Mia. 'She seems so much less abrasive when she's with him. He clearly adores her and brings out a much softer side to her.'

'I think there's more to it than that,' Mia said. 'She's calmer altogether. She's ditched the cropped hair-do, too. If you notice, herself and Tally are so much more at ease in each other's company as well. It's lovely to see.'

'Hello everyone!' Ava and Justin were making their way around the room welcoming all the guests. 'This is Justin, Daisy's father, we're so delighted to welcome you all today,' Ava said.

Mia introduced Aoife and hugged the mother of the bride.

'You are the epitome of elegance, Ava,' Mia said in awe.

'Well, when you enlist the help of Coco Chanel, the rest is a doddle,' Ava whispered. 'Justin brought the dress and jacket from New York last month. He figured that our daughter's wedding called for a really special outfit.'

The understated cream gown, cut on the bias, fell in soft silky folds to the floor. The signature boucle white cropped jacket with navy accented lapels, complete with a long knotted string of pearls, made Ava look like a model.

'Well I'm envious as hell!' Mia said with a smile.

'I know I sound like I'm simply trying to be polite now, but you look like a new woman yourself,' Ava said sincerely.

'I feel it,' Mia said. 'I was in a pretty bad place when we were in Spain, to be honest. I was so focused on the fact that Felicity was moving in with Shane and wallowing in the negative, I think I'd got myself into a state!'

'And how do you feel about it all now?' Ava asked.

'You know, it's all worked out so well,' Mia said, looking genuinely happy. 'Shane is fantastic. I couldn't fault him. I was so hung up on his age and all that, but in reality it's better for Felicity to have a fella who's finished with all the silly young buck behaviour and is ready to be there for her, you know?'

'Totally,' Ava said understanding. 'I had my reservations about

Nathan as you know, but he, too, is one of the good guys. A bit like yourself, I was kind of refusing to allow myself see any of the positive aspects to the poor guy. But Daisy is just so happy and Nathan has proven to be a fantastic support to us all.'

'I think sometimes we all need to take a step back and open our minds, huh?'

'You got it,' Ava said, winking. 'We're never too old to learn and although we often don't see it, our children keep us fresh and continue that process in a way that nothing else ever could.'

'Are you two being all profound over there?' Greta said, standing up to hug Ava.

'I think we are!' Mia laughed.

'Are you trying to upstage the bride?' Greta said good-naturedly.

'I could ask you the same question!' Ava laughed. 'Look at you in your frock. Wow!'

Greta flushed. 'I've never got so much attention,' she said, trying to be all off-hand, but she couldn't hide her obvious delight.

As Justin chatted to Martin and Shane, Ava made her way over to greet Felicity and Tally. 'Hi, girls,' she said, holding her arms out as both rushed to hug her. 'It's really great to see you both.'

'You too,' they chorused and laughed.

'How are you feeling now?' Tally asked.

'Oh, I'm great, thank God. Thank you both for being there with Daisy that night. She said you were fantastic.'

'Not at all,' Felicity said. 'We're just glad you're well again.'

The best man caused a flurry of waves and see you laters as he asked the guests to please be upstanding for the bride and groom.

As Daisy and Nathan waltzed into the room amid the sea of smiling faces, Daisy really felt like she was walking on air.

'Looking good, Mrs Taylor,' Nathan said as he held her hand.

'Not looking half bad yourself, Mr Taylor,' Daisy shot back.

The starter course was served, but Daisy could barely eat a morsel. She was so busy waving and calling out to friends at neighbouring tables, she couldn't bring herself to concentrate on the food.

'If you're not eating that, I will,' Nathan said as his fork hovered over her plate.

'Go for it. I know this is very rude of me, but will you excuse me for a moment? The photographer is over there near the crew Mum and I met in Spain and I'd love a picture with them before we all end up looking worse for wear?'

'Oh, yeah, we're a couple of hours married and you're bored of me already,' Nathan said, smirking.

'I'm sure you'll manage without me for five minutes,' she teased.

'Just so long as you don't behave like one of my friend's ex-wives back in America,' he said.

'Why what did she do?'

'Shagged the best man in a broom cupboard. They were discovered because the bride was being called to join the groom on the dance floor for their first dance.'

'Ouch, what a cow!' Daisy said, trying to stifle a giggle at the thought of it.

'Yup, not the best recipe for a long and happy marriage,' Nathan grinned. 'So chatting is fine, but shagging is off the cards, unless it's with me. In that case, I've already figured out where the nearest broom cupboard is!'

'Deal!' Daisy giggled. 'Why don't you come over and say hello with me, that way there's no danger of any untoward carry-on? Besides, I'm dying for you to meet everyone.'

'Hey y'all,' Daisy said, approaching the table and waving with both hands.

They all stood up to greet the bride and groom, and the girls exclaimed over every detail of Daisy's outfit.

'This,' she said proudly, 'is my husband, Nathan.'

Nathan smiled down at her so tenderly that Tally and Felicity both felt a lump rising in their throats. Daisy looked so beautiful and so in love, and Nathan looked so in love with her, it was impossible not to get caught up in the romance of the moment.

'Daisy, you are the most beautiful bride I've seen,' Tally said, wiping a tear from her eye.

Daisy blushed. 'Thank you,' she said shyly. 'I'm just so happy.'

Introductions were made all round and the girls could have stood chatting for hours, but Daisy was aware that the next course would be coming out soon.

'Would the gentlemen mind if I steal your ladies for a moment?' Daisy asked politely.

'Only if you give them back,' Martin answered.

'I'd love a special photo of all the Spanish ladies!' Daisy explained. 'Mum!' she called over to Ava, 'Spanish reunion photo opportunity!'

'Hang on I'm coming!' Ava called back.

As the wedding photographer assembled them in a group, Tally, Greta, Mia and Felicity cuddled in towards Daisy and Ava.

'Say paella!' Daisy called out and they all burst out laughing. As the camera shutter clicked, it captured six smiling faces of six happy women – mothers and their daughters.